FALSE SUMMIT

THE TRUTH IS HARD TO FACE...

CAM TORRENS

Black Rose Writing | Texas

The author grants the final approval for this literary material.

First printing

This is a work of fiction. Names, characters, businesses, places, events, and incidents are either the products of the author's imagination or used in a fictitious manner. Any resemblance to actual persons, living or dead, or actual events is purely coincidental.

ISBN: 978-1-68513-286-6
PUBLISHED BY BLACK ROSE WRITING
www.blackrosewriting.com

Printed in the United States of America
Suggested Retail Price (SRP) $22.95

False Summit is printed in Minion Pro

*As a planet-friendly publisher, Black Rose Writing does its best to eliminate unnecessary waste to reduce paper usage and energy costs, while never compromising the reading experience. As a result, the final word count vs. page count may not meet common expectations.

ACKNOWLEDGMENTS

It takes a community to write a book. I didn't know this when I began my writing journey, and that might be why it's been such a long haul. My community's support has proven more valuable than the final product. I'd like to thank:

My wife, Linda, for her continued support. My youngest sons, Matt and Josh, who came up with the idea for this plot on a road trip to a middle-school wrestling match. My mother, Susan, and sisters, Amy Torrens-Harry and MaxieJane Frazier, for having to plow through first (and final) drafts. My daughter, Natasha, for helping me with my younger characters, and my sisters-in-law, Donna and Sandra, for their beta reads and positive support.

The Chaffee County Writers and our critique group of fellow authors continue to teach me every week: Linda Ditchkus, Laurel McHargue, Dan Bishop, Susan Bavaria, Wendy Oliver, Robin Hall, Tom Dury, Danielle Frost, and Monica Young.

My beta reader team still with me four years after I started on this path: Liz Brown, Stephanie & Bill Summers, Mary Riley, Terry Williams, Sue & Ben Paganelli, Terry Kelly, Alta Beren, Shane Bumgarner, Scotty Cain, Chris Pike, Penny Martin, Kristy Beardemphl, Chris Kaufman, and Joy Knight.

Brad Grant for sharing his experiences as a Jefferson County Reserve Sheriff and his daughter, Beth Grant Helmke, for serving as an inspiration for the Search & Rescue portions of the book. Bobby Lewis talked me through the Three Apostles and how to use them as a setting. CCSAR-N members: Josh Schwenzfeier, Erik Rasmussen, Rebecca Hinds, and Brandon Ove for supporting my efforts. My friend Eric Meyn for teaching me about cryptocurrency.

Authors Mary Kubica and Janelle Brown for inspiring me to take a turn toward psychological suspense, and Cindy Waskom for helping me shape Kristee as a character.

Finally, Black Rose Writing for continuing to support my work, and Brooke Dillon, editor extraordinaire.

PRAISE FOR
FALSE SUMMIT

"Tyler Zahn is a hero to love – deeply wounded, undeniably flawed, but determined to do the right thing in Cam Torrens' intensely dramatic debut thriller. The stakes of Zahn's search-and-rescue work in Colorado's Rocky Mountains have never been higher, or more personal. Trim your fingernails before you start this one."
–Martin J. Smith, author of the Edgar, Anthony, and Barry Award-nominated *Memory Series* novels of psychological suspense, and the stand-alone thriller *Combustion*

"When a trusted colleague goes missing, search and rescue expert Tyler Zahn relies on his experience and instincts to find her. But the deeper he digs, the more he wonders if he really knows her at all."
–Gail Ward Olmsted, best-selling author of *Miranda Writes* and *Miranda Nights*

"Torrens has done it again! A thought-provoking story about relationships and communication wrapped inside an action-packed thriller with suspects at every turn like a *Knives Out* mystery."
–Lena Gibson, award-winning author of *The Edge of Life: Love and Survival During the Apocalypse*

"Set in the beautiful landscape of Colorado, Cam Torrens' *False Summit* is a mind-bending mystery that will keep you guessing, literally to the last page. Well-paced, and with unrelenting suspense, don't be surprised if you read this story in a single sitting."
–Chris Riley, author of *The Sinking of the Angie Piper* and *The Broken Pines*

"Cam Torrens takes the reader on an edge-of-your-seat thrilling ride through Colorado's The Three Apostles mountain peaks. His book, *False Summit*, features mystery, intrigue, and danger and never lets up in a thoroughly captivating story."
–Christopher Amato, author of *Shadow Investigation*

"Much like a hike up one of the rugged Colorado mountains in this well-crafted story, the tension in *False Summit* gradually builds until readers are rewarded with the view of an inevitable yet still unexpected conclusion."
–Amanda Waters, author of *With You*

"Vivid characters and complex twists propel the plot to a conclusion that no one will expect. An engrossing page-turner, absorbing and skillfully written."
–Carolyn Korsmeyer, author of *Little Follies*

"A fast-moving thriller that keeps the reader glued to the story and turning pages."
–Sherry McNeese Hobbs, author of *Mac: The Wind Beneath My Wings*

"Cam Torrens takes you on an emotional rollercoaster ride as two friends search for different truths to life."
–Stephen W. Briggs, author of *Beside Us*

"You read until your eyes are begging for a break. And then you keep reading."
–Sandra Gardner, author of *The Murder Blog*

FALSE SUMMIT

ZAHN

NOW

A dull bronze lamp illuminates the varnished motel room desk where I am studying my notes from yesterday's Miranda rights lecture. Today's class doesn't start for another two hours.

My phone rings, and my eyes narrow as I see Kristee Li's name across the screen. It's early in the morning for a Kristee call. My gut twists, and I hesitate before answering. *Why rush to hear bad news?*

Kristee and I are close, but family-close, not lover-close. Our twenty-plus-year age difference, multiple missions together with Search & Rescue (SAR), and our mutual love of the outdoors have created a bond between us almost as close as the bond I've forged with my only daughter.

"Kristee? Everything OK?"

"Just needed to check in with the infamous Z-man. Or should I say, Reserve Deputy Sheriff Tyler Zahn?" Her voice sounds glib, as if early morning calls are our norm. They're not. Days start early at the Jefferson County Law Enforcement Academy, and I'm still working to weave this new routine with parts of my old one.

I laugh. "You can keep calling me Z-man. I haven't graduated yet. But your timing is perfect. Class doesn't start for a couple of hours. Everything alright back there?" The last question is a probe, and she'll recognize it.

But it's a reasonable question at this hour. I'm stuck out here on the Front Range outside Denver, wallowing through the Academy while she's back in my adopted hometown of Buena Vista, nestled in the Colorado Rockies on the banks of the Arkansas River. I miss home. And I wonder what's bothering Kristee enough to call me this time of day.

"Everything's great." Kristee pauses. I can almost hear the gears turning as she tries to think up things that are *great*. "The snow's melting, so the river's running high. But the tourists haven't figured it out yet, and the town's still quiet."

"No tourists? Since when does a raft guide think a lack of tourists is a good thing?"

Kristee pauses again. I need to stop with the small talk and let her tell me what's up.

"Yeah, I'm not sure I'll guide this year."

This declaration jars me. Kristee Li is the epitome of the outdoorsy generation flocking like Canada geese to Buena Vista. She guides rafts in the summer and runs a snowplow in the winter so she can afford to live in a location that allows her maximum river and mountain time. When she's not paddling, she's climbing or backcountry skiing, or raising her hand for a SAR mission.

SAR is where I met Kristee. She's the one who watched me fail on my first attempt to climb one of our local fourteen-thousand-foot mountains—*14ers* in the local vernacular—and she's the one who led me to the top of Mt Harvard, my first successful summit.

When we met, I was in a funk. Retired from the Air Force, overweight, and drinking for "medicinal purposes," I latched onto Kristee and fellow SAR member, Deputy Sheriff Rick Perez, and let them rehabilitate me.

"Why not?" I ask. "Is it the business? Still taking too much time?"

Kristee's voice quakes. "Yeah, it's the business. And Randy. And that my mom is here, and Karla arrives tomorrow, and—" She sucks in another breath. "I don't know, Tyler. It's too much. I can't deal with it."

This is not the Kristee I'm used to. Our first SAR mission together, Kristee stepped up and took my place when I told the team leader I wasn't confident treating an injured snowshoer. Her reputation as an expert raft guide and kayaker gives her well-earned rockstar status in our tiny county.

When we met for dinner at the Surf Hotel two months ago, she had shared for the first time a bit about her personal life: problems with the new office space business she ran on Main Street; a hint that all was not right with her boyfriend, US Marshal Randall Williams, stationed in Denver; and the upcoming family visit. I thought Kristee's sharing was a sign we were getting closer as friends, that she was lowering that Wonder Woman persona just an inch or two and admitting she struggled with the same issues as the rest of us mere mortals.

I lean back from my desk. Maybe I had missed this cry for help the last time we met. She sounds—and this is unlike any side of Kristee I've seen before—almost desperate.

"When you first moved here," she says, "you were dealing with all that loss from your Air Force days. Your son and then your aircrew, right? You told me and Perez that our friendship actually pulled you out of your depression, and that being able to talk about it saved you. Remember that?"

"Yes." She's right. I don't know where I'd be now without those two.

"Well, you're the only one I've talked to about my stuff, and some of it's changed since we had dinner. There's something I haven't told you about…" Her voice fades as if she's moved the phone away from her mouth. A familiar beeping sound echoes in the background. Then my phone does the same. It's a Search & Rescue alert.

"Hang on, Z-man. Let me check this out."

"Yeah, I'm looking too." I pull the phone from my mouth and put Kristee on speaker before tapping the Active 911 icon on my home screen.

Ground searchers needed. Party of four hikers missing from a planned route yesterday in the vicinity of the Three Apostles. Report to the bay. There is airlift training in the area, so expect a helicopter for one or more teams.

"Z-man, you still on?"

3

"I'm here. The Three Apostles are way back there, right? Between Huron Peak and Cottonwood Pass? I wish I could do this one."

"I'm responding to this." Kristee's voice has switched to crisp and direct, like one of my Air Force flight commanders briefing an upcoming mission to their boss. Confidence radiates from the phone's speaker. "Especially if they take my team out in the helicopter." Her voice softens. "I'll call you when the mission's over." She pauses. "Tyler?"

I hesitate briefly, as Kristee rarely uses my first name. "Yeah?"

"I still need to talk. You might be the only one who can understand. Will you have time later? With all your Academy stuff going on?"

I assure her I'll make the time. I tell her to be careful, and she laughs at me. I hang up without realizing I may never talk to her again.

• • •

By afternoon, I'm losing my focus. A uniformed deputy teaches our section, and I watch her lips move, but take nothing in. Like I'm drinking from a waterfall with my mouth closed. Not smart on my part.

Deputy Rick Perez, my Buena Vista friend, offered a tip before I left for the Academy, telling me it was more important to pay attention in class than it was to spend evenings in my hotel room studying the written material. The instructors were known to give hints about the end-of-course test questions, while the textbooks and online resources didn't offer such obvious clues.

But I've got Kristee on the brain and I'm unsure whether my distraction stems from her revelation that she's unable to handle her personal life, or from the last-minute SAR call sending her to the outer limits of our county's search jurisdiction. Maybe it's both—knowing she's leading a mission while dealing with personal stress.

Kristee is searching in the Three Apostles, a rugged terrain that earned my respect when I explored it last year. I'd left my truck at the mining town of Winfield and hiked four miles in before setting up camp for the night. The next day, I'd hiked up to North Apostle and taken a stab at the middle Apostle, Ice Mountain, before giving up and returning to camp. I just wasn't comfortable by myself as the climbing turned from Class 3 to Class 4, and without ropes and equipment, I knew climbing it alone was foolish.

Our SAR team also recovered a body out there the year prior. An amateur ultrarunner was training on a rugged route traversing all three Apostles when he slipped and died instantly from a head injury in the fall. Five grueling search days passed before we found his body on West Apostle. Such an ironic name for the jagged peaks thrusting skyward so far from the beaten path. I'd picked up enough biblical knowledge from tagging along to church before Sheila became my ex-wife to understand that apostles spread the word of Jesus—the gospel of forgiveness. Yet, these Three Apostles were the most unforgiving summits in the entire Sawatch Range.

Why am I so worried about Kristee in the mountains? I quickly shrug off my concern. Although we both joined SAR at roughly the same time, only three years ago, Kristee's credentials are known and respected across our organization. She summited all the 14ers in Colorado, climbed every major pitch in our county, and knows the Arkansas river like YoYo Ma knows his cello. What did she say? *Especially if they take our team out on the helicopter.* She automatically assumed she'd be in charge, and rightfully so.

If anything, that's Kristee's sole flaw. She's so damn competent, she intimidates people.

Still locked in the past, I recall one mission where Kristee and I joined SAR member Nathan Hall to form Team 1, while the incident commander worked the phones trying to form a backup team, Team 2. We had found the missing hikers cliffed out on Mt Yale in a position too steep to slide down and too precarious—in their minds—to climb up. We expected to climb out to them and guide them back up to the trail, but they were locked in a situation requiring ropes. We carried ropes, but hadn't expected to use them.

Kristee called Incident Command and announced without discussion that she would rappel to the hikers and send them up in harnesses, while Nathan and I would help haul them up from the top.

Nathan and I just stared at each other, as if she were suddenly speaking a new language. Kristee was hi-angle qualified—meaning she was qualified to perform a rescue requiring climbing gear—but we weren't.

And it all worked out. Kristee rappelled down the cliff—all 5'2" of her, raven hair flashing beneath her helmet—after rehearsing our roles up top. We brought the two hikers up and hiked them down to their car at the trailhead.

That was Kristee. First to raise her hand and say, *Put me in, Coach.* Quick to say, *I've got this.* Unable to say, *No.*

The instructor coughs, and I realize we're ten minutes into the afternoon session, and I don't have a clue about what we are discussing. My phone vibrates, skittering a millimeter on the table. I snatch it as the instructor looks my way and nods. The screen reads *Rick Perez*, the same deputy who talked me into becoming a reserve sheriff deputy, and warned me to pay attention in class.

He, of all people, should realize I can't talk in the middle of the day. Not while I'm in training. I thumb the button for *message* and select *I can't talk right now. Can I call you later?* Reaching forward to reposition the phone, it vibrates again, the sound just loud enough that the instructor glares in my direction. The attention is supposed to be on her, not my table. I twist the phone in my hand and read Perez's text.

No. Call me.

My gut sinks, and I look from the phone to the instructor, who has paused the lesson.

"Got to take this," I mutter.

To her credit, she stares at me with no judgment and says, "Go."

"What?" I'm standing in the hallway outside the classroom, my phone pressed to my ear. "I'm in class."

"Yeah, I figured. But I need to update you on the SAR mission out at Three Apostles."

"What happened? Injuries?"

"No. We got the hikers out and they're all OK. A little shook up, but they'll be fine."

"So what—"

"Some non-standard shit, that's for sure."

I say nothing, waiting for him to continue.

"First off, there was a rockslide. Big one. It's like the whole cliff that makes up the south side of the saddle between Ice Mountain and North Apostle just cleaved off down into Waterloo Gulch. I've never seen anything like it."

"South side? How did you guys even know?" I ask. "I thought the whole mission was on the northern side? That's what the Active 911 text said." I try to picture the terrain from my single visit to the peaks.

"Yeah, we wouldn't have known except for the noise and because the helicopter was buzzing by some hikers summiting Ice Mountain. The pilot saw it go down."

"Did it get anyone? You said there were hikers…"

"I rode up with the helicopter and took a look. The Ice Mountain hikers were traversing over to North Apostle, doing the loop backwards, so they just quit and returned to West Apostle, then down to Lake Ann." Perez coughs. "I mean, it's in a spot where no one would have any business hiking. It's just not hikeable terrain. The party that saw it said it looked like when one of those Alaska glaciers drops off into the ocean." Perez sounds like he's catching his breath. I can tell he's all wound up about this rockslide. "Looks like it picked up momentum as it dropped. There's a big mess at the bottom where the slope flattens out again."

I haven't hiked on the Apostles' southern approach, but I can picture the scenario Perez describes. I've scrambled through other rockslide remnants on my hikes and missions through the Sawatch Range where Mother Nature is always reminding us humans that nothing stays permanent while she has a vote.

I stare at a row of pictures on the hallway wall. Wooden letters above the photos read *Never Forgotten*. These are the graduates of the

7

Law Enforcement Academy who have lost their lives in the line of duty. My eyes focus on one picture, a Deputy Don Tinkham, while my brain tries to work through this phone call. Perez is calling because of a huge rockslide? I don't think so.

"What aren't you telling me? I don't get it."

"It's Kristee. We did a roll call after the mission, and she's not back yet."

My heart feels like it's physically trying to pound through my chest. "What do you mean 'not back?' Who else is with her...on her team?"

Perez's breath rasps on the other end of the phone. He says nothing.

"Rick?"

"She got separated. I talked to her partners. You've met Nikki Kingston, right? And Chad Storms?"

"I know Nikki. I've heard of Chad."

"Yeah, Nikki said Kristee left to check something, but never came back."

I try to recall the last time a Chaffee County SAR member didn't return from a mission. And I realize this is a first.

We've never lost a teammate. And I'm not about to start by losing Kristee.

. . .

I am on the road fifteen minutes later for the two-hour drive back to Buena Vista—or BV, as we locals call it. The Law Enforcement Academy spouted a five-minute spiel about *letting the professionals handle it* when I informed them I was returning home to help search for my friend. Their attempt was half-hearted, I recognize now, because they would have done the same if they were in my shoes.

At the SAR headquarters, I buckle my climbing helmet and grab my 24-hour pack. Flight For Life, the helicopter service shuttling Chaffee County SAR teams in and out of the Three Apostles, just announced that they were five minutes out. Perez stands next to me, taking a day off from his sheriff duties so he can join me as Team Seven of the nine teams we have out searching for Kristee.

The Three Apostles straddle the Continental Divide and form a convenient boundary between Chaffee County, where I live, and Gunnison County, to the south and west. Although the search for Kristee is confined to the northern slopes, and the only thing of significance on the southern side is the trail of debris left by the rockslide, Gunnison has informed us they are sending teams up the southern Waterloo Gulch to assess the slide damage and make sure there weren't any hikers up that direction.

Perez and I listen to Gunnison's plan on the radio and trade glances. Gunnison SAR doesn't survey rockslide damage, nor look for people that haven't been reported missing. They've heard we've lost a member, but haven't yet received a request from us for assistance. They're just trying to get involved because they know what it would be like to lose one of their own, and they can't stand the thought of doing nothing.

"What do you think?" Perez turns to me as we walk toward the landing pad. "You want to look at the rockslide area too? I can have the helicopter do a flyover for a quick look-see."

"You said Kristee and Nikki were descending the north slope from the saddle between North Apostle and Ice, right? I can't picture a scenario where Kristee would climb back up to the saddle and descend the south side." I pause. "Can you?"

Perez's headshake is almost imperceptible, and he says nothing. He shades his eyes, and the sound of rotor blades breaks the silence of the valley. I follow his gaze and spot the black speck moving our direction.

"But?" I know Perez has more to say.

"But where the hell is she? She would have to be between the saddle and treeline, and we've had teams scouring that area for hours. And what? Do we really think Kristee got lost? I mean, Kristee?"

Perez's voice has gone just a trace shrill, which I've never heard in the imperturbable deputy before, and that's when it hits me.

It's not just me who has lost a friend here. Perez has lost something personal as well.

He crushed on Kristee for years before working up the nerve to ask her out. And then, when I set up the two on a group hike to Mt Harvard, Kristee fell for US Marshal Randall Williams instead. Perez has been watching them date for the last year and a half, but that doesn't necessarily mean his flame for Kristee has dimmed. Perez is hurting, too.

"I know," I say. "There's no way she got lost. But maybe she tried a shortcut? Wouldn't be the first time."

Perez turns to me, his lips pressed together in the semblance of a smile, and nods. We both agree that's exactly what Kristee would do if she were by herself and trying to catch up with her team.

We scramble aboard the helicopter within seconds of its touchdown, and a minute later we are weaving west up Cottonwood Pass. The air carries the scent of aviation fuel, and it whisks me back to my C-130 days, flying low level across the Iraqi desert.

The helicopter has enough power to fly northwest directly, but I recognize that our route provides safety options in case we need to land. We crest Cottonwood Pass, then work our way north, following the path where the Continental Divide Trail and the Colorado Trail overlap. The pilot aims for West Apostle, and Perez keys his mike.

"JD, it's Perez," he calls to the pilot. "Can you swing us by the rockslide on the way?"

"Not a problem." JD banks the chopper toward the vertical cliffs highlighting the south side of Ice Mountain.

"You see where it happened?" Perez stabs his finger across my face at the window.

I nod. Even though Ice Mountain is nothing but a stack of massive rock, cliffs, and boulders, the rawness of this fracture leaves its mark. A black-stained new cliff is visible behind the whole mass of earth and rubble that cascaded down the mountainside, leaving a telltale trail, black like the cliffs left behind, highlighted on the edges by the gray rockslides on either side which haven't moved in eons. The slide widens at the bottom, and I see gnarled tree roots, the raw yellow flare of exposed pine, pointing toward the sky where the destructive mass slammed into the forest.

"Thank God there's not a trail up the mountain on this side," I say.

Perez nods. He's already seen the slide, but his eyes are still wide, as if he still can't comprehend the scale of destruction.

"All our teams were on the other side," Perez says, repeating what he told me on the phone. "Gunnison SAR should be on site here in a couple of hours, but we don't have any reason to think any people were down there."

I bob my head in understanding as the pilot veers left to parallel the Apostles. Staring out the window at the jagged spine of the mountains, I pick out my solo summit route to North Apostle, then guess at the spot where I turned around on Ice Mountain. We aren't flying high enough to see the ascent routes on the north side.

We don't get many SAR calls on the Three Apostles. Not for a lack of ignorant hikers—we see plenty of those on the 14ers—but because the peaks are so far out of the way that only the die-hard, more experienced climbers have even heard of them. Die-hards like Kristee, who has soloed the Apostle traverse. *How could she get lost in these peaks?*

Five minutes later, we touch down in a meadow next to Lake Ann. Normally, SAR runs both a command center back at our headquarters in Buena Vista, and a relay command center called Trailhead at the last place we can drive to—in this case, the abandoned mining town of Winfield. But with the Apostles, we're six miles from the SAR truck and surrounded by mountains, with nine teams fanning out from the lake. So, we've established another command link at the lake to coordinate the teams and allow them to check in with handheld radios that might not reach the SAR vehicle back in Winfield.

I thank the pilots as I drape my headset over the seat rail, then grab my 24-hour bag and exit the aircraft. Perez and I duck our heads and make for the SAR canopy set up near a clump of trees about two hundred yards from the landing zone. I suck in a deep breath, the thin alpine air a sharp contrast to the overpowering smell of aviation fuel.

11

Three people with packs are heading our direction, and I assume the helicopter is taking them back to Buena Vista. I recognize the man in the lead, Dave Merrifield. He's with two women, and as they approach, I recognize the last searcher as Nikki Kingston—Kristee's hiking partner on this mission.

I grab Dave and cup my hand to his ear. "Any luck?"

Dave pulls back and shakes his head. "Nothing!"

I clap him on the back and yell, "Thanks for being here." I nod at the two women as we pass and see Perez doing the same.

A tug on the back of my pack slows me, and I turn to see Nikki Kingston, her eyes wide with the black circles of a night's lost sleep highlighting the blue of her eyes.

I'm unsure what she wants, as she pulls me even closer and cups her hand to my ear.

"I don't think she's lost!"

She pulls her hand away from my ear and I stare at her. I don't think Kristee is lost either. But she's been missing for a night in Colorado's most unforgiving climate and terrain. I'm worried she's hurt…or worse. What I don't understand is Nikki's choice of words. *I don't think she's lost.* Implying Nikki knows something that we don't.

"What—" I start, but Nikki has turned back toward the waiting helicopter. She whirls around at my voice and shouts, "I'll talk to you when you get back." Then she turns and jogs to catch the other two.

I stand there staring at Nikki's retreating figure, trying to make sense of what just happened.

KRISTEE

TWO MONTHS BEFORE

"Randy, move your ass! I've got breakfast for you out here." Actually, the only thing Randy can likely smell from my cozy bed is coffee. Not that he expects much more. I'm not what you call handy around the kitchen, and I'm usually far more interested in eating food than cooking it. I even use the stovetop's unused burners to store a stack of folders— paperwork related to my fledgling business venture. At least I'm not storing shoes in the oven like Randy's grandmother.

"Randy?" I leave the almond milk, granola, and two halves of a grapefruit on the small table by the kitchen window and walk the six steps to my bedroom, one of two in my tiny condo. Amore, my rescue mutt, pops up from the couch in the cramped living room and follows close to my heels. Poking my head through the door, I see US Marshal Randall Williams propped up on one elbow, giving me a big smile, his teeth gleaming white in contrast to his dark skin. Amore gives the man in my bed a growl, but it's all bark and no bite—Amore loves Randy.

My first reaction is annoyance. I'm scheduled to meet my new business partner in thirty minutes, and Randy—OK, I get a tickle of a smile there when I remember I'm the only one that he lets call him *Randy*—has to get on the road back to his place in Denver if he's going to make it to work by ten. Not like he's got specific office hours as a Marshal, but he did tell me he had an appointment.

"What?" I ask, staring at his smile, my mouth twitching. I can't help it. Randall Williams spends most of his days as a serious, focused investigator, absorbed in his mission to put away the bad guys. When he does finally loosen up, sharing that wide grin of his, it's ridiculously infectious. Like a yawn at a slumber party, he makes the rest of the room smile in about three seconds flat.

"I just love it when you get riled up," he replied. "It's kind of sexy."

I give up and break into a grin. This is the part where I should run and jump on the bed, burrow under the covers with Randy, and *get a little randy*—our private joke about sleeping together. I'm impulsive, as my teammates on Search & Rescue remind me, and as my fellow raft guides love to point out, but what they don't notice is that my crazy side is almost solely oriented to the great outdoors—the mountains and the water—and that doesn't translate well to the world of romance. Randy is my first venture into the dating game since college six years ago—I was a nervous lover then, and I haven't changed. Randy wants a deeper relationship. I don't know what I want.

"Right. So I'm really sexy now because I've got a meeting in thirty minutes, and you're supposed to be on the road in ten, and breakfast is on the table getting cold?"

Williams—I always revert to his work name when he's heading out my door or talking to me on the phone—looks at me with questioning eyes.

"Well, OK. It's granola and grapefruit, so it's already cold, but we do have to move out," I say.

Williams swings out of bed and looks over his shoulder at me as he heads toward the shower. "Four-minute shower, four-minute breakfast, one big ol' smooch, and I'm on my way."

I throw a pillow at his retreating figure before returning to the dining room table, Amore trailing behind me. He curls up at the base of the chair where Williams will sit.

Four minutes later, as promised, Williams joins me, his shaven head still moist from the shower. He pours milk into his bowl of granola, takes a bite, and looks across the table.

"What was that call last night you didn't want to discuss?" Williams asks. "Perez still trying to convince you that you picked the wrong guy? That a sheriff is sexier than a Marshal?"

"Perez doesn't call me. You know that. He's a good friend." I meet Williams's eyes. "Sure, he hoped for more, but we're good now." I give him a fake scowl. "Besides, he's your friend too."

"Right. You get to hang with my friends more than I do. With Zahn too—he said you all went hiking the other day?" Williams points the end of his spoon at me, laughing.

"Really?" I know he's teasing me, trying to goad me into talking about the call. "I still don't want to talk about it."

"OK—that leaves me three minutes to eat." Williams returns to his granola.

My head still shakes. "It was my mother telling me she wants to come out for a visit the month after next."

"Lord have mercy, Kristee Li's got a family!" Williams sets his spoon on the table and raises his palms like he's praising God at a Sunday service.

"You already knew that."

"I did," Williams says. "But we sure don't talk much about them, do we?"

He's not wrong. He's just the only one who comments on me not talking about my past. My Buena Vista friends like Rick Perez from the Sheriff's Department and Tyler Zahn from Search & Rescue have asked a couple of questions, but they always stop after my awkward, brief answers. Williams, on the other hand, is always needling me for the backstory. It's one of the things I love about him—he cares enough to want to really know who I am. And it's also the thing he does that drives me crazy—I don't like to talk about my time before Buena Vista.

"She let us down." I say, just to give Williams something. "She was a professor at my college—I guess it was more her college than my college—and she got fired."

"Whoa. That sounds kind of harsh. She let you down because she got fired? Maybe it wasn't her fault."

15

"No. It was her fault. I don't want to talk about that." I twist my serrated spoon into the grapefruit. "She just never tried again after that. Never tried to teach again. Never tried to get an actual job. She's been driving for Uber and Lyft for six years now, just making enough for rent and groceries."

Williams nods and says nothing, so I share the part that really bothers me. "I dropped out of school after that."

"Because you couldn't afford it anymore?"

"Yeah, kinda." Actually, wrong. I could have figured out how to stay in school. I dropped out for a different reason, and there's no way I'm prepared to have that conversation with Williams.

"And I vowed I would not let my sister miss out on her opportunity for college just because my mother stopped making enough to contribute." I poke a wedge of grapefruit in my mouth and talk while chewing. "So that's why I have so many sticks in the fire with work. Got to pay Karla's tuition."

"When was the last time you saw your mom?" Williams's eyes turn all sympathetic-like. I can't stand being pitied and try to mask my irritation.

"It's been a couple of years." More like five, I remind myself, and I brace, anticipating Williams's next question.

"So, why is she coming out now? Is she looking for reconciliation or something? Did you invite her?"

"I have absolutely no idea," I say. I think back to our brief conversation and can't recall a single clue from the words my mother said. My heart wants to lean into Williams's suggestion. That my mother is looking to mend the long-broken fences between us. That she wants to beg for a fresh start. That she wants to tell me about how she's returning to the classroom and to her research and to her pursuit of tenure.

But my brain turns off those notions in one fell swoop like the maintenance worker dousing the lights at a football stadium. That's not how my mother operates. When she visits her daughters, she always has an agenda. She's on a mission to fix something that she perceives is amiss with one of her girls. This time her focus is on me, and as I gaze across the table at my boyfriend of color, I have a hunch why she's coming.

Our goodbyes are awkward, as always. Williams has figured out I don't like the long, sweep-me-off-my-feet kisses he imagines are the perfect send-off for another week apart. So he's swung to the opposite end of the spectrum—his new technique involves grabbing my hand and playing with my fingers while we discuss our next planned rendezvous.

I treasure my time with Randy Williams. I'm not much of a conversationalist when it comes to the personal, but when I talk, he listens. Williams charms me in his formal awkward way, and he can be downright funny when it's just us hanging out together.

The sex is OK. Since I left college, there hasn't been a lot of it, and when it does happen, it's definitely different from my school days. What's unique about Williams is he makes it comfortable. Natural. He puts me at ease and makes me laugh.

But these lingering goodbyes? That's not me at all, and Williams knows it. We just shared a fantastic weekend, a quick breakfast together, and now it's time to go to work. Enough already. I pull my hand from his and give him a peck on the lips before he climbs behind the wheel of his black Chevy Traverse.

"See you next week! Call, OK?" I say as he pulls away. He blows a kiss in my direction, and I turn toward my car before realizing I've left my laptop back in my condo.

I grab the computer off the table and Amore follows me to the door.

"I'm just grabbing my computer, silly." The rescue place told me they found Amore with nothing but a nametag on a collar around his neck. I had the best intentions to change his name—a Latin-based word for *love* is about as far away from what I'd name a dog as you could get. But Amore came the first time I called his name, and I ended up reminding myself that it's not always all about me. I scratch his head. "I'll be back in an hour. Hour and a half, tops."

I take the steps down from my condo and spot Jacy, my neighbor's 13-year-old daughter, sitting on the chair they keep next to the front door.

"Jacy," I call, stepping onto the walkway.

She smiles. "Hi, Kristee. Where's Amore?"

"I've got a meeting over on Main, so he's in the condo. I was going to ask, though, are you up for a bit of paid dog-walking next week? I've got some longer meetings scheduled." Oh my God. Listen to me talking like an office wonk. I'm a raft guide, a snowplower, and an occasional gutter cleaner. Now, suddenly, I've got business meetings?

Jacy's eyes light up, and I see a beautiful girl in front of me. It's only then I realize how rarely I see her smile. She goes to school, she comes home from school, and she disappears inside. But, inevitably, she ends up on the porch. Not reading. Not talking on a cell phone. Just sitting there as if she can't stand being in her condo for one more minute.

It must be tough on her. I've met Erik, her dad, and there's no mom in the picture. Erik's a burly guy who works the roads on Highway 50 going over Monarch Pass. Plowing snow, dealing with avalanches, that kind of thing. I've tried to connect with him on the whole *I plow snow too* line, but he hasn't bitten. He's not one to get cozy with the neighbors, or even be friendly.

So, I'm not positive, but I'm guessing Jacy just needs time away from him sometimes, and that's why she's on the porch. What she likely needs is girl time—someone to talk to who doesn't spend all day driving a truck. I tamp down my niggling sense of guilt at not reaching out to her more often, reminding myself that my personality is probably closer to her dad's than to the woman's touch she needs.

"Can I? You don't have to pay me—I'll do it for free." Jacy's blatant eagerness reminds me she's still more girl than teenager, and I return her grin. It's so nice to see what people are thinking rather than having to guess.

"Nope. You either take money, or I find someone else." I wink at Jacy. Her grin disappears for just a second before she realizes I'm joking.

She nods, and the smile returns in full force.

"Can you swing by this afternoon, say four or five, and I'll give you a key? We can talk about how often and where to go and stuff." I pause and tilt my head at the girl. "Should I ask your dad for permission to hire you?"

Jacy's smile drops again, and this time doesn't return. "No. He'll be fine with it. You don't need to talk about it." She turns her head toward the door. "Besides, now's not a good time. He doesn't like to talk when he's getting ready for work."

Her sudden shift in demeanor seems to confirm my suspicions. Everything's not all milk and cookies in the Erik and Jacy household.

ZAHN

NOW

I wake slowly, wrapped in a dream where my daughter Daria is visiting, and she and Kristee are standing over me on a rock-strewn mountain slope, their arms slung over each other's shoulders, laughing.

"Get up," they chant, in a mocking voice. "Get up, or we won't make it to the top." They turn up the trail, Kristee in the lead, pulling Daria by the hand. My daughter looks back at me with imploring eyes. *Get up.*

So I do. I glance at the clock next to my bed and swing my legs to the floor. It's 6:40 in the morning, and the sun is already casting a bronze hue on the tall pines standing sentry over my Elk Trace home. These fifteen minutes—the *golden hour*, though it never lasts that long—highlight the magical experience of the Colorado Rockies. I've vowed never to take these moments for granted, but as I perch on the edge of my bed, struggling to interpret my dream, it is not the dawn beauty that jolts me awake.

It's Kristee.

Perez and I met most of the other teams when we joined the search yesterday at the Three Apostles. No one had seen a trace of Kristee.

I grab my cell phone and thumb to my SAR email account. My first unread message tells me Incident Command called an end to Operational Period 2 at ten o'clock last night, when Perez and I finally rode out on the helicopter.

We were fortunate with the night extraction. Flight For Life usually only flies at night for medical emergencies. But based on our conversation with the pilot on the way back to the SAR bay, we can expect extraordinary assistance from them on this mission. They understand the trauma of losing one of your own and are committed to helping us find Kristee.

The next email solicits volunteers for Operational Period 3 to meet at the bay at 7:30. Three teams will continue the search from the north side, like yesterday, and another will meet at 8:00 for airlift to the south side, where the Gunnison team had searched under the auspices of checking out the rockslide. That we're sending a team to the south side today tells me we've found nothing on the north side and are widening the search.

I glance at the clock again and stand. If I hustle, I've got time to join one of the helicopter shuttles to the south side. If I really hurry, I could join the vehicles driving to the north side. I stare through my bedroom window at the vibrant orange of the Ponderosa bark adorning the trees. *They scoured that north side yesterday, and I talked to almost every team. I don't think she's there.*

I'm dubious she's on the south side by the rockslide, either, but I'd rather try searching there than retracing my steps from yesterday.

"SAR North, this is Deb." A woman's voice answers my call.

"Deb, it's Zahn. Morning."

"Hey, Tyler." Deb pauses. "How are you?" It's the half-second between my name *Tyler* and the *how are you?* that gives Deb away. She's not giving me a greeting. She's worried about how I'm taking Kristee's disappearance.

"Yeah. Just woke up." I'm not ready for a blow-by-blow on my feelings. I rarely am. "Looking at shuttling up with the team headed to the south side. Can I join them?"

This time it's not a pause between words. It's just a pause.

"Deb?"

"Yeah, here's the deal." I hear Deb move the phone away from her mouth and cough before continuing. "Incident Command met last night to review yesterday's results and came up with a rotation schedule. You can join us, but you're on the afternoon shift."

"No. I'm rested and ready to go. Just switch me." *Really?* She's going to deny my request just because it doesn't match the schedule? It's not like a regular mission, trying to find a random hiker.

"No. No switching. That's what we talked about." Deb's voice sounds uncomfortable. I find this odd because Deb never has a problem speaking her mind. While Kristee is the most physical and technically adept woman on our SAR team, Deb is the most *I'm in command—I'll talk, you listen* personality. She rarely goes out on missions—we use her expertise running command and control on the radios back in the SAR bay.

"What?"

"We made this schedule to make sure everyone gets enough rest between shifts. We don't want them to do anything stupid because they're tired. And we specifically put you on the afternoon shift."

"Because you're such an expert on how much sleep I need?" I hate the snark in my response before it even leaves my mouth, but I can't help myself. The Apostles' south side is a long hike. I need the helicopter ride to search for my friend. "Sorry, Deb—"

"No. Don't be sorry. You just showed why we put you on there. We're watching those folks who are emotionally involved in this and making sure you don't burn out. We all know you and Kristee are close."

"We—"

"You know what I mean. Friends close, nothing more."

I say nothing. If it was just Deb, I might talk her into the morning shift. But if my name is on a list, that means the SAR staff was involved, and I'm just going to have to work within whatever parameters they allow me.

"OK," I say. "What time for the afternoon shift?"

"Be here at 2:20 for an expected 2:30 departure."

"Got it."

I hang up the phone, pissed at Deb for bumping me to the afternoon and pissed at myself for losing my cool. I'm supposed to be past all that *losing control* stuff. The mountains and people out here have healed me. Or that's the story, anyway.

It occurs to me that an afternoon search gives me time to update people on what's happening. I can call the Academy and tell them I won't be back for a few days. Find out if they will disenroll me.

And I can meet Kristee's mother, Lin Li. Perez filled me in while we were searching yesterday. Kristee's been stressing about the visit for two months, and her mother just arrived four days ago. Kristee's sister, Karla, flew into Denver late last night and stayed in a hotel. Lin Li is picking her up from Denver, and they are due to arrive later this morning. Now I'll have time to meet them before heading back into the field.

I have nothing useful to tell them. *Your daughter was the first to raise her hand for one of the most remote missions of the year, and now she's disappeared, and we have no idea where she is.* I dreaded this duty during my Air Force days—providing comfort rather than hope to those who lost loved ones.

I move to the kitchen and flip on my coffee maker. My breathing slows as the first drips of coffee fill the kitchen with the smell of fresh grounds. I'm no longer angry at Deb and her made-in-concrete search schedule—or myself.

Damn it, Kristee.

It's her fault. She jumped at the mission. She's the one who is such an expert in the field that her teammates had no qualms about letting her split from the group. She knows what to do in these situations. And now?

Now she *is* the situation.

I pour myself a cup of coffee before the machine finishes. I'll need it strong today.

What am I supposed to do? I don't run Search & Rescue. I'm just another member and have no say in where we look, how long we try, and when we terminate the search.

I'm not law enforcement. In fact, if we don't find Kristee in the next 24 hours, I'm going to have to decide about the Law Enforcement Academy—whether to give up on Kristee and return to the Academy, or drop out and continue to help with the search.

Hell, I'm not even related to her. She might be like a daughter, but she's not my daughter. She sure as hell isn't my girlfriend. Marshal Randall Williams owns that piece of her heart.

Shit. Randall.

I grab my cell phone and press speed dial for Perez.

"What's up?" Perez says.

"I'm going back out to search today."

"Not this morning, you're not." Perez replies, and I can tell he's been talking to the SAR leadership.

"I know. This afternoon. That's not why I called."

"What's up?" Perez says.

"I forgot about Randall. We've got to tell him what's going on with Kristee. He's probably not foremost in your thoughts, but he deserves to know."

Perez says nothing.

"Do you want me to call him?" I say.

I hear him sigh into the phone. "He'll be here this afternoon." Perez says. "I doubt he's going out to the Apostles, but we're meeting him at the office to give him an update, and then he's going to introduce himself to Kristee's mother."

"Oh."

"Come on, man. I called Randall before I called you. They're boyfriend and girlfriend—I think, anyway—and both friends of mine. You're the only one imagining I'm still pissed about that."

He's right. I'm an idiot. But what did he mean by *I think*?

"Yeah, sorry. I should've known you'd have that all taken care of."

I can almost hear Perez nodding. "Yeah, you should've." He pauses. "So." He shifts topics like the President at a press conference. "Are you going back to bed, or moping around your house all day?"

"I won't sleep," I say. "You got something for me?"

"Yeah. Not sheriff stuff. Friend stuff."

"You got it."

"So we talked about Kristee's mom and sister coming in this morning from Denver, right?"

"Right. I was thinking I'd go introduce myself."

"Great idea. You know Kristee's mom has been staying at the Super 8, right? How about you head over and check Kristee's condo and make sure everything's squared away for Karla, the sister, to stay there? Make sure Kristee didn't just up and leave the place a mess when she left on the mission. Maybe throw a couple of things from the store into the fridge."

I realize my friend Perez is miles ahead of me—not just in the sheriff's job—but in the friend department.

"I probably should have thought of that."

"Whatever. Swing by here and grab the key. I went by to see about Amore, her dog, and ran into the neighbor girl Kristee hired to walk him. She gave me the key." Perez paused. "You can let Amore outside for a bathroom break, as well."

"Got it. I'll see you in about 20 minutes. Thanks."

I hang up my phone and stare at my untouched Folgers before heading toward the shower. I realize my anger from this morning has tapered like the temperature of my lukewarm coffee. I've finally been given something to do.

An hour later, I'm remaking Kristee's bed with clean sheets. Amore sprawls in the bedroom doorway with his chin between his paws like he's inspecting my technique and trying to decide whether to keep me. I've been around Amore enough to earn his trust, and he's not much of a guard dog. He sneezes and I wonder if I've overdone it with the Febreze.

I hear a tap at the door and pause my efforts, high-stepping over Amore as I make my way toward the entry. Through the door's side window, I see a young woman about my daughter's age with her hands cupped against the glass, peering inside. The tapping continues, and I realize she's not alone. I assume this must be Karla, Kristee's sister, and her mother.

Waving at Karla, I stride across the floor and open the door. A petite, middle-aged woman with jet black hair stands before me, her hand in midair getting ready to knock again. She drops it when she sees me.

"Hi. I'm Tyler Zahn." I extend my hand in greeting. "Kristee's friend."

The woman looks up into my face as if I'm not what she expected, but she nods anyway, ignoring my hand.

"Hello, Mr. Zahn. I am Lin Li. I am Kristee's mother." She steps forward, and I move to the side as she enters the living room. "Thank you for preparing Kristee's place."

The young woman pauses in the doorway and grabs my hand, giving me an apologetic shake of the head. "I'm Karla," she says. "Kristee's sister. Do you mind if we come in?"

I open my mouth, but Lin Li speaks first. "Of course we can come in. This is my daughter's house."

"Right," I say. "I was just checking on Amore and making sure everything was ready for your arrival."

I close the door after Karla enters and turn to the two women standing in the middle of the living room. Lin Li, who has already seen Kristee's condo, watches Karla take in the single couch, the single picture of a mountain on the wall, and the tiny dining room table with two chairs where the living room opens to the small kitchen.

"It's so Kristee," Karla murmurs.

Lin Li shakes her head.

"I'm so sorry about what's happened," I say. "And so sorry we don't have more information about Kristee."

Karla looks at her mother before turning to me. "We stopped and talked to Rick before coming here. That's how we knew to expect you, Mr. Zahn."

I'm surprised at the familiar way Karla uses Deputy Rick Perez's name. "You can call me Tyler." I hold out the key Perez gave me. "This is the key the neighbor girl used when she walked Amore."

Karla takes the key and puts it in her pocket.

"Had you already met Rick?" I say.

"Yes. I was out here a couple years ago visiting Kristee in her first apartment, and we met then." She gestures toward Lin Li. "But this is my mother's first visit to Buena Vista." She pauses. "Rick was trying to be optimistic, but it didn't sound very promising, with Kristee missing this long."

Lin Li whirls around at Karla's low voice and raises her finger as if to make a point. "She's lost." The woman steps between Karla and me. "That girl. She's always got to be different. Normal girls want to swim, and she wants to ride boats. Normal girls finish college, and she quits. Normal girls are married by now, and she just plays around."

Lin Li turns her head to Karla. "Your sister is not a normal girl, and it is finally catching up to her. She's lost out there, and her friends are going to find her—" She pivots back to me, and I involuntarily step backwards. "Right, Mr. Zahn?"

"Right," I say, reluctantly spouting a half-truth. I honestly believe we will find Kristee. Like Lin Li, I'm of the opinion that Kristee is not a normal young woman. But unlike her mother, I have absolute confidence in Kristee's outdoor expertise. She's unlikely to get lost, and even if she did, there's no way she would stay lost. When Kristee didn't return from the mission, it meant she was hurt…or worse. As to Lin Li's question about whether we will find her? The answer is yes. I'm just not convinced we'll find her alive.

Kristee's mother nods her head at my answer and stares at me as if she's made a decision. "Thank you, Mr. Zahn, for preparing the condo for our stay."

I try to explain that I only made up the one bed, but Lin Li interrupts. "I will walk you to your car now."

Karla turns to me and gives me a small shrug, a raise of the eyebrows, and a subtle head shake. She bends to hold Amore's collar as Lin Li motions toward the door.

"OK," I say, and I open the front door to let Lin Li lead me out.

From the stairs, Lin Li a step ahead of me, I spot a young girl sitting in a chair outside a first-floor condo. She turns a tear-stained face in our direction at the sound of our steps.

Lin Li ignores the girl as we walk past, but I keep my eyes on her, trying to see if she is hurt. I nod and say hello, and she answers with a soft "hi."

I pause. "Are you alright?"

The girl nods. "I'm fine." She stands and disappears into her condo, leaving me facing an empty chair.

"Are you coming?" Lin Li calls.

I nod and rejoin Kristee's mother, now waiting in the parking lot. She grabs my arm and pulls me a few inches closer.

"What about the African American man?"

I scan the parking lot, trying to find the source of her question. You can count the number of Black residents in BV on one hand, and I am unsure why she's asking me this.

"What?"

"Kristee's boyfriend. She still dates the Black man?"

US Marshal Randall Williams. At least now I recognize who she's talking about, even if I'm unsure why. And how should I answer her question after Perez's *I think* comment about their relationship status?

"Randall?" I say. "Yes, they have dated." Kristee told me her mother has lived in the US for over thirty years. I wonder if she picks up on my verb tenses.

"Where was he when Kristee disappeared on that mountain?" She doesn't release my arm.

"Nowhere near here. He's going to be here this afternoon to get an update from Deputy Sheriff Perez. Would you like to meet him? I can bring him by and introduce him to you and Karla."

Lin Li releases my arm and steps back. Her eyes drop from mine, and she shakes her head. "It's been a long trip. Perhaps it's best if we meet him at a later time."

I nod and say goodbye before turning to my truck. I open the door and Lin Li calls out. "Mr. Zahn?"

I turn back toward Lin Li.

"Why is her boyfriend getting involved in the case?"

I stare at Lin Li without expression before responding. "He's coming out because a woman he cares for, your daughter, is missing. I doubt anyone could keep him away. It's not a *case*. Kristee is lost or hurt, and we're going to find her. Randall is a US Marshal. He's a good guy to have helping us if we need to bring in more resources."

Lin Li nods her head and drops her eyes.

"Do you have any concerns about Randall? Anything we should know about?" I say.

"No. Thank you, Mr. Zahn. Thank you for helping find Kristee." Lin Li turns and walks toward her daughter's condo.

What the—?

•   •   •

"I'm pissed at her." Perez rests his hands on the table at the Elkhead and stares at his uneaten quiche.

I don't smile, but I'm struck by the similarity of our emotions. Perez is experiencing the same anger toward Kristee I felt when I woke this morning. How could she do this to us, her friends? How could she put our rescue team in this situation? And I can tell it's hitting Perez hard. Usually, he's talking nonstop. Today, he just sits there staring at the wedge of egg and cheese, while I devour a raspberry-orange scone, washing down the crumbs with black coffee. My interaction with Lin Li has left me confused. And hungry, longing for comfort.

"It's not the first time she's left a team, you know?" Perez says.

"No. I don't know."

"She's always been a bit of a lone wolf. She left us the first time we met her. Remember? The snowshoer?"

"Bullshit. That's not how it went down, and you know it." Perez, Kristee, and I met on a training mission where Perez was our instructor, and Kristee and I were students. A real-world call came in, and we were the closest team to the injured party. Kristee jumped at the opportunity to treat the patient, after I had declined. By the time Perez and I returned from the truck with the litter, Kristee had the woman's leg in a splint and a cup of hot tea in her hands.

"Yeah, alright. Maybe that was different. But I've heard about other times. You know how she is."

I stare at Perez and shake my head. "Come on. Are you trying to say it's her fault? Are you looking for someone to lay the blame on?" I lean closer and before I can think better of it, I say in a low voice, "Got to have someone to finger, right? That's what you do in law enforcement. Quit hiding behind your badge, and start acting like a friend."

Perez turns his fork sideways into his quiche and pries off a quarter of the slice. He stabs the piece and raises it to eye level. "You know how you always shut down when anyone tries to talk personal with you, Zahn?"

I nod. He's right. I am that way. He's also pissed, or he would have called me Tyler.

"Well, I'm not shutting down. Here's my answer." He shoves the fork's contents into his mouth, chews for about five seconds, then says, "Fuck." He chews twice more. "You."

And my theory about pushing Perez too far is confirmed.

We sit in silence. I'm not planning to apologize because I'm tired of hearing how it's Kristee's fault she disappeared, even though I suspect it could be true. Perez will not apologize because that's not how he rolls. He generally likes a full-day separation between saying something he regrets, and working his way up to a "sorry."

A blast of cool air hits my back, and I see Perez's eyes lift to the door behind me. The flicker in his eyes makes me turn, and I see Nikki from SAR striding toward our table.

I'll talk to you when I get back. I remember her last words before she climbed aboard the helicopter at the end of her search shift at the Three Apostles. Between my scant hours of sleep and Kristee's family arriving, I had forgotten the message she'd cupped into my ear. *I don't think she's lost…*

Perez rises as Nikki approaches, and I push out of my chair, but she shakes her head.

"I'll sit." She pulls out a chair between us.

"Do you want—?" Perez starts.

Nikki turns to me, talking over Perez. "You didn't call." She doesn't wait for a reply. "I thought I could talk to you guys because you know Kristee outside of SAR. She said you guys were all friends."

"We are," Perez says. "What do you need to say, Nikki?"

"You said you didn't think she was lost," I say. "What did you mean by that?"

Nikki places her palms on the table and sighs, like she's annoyed she had to find us, instead of us coming to her.

"I meant Kristee had some personal stuff going on. Real personal, and real deep, you know." She scratches at a groove on the wooden table, then fixes her eyes on me. "So, I'm just saying that maybe she didn't accidentally get lost." Nikki pauses.

I look past Nikki to Perez and catch his eyes. He squints slightly as if he's trying to decipher Nikki's words.

Reaching out, I lay my hand on Nikki's jacket sleeve. "What aren't you saying, Nikki?"

The woman lets out a deep breath. "Maybe she disappeared on purpose."

KRISTEE

BEFORE

I have always imagined my life as a book—a continuous narrative arc. I never dreamed it could pivot in an instant, as if someone ripped out the middle chapters of my life.

Before. And after.

This Rocky Mountain tableau of mine approaches perfection—it fulfills my idyllic dream of rafting the roiling rapids of the Arkansas River in the summer, and bagging peaks on the off days. Backcountry skiing in the winter and then scraping up enough money by plowing snow and cleaning gutters to do it all over again in the summer. This is the dream life. A dream that allows me to forget where I come from and the pain I leave behind.

The only care or concern I have in my life is Karla, and trying to give my sister what our mother fails to provide—enough of a monetary boost to pay what her partial scholarship at Duke doesn't cover.

If I were to reflect too long on my fledgling business initiative, my love life, and my screwed-up mother, my thoughts would pile on one another like angry storm clouds rolling over our valley on a summer afternoon. And just as the storm announces itself with a bolt of lightning and a crash of thunder, this day will flash in my memory like a garish neon sign—IT STARTED HERE.

• • •

I'm talking with Jacy about dog-walking dates and times outside her condo, while trying to think of a subtle way to ask her about a bruise on her cheek, when my phone blurts a staccato ring that I recognize as my man Randy Williams. I promise Jacy to reconnect on the Amore schedule soon, and then accept the video call request on the way up the stairs. Amore's yapping stops at the same time I see Williams's face. I haven't figured out yet whether Amore can actually hear Williams on the phone or whether he recognizes the ringtone, but he knows it's Williams, and he seems to enjoy hearing us talk.

"Hey." I unlock my door and Amore bolts through my legs.

"Hey. I saw the sky, and now I see your ceiling. Is this a bad time?"

I laugh, hanging my keys on the hook and framing my face on the phone. "Just got home. Let's talk." I plop into the recliner, which stands sentry over the entire condo.

We'd texted the night before, so I know he made it to work on time yesterday. He'd asked about my meeting, and I'd told him it could wait for a call. This is the call.

"So, give me the rundown. I thought you would have called last night if all was good," Williams says. "Tell me about the secret lives of office space entrepreneurs."

"It went OK. Mostly how I'd expected." I'm delaying getting into it because of the wrinkle I hadn't expected.

"OK, girl. I'm a simple guy, but I can still recognize when you're saying one thing and meaning another."

I smile. Randall Williams is anything but a simple guy, but he's not the most intuitive partner in a relationship. Maybe that's why we get along so well, since I'm self-aware enough to know I have the same problem. So Williams recognizing my subtext probably surprises us both.

"It's a space issue. I based our profit potential off a model of four single offices and a meeting room. That was in the business proposal Travis agreed to when we partnered to buy the building."

"And?"

"And now Travis tells me something's come up, and he'll need access to one of the single offices for his other business. That leaves us only three offices and the meeting room." I sigh. "It changes all the profit margins. I'm not sure I would have gone through with the deal if I'd known about this."

"Just say no, Kristee. He bit off on your proposal, so he has to stick with it."

"It's not that simple. We signed off on the purchase agreement. Not the business plan. The plan was just a handshake."

I watch Williams tilt his head.

"How about this?" he asks. "How about he co-shares the office, like anyone else, but doesn't pay? At least then you can advertise the fourth office and take in the money from when he's not there."

Now I'm nodding, impressed Williams has paid enough attention to my business venture to come up with the same idea I had proposed after telling Travis I didn't want to give up the office.

"My thought, exactly. That's better than losing the office. I ran that idea by him, though, and he didn't bite. Said he needed total access to the office, and he couldn't share it."

"What's he doing? In his other business?"

It's like I'm reliving yesterday's meeting. Williams is asking all the same questions I had peppered at Travis. "Something to do with cryptocurrency."

"Oh, shit. It's not just the space, then, you'll need to talk about the power bill, too." Williams laughs. "And that pretty much sums up my crypto knowledge. The Marshals have a contractor who manages the custody of the crypto we seize, but I don't know Jack about how they do that."

"Yeah, he says he doesn't mine it, so no power issues. He's some kind of intermediary."

"So push him. This messes up your plan, right?"

Williams knows how thin I'm stretched. I've made payments to get Karla through this semester, but need to turn an immediate profit to pay both my mortgage and the rest of Karla's spring tuition.

"I'm going to talk to him again. It'll be close, otherwise. We'll need to fill those other spaces pretty damn quick."

Williams tilts his head like he does when he's come up with an idea. "You said your mother's coming soon, right? Maybe she can lend a hand?"

I watch Williams's eyes widen, and I realize he must have seen my face freeze on his screen. He knows I'm in charge of Karla's tuition. And he knows we don't talk about my mother. But he doesn't know why.

Even Amore senses the tension because he gets up from beside my chair and pushes his head against the front door with a whine.

I force my face into a grin like a woman testing her Botox treatment. "Amore's got to pee, Randy. Catch up with you tonight?"

He's nodding on my screen, mouth opening to reply when I end our call.

ZAHN

NOW

Afternoon finds me and Team 2 scouring the north side of the Apostles again, retracing the routes already searched that morning and poking deeper on possible off-trail detours for a hiker seeking a shortcut. Nothing. The morning teams came up empty on the southern search, as well.

Nikki's drama pisses me off. First it was: *I don't think she's lost.* Then she hit Perez and me with the: *maybe she disappeared on purpose.* But Nikki never elaborated on Kristee's deep issues, even after Perez went all deputy sheriff on her. She stubbornly clung to the same mantra: *I promised I wouldn't compromise her personal life...* while insisting we needed to dig deeper into Kristee's disappearance.

By evening, I'm parked at my dining room table, two beers into a six-pack of Eddyline's Summer in the Citra IPA, trying to ignore a twisting worry in my gut. Part of me fears Kristee may already be dead. I try to consider objectively what Nikki said, that Kristee might have purposely decided she'd had enough. But, *Kristee?*

The second beer numbs the adrenaline coursing through my veins, and I mull over what *had enough* would look like in her mind. Assuming Nikki isn't a conspiracy wacko, is she implying Kristee used the SAR mission to disappear? Or that she used the opportunity to kill herself, perhaps hoping she could do it in such a way that no one ever would ever find her?

Neither scenario fits the Kristee I know. I've never seen her run away from anything, especially trouble. And I can't imagine any situation so bad she'd end her own life.

I pause on that one. If things were that bad and she decided to end it all, I *can* imagine her trying to disguise a suicide as something else. Even in death, I doubt she'd want anyone to believe she'd run into a problem she couldn't handle.

By my third beer, I've convinced myself we need to keep talking to Nikki, and by the fourth, I realize I'm drunk and go to bed. I dream of nothing.

I wake before six, my head pounding in rhythm with my heart. The panic I felt last night—before the beer numbed it into submission—is back. If we don't find her today, she's dead. I'm confident she could survive for weeks in the wilderness, a reality show's dream contestant—but why would she? Why stay gone? Something must have happened to her.

As I down a bowl of generic oat square cereal, I eye the two remaining beers in the middle of the table. The beer had been like lancing a boil with a dirty needle. Immediate relief, followed by lingering pain that worsened instead of improved.

I seize the dangling plastic ring I'd pulled the beers from last night and toss the remaining cans toward the waste bin about ten feet to my left. The remnants of last night's pity fest tumble in two neat rotations before landing in the trash with a thump.

Score. At least something is going right.

I'm back on the schedule for another afternoon search—this time on the south side. Gunnison SAR has been up that direction twice, and our team was there yesterday. No one found anything. The teams spent most of their time at the bottom of the rockslide, and our SAR leadership wants us to take a look at the sides, just in case Kristee descended the Apostles in the wrong direction with no trail. It doesn't make sense, but three days into a search with no clues, and that's what you do. Check out the stuff initially ruled as implausible.

Nikki's rantings about Kristee's personal problems are still rattling around my head, and I consider trying to pry more out of her. That last dinner with Kristee was almost a month ago, when I first sensed that she needed to unload. I remember her staring at me for a good ten seconds after I offered to lend an ear before she finally nodded.

"Talking might help, Z-man," she had said. "Thanks for being here."

Kristee finally started talking, but I sensed her holding back. She brought up problems with Williams, which came as a surprise—but nothing else. Nothing of the magnitude Nikki is implying.

I finish my cereal, and as I rinse the bowl in the sink, I spy a buck, two does, and a fawn browsing near my back porch, poking through the pine needles for blades of green. A flash of movement near the second doe catches my eye. Another fawn, perfectly camouflaged against a tree trunk, stands motionless, eyes fastened on my back door. Maybe it's not that hard to disappear.

Was Kristee's problem with Williams the culminating event Nikki was talking about? Had something happened over the last month with this whole Williams-Kristee-Perez thing?

I've spent the last two days with Perez, and he hasn't hinted at any personal issues with Kristee. I need to talk to Williams.

I call his cell phone and end up in voicemail, which is odd for a US Marshal, even if he is off duty. I remember Perez mentioning Williams would be helping with the search effort. He's probably out at the Apostles without a phone signal. I confirm with Deb, who's still running the day shift at incident command. Williams won't be back until past two this afternoon.

My cereal and coffee dull my headache. I lean back and think about who else might have insight into Kristee's relationships.

She is still dating the Black man, right? I remember Lin Li, Kristee's mother, asking. Why did she say *still*? Had she also heard of a problem in the relationship?

I push back my chair and head for the shower. Lin Li might be prickly, but I need to talk with her again.

. . .

"We found this in Kristee's dresser." Karla hands me a note, folded in half. She lowers her eyes. "Rick—er, Deputy Perez asked us to check through her things for clues as to why she would leave her team on that mission. Like if she was upset about something."

I look from Karla to the note. Amore has positioned himself at my feet, gazing at me like a long-lost friend. Lin Li sits in front of the dining room window staring at the Collegiate Peaks to the west.

Perez hadn't mentioned this request to me—having Kristee's family search the condo. But then, again, I'm not a law enforcement officer—he doesn't need to tell me anything. And Kristee's sister and mother don't need anyone's permission to go through her possessions.

"Go ahead, read it," Karla says.

I unfold the note and read the sentence inked inside: *You deserve better—R*

How ironic is that? The same Rick Perez who asked the women to search the condo left a note sometime in the past telling Kristee how to solve her boyfriend problems with Williams.

"See?" Lin Li turns her head from her seat at the dining room table. "The Black man must have done something wrong and left the note. I knew this relationship was wrong."

R for Randall. Why did I immediately assume Perez wrote the note?

Karla gives me an embarrassed glance and turns on her mother. "Mama, you can't do that. You can't just refer to Kristee's boyfriend as *the Black man.*"

Lin Li rotates her chair a half-turn so she's partially facing us. "Fine. The African American then. Whatever. The point is—"

Amore whines at my feet as Karla interrupts her mother.

"No, Mama. You know his name. At least use it—out of respect for Kristee."

Lin Li says nothing and Karla prods her again. "Randy. Randy Williams."

Lin Li doesn't acknowledge her daughter, instead addressing me. "Maybe Kristee was upset about this, right? This relationship problem. Maybe she left her team because she needed some time alone. And then she got lost."

You deserve better.

Could Randall Williams have written this note to Kristee?

I nod, still trying to decide if the note has anything to do with the disappearance. Kristee wandering off and getting lost because she's torn up about a love note makes no sense to me.

"We're going to give it to Deputy Perez after we finish looking around," Karla says.

"I'm driving right by the annex on the way home. You want me to drop it by?" The question is out of my mouth before I've fully considered the situation.

Why would Perez want these women to find a note he wrote to Kristee? He wouldn't—but perhaps he doesn't realize Kristee kept the note. If he even wrote it.

I need time to process this.

The rational—make that rationalizing—part of my brain, the part that always straddles instinct and logic, whispers in my ear. *This is not a criminal investigation.* I'm not necessarily morally right in keeping this note while I check things out, but I'm not legally culpable, either.

"Sure, please take it." Karla says, and when I glance at Lin Li, I see her nodding while looking at the papers spread across the table.

Karla follows my gaze. "Mama is reading the life insurance policy. We found it in her files when we were looking around."

I'm taken aback. It's one thing for me to sit at my dining room table and contemplate Kristee's death. But with no clues, no body, and no explanation, I find it hard to accept others assuming she's gone forever.

"Mrs. Li," I say.

"Stop, Mr. Zahn." Lin Li meets my stare and rests her hands on the loose pages. "I am aware of how this must appear to you. The insensitive mother poring over her missing daughter's assets before she's even found."

She's right about that, but I say nothing.

"It's about my college," Karla says.

I turn at Karla's comment, then shift my eyes back to Lin Li when she speaks again.

"We will use her college fund to get her through the rest of this semester, but Kristee was involved in Karla's tuition payments." She glances down at the paper directly in front of her before returning her eyes to me. "If Kristee can't pay in the future, we must decide if Karla can continue school."

I nod, somewhat ashamed of the first thought crossing my mind. That Lin Li was already counting on Kristee's assets for herself. I don't even know this family, and already I'm jumping to conclusions.

"I just wanted to say that we have to assume she's alive." I glance at Karla, then back to Lin Li. "We don't have proof she's not."

Lin Li nods. "And for my other daughter's future education, I at least have to plan for the fact that she might not be alive. I'm sure you understand that." She looks straight at me.

I nod and say nothing.

"Thank you so much for stopping by, Mr. Zahn. Is there anything else?" Lin Li stands and so does Amore, as if affirming the woman's decision that it's time for me to leave.

There is something else, but I'm unsure the answers are here, and I'm positive I don't want to bring up the topic. I've come here to find out more information about Kristee's relationship with Williams. But I won't get an unbiased opinion about that subject from Kristee's mother.

"Nothing else. Call me if you need anything," I say.

"I'll walk you out," Karla says, as her mother returns to the papers at the table.

As we descend the stairs, I scan the walkway for the girl from yesterday—the one crying. No one is in sight.

"There is no college fund," Karla says from behind me on the stairs.

I stop and turn back to her, but she points toward the parking lot for me to keep walking.

41

"I don't want her to hear."

We round the utility closet at the landing, and Karla moves forward to my side. "I work part-time at college but that just pays for food. Kristee pays for all my college. Mama and Kristee are not close."

"Yeah, Kristee mentioned that to me. She didn't like to talk about it, though."

"She doesn't like to talk about that time with anybody. Even I don't know all the details."

I frown. "What's the story with 'that time?' I thought they just didn't get along?"

"No," she says, as we approach my truck. "It's more than that. Kristee left school, and my mother stopped working at the same time. She was a computer science professor at the same college Kristee went to." Karla pauses. "Something happened."

"So, if there's no college fund, why does your mother—"

"My mother believes there is a fund. Kristee said she used the refunded money from the semester she quit school to start a college fund. That's what she told me to tell Mama. But Kristee's been paying everything herself. From money she makes working."

"So, is it true you're paid up for this semester?"

Karla stops next to my truck and stares at my feet. When she looks up, her eyes are full of tears. "No. Partially paid." She sniffs, and I see a tear squeeze from one eye. "But I don't care about that. About tuition and staying in college. I just want my sister back."

KRISTEE

BEFORE

I'm not happy with how Randy and I left things, but I can't help a small smile as I turn the corner onto Main and spot our two-day-old business sign. *THE AERIE.* I came up with the name and my new partner, Travis, instantly agreed. An eagle's nest is a perfect metaphor for our entrepreneurial dream. We want to attract customers who can't stay away from the mountains guarding this valley, but who also need a place to take care of their personal business concerns.

This shared office space concept is exploding outside Ft. Collins, Denver, and Colorado Springs—the Front Range. People fled the cities for a simpler life, but soon found the daily commute unbearable. Many experimented with teleworking from home, but that solution uncovered its own unintended consequences, including the constant distraction of kids on snow days and spouses with to-do lists. Not a problem for me, but evidently a genuine concern.

Rent-by-the-hour offices with seamless connectivity proved a practical solution, and their popularity is spreading west. Last summer, I met a couple who runs shared offices in Breckenridge, and they convinced me it was a sure-fire real estate investment. I spent a morning touring their offices, then stopped next door in Frisco to check out another similar business. Returning to Buena Vista, I gave up a night out drinking with my SAR teammates and drafted a business plan.

My eyes lower and my smile disappears as I spot Travis through the front window, working on a project behind the reception desk. It's going to be a rough day. First Williams mentions my mother, and now I have to confront Travis again over his office takeover.

The two issues are related. I desperately need money and am gambling on this venture's success. My need for money springs from my relationship troubles with my mother, who I haven't talked to in five years. She thinks my silence is her penance for the mistake she made. But I'm the one being punished. Now I'm putting my sister, Karla, through college because my mother can't. I'm the one taking financial risks to get her through to a degree.

Karla suggested student loans as a solution, but I won't let her do it. I don't believe in the screwed-up system offering high-schoolers so-called scholarships from universities that have doubled their tuition twice in the last ten years. *Congratulations, we're offering you a grant scholarship for half tuition—sign here to accept.* Then you read the fine print and realize they've dressed up a student loan as a scholarship.

Not fair. Not right. Not happening on my watch. She's already got a legitimate scholarship paying half her tuition. I'll figure out the rest.

But financing these last two years is like paddling upriver on the Arkansas—no matter how hard I work, I'm getting nowhere. I know snowplowing and raft guiding won't get me—and Karla—to the finish line.

This office space gig solves it—but only if my business plan works. I'm up shit creek (without my proverbial paddle) if it doesn't, because I used part of this semester's college savings, all of next term's, and my life insurance conversion to make the down payment on the office building.

The problem with these mountain paradises rests in the property investment. Real estate might see-saw on the Front Range, but once you hit these towns within forty-five minutes of a ski resort or a whitewater river, prices only slant one direction. Up.

Armed with my draft plan, I had scoured the commercial real estate listings in Buena Vista (OK, it only took fourteen minutes) and immediately given up. Nothing listed for less than half a million—well out of my range. But the following night, drowning my sorrows at our local hangout, I met up with fellow rafting guide Travis, and fortune tapped my shoulder.

Long story short: Travis's parents aren't happy with Travis's river rat lifestyle. They offered to front two-thirds of the down payment on a Main Street property and pay the first six months' mortgage payments if Travis developed a viable money-making plan and found another investor.

When I met Travis at the bar that night, he had neither. By the time we went home (not together), we were partners.

As I watch Travis now through the window, my phone buzzes, and I pull it from my back pocket. I love living in a town where a businesswoman's attire includes back pockets.

The text is from Nikki, one of my SAR teammates. She's been after me to grab a drink sometime.

Hey, girl. Tonight?

I sigh. Between my Williams goodbye and my impending Travis conversation, I need a drink right now—and more than that by the end of the day. But odds are against Travis budging on his demands, and I suspect I'll need time tonight to revise my earnings estimates.

But I've already put Nikki off twice. And I like her.

Tomorrow night? I'm slammed tonight. How about The Lock-Up at 8?

Buena Vista's packed with old buildings, but only one serves drinks in a 100-year-old former jail.

Deal. See you then 😊

•　•　•

"What's up, pardner?" Travis drawls in his faux Texan voice. I force a smile, but remind myself that we are past pretending yesterday's conversation didn't happen.

"Partners means people who discuss things before changing plans," I say. "Let's talk in the meeting room."

Travis's expression sobers. He nods and rests his hammer on the reception counter before unbuckling his carpentry belt.

"This whole human relations shit's a lot easier on the river," he says. "Cut me some slack."

I spin around and point my finger at him. "No. It's just like the river. If you don't know what you're doing, people can get hurt. You made a decision without considering what it will do to me."

Travis ducks his head and aims for the alcove next to the meeting room. "I'll get us some coffee."

When he returns, I sit at the head of the table, Travis to my right. I tip my cup toward his.

"Thanks." His trip to the coffeemaker gives me time for a deep breath. I remind myself I'm losing this argument if I open with a raised voice and a scowl.

I open my mouth, but Travis speaks first. "Look, Kristee. I appreciate the fact that we wouldn't even be meeting if it wasn't for you. I needed a plan…I needed the investment…and you came through."

I nod, hoping this is the part where Travis says he's changed his mind about the office space he has declared as his own.

"I just didn't imagine one office would be a deal breaker. The problem is that I'm committed to another contract. With my crypto gig. I need the space."

Shit. So much for reconsideration. Time for mitigation. "And what about my suggestion? The one where you rent the office at a reduced rate, so I at least get something for losing revenue, and you allow it to be rented when you're not using it."

Travis is shaking his head before I even finish.

"Nope. I need the space for what we're doing. For security purposes."

Travis isn't even looking at me. He's already decided.

"I have an issue there." I center my coffee cup and lace my fingers together. "You said crypto equipment yesterday. Today you're saying security. So that makes me think you're going to be doing some mining in there. It's one thing if you steal one of our offices...partner. It's another if you think I'm going to pick up the tab for the power bill that comes with mining that stuff."

Travis starts in with the head shaking again and looks me directly in the eye.

"Let's clear the air right now. I'm using the office. I'm not mining. You need to back off my shit and figure out how to make this work." He raises from his chair and leans forward with his hands on the table and his head angled toward me. "You mess with my end of things, and we're going to have problems keeping this whole thing afloat."

Travis exits the meeting room, and a moment later I hear an electronic chime echoing in the foyer as the entrance door opens. He's gone.

I don't really have any recourse. I've committed everything I had saved for Karla on this venture—a sure-fire investment designed to earn everything I need to get my little sister to graduation. It has to work.

But I'll be damned if I'm going to start a business with a partner whose opening play is to go all cloak and dagger on me. "I need the office for what we're doing," Travis had said. Well, what the hell are they doing?

•　•　•

"Anything else, Kristee?" Walt asks, handing me a fresh-cut key and looking around the inside of Travis's office.

"That's it. Appreciate you coming on short notice. See you Tuesday at the SAR meeting?" I had pulled in Walt, BV's only locksmith, through our work together in Search & Rescue. We both knew he wouldn't have dropped everything and made me this key without our shared experiences looking for lost hikers above eleven thousand feet.

Walt points his finger at me, thumb raised, like a pistol. "Tuesday. It's a date." He heads out the door.

I like Walt. Mid 60s with lungs like a whale and a personality like everyone's favorite grandfather. Not a hint of flirtation in his *date* comment.

Yesterday, I would have been surprised to discover that none of my keys worked on Travis's new office door. After our conversation in the meeting room this morning, though, I almost expect it. Three keys on my ring. Front entrance, the office master key, and the storage key. I called Walt because the master key didn't work for Travis's room.

Now I stand in the contested office and wonder what I hope to find. Travis has started with just the bare necessities. There's a laptop on the desk, plugged in, but no visible lights indicating it's running. Two cardboard boxes sit under the table, stacked on one another.

I lift the screen of the laptop and lower my finger toward the power button before pausing and stepping back from the desk. Yes, I'm pissed at Travis. No, I don't think it's a fair way to begin a business partnership. But am I really going to snoop on his private computer?

I close the laptop and kneel below the desk, opening the flaps of the top cardboard box. A yellow legal pad rests atop a stack of papers, pen scribbles decorating the front page. The inked notations are letters and numbers, and even though I can't understand what they mean, I recognize they are just what I'd expect from someone doing something with crypto. Codes and shit. Blockchains? I'm not even exactly sure what a blockchain is, but I've seen it in the tech headlines of the articles I don't read.

I set the legal pad on the chair next to me and thumb through the stack of papers. Six different forms, but common in purpose—leases for storage units. I see one in Salida, one in Alamosa, one in Minturn, each with one or two keys clipped to the lease copies. I thumb through the pile to the bottom before I see a familiar name. Hi-Alt Storage operates just four blocks from our office here in Buena Vista.

I'm unsure what I expected, but even after sneaking into my partner's office—*our* office, I remind myself—I don't have any better idea why Travis is insisting on taking this space. I snap a picture of the top page of the legal pad and return it to the box before heading toward the office door. Closing the door behind me, I insert the key and lock it just as I hear the electronic chime of the main entrance door.

Travis freezes as he looks through the foyer to where I stand outside his office.

"What the hell are you doing, Kristee?"

ZAHN

NOW

I'm two days back at the Academy in Jefferson County and my focus sucks—like a 60-year-old man with a newspaper and no reading glasses. Studying in my motel, I fixate on the words in my lecture handouts but can't force myself to read. I sit wide-eyed facing the instructors during class, but I cannot hear.

My mind remains in the mountains where I've left Kristee alone and lost. Teams still search, but now it's one team a day for a six-hour shift. Two theories dominate. Either Kristee wandered off and died of exposure, or somehow the rockslide on the south side of the Apostles got her.

I'd still be there, searching, except for the prod from my daughter, Daria. She called me from college for an update on the search. She and Kristee are friends—they spent time together last year during Daria's extended spring break, and quickly bonded. They still stayed in touch by text. Or at least they used to.

Daria clearly alerts on something familiar in my dull monotone and starts in on me.

"Dad, go back to the Academy."

"Says the one who called me for an update?" I sip my second beer of the night, Elevation's First Cast IPA. "How am I going to help find Kristee if I leave?"

"Do you think she's alive?"

I'm silent at Daria's question. Parental instinct screams, "Never show them pessimism." But Daria's an adult. We've both lost someone. My son. Her brother.

"No," I finally admit.

"Then you need to take the first step in moving on, Dad. You don't need to be the one who finds her body. The longer you stay, the more obsessed you'll get with what happened to her. You know how you get." She pauses. "Are you drinking?"

"That was different," I snap. "That was a one-time thing, and I fixed it. I can handle this."

Daria whispers something like...*ears,* and I call her out on it.

"What?" I say, evenly. "Say it louder."

"I said, 'you fixed it...but it took you seven years.'" She sighs. "Look, I don't want to fight. I just think it would be good for your mental health to return to the Academy."

"I'll think about it."

She hung up, obviously not wanting to argue. I sat at the table pondering the wisdom which sometimes pours from the lips of our children and then did some pouring of my own, dumping the rest of my beer in the sink and packing to leave.

Daria was right about the Academy thwarting my probable slide into depression. I haven't had a drink since returning to my studies. She just got the whole *focus on something else* wrong.

I wish that I could.

I can't stop imagining Kristee alone on the slopes of those rugged mountains, freezing wind permanently chilling her unmoving body. And I can't stop asking the questions...*How? Why?* How did our most qualified Search & Rescue member wander off from her team, get lost, and die in an environment where she was better trained than almost anyone to survive?

•　•　•

Phone calls from Perez, and then Karla, Kristee's sister, save me from failing an end-of-block exam. Perez and his team called off the search yesterday. After a week of scouring the mountainsides of the Three

51

Apostles in ever-widening search patterns, our search teams came up with nothing.

Zero.

Zip.

It hurt to hear it from Perez. He cared for Kristee, too. In a different way.

Karla's announcement jars me. "We're going to have a memorial the day after tomorrow," Karla says when I answer her call. "We'd like you there, if you can make it. You were close to her."

I nod, even though Karla can't see me, the lump in my throat preventing me from speaking at first. It was one thing when I quit the search, which was essentially acknowledging the unlikelihood of Kristee's survival. It was another when Karla uttered the word *memorial*, which was admitting Kristee was dead.

"Tyler? Are you still there?"

I cough. "I'll be there. Sorry. Can you text the details?"

I hang up after she agrees, unwilling to break down in front of a sibling whose loss is magnitudes greater than my own.

My phone buzzes with an inbound text.

Thursday. 1100. At Lake Ann. Sheriff Perez has arranged a helicopter for Mama & me. And you, if you can come.

I'll be there, I text. *I'll meet you at the lake.*

I'm not taking the helicopter. If I'm going back to the Apostles, I'm going to walk the terrain. Look for clues on the infinitesimal chance I can find something—anything—that scores of teams have missed over the past week.

The Academy isn't as accommodating as last time.

"It's a memorial," I say. "For my friend." I try to squelch the pleading tone of my request. These people should understand honoring a first responder's death. "I'll be back for class Monday morning."

"It's not that, Zahn," the director says in a quiet voice. "You've been back for two days, but you're not really here. Your instructors say you're not focused." He pauses. "The material we're teaching may seem dry to you, but it keeps you alive out there." He waves toward his office's single window, and I follow his gesture.

"I know—" I start, before he brings his hand back and raises a palm.

"Of course you can go, Zahn. We all understand you have to." He lowers his hand and looks at me, his eyes matching his voice's gentle tone. "But pack all your stuff and take it with you."

"But—"

"I'm not kicking you out of the Academy. I'm removing you from this class."

My mouth opens, but he does that palm thing again, and I shut up.

"Do the memorial. Take a couple months to fix your head. Then call me, and we'll see about getting you into another class."

I nod as he finishes his sentence. Once I realize he's not kicking me out, but washing me back, I can see the situation from his eyes. He's right. My brain still focuses on Kristee, and my heart is inoperative. I shouldn't be here right now.

• • •

The sun still hides behind Huron Peak Thursday morning as I crawl my Tacoma up the rocky four-wheel track toward the trailhead, the scent of my second cup of coffee easing my headache. I've started early on purpose. The hike is less than two hours, but I want the extra time in case I find something. Which is unlikely.

If I'm honest with myself, I crave the alone time in the mountains. Sure, I spent last night with me, myself, and I, unpacking my gear and settling in. The stillness of my house is bearable with a beer in hand and more in the fridge. Just six hours before, I polished off the rest of that six-pack left from my last talk with Daria. A different kind of alone time.

Now, with my 24-hour pack slung over my shoulders, and a burn in my legs from the slight climb up the river valley, I can think—instead of anesthetizing myself so I won't.

And for the first time since Kristee disappeared, I cry. I came close during Karla's call, but now fat tears blur my vision, and I'm brushing them away with alternating hands as I climb the trail. My first instinct is to stop and get myself under control. That's who I am. How I respond. Even when my son passed, I didn't cry until months later. I had too many responsibilities to handle—I couldn't be the one who lost control. I was an Air Force officer with a squadron to command and a wife and daughter to comfort. Crying was for others—those who depend on me.

But today I don't stop hiking, and I don't stop crying. I let myself sob for all the wrong reasons. Instead of acknowledging my grief, I rationalize my aberrant behavior as a cleansing before the memorial. *Get rid of the tears now, so I can be stoic later.* So I can be strong if Karla needs a shoulder. Or her mother.

I snort at that thought and pull up short because the crying and the snorting and picturing ice queen Lin Li needing my shoulder to cry upon, triggers a coughing fit. I pause with one foot resting on the trail, the other on a tree root, and catch my breath. Get my shit together.

"You alright?" A voice calls out behind me.

I turn and see another hiker, wearing a red Search & Rescue jacket, fast approaching. I recognize him from our monthly meetings—Chad Sterns, or Storms, something with an S-T on the front. About half my age, I estimate. We haven't been on a mission together yet.

"Taking a break," I say, moving my foot off the tree root and returning to the trail. "Chad, right?"

"Yeah. That's right. We met at the meetings."

"Are you up for the memorial?"

Chad looks down at his SAR jacket and back up at me, nodding, and I realize my question's absurdity. Why else would he wear our uniform out here in the middle of nowhere?

"Want to join me?" I say. "I'll follow you." I stay to the side of the trail as Chad passes.

"Cool," he says. We hike a couple minutes—Chad obviously slowing and me picking up my pace—before he speaks again.

"Yeah, I didn't know Kristee that well. We did one other rescue together, but not on the same team. Never lost anyone on a mission before. I felt I needed to be here, you know?"

I don't answer right away. Not because I haven't lost a teammate. I have. Eight crewmembers in a crash in Kuwait.

I pause because I hadn't remembered Chad was the third member of Kristee's team. Nikki, Kristee, and Chad. Didn't Perez tell me that at the start?

"I guess I didn't realize you were with her. What happened?"

Chad twists his head back and looks at me with a questioning glance. "Didn't Rick Perez give you the rundown? Rumor around SAR is that you guys are thick as thieves. That you've helped put a few bad guys away the last couple of years."

"Rundown on what? He said he interviewed the two other members on the team. Nikki and—I guess—you. He didn't mention you by name. Nikki said she didn't know how Kristee disappeared, but said Kristee was dealing with some personal issues." I pause a beat. "He didn't say anything about your interview."

Chad stops in his tracks and turns to face me. I come to an abrupt halt to avoid crashing into him.

"Nikki told him that? That she didn't know what happened with Kristee?"

"That's what she said. I talked to her myself. She wouldn't tell us about the personal stuff."

Chad met my questioning look and squinted his eyes. "I guess technically she's right. She doesn't know how Kristee disappeared. But she knows why Kristee left us. I'll tell you what I told Deputy Perez."

I nod, staring back at Chad.

"They were fighting," Chad says. My eyebrows raise, and Chad nods. "I know, on a SAR mission, right? Never seen anything like it."

"Fighting? Like—"

"Not like punches. I mean like verbal sparring. Kristee said something, and Nikki went off, yelling at Kristee. It got all emotional, real quick."

"What were they fighting about?"

"I don't know. We were on our way back to the helicopter landing site. They started yelling at each other, and I hung back. When Kristee looked back at me, I told her I'd catch up. I didn't want any part of it."

I'm still staring at Chad, and I realize my mouth has dropped open. He probably suspects I doubt his story. But that's not the issue. What floors me is Perez not telling me this part of the interview. It's not like it's a criminal case or under investigation. Why wouldn't he tell me about the fight? Even Nikki didn't mention it, which makes me wonder whether she told Perez about it.

I lower my eyes and try to wrap my head around Chad's story. If he told Perez about the fight and Nikki didn't, Perez needed to circle back to Nikki and question her again. And if he had already done that, he didn't share those results with me, either.

"So then what? What happened next?"

"You want to keep hiking, dude?" Chad asks, and I nod. He turns up the trail, his head swiveling back to talk to me while he's walking. "So, I hear their voices but no words as I'm trailing along maybe a hundred yards back, and suddenly there's like…silence. I think to myself, OK, they've hashed it out, and I pick up my pace to catch up, you know?"

"Uh-huh," I say between breaths. Chad hikes faster as he nears the end of his story.

"And then, boom. There's Kristee walking back up the trail. I stop to ask her what's up, and she gives me this big smile. Not like a real smile—more like when smiling is the last thing you want to do. She grabs my arm and says, 'Catfight, Chad. Sorry you had to listen to it.'" Chad turns his head farther and shrugs. "I start to tell her I didn't really hear anything, but she interrupts. She lets go of my arm, heads back up the slope and says, 'I need some space—catch up with you guys in a few.'"

Chad stops, turning with his hands spread. He's not crying, but I see his chest heaving from something besides our climb up the valley.

"Dude, that's why I'm here. That's why I have to go to the memorial even though I don't know her that well. I may have been the last person to see Kristee Li alive."

• • •

Williams is still in Buena Vista, and I invite him and Perez to coffee. The first to arrive, I nab a four-person table at the back end of the shop. The Elkhead is a tradition for Perez and me—and Williams if he's in town—it's a time to catch up and trade local and state gossip. Rarely able to contribute, I do most of the listening.

We won't trade gossip today.

I expect Perez first—I've given the two men different meeting times. I need to speak with the Perez alone.

The entrance bell jingles and the lean, dark-haired deputy scans the tables before spotting me. I catch his eye, and he nods my direction before ordering at the counter. With foresight, I could have ordered for him. One wedge of quiche and a black coffee with room for cream. Same order as the first time I met Deputy Rick Perez. Same order every time. I know this man, ten years my junior, like the brother I never had. In two short years, we've put domestic terrorists behind bars and taken out a child trafficking group. I trust him.

But I can't figure out why he's keeping the argument between Kristee and Nikki from me. It makes no sense.

Perez sits across from me, wedging a forkful of quiche into his mouth and talking between chews.

"Where's Williams?"

"He said he'd be here. Maybe he's running behind." I keep my separate arrival times scheme to myself. Perez likes to be in control.

Perez shoves another bite into his mouth and stares at me while chewing.

"Any updates?" I say.

My companion knows better than to ask which case I mean. We've both lost a close friend. The memorial service yesterday was supposed to provide closure, but I suspect Perez feels the same way I do. Closure comes with a body. Kristee might be dead, but she's still out there. We still need to bring her home. We owe her that.

Perez looks down. "No. The search is officially halted." He swallows. "Doesn't mean we can't keep looking on our own, but we're done committing county resources."

"Was that your decision?" I ask, shaking my head. I thought I was the master of compartmentalization, but here's Perez giving me the bureaucratic *resources* line, as if Kristee is just another lost hiker.

"No. I asked for another week." He pauses and stares at me. "Come on, Zahn. Do you think you're the only one hurting here?"

I don't. But I'm pissed at Perez, and I'm pissed at myself for turning the conversation negative before I even worked up to the question I intended to ask.

"When were you planning to tell me about the fight?"

Perez lays his fork on his plate. "What fight?"

"Nikki? Kristee? The fight before she broke off from the group. I talked to Chad yesterday on the way up to the service. He said he told you about it."

"I'm not sure I would call what he described as a fight. More like an argument." Perez grabs his coffee and takes a swallow. "Did he say why they were fighting?"

"Wouldn't he have told *you* that? He told me he didn't know. Said it sounded personal, so he backed off."

"Yeah. He told me the same thing. I wanted to make sure he didn't add anything else."

"So?"

"So what?"

"So why didn't you mention the fight—the argument? Is this turning into something bigger than a lost SAR member? Is this a law enforcement thing now?"

The entrance bell jingles again, and Perez looks over my shoulder. I turn and see a tall Black man in black cargo pants and a black collared shirt striding toward our table. He wears a grimace on his face, and I realize he's trying to smile a greeting, but can't quite get there.

I watch him approach and my gut twists. US Marshal Randall Williams, still wearing the same clothes he wore to the memorial the day before, has lost the woman he loved. They might have been having problems, but obviously the loss has hit him hard.

Williams is almost at our table when he notices we've already ordered and spins back to the counter. Perez coughs, and I turn back to him.

"I didn't tell you because I didn't think to tell you. I don't see how it's relevant, either. We know she left the team. As Chad probably told you, she said she needed a minute."

"Not relevant?"

"She left, and she got hurt or she got lost. That's where we are focusing. Not on a petty argument that won't tell us which way she went or how she got hurt."

Perez glances up again and I see Williams heading our way, foofoo coffee and scone in hand. Tragedy has struck our small town, but my friend's eating habits haven't altered.

"And I don't see how telling the SAR team, her mother, and...him—" Perez nods toward Williams. "—is going to make anything better. Do we really want to tell him she had an argument on a mission? Why tarnish her memory?" Perez looks back to me. "Not professional."

"What's not professional?" Williams says, sitting next to me and staring at Perez. I shift my eyes to Perez, as well. I'm not bailing him out of this one.

"Randall." Perez takes a deep breath. "We're talking about Kristee and her team. Letting her walk off by herself wasn't professional." Perez is telling the truth and lying at the same time.

Why?

"You ever try to stop that woman from doing what she wants to do?" Williams says, shaking his head. "Never met someone so stubborn."

Williams sips his coffee before setting it on the table and fixing me with his gaze. "Thanks for coming to the memorial."

I nod and gesture toward Perez. "We wouldn't miss it. You know how much she meant to us."

"Oh, I know." Williams turns his gaze toward the deputy. "Don't I know, Perez?"

"Whatever," Perez says, focusing on the last two bites of his quiche.

I realize I've been a little slow on the uptake. The tension between these two men is as thick as mountain lake ice, and I'd missed it when Williams arrived.

"Do I need to make you guys hold hands?" I say. "What the hell is going on?"

Perez raises his eyes from his plate to Williams and fixes him with a stare. Williams doesn't flinch.

"Nothing that matters now," Williams says evenly. "She left her team, she got lost, and now she's dead. That about sum it up, Perez?"

"We still don't understand what happened, Williams." I notice Perez has switched from using Williams's first name to his last. "But you're right. That's the theory."

"And why does the mighty Chaffee County Sheriff's Department— all what, five of you?—think a professional like Kristee would leave her team?" Williams's lip curls, and he takes another swallow of coffee. "Or should I ask it in a more personal fashion, since you've been spending so much time with her? What does Rick Perez imagine would cause Kristee to pull a stunt like that?" He picks up his coffee then bangs the cup on the table, liquid splashing over the rim.

"Go ahead, Perez. I'm listening."

Perez glances at me before turning his eyes back to Williams. "Look, man. Randall." He shakes his head. "You're devastated. I know there's nothing I can say that can change that. If you feel better directing your anger at me, then bring it on. I'll take it."

"Answer the fucking question."

"The Sheriff's Department has terminated the investigation. You know that." Perez pauses and sucks in a breath before speaking again.

"As for me? Yes, I talked to Kristee last week. As a matter of fact, I talked to Kristee the whole time she dated you." He gestures toward me with his hand. "Just like Zahn talked to her the whole time you dated. She was our friend. She was dealing with problems, and that's what friends do. They help each other."

I'm out of the loop here. Yes, Kristee and I talk. Probably at least once a week. But not personal, like Perez intimates.

"You mean her mother?" Williams's voice is flat. "The family stuff that she's always so tight-lipped about? I know about that already. She talked to me about it." I cringe at how Williams feels the need to prove Kristee shared secrets with him, as well. I'm not used to the vulnerable side of my Marshal friend. I eye Perez, who is shaking his head. His eyebrows raise at Williams's question, and his head switches to a nod.

"Right. Then you know how she needed to get that stuff off her chest. Especially since she was coming to visit. I was kind of like a sounding board while you guys weren't getting along," Perez says.

Williams squints his eyes at Perez and I can't tell whether he doesn't believe him or if he's pissed that Perez brought up their relationship problems. And I won't find out during this conversation because Williams abruptly stands up, his chair scraping backward across the floor. The people at the neighboring table turn our way as Williams leans into Perez, lips pressed together and says in a calm voice, "Sounding board? Right. Hope you feel good about yourself, Perez."

Williams nods my direction. "I'm out of here. See you."

I nod back at Williams and glance over at Perez, whose gaze returns to the remnants of his uneaten breakfast.

"What the hell was that all about?" I ask.

Perez lifts his eyes back to mine before shifting them over my shoulder. I turn, expecting to see Williams returning to our table. I see nothing.

"What?"

"Just a sec." Perez moves from his seat toward the window facing the street. He rests his hands on the empty table next to the window without moving. He must have something sensitive to share if he is waiting to make sure Williams is gone.

Perez returns to the table, sliding into his seat. I wait. He picks up his fork and gamely stabs at a piece of flaky crust, looking as if he's just going to finish breakfast. Move along. Nothing to see here.

There's no way in hell I'm going to beg him to talk. I wait, while he returns his fork to the plate and chews. His eyes catch mine.

"What?"

"Where do I start? You lie to Williams, have a pissing contest with him, then you peek out to make sure he's left. What the hell?"

Perez gives a thin smile. "I was watching someone else out the window."

I recognize the deflection away from Williams, but at least he's talking. I raise my eyebrows.

"Lin Li. Kristee's mother. She just passed by, and I was checking if she was going to The Aerie—Kristee's business," Perez says.

"And?"

"She was. She's in there now."

"And why do you care?"

"Because I'm worried about Lin Li dealing with Travis Richmond on her own. Do you know the guy?"

I do know Travis. Not personally, but Kristee has definitely mentioned him before. He's the guy she partnered with to buy the building at a discount because of his family connections. The one who caused all the drama when he commandeered one office after the building deal closed.

"Not personally. Kristee mentioned some growing pains when they opened up."

Perez snorts. "Yeah, right? I know the kid, and I've never been impressed. He runs the river with Kristee. Same company. Know the parents, too. They're long-timers here in BV." Perez looks up again and I instinctively turn.

He touches my arm, and I turn back. "I didn't see anything," he says. "Just looking at the building."

"What are you worried about? Lin Li strikes me as someone who can hold her own."

Perez chuckles. "Oh, you're spot on there." He shakes his head. "It's just that Kristee's talked to me about that rough start, too. With the business."

I nod.

"She mentioned that there were other things happening with the space. Strange guys going in and out. Travis working late hours."

"Isn't he doing computer stuff? Kristee mentioned codes or something."

"Not codes. Crypto. Crypto currency is what she said. You familiar with that?"

"Not really. Blockchains. Bitcoin. They're mostly just words to me."

Perez nods. He doesn't appear surprised that I'm out of touch on this. "I'm worried about Lin Li getting her fair share of Kristee's investment, and I've got a bad feeling in my gut about Travis's side of the business."

"Why?"

"I ran plates on the vehicles parked outside during the whole 'these guys look suspicious' visit. Kristee copied them down and gave them to me." He tilts his head. "Two of the three were nothing. But the last one? Owner is on parole. For running drugs."

"Did you pick him up?"

"For what? We've got a partner in a business acting all sneaky with his private office and a cryptocurrency gig and a suspicious ex- (maybe) drug dealer visiting him. Enough to think…hmmmm. But not enough to do anything about it." He looks past me again.

"I'm not turning," I say.

"It's Lin Li. Looks like she's heading back to Kristee's."

"You going to go talk to her? See how it went?"

Perez sighs. "I don't think she likes me. Or maybe it's my skin color—I feel that vibe."

"Does she know about you and Kristee?" I gamble.

"Don't give me that bullshit, Zahn. I expected it from Williams, but not you. You know me better than that."

But do I? Kristee and Williams were having problems. An opportunity for Perez. I don't voice my thoughts and instead make a proposal.

"How about I go talk to her? I wanted to check in on her and Karla, anyway."

Perez nods and gives a thin smile. "Yeah, that'd be great. I'm kind of curious about the business thing and how they're planning to handle that without Kristee." He raises his eyebrows. "You'll let me know?"

My smile is thinner. "You bet, Rick. After all, we've got a conversation to finish, right?"

• • •

I catch up with Lin Li by cutting through an alley that shortcuts to Kristee's, and jogging a half block toward her slim figure. She's not wasting any time—she has either quickly acclimatized to BV's eight-thousand-foot elevation, or she's in awesome physical condition.

"Lin Li," I call.

Kristee's mother stops in her tracks and turns in my direction. Her cool eyes evaluate me before she nods.

"Mr. Zahn. Nice to see you. Thank you for coming to the memorial." She pauses. "May I help you?"

Lin Li—cutting straight to the chase. I've given up on asking her to call me Tyler. I've known this woman for three days, and I don't think I've seen her smile once. I chastise myself. Passing judgment on a woman who has just lost her daughter. Why would I expect her to smile?

"No, ma'am. Just wondered if you needed any help? Around the condo? Or with Kristee's affairs?" I catch up with Lin Li and gesture with my hand for her to continue walking if she wants.

Lin Li looks at me sideways and does that top-to-bottom scan again, like she's evaluating livestock at an auction before placing a bid.

"No," she says. "I don't think so." Her eyes return to the sidewalk, and I quicken my pace to keep up.

She pauses, and I'm three steps ahead before I realize what has happened. I step toward her and ask, "What is it?"

"Maybe I do have some questions. Do you know anything about her business? The office-sharing thing?"

"I doubt I know much more than you," I say. "We discussed what her plans were when she bought into it with Travis. She said it was going okay—except that glitch with Travis taking extra space. People were coming in." I pause. "Why do you ask?"

Lin Li stares into my eyes, nodding as I answer her question. But when I ask my own questions, she lowers her eyes to my chest as if pondering her answer.

"I have talked to Mr. Richmond. This…Travis. About selling back Kristee's share of the business. He's interested in buying it, but he says it's impossible to do right now."

I nod. "He doesn't have the money?"

Lin Li shakes her head. "He says that he could buy it, except Kristee still owes him money. He loaned her money—he didn't say how much—based on projected profits for the next quarter." Lin Li pauses and looks back up at me.

To fill the awkward silence, I ask the obvious question. "I don't know the amounts we are talking about, but can't he just apply the loan money owed against Kristee's share?"

Lin Li walks, and I fall in beside her. She's shaking her head again. "Perhaps I'm asking you the wrong questions, Mr. Zahn. Let me be direct. Do you know where this money is?"

"Oh." *That was definitely direct.*

"Karla and I have been in contact with her local bank. We've also asked questions to the investment company about money on deposit. Neither will give us information about her accounts without a death certificate."

"I thought you had that? Wasn't that one reason for proceeding with the memorial?"

"No." Lin Li's mouth tightens. "Even though we know she is gone, Deputy Perez says the absence of physical evidence means we have to wait for a longer time."

Another surprise Perez kept from me. There's a reason he didn't mention Kristee and Nikki's fight. But this death certificate thing is fuzzier. It's not as if I expect Perez to share every piece of paperwork he completes. But he knows I'm personally involved in this disappearance.

After the memorial, I had hiked down from the mountain with Kristee's death weighing on me more heavily than the backpack I carried. Now her mother is reminding me that, legally, Kristee's not dead yet. I don't appreciate being jerked around. Especially with emotions. I can handle bureaucratic buffoonery—I'm a military veteran, after all. But messing with my feelings? I don't even like to admit I have them.

I glance sideways at Lin Li, at her lips pressed together. She probably likes it less than I do.

Lin Li says, "I don't know that the certificate is necessary in this case. We have her computer, and we can see her statements. There's no evidence of this money in either account." She looks up at me. "Any ideas? We can't decide about the business without it. I would have to make some arrangements with Karla's college fund if we don't find it."

I recall Karla's words outside Kristee's condo. *There is no college fund.*

I try to square her words with the no-nonsense woman standing before me. She doesn't look a mess. She doesn't look broke. Lin Li's not going to win any congeniality contests, but she's different from how her daughters have portrayed her.

What am I missing about this family?

KRISTEE

BEFORE

I stand with our contractor on the second floor of The Aerie picking out trim for the upstairs offices. Esthetics matter in this line of business, and I try to focus on the four strips of molding Donny displays like a vintner at a wine-tasting.

"Your call, but I think these off-whites here match the carpet we've laid," he says.

God. He's lost me at *off-white*. I nod, but my mind is on yesterday's confrontation with Travis. He caught me at his office door, but he didn't discover that I'd been inside. I switched the key on my ring to the office master—the one that didn't work—as he approached.

"Trying to get in, but the master key doesn't work." It's a bluff, but fuck him. I'm part owner of this building too.

Travis's face was firm, like those Easter Island statues. He wasn't happy. "That's because it's not a shared office." He stepped between me and the door, and crossed his arms. "What part of our conversation this morning did you not understand?"

I stepped back and shook my head. "Yeah, you were crystal clear. But Donny and his guys are coming in for the trim match tomorrow, and I'm checking the measurements. You want to let me in?" Travis had glared at that. "Or are you planning to pick out the trim tomorrow?"

I'm pretty sure Travis left last night believing my story. I left, however, with an even stronger gut feeling that there was something wrong with how very private he wanted his private office to be.

"What about scuff marks?" I ask Donny. Not that I really care what trim we select, but I want him to believe I'm paying attention. I walk across the room to the window and gaze north up the Upper Arkansas River Valley, framed on the west with the Collegiate Peaks and on the east by the red-rocked canyon cradling the river. Who wouldn't want an office with these views? I turn back to Donny after asking my question.

Donny stares at me like I've got something growing out of my forehead. I instinctively touch above my eyebrows, even though I recognize it's my question that puzzles him.

"Shouldn't be a problem." Donny scratches his own head and I wonder if head-touching is contagious like a yawn. "Most folks don't walk close to the walls in offices. As long as your cleaning service doesn't ram a black vacuum cleaner into the baseboards, you should be fine."

He's holding one of the off-white samples in his non-scratching hand, and I gesture toward it. "That one's good. Let's go with that."

I return to the window, my eyes catching movement in the alley below. A silver Toyota RAV-4 has pulled behind our building, and a stranger stands next to the open hatchback, talking with Travis.

"OK, I'll let the team know." I hear Donny packing up his samples behind me, and I nod without turning. Below me, Travis has his head stuck in the cargo compartment of the car, and I see him opening a cardboard box and pawing through the contents. I can't tell what's in the box.

Travis pulls his head from the back of the car and scans the alley. I step back from the window in case his next glance is in my direction. I'm unsure why I feel the need to stay out of sight. It's not like I don't own the office in which I stand.

"Thanks, Donny," I say and walk him to the door, closing it behind him. Returning to the window, I tentatively peer out from the side. The stranger thumbs the contents of a business envelope and even from this distance, I can tell he's counting bills. Travis holds a box, and I assume it's the same one from the car.

I sort through the reasonable explanations for what I've just seen.

Perhaps Travis is taking an office supply delivery in the alley? So why didn't he use our brand-new business credit card?

Or maybe Travis ordered takeout. What? And paid in ones? That envelope bulged like a rainbow trout caught at summer's end.

My meager guesses make little sense. I have a partner with a fetish for a private office taking strange deliveries in the back alley of my building.

I don't like it.

. . .

I don't put up with shit I don't like. When I'm guiding on the river, plowing snow, or scraping gutters, if I have a customer giving me a hard time, I'll give them one strike—not two. The second time they start ruining my day, I send them out the door. Pick another raft company. Find someone else to do maintenance on your house.

I'm the same way at Search & Rescue. You better have your shit together and pull your weight, or I'm going to kindly ask you to step to the side. Most of my teammates roll the same as me—we all had the same training, so all of us should be competent. But I'll admit, my attitude can rub a few of our team members the wrong way. SAR leadership has informed me that several members asked not to be paired with me. Evidently, I'm too intense.

That's OK. SAR is a volunteer organization. But my business venture is not, and I can't just ignore my partner.

Travis is already at strike two. He screwed me on the business plan when he annexed his own private office. Now he's accepting cash payments in the back alley of my business? I don't care if it's legit or not—perceptions matter.

I need answers.

"Hey," I call, rounding the stairs as Travis steps through the door to his office. "You got a sec?"

Travis pauses in the doorway, staring at me over the box, like a kindergartner who just pulled a cookie jar from the top shelf. Maybe he hopes I won't notice? "Kristee, hey. Kind of busy right now." He nods and ducks through the doorway as I approach.

The door swings back my direction, Travis using his foot to close it since his hands are full. I stick my shoe between the door and the frame and smile at Travis.

"Well, I kind of have to talk to you. Right now."

"Right." Travis sighs as I push open the door. He skirts his desk, laying the box next to the other box I'd found yesterday, then pulling out the only chair in the room. Travis sits and spreads his hands on the desktop.

I'm reminded of my Psych 101 course and a case study we did about office power politics. The two-thirds owner leaning back behind his office desk while his one-third partner awkwardly glances around for a chair. But that's not how I'm playing this. I'm only a couple inches over five feet, but I can make those inches count. I walk toward Travis and lower my hands to his desk, looking down at him. A bead of sweat drops from his face, and he smells a bit like our raft company's life jackets when the customers return them.

"Okay. I've had a day now where I've put up with your bullshit about needing a private office, and I haven't brought it up again."

Travis nods, looking around his bare desk like he's searching for something else to concentrate on, or maybe he thinks he needs to take notes.

"Today, I'm gazing out our top-floor window." I nod toward the ceiling. "Beautiful view until I see you hand over a wad of cash to some guy in the alley." Travis's head freezes, and he stops his hunt for something to do, meeting my eyes. "He takes your cash. Hell, I don't know, it could be my cash, right? We're partners. Anyway, he takes the money and gives you a box. That one behind your desk there."

Travis nods, but says nothing. I haven't said anything he doesn't already know—except that I saw him—and I keep talking.

"So I think to myself. There's nothing illegal about that. Maybe it's a box of potpourri for his new private office. Or tulip bulbs to grow next to his window." I gesture to the sunlight angling through the single window, and when I look back, I recognize a flicker of relief in Travis's eyes. I replay my words and realize I've played this wrong. He thought I saw something. Now he knows I didn't.

"Kristee, let me—"

"No, why don't we start with what's in the box rather than some weak-ass explanation of what's going on here?" I figure since I played the box thing wrong, I might as well take the offensive.

Travis's relief morphs into confidence, like those hi-speed films of a plant responding to water. He breaks into a smile and pushes his chair away from the desk. He walks toward the window, then turns back to me.

"Tell me what you think I'm doing, Kristee." He raises his eyebrows.

I'm not sure what he's doing. The private office, the crypto, the cash…I have seen nothing illegal, but something feels sketchy. I throw him the first thought that comes to my head. "I think you're going to mine crypto and you don't want me to find out, so you're taking secret deliveries in the back alley." I walk around the side of the desk and stand above the box he laid on the floor. "And whatever's inside this is part of it." I bend toward the box.

"How about ten thousand dollars to just stop there and listen to what I have to say?" Travis barks the question in the same tone he might have said *back away from that box, and no one gets hurt!*

I freeze, stand erect, and take a step backwards.

• • •

Travis and I walk the river trail on the east side of the Arkansas. This side of the river also sports a more popular and well-worn trail, but it's obvious that Travis is demanding privacy. If it were me, I would have just stayed in his office. No one to bother us there. But I suspect he wants me away from that box.

Funny how Travis knew to throw out the *ten thousand* dollars to grab my attention. Must have been my tantrum after he screwed up my planned profit margins. Besides my brief loss of control, I haven't given him any specifics regarding my money issues. He doesn't know that I took a risk in buying into our business because my current finances would not keep both Karla in school and me afloat here in Buena Vista. I ran the new numbers last night, instead of joining Nikki for that much anticipated drink, and figured his little office grab puts me short for Karla's next two school payments.

I'm listening. If he's serious about the ten thousand dollars—and it's legal—then I'm interested. But I'm also wary. I don't know my new partner too well, and he's already screwed me once. I need to tread lightly and keep my eyes open.

"I'm not mining cryptocurrency. I'm tumbling it." Travis stays a step ahead of me so we both fit on the trail and can carry on a conversation.

"Speak English."

Travis gives a short laugh and turns his head. "How knowledgeable are you on crypto? Besides your fixation on the electrical bill?"

"Nothing. Some short articles on *Apple News* that I remember nothing about. What's tumbling?"

"Let me start with some basics." The trail widens, and Travis tucks in beside me, his hands gesturing. I've seen his eyes light up when we raft, but not like this. He's downright giddy.

"These transactions all have some computer code attached to them called blockchains."

I nod. "I've heard of those."

"Well, the blockchains use open-source code. Anyone with computer skills can see who transferred money to whom. It's not really as private as the word 'crypto' implies."

"Neither is your credit card or check. Why's that a big issue?"

"Some people believe they have a right to financial privacy. That they don't have to disclose how much money they spend or where they spend it." Travis pauses. "Or they may not want others to track the source of their income." He gestures with his hands again. "This is where my work becomes important. I'm a tumbler."

"I'm guessing it doesn't involve somersaults?" Travis doesn't laugh, and I don't blame him. "So you make the transactions private, then?"

"Exactly. I've got various customers, right? I take one customer's exchange, and I mix this exchange with the exchanges of my other clients by sending crypto coins from all the different contributors into my tumbler. In the end, my clients receive random coins back from the tumbler, making them virtually untraceable. They've still got blockchains, but the people with the tools to read the data can't decipher them. Does that make sense?"

On a conceptual level, I understand the part about turning traceable exchanges into untraceable exchanges. What I don't understand is the mechanics of how he actually does it. The buttons he presses on the computer.

"I think so. So you're just moving crypto and not mining it. No big power bills?" A tiny sensation of relief trickles through me, but as I detect Travis's shoulders relaxing, I realize I'm not asking the right questions. If it's all so simple, then why is he so secretive about it?

"Wait. Is this tumbling thing legal? And if you can do it on your laptop, why not do it at home?"

"Completely legal," Travis says. "That's one reason I need a legitimate office. How am I going to attract clients if I'm running this thing out of the spare bedroom in my double-wide down by the river?"

I laugh. Not because it's not true. Travis does live in a double-wide on the Arkansas River. But he's living on his parents' lot, and the land is worth over a million dollars.

One thing still puzzles me. "What kind of businessmen need to keep their transactions so private, Travis? What type of businesses are they running?"

"Ding! Ding! Ding!" Travis stops walking and I stop with him. He turns to me and grabs at my shoulders. "That's the crux of this thing, Kristee. What I'm doing is completely legal. But I don't have any idea what my clients are doing. I figure as long as I don't ask, I'm completely safe."

I stare at Travis, trying to rationalize whether what he's saying is true. Innocence through ignorance. Is that even a defense?

"Do I have my suspicions?" Travis says. "Yes, I've got some clients buying land here in the valley and trying to interconnect some plots without the local government figuring out it's one entity buying up all the land. Got another doing something with mine claims he doesn't want made public, for whatever reason." He smiles. "But I don't ask. And they don't tell. They just make the exchange and I tumble it."

"And they pay you to do that?" I say.

"They pay me quite well to do that."

"So back to the ten thousand dollars..." My voice starts out loud and trails away.

Travis is still nodding. "I thought I could just do this without involving you. Because I'm running it out of my office, and I'm a two-thirds owner and all that. And I didn't want to share the proceeds...actually, I still don't. I need the money, Kristee. You're not the only one trying to make a buck."

Now it's my turn to nod while he keeps talking.

"I'm not scaled up enough to include you as a partner in this—"

I interrupt. "I'm not interested in getting into the crypto business."

He pats my arm in a way I'd normally find patronizing. Except, I sense he's getting ready to make an offer.

"You get off my ass about the office. You stay out of the office. And you don't interact with my clients."

"And you'll give me ten grand?" Something about this is wrong. Why does he want me out of his office? It's not like I'll go in and get on his laptop and tumble stuff myself. "What was in the box?"

"That's what I'm talking about." He pulls out the same type of envelope I saw in the alley and thumbs through 100-dollar bills. I watch as he keeps thumbing. Finally, he pulls a segment out and hands it to me. "There's $5k. There's nothing in the box. In two weeks, there will still be nothing in the box. And you'll get the other $5k. Do you understand?"

I stare at the money before eyeing Travis. His eyebrows rise, and my gut burns as I hear a question hammering in my head. *If this is legit, why am I accepting cash on an isolated trail near a river?*

The right side of my brain overrides the question. *10K gets me through to Karla's fall semester. Buys enough time to earn the rest of the money.*

Stuffing the money in my down jacket breast pocket, I answer with a question of my own. "What box?"

ZAHN

NOW

I huddle at my dining room table bundled in a fleece pullover, a beanie covering my thinning hair. An 8-inch electric heater funnels warmth to my feet, but the rest of my body still shivers. Moving my ass off the chair and out the door might help, but instead I sip a late morning IPA and consider fate, karma, Murphy's law—whatever you want to call it. When things can't get worse, they get worse.

A cold front blasted the valley last night, delivering three inches of snow here in Elk Trace and an inch downtown. Anywhere else in the country, snow in June makes national news. But here in the Rockies above eight thousand feet, it's par for the course. But I'd missed the forecast and when the temperature dropped like an amusement park ride, my heating system failed.

The Air Force tested me every year on my ability to fly multimillion dollar aircraft and evaluated me on my knowledge of the plane's complicated systems. But fixing the heat in my house is a different matter. I stretched my home repair skills by restarting it, then located the breaker and reset it. I even tunneled into my musty crawl space to confirm what I suspected. No glow of flames from the gas burner. I bribed Mike, my neighbor, with beer and dragged him under the house with his voltmeter. More bad news—everything electrical worked, but the gas valve was broken.

I tilt my Green Chile Ale from the Soulcraft Brewery and drain it. Others might label a lunch-time beer unusual, but there is no one here to judge. And it's got chiles in it, so it's kind of like a meal. I need something familiar—something comforting. Something to remind me that this house, this town, and these mountains still anchor me. Because right now my world is upended.

I can't shake the sense that there's more to Kristee's disappearance than her just wandering off. The niggling feeling began when someone used the words *lost* and *Kristee* in the same sentence. It's hard to fathom. But I also recognize my admiration for my friend might blind me to reality. Even the mighty can be knocked down a notch in the rugged Rockies.

But when I toss in Nikki's obscure references to Kristee's personal issues and Chad's description of their fight on the mountain—and then sprinkle Perez's odd behavior on top—these unanswered questions are suddenly turning my nascent unease about Kristee's accident into a full-blown suspicion that something else is going on.

Here's the problem, though. What can I do about it? The events of the past two years have graced me with a reputation as a problem-solver. But those were physical responses. Chasing terrorists in tunnels and child traffickers in the mountains didn't really involve that much investigation—and when it did, I had Perez and the sheriff's department as resources.

Now I've got Perez stonewalling me, and I can't decide if he's doing it personally—because of his relationship with Kristee—or on behalf of his superiors. For Randall Williams, Kristee's disappearance is personal, but I can't take advantage of his Marshal badge because there's nothing to involve the Marshals in this case…yet.

Even if I went to law enforcement, bypassing Perez and Williams— what would I tell them? *You know that Search & Rescue gal that disappeared two weeks ago, Kristee Li? I've talked to a hysterical friend of hers and two jealous love interests, and although none of them have told me anything concrete, I suspect something suspicious about Kristee's disappearance.*

Shit.

I head to the fridge to get another beer. Just listening to my internal thoughts is making me question myself. I need to calm the nerves.

Halfway to the kitchen, my pocket vibrates and I hear my phone's muffled ring tone. Snatching it from my pocket, I scan the screen.

Daria Zahn.

I instinctively smile and move my finger to accept my daughter's call. But then I pause. The last time Daria called, she urged me to saddle up and return to the Academy, dive into the books, and put Kristee's disappearance in the rearview mirror. She was trying to prevent a slide into the cesspool of emotions like before—those bad years after Jacob died and my family disintegrated.

I shift my gaze from the phone back to the empty beer can serving as a poor man's centerpiece on the table. The day is only half over.

I can't talk to my daughter while I'm wallowing in self-medication. I need to get my shit together. Fumbling with the phone, I press a button next to the one that answers the call and review my options: *"I'm on my way," "Can I call you later?" "Sorry, I can't talk right now."* I choose the last one because it makes the most sense even as I'm aware it translates into *Sorry, I'm your father. I'm retired. And I'm too busy to talk with you right now.*

Rude. She instantly replies, and I recognize she's kidding. But my guilt at ignoring her call is no joke. Stuffing the phone in my pocket, I bypass the fridge and my second beer for the keyring in the utility room. I need to get away from this frigid house, my paranoia, and my default coping medicine.

·   ·   ·

As I drive to Buena Vista, the snow veneer dissipates as quickly as an ice cube on a frying pan. This winter/summer climate mix is just one of the features luring tourists to our town. In the winter, you can drive forty minutes to the mountains ringing our valley and ski, then come back to town and mountain bike in the bare hills east of town. Snow doesn't hit downtown, all four blocks of it, that often—maybe only four or five times a year. The front that dropped three inches on my house last night barely dusted the town.

I'm aiming for The Ranch, a development of tiny low-cost houses set between the town and the correctional center. When real estate prices started climbing, speculators saw the writing on the wall and bought large swathes of land still available within city limits. Several of our Search & Rescue members, especially the young ones, have bought these two-story, two-bedroom houses. They're pressed tight together, contain less than 1200 square feet, and don't have garages, but they're the only thing a normal thirty-year-old could afford in this town besides a one-bedroom condo with a two-year waiting list—like what Kristee lives in. Or used to.

Nikki lives here. I'm sure of this because I pulled her address off the SAR shared drive on my computer before I left my house. Although Nikki assured Perez and me that she wouldn't elaborate on Kristee's personal issues, my Spidey sense tells me she's holding back something she wants to say. I'm hoping she might be more willing to say it without Perez around.

A gentleman would have called first, but I don't relish the idea of Nikki getting worked up on the phone and me trying to decipher her words and her tone. Besides, gentlemen don't drink beer for lunch alone at their dining room table.

The narrow two-story houses overlook a grassy common and sit back from the street, designed for residents to park in the alley and enter through the rear. It's not obvious where guests park. I maneuver into the alley behind Nikki's house and pull in behind her black Honda CRV with the SAR decal on the back window. I spot a gate in the wooden fence appearing to lead to her back door. If I circle to the front door, I have to walk through the common area, passing other houses on my way. Not a big deal, but still—I'm uncomfortable doing it. A divorced man knocking on a 20-something woman's front door midday? People might talk. Maybe I am a gentleman, after all.

I call her on my phone.

"Nikki, it's Tyler Zahn. From SAR."

"Tyler—what do you want? Anything new on Kristee?" Her voice sounds suspicious.

"No. But I want to talk with you more about her." *Why else would I be here?* She's the only thing we have in common.

"Have they opened an investigation into her disappearance?"

I sigh. I'm having a hard time admitting my suspicions to myself, so there's no way I can bring myself to discuss them with Nikki.

"She's dead, Nikki. We've had the memorial. You were there."

"Bullshit." Nikki says. "There wasn't a body." She pauses. "And you're wanting to talk. I doubt you want to sit around with me and sip Mai Tais, talking about our common friend. You think something's going on too."

I say nothing, but if she could read my mind, she would have heard *you had me at Mai Tais...*

"I've said all I'm going to say about Kristee," Nikki says. "I promised her I wouldn't talk about her private issues. You're wasting a trip if you come over."

"Too late. I'm parked behind your house right now. In back of your car."

Her silence carries its own sound. It drags on, and as I wonder if she's just left her phone somewhere, the back gate opens. She glares through my windshield before lowering her head and ending our call. I open my door to climb out of my truck, but she raises a palm toward me like a crossing guard at the elementary school.

"I'll get in."

I lean across to the passenger side and pull the handle. Nikki climbs aboard and I catch a waft of citrus.

"Creepy. Why didn't you ring the bell at the front door? I mean, instead of like hanging out in the alley behind my house?"

I rest one hand on the steering wheel and look at her while shaking my head. "I don't know. The neighbors might talk. You know, an old guy calling on a younger woman." I see Nikki shaking her head as well and figure she's thinking I'm some old-fashioned throwback more suited for her parents. "And now we're sitting alone in my truck in your back alley where everyone can see us. That's worse. Want to go for a drive?"

"Are you really that clueless?"

"Well, probably more of a traditional guy than you're used to, but I wouldn't say clueless."

She stares at me and her jaw shifts lower, her mouth opening, before she speaks again. "You do know I'm gay, right?"

I don't know this. I mean, I'm not shocked at the news because declaring your sexuality wasn't uncommon in the military I left, and is completely normal in the civilian society in which I live.

So am I shocked to find out Nikki likes women? No. I'm just surprised I hadn't discovered it earlier. And from the look on Nikki's face, she is as surprised as me.

"God, Tyler. You need to get out more. I thought everyone in SAR knew." Nikki gazes out my truck window at the houses abutting her own. She gives a beauty pageant wave, then turns and leans across the center console to give another wave out my window.

"See, I don't give a shit who sees me. None of my neighbors are going to think I've suddenly gone straight." She gives me a manic grin. "You're lucky no one your age lives here, or they'd be starting rumors about you."

I say nothing and try to smile at her. I'm not in the mood.

Nikki seems to recognize my discomfort, and her smile fades. "So, why are you here? I told you I'm not going to talk about Kristee's personal problems."

"Right. You've been clear on that. But you've also been spouting off about how you think her disappearance is no accident." I drop my thin smile. "Which isn't fair to Kristee's family and isn't fair to her friends who are grieving." I watch Nikki shift in the bucket seat. "So either you have a reason to think someone wanted Kristee to disappear, or you're just trying to get some attention. Which is it?"

At my last comment, Nikki stiffens and turns an incredulous face toward me.

"Trying to get attention?" Her voice is icy. "Fuck you, Zahn. Mr. 'I'm the only hero in Buena Vista.' Everyone knows about all your heroics in the last couple of years with Perez. You think *I'm* the one trying to get attention?"

I'm not sure what Nikki is getting at or how to respond—and she's not finished. "Kristee had a lot going on. Head stuff, heart stuff—and here." Nikki leans forward and taps her backside.

Head, heart, and butt? I give Nikki a puzzled stare.

"The pocketbook, the wallet, whatever…she was dealing with money issues." Nikki taps her back pocket again before opening her door and exiting. I see her shoulders rise like she's taking a deep breath, and then she turns to face me, leaning into the truck.

"Honestly, I have no idea who would be involved in making her disappear. But there was enough stuff going on in different areas of her life that it could have been one of several people. And since I'm not telling you about the issues of the heart, I guess you'd better focus on where her head was. And you might consider the money thing. It's no secret that she was trying to make enough money to pay for Karla's college."

"Nikki, I—"

She exits the truck before I can get the words out, slamming the door and aiming toward her house.

Damn—that didn't go well.

I pull away from Nikki's housing development, mulling over my new information. Which isn't much. Kristee was having money problems. I knew that—that's why she started the business and was so stressed about it. Kristee was having issues of the heart—I knew that, as well. She and Williams were having relationship challenges. Probably Perez was still in the picture. Was he the one who left her the note? You put the money issues together with the heart issues and, yes, I'm sure Kristee's head was pretty messed up.

I still think Nikki's a bit wacko. None of these issues explain someone wanting Kristee to disappear. Not in the world I live in.

. . .

Driving through town on my way home, I spy Karla walking the sidewalk toward Kristee's condo, a bag of takeout in one hand. Her eyes are on the mountains, and I wonder if the love of the outdoors runs in the family. I maneuver into an empty parking slot a half block ahead and exit my truck as Karla passes.

I note a flash of recognition in Kristee's sister's eyes as she stops and breaks into a smile. Which is nice. And unexpected.

"Thank you for being at the memorial. It meant a lot to us."

"I wouldn't have missed it. She was very special to me." I wonder if I should explain further.

Karla nods. "She told me how you were someone she could talk to. She admired you." Her smile fades. "We didn't grow up with a father."

"Do you mind if I walk with you?" My mouth waters at the scent of roast garlic from the bag. "Smells like Italian—I can carry the bag."

"I got it. Spaghetti *aglio e olio*." Karla twirls the bag on her wrist. "But, yeah, you're welcome to join me."

I pull up alongside her as she walks, claiming the space between her and the street.

Karla looks at me. "We thought you were at the Academy."

"I'm taking a break. It was hard to concentrate back there."

Karla nods. I can't find a subtle way to ask my question, so I plow forward.

"You said you don't have a college fund. That your mother stopped paying for college. Why is that?"

"Kristee never told you?"

I snort. If there's one thing Kristee's friends understood about Kristee, it was not to bring up her mother. Taboo subject. "Uh, she didn't talk about your mother much."

Karla's laugh falters. "Family drama. Are you sure you want to hear it?"

"I think so," I say. "Not because I'm into family gossip or anything. She had something on her mind and I'm trying to figure out what it was. She called me the morning of the mission to talk, and I got the sense it was personal. But then came the SAR call, and I never spoke to her again."

"I doubt it was the issue with my mother and the college money." Karla pauses, and I turn my head to her. "Sorry. I was thinking it was more likely she was calling to tell you how stressed out she was about Mama's visit. This would have been their first real talk since 'the incident.'"

I nod.

Karla glances my way before continuing. "You might have noticed our mother is a little protective about who Kristee dates. She's that way with me, too."

I say nothing, still nodding, and remember Lin Li's question when she first arrived. *She's still dating the Black man, correct?* The way she depersonalized Williams made it clear she did not approve.

"That's what happened with Kristee at college. Kristee was a sophomore at the University of Denver, the same college my mother taught at. She started dating someone who was—how would you put it?—sort of unconventional. Mama hit the roof when she found out and demanded Kristee put an end to it."

"I can guess how that turned out." I smiled at the thought of anyone telling Kristee who she could date.

"I bet you can't." Karla's face is solemn. "Yes, Kristee ignored my mother. When Mama started threatening to cut off the college money, Kristee just got a job. She wasn't going to end the relationship."

This is the Kristee I remember.

"But things got a little crazy. Mama set up Kristee's partner."

"What do you mean 'set up?'"

"I mean she had access to the learning management system and could change assignment submissions."

"What's a learning management system?"

"Like Canvas or Scholar. The computer system that allows you to submit all your assignments online."

I nod, understanding the concept, but not familiar with the names. My daughter doesn't provide these details when I ask her how school's going.

"Anyway, Mama doctors up the assignment and gets Kristee's partner kicked out for plagiarism. Like overnight." We are approaching the parking lot in front of Kristee's condo, and Karla slows. I'm guessing it's so she can finish the story, but as I watch her scan the balcony, I realize it could be she doesn't want her mother to see us talking.

"And that's when Kristee stopped talking to your mother?"

Karla stops at the edge of the parking lot and turns to me. "No. That's when Kristee quit school. She didn't realize our mother was involved in this. She just knew she'd lost someone she cared about for a reason she didn't understand. It broke her heart. That's when she headed out here to the mountains."

I'm familiar with fleeing to the Rockies when your life goes to shit. Kristee had pulled a Tyler Zahn before I had.

"All the stuff with my mother came out later. An investigation uncovered what she had done. She got fired and hasn't worked a professional job since. So it's not that she wouldn't pay for my college. It's that she can't. And she's not proud of that."

"But Kristee knows…?" I pause, then try again. "I mean, she knew what your mother did?"

"Oh, yeah. The university kept it quiet because they were embarrassed, and Mama would never tell her." She pauses. "But I did. And they haven't talked since." She gives me a sad smile and spreads her hands at her side. "This was supposed to be the big reconciliation."

I pause, remembering Lin Li's attitude toward Kristee's relationship with Williams. Was that why Kristee and Williams were having issues? Because Kristee wanted to mend her broken mother-daughter relationship and Williams was the obstacle to reconciliation. Another man Lin Li could not abide?

"No wonder Kristee was stressed," I say. "She's having relationship issues with both Williams and your mother, while trying to figure out how to make enough money to keep you in school." I pause. "That's a lot."

Karla lowers her head as if it's her fault. I remember a question I had for her.

"Why didn't you apply for student loans? I'm not passing judgment here, and I'm not a fan of student loans, but it seems like everybody's using them. Why didn't you?"

Karla nods. "I would have, but neither of them would co-sign. My mother refused on principle. Like a cultural thing. She was raised in mainland China, where school debt was literally a foreign concept. She would never allow me to borrow money for school."

"And Kristee?"

"You know Kristee. When I asked her about it, she also refused, insisting she could pay for the school herself." Karla sighs. "Both of them are very protective. They just go about it in different ways."

A diesel truck roars into the parking lot, pulling into a spot facing Kristee's stairwell. Karla and I pause and watch as the downstairs neighbor—the girl who watches Amore for Kristee—gets out and makes a run for the door of her condo.

The truck's other door opens and the driver, a large man, steps out.

"That's Jacy's dad," Karla whispers, staring at the man's back across the lot. "Kristee had some run-ins with him. She says he's an asshole." She turns to me, her eyes glistening. "Said. Not says."

We hear the man's voice boom across the lot. "Jacy, get your ass back here. I ain't finished."

The condo door slams and Jacy disappears.

"Shit." Jacy's father pulls off his hat, turns around, and slaps it against the truck. He spots us on the other side of the lot and freezes. "What the fuck you looking at?"

We say nothing, and I step forward in front of Karla. The man squints my direction and shakes his head. He turns around, slams the truck door, and aims for his condo.

Karla and I wait until he's inside before resuming our conversation.

My voice is quiet. "You said Kristee was distraught when she came out here to the mountains? After college. Running away because she couldn't handle everything that was happening?"

"She was. I remember it was so strange, because Kristee usually can handle anything."

"Maybe she did the same thing this time? You know…left?"

Karla flashes her eyes at me. "What are you saying? Like she staged her disappearance and just ran away?"

"I'm not sure what I'm thinking. You're right, that doesn't sound like Kristee. She wouldn't run."

I remind Karla I'm available if she needs to talk. She nods and walks across the lot toward Kristee's stairwell. I stay where I'm at, making sure Jacy's dad doesn't reappear.

Karla waves from the balcony and disappears, leaving me pondering the many ways one can run away. After hearing the story of Kristee's past and discovering what she was dealing with, I wonder if the pressure overwhelmed her. I'm frightened Kristee believed leaving the mountains wouldn't solve her problems and instead decided to leave her life. To end it.

KRISTEE

BEFORE

I sit on the edge of my bed, my fingers kneading Amore's head, my eyes zeroed in on my bedroom dresser. The five thousand from Travis is stacked in the third drawer. My brain screams, *use it to pay the rest of Karla's spring tuition,* while my gut counters with *what the hell are you doing?* This is so not me.

Yes, diving into this business venture, using money I had set aside for Karla's tuition next year is a risk. But my motives are pure. I'm forecasting past next year and planning how to get Karla through the rest of her undergraduate degree. Maybe even beyond. The kid's smart enough for grad school, and she's talked about it.

The Aerie's start-up costs were a different gamble than accepting cash to ignore Travis's work. Externally, I present an aura of the self-assured, self-made woman that doesn't take shit from anyone. That's how all of Buena Vista sees me. And then there's the internal me, recovering from a controlling mother who lacks the capacity for love, and a cultural and familial obligation to my sister's college dreams, keeping me on the edge of broke every day.

But if I'm honest—and really, why shouldn't I be?—accepting that money from Travis doesn't fit either of those personas. It's not who I am. It's not what I stand for.

I flop back on my bed and listen to Amore scramble to his feet and turn in circles. I smile, recognizing what's coming. Rather than let him break the rules, I change them.

"Up."

Amore leaps onto my bed and sticks his face into mine. A rare treat for my best friend, but he seems to know I need some loving right now.

The whole loving thing brought me to this point in my life. If it hadn't been for my college days with Terry, my first love, I wouldn't be living out here in the heart of the Rockies. If it hadn't been for the mother who refuses to love me, I wouldn't have stayed this long. And if it hadn't been for the man I may love, my mother wouldn't be visiting. She's not coming for a reconciliation, or to forgive. Instead, she's seizing an opportunity to run my life once again. Somehow, she's discovered my relationship with Williams, and she's on her way to put an end to it.

That's what Williams didn't understand when I shut him down. He thought it was because he brought up the taboo subject of Mama Li—he was supposed to know better. But the real reason I clammed up was because her impending visit is about him. A man she doesn't even know, but judges only by skin color.

Why does the thought of discussing this with Williams unnerve me? Even though we're both people more attuned to action than long conversations over a candlelit dinner, we still talk. Well, some. I knead my fingers into Amore's fur again, remembering how Tyler Zahn tried to set me up with Rick Perez after the two of them—actually, Randy too—stopped that terrorist thing at the Dillon Dam.

The four of us had driven up North Cottonwood Creek and set off to climb Mt Harvard, one of Buena Vista's closest 14ers. I talked with Perez for the first third of the climb. He's a great guy and thank God he's still my friend. But then Randy moved up the hiking line and slipped in behind me. We started talking and never stopped.

There's a connection between us. I'm unsure whether it's the common frustration with our upbringing—Williams raised as a city boy, and me with an overprotective mother—or our mutual appreciation for outdoor exercise, but we've bonded. We're comfortable together.

However, I've discovered from my limited pool of girlfriends in town—Nikki from Search & Rescue, and April and Savannah from rafting—that *comfortable* isn't necessarily what satisfies others in a relationship.

"I need a man that knows I'm in charge, but makes me forget it when I'm in the sack," April once told me.

"Me too, except a woman." Nikki said, when I told her about April's statement at The Lock-Up the night after Travis shoved his money at me. Right before we ordered a round of shots. The night was blurry after that—but in a good way.

The truth is, me and Williams are just OK between the sheets. There's a TV ad that always reminds me our sex lives might lack some spice. The narrator explains, *just OK, is not OK.* Like every experience needs to be an out-of-the-park home run.

That's not how it is with Williams and me. We like to be close. We have sex—but not every time he comes to visit. What we do best is what we don't do with others—open up. Most of the time.

I missed that opportunity the last time he visited. We'd just made love, and there was a moment when he propped on his elbow, leaned over me, and locked his eyes on mine. I'd lifted my head from the pillow and nibbled on his bottom lip, giggling as his sudden smile pulled his lip from my mouth.

"Wait," he said. "Do it again."

I laughed and pushed his chest. "Out. You've got work. I've got my meeting with Travis. We're going to be late."

Williams had pushed up and straddled me, his hands pressed into the mattress by my ears.

"Go!" I laughed. But he didn't move. For the next minute, he told me how proud he was that I was starting the business. How he always respected my work ethic—plowing snow in the winter and guiding rafts in the summer—but that running a business took it to a whole new level.

"You're turning yourself into an honest woman, Kristee," he said in a teasing tone. And then we had parted—Williams back to Denver and me to my new office.

I jerk upright in my bed, my legs dangling off the end, and Amore scrabbling at my lap, trying to figure out if his rare bed privileges are in danger. Through the window, Mt Yale and Mt Columbia form a vee, like a gunsight. Mt Harvard juts skyward out of sight at the end of that gap.

"Right there." I point at the window and turn to Amore, who follows my finger without understanding. He jumps from the bed and stands by the window, whining.

"Right there," I repeat. "Me and Randy Williams hiking up that mountain. That's the last time I was an honest woman."

I failed twice. I didn't tell him about Mama's visit and her little racism problem, and I've made a mockery of his admiration for me. Sure, he was joking about the *honest woman* thing—rafting and plowing are honest ways to make a buck. But he was also proud of me for stepping into the challenge of turning a fledgling enterprise into a respected business establishment.

Except now I have $5k in cash stuffed into my underwear drawer and another cash delivery scheduled in two weeks. For something I've agreed to ignore.

Honest woman, hell.

• • •

That night I can't sleep. At 4:30 in the morning, I give up and take Amore for a long jog. The sun angles off the Collegiates by the time we return. Before I head to the office, I scribble a note to Jacy, letting her know I exercised Amore for the day and she can skip his walk if she wants.

A door slams as I descend the steps and I catch sight of Erik, Jacy's father, heading toward the parking lot.

"Morning," I call, falling in behind him on the walkway.

Erik whips his head around. I hear him grunt, and as he turns back toward his truck, I speak again.

"I'm Kristee, from upstairs? Jacy's watching my dog, Amore."

He turns and faces me.

"How much are you paying her?"

I haven't paid Jacy yet. She said she'd watch him for free, but of course I'm paying. We just haven't discussed how much.

So that's what I tell her father.

"You'd better figure it out," he says. "Otherwise, you're keeping her from a better paying job."

He wheels around and heads for his truck.

"Nice to meet you, too," I call. Then I add under my breath, "Erik."

I must have said it louder than I planned, because I see his shoulders flinch. But he doesn't turn.

•   •   •

Lights shine from inside The Aerie, but the front door is locked. My reflection greets me in the glass door as I twist the key and enter. The entrepreneur stepping into her domain. The contractors finished the trim yesterday, and the just-cut wood and new carpet emit a fresh smell. Like when you drive a new car. I wonder how long it will last. The aura of new, that is. If I don't get my shit together, the scent will last longer than my business license.

I made the decision during my early morning jog to return the money Travis gave me. It's in my backpack. No matter how you look at it—and I've been turning it over and over in my head like a pig on a spit for a day now—this is hush money. Keeping the cash is not who I am or what I stand for.

I see Travis's office door closed, a sliver of light winking between the carpet and the door. When I rap twice, I get no reply.

"Travis, you in there?"

A breeze tickles my neck, and I turn to the rear entrance. A brick props the door open and now I know where to find my business partner. Aiming for the exit, I watch as a foot thrusts through the frame and maneuvers the door open. It's Travis, and he's got his arms cradled around another box. He nods at me as he steps through the door, then turns and nudges the brick outside. He greets me as the door clicks shut.

"Kristee." He grins.

"Another box? Through the back door?"

Travis keeps the grin plastered on his face and replies, "What box? Remember?" Then he leans the package against the wall and fumbles in his pocket for a set of keys. He eyes me again and tosses the key ring to me. "The silver one. Can you open the door for me?"

I shuffle through the keys and choose the only silver one. The one that matches the key Walt made for me. I open the door.

"Thanks." He steps past me and lowers the box behind the desk in the same spot where he'd left the other box the day before. When he stands, I toss him the keyring and block the doorframe, hands on my hips.

Travis looks at me, and I see a question in his eyes.

"What's up?"

I take a breath and remove my backpack. I see his smile disappear as he watches me unzip the pack and dig through it.

"What's going on, Kristee?" Now his eyes reflect a flicker of fear.

I pull the envelope of cash from the pack and step forward, placing it on the desk between us. "Here's the money. I can't take it." I pause. "I won't take it. I will not be a part of whatever this…" I spread my arms wide. "…is. And I can't ignore it if it's happening in our building."

I watch Travis's shoulders slump and at first, I guess he's going to be upset that I'm kicking his operation out of our building. But when I see him offer that stupid grin again, I recognize relief slumping his shoulders, not dejection. *Did he think I had a weapon? Holy shit.*

"I'll keep quiet," I say. "Speaking as a friend, I'll remind you that anything requiring you to sneak around can't be legal…or smart. But I'll leave that to you as your business. It's not my business, and I want it out of our building."

Travis is nodding at me, still wearing that stupid smile.

"What?" I'm confused.

"I'm agreeing with you." He reaches into his pocket and pulls out his phone. He taps the screen twice before returning his eyes to mine. "Actually, I'm agreeing with some of what you're saying. Like the part about you not mentioning it to anyone. You got that right—you won't mention it."

"And the part about you moving it out of here? I'm serious about that."

Travis lays his phone on the desk next to the envelope of cash and hits another button. The sound of his voice comes from the phone.

"There's $5k. There's nothing in the box. Two weeks from now, there will still be nothing in the box. And you'll get the other $5k. Do you understand?"

And then I hear my voice. Not shy, not innocent. Kind of snarky.

"What box?"

"You taped us? You fucking taped us exchanging the money?" Bile surges in the back of my throat, and I can't wrap my head around Travis's logic. "What good does it do you to have me on tape if you are the one buying me off? If you used this, you'd get in more trouble than I would."

Travis nods. His smile disappears, and he returns the phone to his pocket. I squint at the phone as he does it, making sure he hasn't started to record again. *Fool me once...shame on you...*

"I think you might be right, but that's OK. You know why?"

I have no idea why—I've chosen the business partner from hell and I'm in over my head.

"I'm a part-time raft guide who's living on his parents' dime—hell, I'm just an accident waiting to happen," Travis says. "But you? You've established yourself in this community. You're on the Search & Rescue team. You're friends with the cops. People are talking about you as the 'budding entrepreneur.' Hell, you're on track to be business owner of the year. What's that? #1 out of 12 businesses in town? Yee-haw."

"What's your point?" But I realize he's already made it. If he takes that tape to the cops, I'm guilty of accepting his money. It doesn't matter what they do to Travis, I'm ruined in this town and probably facing charges for ignoring Travis's wrongdoings. And they'll never believe I don't know what he's up to.

I lower my eyes.

"Oh, you get my point alright." Travis's voice is flat. "Don't you?"

I say nothing.

"Come over here and take your money. Get out of my office."

So I do.

• • •

Adrenaline floods my veins as I speed walk home, aghast at how far I've fallen on the ethical scale. When Travis had played that recording, my stomach dropped, the same feeling I have when the pilot gives up on the landing five feet above the runway coming into Denver. I just wanted a do-over with Travis. *Here's your money. I don't agree with your shit, but I'm over it. Let's move on.*

Instead, I'm in the thick of it. Tears form in the corners of my eyes, and I brush them away, focusing my eyes on the jagged outline of the Collegiate Peaks across the valley. So regal, majestic…so right.

The mountains and the river behind me drew me to this town with their promises of both livelihood and adventure. They represent everything good in my life since my move. I've opened my heart to the outdoors, and the Colorado Rockies have filled it. I wipe my eyes again, turning my gaze back to the sidewalk. I don't deserve to look at the mountains.

As I climb my condo stairs, Jacy exits my door. She freezes mid-stride as she sees me and widens her eyes.

"I saw the note, so I didn't walk Amore." Jacy shrugs and twists her palms up like I'm going to berate her for not doing her job. "I just fed him." She pauses. "And petted him for a while."

"You did exactly what I asked, Jacy. Relax." I give her a tight smile, hoping she'll take my words to heart.

She nods and shifts her eyes to my feet. "Same time tomorrow? I've got to run to school."

"Same time. And he'll probably need that walk tomorrow. I doubt I'll be out as early as I was today." Actually, I have no clue what I'll be doing tomorrow. Whether I'll still go to my job. Whether I'll be turning myself into law enforcement. Whether I'll be locked in my bedroom trying to figure out what to do. But that's not Jacy's concern. She just wants the job. And probably an excuse to avoid her father.

I reach out and gently grasp Jacy's wrist. "Is everything alright?"

I see her hesitate and she keeps her eyes on mine. Is she going to trust me with her story? Or is she simply looking for a friend?

Or maybe I'm just finding drama around every corner. I drop her wrist before it gets too awkward. Jacy steps backward and gives me a nod.

"Going great," she says brightly. Too brightly. "I love seeing Amore before school." She raises her hand to me and turns to the stairs. "See you," she says as she starts the descent.

Amore greets me at the door, and I crouch and scratch his head, looking past him to the sparse living room. I picture lying on this couch all morning trying to solve my dilemma. Not how I generally deal with my problems. I cup Amore's chin and pull his face up so I'm looking him in the eyes.

"Up for another run?" Amore pulls away, dashing to the rack where his leash dangles, and turning circles beneath it. I laugh. "Give me a minute to change," I call, aiming for the bedroom. Five minutes later, we're jogging to the bridge at the River Park and the trail network on the other side.

It's the variety that draws me to the trails. Not just the way they undulate beneath my feet, wind me in unanticipated directions, or change with the seasons, but also how I can attack them differently, depending on my mood and my purpose.

If I run a trail to escape the troubles of my day, I run fast. My attention focuses on where to plant my feet, leaving no time for other thoughts. If I'm running with a friend or Amore, it's usually a steady, slower pace where I can keep up a conversation while still watching foot placement. But if I'm using my trail run to get my thoughts in order, I go slow. I'll power hike the uphills and let gravity guide me downhill. I'm careful and consistent, because I need to do two things at once: keep myself from rolling an ankle and concentrate on whatever issue has brought me to the mountains.

That's how I run today. Slow, steady, and careful—partly because I don't want to run Amore ragged after his early morning jog, but mostly so I can figure out what to do about Travis.

I need to do the right thing. Go to the police—or Perez. Explain that my business partner paid me money to ignore his illegal activity, and I agreed to his proposition. That I know I made the wrong choice and I'm turning myself in. That's what right looks like.

But here's the problem. It's not just my reputation at risk here. I'm frightened about what turning myself in would mean for Karla. My business will collapse after Travis is arrested—regardless of what happens to me—along with my long-term solution for getting Karla through school.

I have no money for the short-term. Karla's going to have to drop out.

I don't know how much trouble I'm in for accepting Travis's offer, but I do know that if I go to jail, then I'm all done helping my sister.

"Come on, Amore." I tuck his leash in my pocket. "Let's go." We cut off the trail, and I power hike up the mountain, Amore scrambling in the lead. He loves bushwhacking.

I press my palms on my knees, pushing them into the slope, and block out the conflict roaring in my head. Instead, I focus on my breath. My quads burn and I increase my pace. Alternating my steps, an involuntary mantra escapes my lips.

Tell the cops. Right foot forward.

Take the money. Left foot forward.

I plow the last thirty yards to the ridgeline, the dichotomy ringing in my head, and gasp as I summit. Amore is waiting and circles my legs as I rest my hands on my knees. I stand erect and turn, staring across the valley at the silhouette of the Collegiate Peaks.

"God, what do I do?" I yell. My voice's echo is my only reply.

I don't believe in God. Yesterday, I believed that as long as you lived right and believed in yourself, the rest would take care of itself. Now I'm relying on instinct. And it's telling me to take care of my sister.

Take the money.

ZAHN

NOW

Nikki's words echo in my head over the following days as I try to reestablish my home routines. Now that I've left the Academy, I drift between my house and town, searching for a purpose. Search & Rescue knows I'm available for calls, and I've checked in with Ruth at yoga to make sure class times haven't changed. But I have no anchor. Like a ship cut loose from its harbor moorings, I bump around Buena Vista, groping for something firm.

Consider the money thing. Nikki dropped those words after I'd blatantly accused her of just looking for attention. Karla reaffirmed that money was an issue when I talked to her.

As each day passes, Kristee's memory fades from the town's consciousness. A local death always strikes a small community hard, but I sense Buena Vista is rebounding quickly. There are businesses to run, families to feed, and lives to live.

But Kristee disappeared only days ago, and I'm still numb.

Am I the only one? I know Randall is hurting, but he has returned to the Marshal's office in Denver. Perez has stopped taking time off from work. They've both gone back to their lives, giving the impression they've adjusted to her absence. So why haven't I?

It's unfair to assume that I bear Kristee's absence alone. Karla has delayed returning to college and surely grieves far more than me. And her mother hasn't left BV either. It's hard to imagine Kristee's mother feeling anything, but who am I to judge? I've seen parental panic when a child disappears, and I've borne the pain of losing a child forever. I know she's hurting.

I make it to 3:30 without a beer. I jot notes from my discussions with Nikki and Karla, try to piece together the odd relationship between Perez, Williams, and Kristee, and ponder the rift between Kristee and her mother. Nothing connects and I give up, cracking the fridge in search of inspiration. Or solace.

I finish my first can of Backside Blond, discouraged at my lack of progress, but inspired at my empty can's three-point trajectory—a bank shot off the side of the fridge into the trash. Kristee hadn't shared all the drama in her life with me. I'm surprised at what I've discovered and a bit hurt. Kristee and I didn't discuss her love life—or mine, for that matter—but we talked about everything else. Or, so I thought. She described the challenges she faced as a woman in this testosterone-charged town: guiding rafts, plowing snow, and cleaning gutters. I opened up about finding purpose in our small community and attempting to shed the pain, loss, and apathy I still carried from my troubled past.

We didn't discuss Kristee's financial situation, and we didn't talk much about our mutual friend, Perez. Randall Williams fell under the love-life category, so I kept my Williams questions focused on his US Marshal job. I guess we avoided day-to-day problems in favor of our existential issues. From *why are we here* to *what mountain should we climb next?*

When she started the business, I was proud. But I certainly didn't pepper her with entrepreneurial questions. Wouldn't have known where to start.

I reach for a second beer, then pause as I consider The Aerie. I glance at my watch and decide it's not too late to return downtown for more questions. Maybe her business partner, Travis, has more insight on Kristee and her problems. *Consider the money thing,* Nikki said.

The drive from my house in Elk Trace to downtown Buena Vista is only eleven minutes. Daria always admonishes me to bike the six miles to stay in shape. I tried it once and surprised myself when I reached downtown in thirty minutes. It's mostly downhill. But the return trip is no joke. Buena Vista sits at eight thousand feet elevation, and my house is six hundred feet higher. Riding home took an hour, and I pushed the bike the last mile. I've stuck to my truck ever since.

Scattered businesses fly by my window as I rehearse questions for Travis. Just north of town, my peripheral vision catches a Search & Rescue sticker plastered to a Honda parked near the highway. My eyes shift to the business establishment, and I recognize the Planned Parenthood clinic. I ease my foot off the gas and check for traffic before whipping my head back toward the car again. It's Nikki's Honda, the same one I parked behind at her house.

Turning my attention back to the road, I pass under the first of our town's two traffic lights and consider what I've just seen. The logical part of my brain tells me I don't know Nikki that well—she might work there. Whatever the other part of my brain is called—the conspiracy side?—is what caused me to double-take, though. Nikki doesn't work there—I don't think—so why is her car parked outside? She just told me she's not heterosexual, so it's not as if she'd use this service to *plan parenthood*, right?

I might be familiar with same-sex couples, but my imagination somewhat freezes when I try to come up with a scenario where Nikki needs help from this clinic. So why is she there?

I shake my thoughts from my head and pull into an empty parking slot in front of Kristee's business. Or her ex-business? I'm still uncertain what Kristee's death means to the enterprise.

Striding toward the glass doors, I see Travis behind the counter of the reception desk. I've met him once through Kristee and have seen him in town. Based on the blank stare he trains my direction as I reach for the door, I'm unsure he remembers me. I enter The Aerie, and Travis greets me with a smile.

"Hey, welcome to The Aerie. Can I help you?" He looks at my empty hands and I realize he probably wonders what guy comes in to use a temp office with no office supplies—a computer, paper, that sort of stuff.

"Travis, right? I'm Tyler Zahn. Kristee's friend?"

Recognition dawns in Travis's eyes, and his grin fades. "Right. From Search & Rescue. I remember." He nods and stands. "Sorry, dude. She was your friend, right?"

I nod. "Yeah. Sorry for you too. You lost a partner. That must be hard."

"In more ways than one. We were just getting to know each other, so that was pretty tough. I mean, I've lost friends on the river before. That's part of river life, you know? But this? Just came out of nowhere."

I nod and say nothing.

"Then there's the whole business side of it. I'm new to all this, and Kristee was the one doing most of the paperwork. So she still owns her part of the business. But she's considered dead." Travis spreads his hands out, as if at a loss. "But there's no death certificate, and her mom was here, but she knows nothing about the business." Travis pauses, like he realizes he's rambling. "It's all fucked."

"Sounds like maybe you should ask someone about it. You have a lawyer or anything?"

"Why would I need a lawyer?" Travis's voice turns sharp. "I'm not doing anything wrong."

I squint my eyes. "I didn't say you were. But it sounds like you could use some advice. Lawyers do that, too, you know?"

Travis shakes his head as I talk.

"What?"

"Can't afford that kind of advice," he says. "Kristee and I were operating on a shoestring as it was. If I can keep these offices filled and expenses down, I can just break into the black. I figure if I do that for a couple months, I should be able to buy out Kristee's portion from her mom or sister or whoever ends up owning it."

"Did she talk to you about why she was starting the business?"

Now it's Travis's turn to squint. "Not specifically. She had some payments to make. She was always interested in turning a profit from the start."

I think back to the offhand comment Kristee made when we shared the beer at the Surf. *Travis is running his own business inside of ours. I wasn't planning on that. But I've adjusted.* I paid little attention to her comment at the time. I wasn't actually that interested in the details of her venture. Simply proud that she seized the opportunity.

Travis still has his eyes narrowed. "Why? Did she ever talk to you about the business?"

I consider asking him about his *business within a business* but decide against it. He already looks nervous.

I spread my arms wide. "I'm an old retired military guy. Do I look like I fit in around offices?"

Travis seems to relax a bit, but not completely. "So, why are you here?"

"I care about the family. I've met her sister, Karla, and I think Kristee was planning on using the money from this place"—I raise my palm toward the roof—"to pay for her college." I smile. "I just wanted to check and see what was happening with Kristee's business."

Travis nods. "That's cool. I can respect that." He spreads his palms across the reception desk. "Look, I told you I'm working through the mechanics of Kristee's share of the company. And you told me you're not business savvy. What I can tell you is this. I won't cheat Kristee's family out of what they are due." He paused. "I guess I might consider a lawyer for that advice you talked about. But I'll be fair."

My phone's ringtone blares, and I grab for my pocket.

"Go ahead, man," Travis says, turning back to the computer at the reception desk.

I nod at him and spin toward the door, glancing at my phone. The screen reads *Rick Perez, Sheriff's Office.* I push the glass doors out toward the sidewalk.

"What's up, Rick?"

"What's up with *you*? I had business up in Elk Trace and stopped by to say 'hey.' But you ain't here."

I turn and look back at Kristee's business and watch Travis tracking my progress. "Yeah, out doing errands," I say. I don't need to offer

Perez details on my movements. I'm still pissed at him for holding back on the Kristee-Nikki fight.

"Want to meet up? Got something new on Kristee."

"What do you have? I thought you all shut down the case." I squeeze my phone and stop walking.

"I'll meet you down at the Elk Trace entrance, at the bus stop. Ten minutes?"

"I'll be there." I hang up and head for my truck.

What does Perez have? Did they find physical evidence from Kristee or new information from someone else? Another question pops into my head. Why is Perez suddenly turning cooperative? Does he feel guilty for leaving me out of the loop?

Perez waits at the entrance, his department Tahoe pointed straight at me as I pull in next to him. By the time I stop, he's out of his vehicle and leaning against the door. I exit my truck and stand facing the deputy.

"What you got?"

Rick stares at me a minute before nodding. "Yeah, I'll brief you on it." He pauses. "Let me ask you something else first."

"What?"

"What's going on with you and Nikki Kingston?"

I stare back at Perez, wondering how he knows I met with Nikki. "Nothing's going on. Why do you think there is?"

"You haven't been talking to her since Kristee disappeared?"

Now I'm pissed. "You know I have, or you wouldn't be asking." I put my hands on my hips and take a step back from Perez. "What? Are you following me around town now, or do you have one of your deputy deputies doing that?"

Perez gives a short laugh. "Come on, Tyler? What's happening here? Since when are you and I not together on this stuff?"

I bristle. "Since you didn't tell me the full story about Nikki and Kristee having a fight. Since you've obviously got folks tracking me because you know I went to talk to Nikki again. Jesus, Rick. What's going on?"

"We don't have anyone tracking you. We did a check-in with Nikki, and she told us about your visit. Actually, she berated us about your visit. Accused us of doing nothing more on Kristee's disappearance. Said the only one still showing interest in it was Tyler Zahn."

"Why check in on Nikki? That doesn't make sense."

Perez nods. "You really want to know?"

I don't like Perez to catch me off-guard, but I can't keep the incredulity off my face. "No. Not interested at all about my missing best friend."

I see Perez flinch a fraction. Not at my sarcasm. Probably at the fact that he figured himself as my best friend. A week ago, he would've been right. Now I'm not so sure.

"Kristee had a restraining order on Nikki. That fight on the mountain wasn't their first altercation."

"What the hell?" Now I'm just confused. Perez watches me as I grasp what he's saying. "Why were they teamed up?"

"Nikki said that's the way the teams shook out, and they mutually agreed to roll with it."

"But I don't understand. What could they be arguing about that was so important Kristee sought legal protection from Nikki?"

Perez's eyes meet mine before shifting sideways toward my truck. "Don't know. They had an altercation at Kristee's place. BV police came by. Kristee filed the restraining order the next day. She claimed irreconcilable differences that caused her to fear for her personal safety."

Perez isn't telling me everything. I can tell. And it makes no sense to me. I wasn't even aware Kristee and Nikki had such a stormy friendship. My daughter joined them once at the Lock-Up, but never mentioned a problem. I remember they had done a couple of SAR missions together. That was the whole of my Kristee-Nikki knowledge.

"So that's why I'm asking about you and Nikki. You seem to think I'm keeping stuff from you, so now I'm sharing. Kristee is an emotional topic for Nikki. Maybe you should watch your step if you decide to talk to her again. If Kristee didn't think she was safe around Nikki, why should you?"

I try to sort everything Perez has told me. "This is why you called? I thought you had a break—some clue, or something. Sounds like the restraining order is old news."

"This isn't why I called you. The restraining order isn't relevant to the case. Nikki couldn't have done anything to Kristee—Chad was right there the whole time. But when I heard you were contacting Nikki, I decided you should know."

"So, why did you call?"

"It's the landslide. The one that happened the day Kristee disappeared—on the south side of the cut between North Apostle and Ice Mountain."

"What about it?"

"Some hikers were up there yesterday. They found Kristee's phone."

KRISTEE

BEFORE

The Aerie sucks the joy from my life like a vacuum. I was so excited about starting the business, offering my community a new opportunity and me a chance to try something new and make more money. Our venture has kicked off, and clients are renting our space—but where is the joy? Travis and I aren't talking, which leaves me bouncing in and out all day, checking in with Bree—our reception desk new-hire—about how things are going. I avoid Travis's office and ignore the back alley.

Daria, Zahn's daughter, arrives for a visit and asks me to join her and Zahn for a hike to Harvard Lakes. I jump at the invite. Snowplow season is over, my customers' gutters are clean, and I'm the third wheel at work. We agree to meet at the Three Elk trailhead at eleven and enjoy a picnic at the lakes.

Zahn and Daria are already parked at the trailhead when I arrive. I wrap Daria in a quick hug and step back, shaking my head.

"Look at you out hiking the mountains. Thought you were supposed to ease into recovery?"

Daria experienced a double whammy last year—first, a fall from a horse near the Colorado Trail and then a severe leg injury during her abduction by a local lunatic. It was quite a visit for her.

"Girl, it's been like ten months. I'm ready to go." Daria grins. "How come you haven't been out to the Front Range for a visit?"

I hang my head. I've visited Denver twice this past year, but not up toward Boulder. I could've seen Daria, but I'm always in such a hurry to return home after a trip to the city. Home to my mountains and my river—not to cars and people.

"Guilty." I grin back. "But I'm ready to go today." I punch Zahn in the arm and give him a smile. "What? We're bringing the old man so we don't push ourselves too hard?"

Zahn's eyes crinkle and he shakes his head. "Something like that. Good to see you, too, Kristee."

We hit the trail at a steady pace, comfortable in each other's company. The Zahns are family to me. Tyler and I hit it off from day one of our Search & Rescue training and have remained close. I know him better than I do Daria. His daughter's visit last year was the first time I'd met her and her first visit in something like seven years. I don't know all the details, but Zahn just refers to that time apart as the *bad years*.

Perez and I were there when Zahn moved to Buena Vista, with all his bottled-up personal troubles. Mountains are supposed to soothe the troubled soul, but people forget about Boyle's Law. Whatever you have bottled up expands the higher you go. That's what happened to Zahn. Everything inside of him eventually released, and Perez and I—and Randy toward the end—were there to help him deal with it. We helped bring him to a point where he was comfortable reconnecting with his daughter.

My friendship with Daria has been a surprise. Our mutual love of the outdoors hinted at our compatibility, but there was something else as well. Two women of color in a predominantly white county—Zahn's ex-wife, Sheila, is African American and I'm ethnically Chinese—creates a bond. We both enjoy the surprised expressions people give two women of color strolling all four blocks of Main Street, confident in our status as locals. Okay, Daria's not a local, but when she's with me, I treat her like one.

The hike today is familiar and challenging, the trail weaving across the Three Elk drainage several times before sticking to a rocky spine the last half mile to the lakes. We make it in just over an hour and kick back next to the water, enjoying our lunch. We haven't talked much during the climb, but none of us are out of breath.

I quiz Daria on school and men, but she deftly turns the conversation back to life in Buena Vista. Daria's mature for her age. She takes her studies seriously, but doesn't lose much sleep over the drama of daily college life. Zahn sits back and sips from his water bottle, appearing to enjoy our banter. He's always one for letting others talk. I watch him lean forward, however, when I grill Daria about her friend Kevin, the guy she'd started dating last year during her visit.

"He ended up moving back to southwest Virginia. Took a job as the activity director at a large church camp near Marion. You know where that is?"

I shake my head.

"South of Virginia Tech by about an hour. Anyway, we kept things going for a couple months after he moved before we decided to just be friends. Long distance romance...ugh."

I see Zahn settle back with a handful of chips. I wonder how much he is hearing for the first time. Although I'm no *dad* expert, having hardly known my own, I remember Zahn's struggles during Daria's visit last year. Trying to win her back by serving as her tour guide and activities director, rather than giving her what she wanted—a father.

"I want to hear about the business," Daria says. "Are you going to give me a tour?"

I force a smile. "I can do that. In fact, I can show you through the building tonight before we go out."

Daria's smile curls, and she glances at Zahn. "Go out?"

"Yeah, I'm meeting my friend Nikki for a little live music at the Lock-Up, and I'm thinking you didn't come all the way out to Buena Vista to stream old *Longmire* episodes on TV with your dad, did you?"

"Hey, now—" Zahn leans forward again.

"You are so right," Daria says, and pushes her father gently back with a smile. "Give me a time to meet you guys when we get back to the car, OK?"

I consider texting Nikki to tell her Daria will join us, but I have no phone service. No surprise at 10,500 feet, and fewer than three miles from the Continental Divide. Looking up, I see Zahn laughing.

"What? I've had reception up here before," I protest.

Zahn shakes his head, still chuckling. "No, I'm just laughing at how fast you turned into a businesswoman. Used to be the only thing you used your phone for was the compass."

I return Zahn's smile. He's not wrong, even if I was texting a friend and not Travis.

Travis. My gut twists, thinking about the money and his phone recording and my predicament. I watch as a robber jay lands five feet from our picnic lunch and begins hopping between us looking for food.

"Have you ever worked in business?" I realize I've never talked much to Zahn about his life after the Air Force.

"Nope. Never had an interest." Zahn's laugh fades to a smile, and he keeps his eyes on me. "But I respect those who do it right."

"Well, we've got a long way to go before we're doing it right. Before we're in the black and making good money." My eyes follow the inquisitive bird in search of a meal. *A long way to go.*

I steal a glance at Zahn, and now he's the one shaking his head. "That's not what I meant about doing it right, Kristee. You've got to be smart and business savvy to make money in business. I know you can do that. Doing it the right way is something different."

Staring at Zahn, I wonder if he senses my tension. There's no way he knows what's going on between Travis and me. No one does…as far as I know.

Daria leans back, her head on her backpack with sunglasses covering her eyes. She wears a small smile, like she's heard Zahn's impending soliloquy before.

"Doing it right means imbuing your business with your personal integrity." Zahn stares at me. "So your customers are convinced they're not dealing with a corporation, but with Kristee Li. You put service in front of profits and produce a product so excellent that your customers can't imagine going anywhere else."

He makes it sound so simple, yet I can't even meet his eyes.

"I thought you didn't have any experience in business," I say. "Sounds to me like you know what you're talking about."

"Nope. No business savvy on my part. But I've had a lot of experience leading people, and I picked up a few things along the way."

Daria snorts, but I can't see her eyes behind her sunglasses.

"What?" I push Daria's leg.

"He led a squadron of 16 planes and 500 aircrew and maintenance troops during the invasion of Iraq. That's where he 'picked up a few things.'"

I look back at Zahn, and his smile is gone. Daria slides her glasses down her nose and looks across at her father.

"Sorry, Dad."

Zahn nods and says nothing. I'm not sure what Daria said wrong, but I recall the Iraq War was around the time the wheels started coming off for Zahn. When his son died. And another tragedy. He lost an aircrew under his command to an Iraqi missile.

I try to steer Zahn back to the topic, even though I'm too embarrassed to meet his eyes. What do I know about integrity? My partner bought my silence for money, and I'm too greedy to find out why he wants to keep me quiet.

"What if you're in an unequal partnership?" I say. "I'm only a one-third partner. Travis is the majority owner."

Zahn focuses his eyes back to me, and I see him snap out of whatever trance Daria's comment triggered. "Right. Unequal partnerships are only a challenge for accounting. You've got to figure out your capital investment and calculate your earned profits—how to split that all up." Zahn tilts his head. "But regarding character, you two have to operate as one. The company can't be one-third about character and two-thirds about just making money. Integrity requires you to be on the same sheet of music. When people hear about Kristee Li and her new company, they don't care who owns how much of the company. They trust your name."

I raise my eyes to the Search & Rescue emblem on Zahn's t-shirt and reflect on his words. The Aerie's doors have barely opened, and already I'm living a lie within my own company.

Daria has gone silent again, and I can't tell if she's asleep. For a moment, I consider telling Zahn what's going on. He'll know what to do.

But I don't. Because I know what he'll say. Take my situation to the police. Accept responsibility for my errors and deal with the consequences.

Except I don't want to pay the consequences. I want to finish paying for Karla's spring semester. If I can just get her through the year and get the rest of the business—the part that doesn't appear to concern Travis—up on its feet and making money, then I can just ignore the trouble with Travis.

I'm not telling Zahn.

• • •

I need this. The Lock-Up pulses tonight with music and people and a palpable energy unusual for our sleepy mountain town. The local band opened with bluegrass, but something happened as the crowd buzzed, and suddenly the band riffs pop music with a woman from the crowd clutching the mike and crooning Beyoncé. She's actually not terrible, and I find myself on the postage-stamp dance floor, moving and grooving with Daria and Nikki.

"How have I been missing BV's dance scene?" Daria yells.

I grab her hand, pulling it over my head, and give her a twirl as Nikki raises both hands and swings her hips to the music. Nikki's the spark plug for the crowd's mood shift. Some people wield dance moves best admired from a distance. Nikki's infectious laugh and twinkling eyes, combined with her body rhythm, cause the opposite reaction. When she takes the floor, people flock to join her.

"Because we don't usually have one," I say with a laugh.

The Lock-Up is a beer pub, but the bartender runs a blender behind the counter with something pineapple mixed with something rum. All three of us are partaking, but there's only one blender—a pacing mechanism keeping us buzzed but not drunk.

I'm not much of a dancer, and I can count the number of times I've been out with girlfriends tearing it up. It's just not how I roll. But this is nice. When I'm dancing, lost in the music and laughing with friends, it's like I forget everything else. The Aerie looms only a block away, but tonight I choose to forget I'm part owner of a business. I block out my unreliable partner's mystery schemes. Tonight, it's just music, alcohol, and good company.

By midnight, the lead singer has reclaimed the mike and corralled her band back to their native genre. The bluegrass charges the crowd, but in a different way—the twirling group of locals shouting above each other has given way to older couples, laughing as they demonstrate their practiced moves. The bartender has obviously run out of fruit because the blender is gone.

"What do you say we move this to my place?" I remember I need to let Amore out. "It looks like things are winding up here."

"I'm in," Nikki says. Her face is flushed, and it's obvious she's having as much fun—or more—than I am. She and Daria are hitting it off, and that enhances the night's glow. I love it when my friends who haven't met before become friends. It's like a validation of my friend selection process or something.

"I'll walk with you guys, but I'm going to give my dad a call and have him pick me up there so he doesn't have to stay awake any longer," Daria says.

Zahn has offered to drive us home. It makes sense for Daria, since Zahn lives six miles out of town, but my condo sits only four blocks off Main Street, and Nikki lives just over a mile away.

"Guess he won't come inside for a beer if he's the driver," I say. "Too bad. He and I hardly ever chill. It's either Search & Rescue or hiking."

"That's why you got me." Nikki gives me a squeeze. "And I'm ready for another drink, girlfriend."

"He enjoys your company, Kristee." Daria smiles. "It's not like he has a ton of friends out here. I'm glad he's got you and Perez."

We walk the four blocks, not stumbling, but with a lot of giggling and a bit of skipping. A truck pulls alongside, as my condo block comes into view, and I recognize Zahn waving at us through his window. He points to my parking lot and pulls forward.

"He didn't waste any time," I say to Daria.

"Probably ready to get back home and to bed." She glances at her watch. "I think we're sitting at three hours past his normal night-night time."

I introduce Nikki to Zahn and badger him with a couple of my old man jokes while Daria climbs in the truck. I turn to Nikki as he pulls away.

"Still up for that nightcap?" I hope she is. This entire night has been an escape, and I'm afraid that when I'm alone, all the Travis and business drama will crash through the mental block I've enjoyed tonight.

Nikki grabs my hand and pulls me across the parking lot, laughing. "If a bear craps in the woods, can you hear it?"

I snort, ready to call her out—but I can't decide what you call her question. A mixed metaphor? A botched rhetorical question? So I just snort again. Her hand is warm, and her laugh carries the same effect as her dance moves. I want to join her and absorb her extra joy.

"Whatever," Nikki adds, and she tugs me in front of her. "Lead on, sweetheart. The night is young."

Wow. I'm ready for more, but not an all-nighter. Zahn's bedtime might have been three hours ago, but mine isn't that far off. I dread the thought of waking up to the fuzzy aftermath of the Lock-Up's pineapple surprise.

Nikki seems set on keeping the night going. And honestly? What the hell...I'm game for a little more. I squeeze her hand, then drop it and mount the stairs to my condo.

• • •

When I wake the next morning, I'm back at college. Or I imagine I am, for the first five seconds. It's not the arm draped across my neck—that should have made me think of Randy—but the scent of another female. I'm not much for perfume, but Nikki is. And she's lying in my bed. And for those five seconds, I'm whisked back to my sophomore year in college. Waking up with Terry.

And then...poof—it's gone. I move my eyes from Nikki's hand to the window, admiring my mountains as they stretch skyward to seize the day. I'm here, in Buena Vista, sharing my bed with Nikki.

*If a bear craps in the woods...*I snort again and I sense Nikki stiffen behind me. She jerks her arm away, and I roll onto my back, turning my head toward her with a smile.

"Sorry!" she says.

I laugh. It's not like we were so drunk I can't remember what happened last night. And what happened was...nothing. Nikki and I enjoyed two nightcaps, not one. We talked for over an hour before we both started nodding off on the couch.

I couldn't see letting Nikki walk the mile to her house, and neither of us was in any shape to drive her car. So I invited her to spend the night. When she insisted on the couch, I insisted my queen-size bed was plenty big enough for the two of us. And that was it. We were asleep within five minutes. Or at least I know I was.

"For what?" I laugh.

"The arm thing. I was asleep, I think."

"Oh my God, Nikki. Relax. Between Amore's paws on my back, and Randy rolling over on me in the middle of the night, do you think I'm not used to being mauled in my sleep?"

Nikki's mouth twitches at my teasing, and she turns on her back, grinning at the ceiling. "That, my friend, was a pretty epic night for Buena Vista, don't you think?"

"Uh-huh."

"And I'm not even hungover." Nikki turns her head back to me. "What are you doing for the rest of the weekend? Want to hang? Hike or something?"

My gut twinges when Nikki asks about my plans. I'd gone the entire night—and most of the morning—without thinking about The Aerie. Nikki—well, Daria too, but mostly Nikki—had done the impossible and distracted me from the number one stressor in my life.

My cell phone rings and I grab it from the nightstand. The screen reads *Randy*. Now the pang doubles down as I remember my first five seconds this morning. College memories of the woman I loved, her limbs entangled with mine, and a desire to stay in bed with her forever.

Waves of guilt smack me as I review the day ahead. I can't talk to Randy until I've processed my night with Nikki. The night where nothing happened. But still…I thought I had blocked my college years. Suppressed the pain of losing Terry. Escaped the memories of the relationship my mother destroyed. Created a new life here and a new Kristee.

Even if I push that aside and answer the phone, Randy's likely more interested in asking me how it went with Travis than listening to my bar dancing stories.

I glance at Nikki and find her staring at me. I hit the message button on the phone and select *Can I Call You Later?* before returning the phone to the nightstand.

"Parents?"

"Boyfriend."

I've got plenty of granola and yogurt, but my post-party appetite screams for a meat and potatoes breakfast. Nikki agrees, and I scramble up eggs with sausage on the side.

We share breakfast in a comfortable silence, Amore stationed to Nikki's right, alert to the possibility of a newcomer providing scraps. I'm used to eating alone, unless Randy is in town, and accustomed to the quiet. I wonder if Nikki is as comfortable as I am with the lack of conversation.

As if reading my mind, Nikki asks, "So, what do you think? Want to hit the Broken Boyfriend loop?" She's referring to my standard route across the river, and it's a great day for it. But I drag myself back to reality.

I need to address this Travis thing. I need to call Randy back. Last night's *cut loose* interlude with the girls is over, and it's time to rejoin the real world. I meet Nikki's questioning eyes and realize I want to get to know her better. I want more of that relaxed, safe, and secure feeling that enveloped me when I woke this morning.

But that's not who I am. Not anymore. It's time to cowboy up and face life head on, the way Kristee Li is expected to.

I reach across the table and grab Nikki's hand. "Nikki, Nik…I had the best time in, like, forever last night. I can't thank you enough for getting me out."

"But…"

"But I've got stuff going on. Stuff at work with the new business. Stuff with Randy—that call this morning. You know." I pause. "I need to take care of it. But I had a blast, and I think we should schedule a repeat."

Nikki's face creases into a grin, and she turns her wrist so that now she's grasping mine. She gives it a squeeze. "That's all I needed to hear, girl." She slides her hand across my palm, then reaches over to scratch Amore between the ears. "What about you, boy? You got a busy day scheduled, too?"

Amore looks from Nikki to her plate, expecting scraps, then settles for a head scratch. After a moment, Nikki rises and retrieves her jacket from the couch.

"You'll walk me out, though, won't you?"

"Does a bear make a noise if it falls in the forest...?" I try to remember her words from last night.

Nikki giggles and gives me a hug. "Exactly!"

I watch from the edge of the parking lot as she pulls away in her CRV. I would have followed her to her car, but I'm barefoot and it's chilly. Besides, after the hug upstairs, another at the car might have gotten awkward. I mean, Nikki and I have been friends for a while, but last night was the first time we'd really talked. And then there was the whole morning thing. I'm still processing that.

As I watch Nikki's car turn the corner, I gaze up to Sleeping Indian Mountain and shake my head. Why did I turn down Nikki's suggestion for a hike? It's one of those Colorado days where you wouldn't leave without your jacket, but would be tying it around your waist within ten minutes if you were moving uphill. A perfect hiking day.

A shout breaks my reverie.

"Jacy!" A man's voice reverberates behind me. Downstairs, I watch my neighbor, Jacy, halfway out the door of her condo, while a hand from inside tugs on her arm. Jacy disappears momentarily, then bursts through the screen door again, this time free of the arm. She runs forward to the sidewalk, before turning back toward the condo.

Her father explodes from the door in pursuit, making a beeline for Jacy, before he spots me. He pulls up short, almost to a complete stop, and looks from me to Jacy. Jacy must see his eyes shift because she turns her head and looks at me.

I raise my eyebrows and say in a low voice, "Are you OK?" Obviously, I'm too loud because her father answers for her.

"She's fine." He turns his attention from me back to his daughter. "Back inside. We'll finish talking, and then you can go wherever you want to go."

Fury rises from my gut to my chest as I picture the way he yanked her back into the condo. Yes, it's a family thing. But there's a power dynamic here, and there's nothing okay when an adult male manhandles a young woman.

"Actually, Jacy, do you have a minute? Would you mind coming up to my place to talk about Amore's feedings?" I fumble for a legitimate reason to get her away from her father. "I'm trying a new brand and want to show you how much to give him."

Jacy turns to her father, who stares at me.

"Actually, no." Her father sneers. "You can mind your own fucking business, and let us settle this little family issue." He stares at me. "Don't you have somewhere to be?"

Something inside me snaps, and I stride toward Jacy's father with my finger out. I can almost see myself from above, like I'm watching a security camera. A superhero in the form of a 5' 2" Asian woman making the world safe for young girls everywhere. Christ, I've turned into my mother.

"You listen to me," I say as I pull up short of the man. "You just made your business my business when you assaulted your daughter. I watched what you did when she tried to leave. I'm a witness." My chest is heaving, and Jacy's father is scowling like a grizzly bear who's been stunned with a two-by-four backslap across the face. "So you either tell me you understand you'll keep your hands off her, or I'm going to the cops and reporting your child abuse."

"Kristee! Kristee!" Jacy calls, and I turn my head toward her. "It's OK. I said something to him I shouldn't have. I was disrespectful. But it's not what you're saying."

Erik's voice barks behind me. "Get in the house, Jacy."

Jacy passes me and gives me a blank glance as she aims for the door.

"Jacy," I call, but she doesn't turn. I shift my attention to Erik and his eyes are almost twinkling, a faint smile on his lips. The screen door clicks shut behind Jacy, and whatever warped attempt at humor he was feigning disappears like the charm of a used car salesman after he's made the sale.

119

"Go ahead," he says.

"Go ahead, what?"

"Take it to the cops. See what they say about me trying to protect my teenage daughter from harm."

"You were—" I sputter before Erik interrupts.

"And just know that if you do, I will turn my attention from my daughter to you."

My jaw drops, and for a moment I'm speechless. Then I recover my voice. "Did you just threaten me?"

Jacy's father says nothing. His lips press together, but the faint twinkle in his eye returns. He stares at me for a moment, then turns and disappears into his condo.

ZAHN

NOW

Perez's news about finding Kristee's phone jars me. "Where did you find it? What's on it?"

The deputy shakes his head slowly, and frustration simmers inside me. Is he just going to obfuscate again? There's something about this whole non-investigation he's not revealing, and it's nagging at me like a string from a celery stick wedged between my teeth. Kristee's disappearance is more than a SAR mission gone bad, and I'm determined to find out what it is. Especially with the discovery of the phone. How in the hell did Kristee end up on the opposite slope of the mountain?

"We can't examine it without permission from Kristee's family. It's not a criminal investigation, and we don't have a reason to request a search warrant," Perez says.

"Can't you just ask them? I'm sure they'll let you keep it while you check for clues."

"You're right. Sort of. I delivered it to Karla, and she said we could look at it...after she does. Might be a day or two."

"What about Lin Li? Kristee's mother?"

"She wasn't there."

I say my goodbyes and swing my truck back toward town. Perez's Tahoe leads the way, and I watch his head tilt to the rearview mirror. I'm close enough to see him shake his head. He's probably guessed where I'm heading and isn't happy.

121

I don't really care. Law enforcement can't take the phone, but I've got every right to ask Karla for a peek at it. Nikki keeps bringing up everything Kristee had going on. Some of those things should be on her phone if my friend is anything like my daughter.

I park my truck near the condo, and take the sidewalk toward Kristee's stairs. At the landing, I see a teenage girl with Amore on a leash.

"Jacy?"

The girl pauses and the look she throws my way is not trusting. She says nothing.

"I'm Kristee's friend, Tyler Zahn—from Search & Rescue?" I rush my words, attempting to erase the wary expression she still carries. "She told me about you. You're the one who takes care of Amore when she's working." I pause, realizing my verb tense is off. "When she worked."

Jacy nods and I throw in another legitimizing question. "So, are Karla and Lin Li still asking you to help with Amore? That's awesome."

My familiarity with Kristee's family seems to break the ice. Kristee had described Jacy as a nervous girl from a broken family. Maybe she's wary around everyone.

"Hi," she says. "Are you Z-man?"

I nod.

"I remember her talking about you. I didn't know you were so old."

*Out of the mouths of babes...*I sigh. "Yeah, we were like outdoors friends, you know? Did a lot of hikes and that type of stuff. Not like dating friends."

Jacy smirks. "I figured that." Her smile fades. She takes a step away, tugging Amore, then stops. "I miss her. Kristee."

I was raised to believe guys' hearts don't melt, but it's happening right now. I don't know Jacy well enough to hug her, but she certainly needs comfort. Instead, I nod at her.

"I do too, Jacy."

"She was the only one who understood me. And she was brave. She wasn't afraid to stand up for me, even if it meant getting hurt."

I freeze at this. What the hell is Jacy talking about? I spy movement over her shoulder, and watch a man step from the downstairs condo. The screen door shuts, and Jacy turns at the sound.

"Hey, Dad."

"What the fuck you doing yakking out here? If you got a job, then do it. Those people ain't paying you to stand around jawing with strangers."

Jacy tugs on Amore and sidesteps me. "I've got to go."

"Wait," I say, but she's already three steps out toward the parking lot.

"Can I help you?" The man's voice is loud behind me and definitely insincere. He doesn't want to help me—he wants to confront the man talking to his daughter.

I walk toward him and see his arms widen at his side like a cobra spreading its hood before a strike. Shaking my head, I answer his question. "Heading upstairs. Visiting the family." I assume the man knows about the Kristee situation—it's a small condo complex.

He grunts and I watch his posture relax slightly as he turns back to the door. No more words. This is not a man endowed with social graces, and I doubt he's been delivering casseroles to the grieving family.

Karla answers the door, and her eyes widen as she recognizes me. She steps across the doorframe and grabs my wrist, pulling herself toward my ear.

"Don't mention the phone."

As I enter, Lin Li rises from the living room couch, a puzzled expression pursing her lips. She's probably trying to guess how Karla suddenly knows me well enough to greet me with an ear nibble.

"Can we help you, Mr. Zahn?"

I've almost given up convincing Kristee's mother to use my first name. I glance back at Karla and she gives me a shrug.

123

"No, Ms. Li. I'm just checking to see how you all are doing." I offer a small smile. "I wanted to know if you needed anything."

Lin Li opens her mouth, but Karla interrupts. "Sit down. Stay and talk for a while."

I shift my focus back to Lin Li, who's pressing her lips together as if Karla's suggestion is the opposite of what she wants. She's not the only one uncomfortable. I'm hoping to discuss the very thing Karla asked me not to mention—the phone.

Lin Li watches me lower myself to the couch before speaking. "Karla, I forgot to tell you Travis called and asked if I wanted to get some of Kristee's personal items from The Aerie. I think I'll go take care of that now."

Before Karla can speak, Lin Li turns to me. "I'm sorry to leave so soon, Mr. Zahn, but I'd like to take care of this right away." She pauses. "I'm sure you understand."

What I understand is that Lin Li has no wish to sit and make idle chit-chat with me. What a coincidence—it's the last thing I want either.

"Mama—" Karla cuts herself off as if it's dawned on her that her mother's departure isn't such a bad idea. She starts again. "If you wait a bit, I can go with you."

Lin Li grabs a coat from the rack. "It won't take me long." Karla and I exchange glances as the door shuts.

"Sorry," Karla says. "Subtlety has never been her strong point."

"No need to explain. You both are going through a lot. And I do want to know if I can help."

Karla's hands fidget in her lap, and she glances at them as if suddenly aware she's acting nervous. She grasps her left hand with her right and looks at me. "And I appreciate that. It's just…well, I thought you were here about the phone. Did Perez tell you about it?"

I nod. "He did. He told me the Sheriff's Department asked to examine it, and you said you preferred to look at it first."

Now Karla nods. She says nothing.

"Did you? Did you look at it?" My breath quickens. Kristee did not wander off and get lost. Not the Kristee I remember. Karla's silence says more than words could. She's found something on the phone proving Kristee's disappearance was no accident.

Karla's nods as if she's reading my thoughts.

"It wasn't an accident, was it?" I prod. "Why are you keeping it from your mother?" I pause. "And why are you keeping it from the Sheriff's Department?"

"No. It's not that. Not about Kristee and the mountain. It's about something else."

What? I should be relieved that there's no conspiracy of silence, or criminal action, or a sinister plot behind my friend's disappearance. Instead, my ego is in control. I'm disappointed I haven't been proven right. What kind of man am I?

Karla's eyes glisten as I speak, "What 'something else?' Something you can share with me?"

"Yes. I need some advice." Karla rises from the couch and opens a closet door between the living room and Kristee's bedroom. Cardboard boxes rasp against each other, and a moment later she reappears with a cell phone. "It's booting up."

"How did you get the password?"

"I know what she uses. She probably remembers mine, too. We're sisters." She gives me a weak smile, then checks the phone's screen. She thumbs something into the phone, then presses her finger on the screen before handing it to me.

"Read this text string."

I take the phone. A green bubble with white text sits in the screen's center, the initials NK highlighted at the phone's top. I read the text.

Stay away from me. No more contact. Period. You're making me uncomfortable.

"Stay away from me?" I look at Karla. "Why do you say it's 'something else?' This sounds like someone who could harm Kristee." I throw in another question. "And who's NK?"

Karla reaches for the phone and I hand it back to her.

"Sorry, I meant for you to start toward the top of the text exchange, not the bottom." She runs her finger up the phone's screen, then pauses and hands the phone back to me. "Start here."

I take the phone back and begin reading. Karla interrupts. "NK is Nikki Kingston. You know her, right?

I nod and read the texts.

I can't stop thinking about last night.
Me either. When can I see you again?
I need some time to think.
What's there to think about, K? Stop thinking. Start feeling.
I've already started feeling. That's the problem. You're not the only one I have feelings for.
There's another woman? (gasp) ☺
Stop it. I need to discuss this with Randy...

The combination of the texts and Karla's expectant stare confuses me. The words read like a morning-after conversation between two lovers, and I don't understand why Karla imagines it's important for me to see this.

"Karla," I say, shaking my head. "This seems like an awfully personal conversation to share with me. Maybe you're misunderstanding how close Kristee and I were."

"No, Tyler. I'm sharing this because of your relationship with Perez, not your relationship with Kristee."

Now I'm even more confused. "You don't want to share this with Perez? What about Kristee's last text? *Stay away from me.* What if Nikki was upset about that? Maybe she was somehow involved in Kristee's disappearance?"

As I say these words, desperation creeps into my voice, like I'm trying too hard. Chad Storms, the third member of their search team, heard the altercation between the two. Kristee left. Nikki continued on the trail with Chad. Nikki couldn't have harmed Kristee. And she

126

couldn't have arranged for someone else to hurt her because she couldn't have known Kristee would take off after their altercation.

Karla nods in agreement. "I agree. Perez and his guys need to see this. But I need them to keep it quiet. I don't want this released to the public if they determine it's not relevant."

I nod slowly. There's something more here than Kristee's relationship with Nikki. Something deeper.

Karla seems to sense my dissatisfaction with her explanation. "What did you think when you read the texts?"

I pause for a moment and study my hands before meeting Karla's eyes. "It read like she might have had some kind of relationship with Nikki. And then it went south somehow. She became uncomfortable with it."

"And?"

"I don't know what you are after here, Karla. I didn't know about this. Are you asking me how I feel about Kristee having a relationship with another woman?"

"Exactly."

I meet her eyes. "Am I surprised? Sure. I've known Kristee for a couple of years. Seen her dating men and specifically Randall Williams. So if she's gay, or bisexual, or whatever the right word is, I didn't know it."

Karla stares at me as if she's expecting more.

"But don't expect me to judge her. Just because I'm old doesn't mean I disapprove." I shake my head.

"What?"

"It's kind of funny. I just had this conversation with Nikki. It's like you young folks assume us middle-aged folks can't handle modern society."

Karla stands up and walks to the window overlooking the parking lot. Then she turns to face me. "That's the thing. Not all of you can. Like my mother, for instance. That's why I need you to talk to Perez."

I give her a blank look, and she keeps talking. "The situation when Kristee was in college—the unconventional relationship my mother didn't like?"

Clarity strikes me like the discovery of the last puzzle piece under the living room couch. "That was a woman? That's why your mother was upset? She didn't want Kristee dating a woman."

"Exactly. My mother has very definitive thoughts about who her daughters should date and who they shouldn't. She was born and raised in China. She never met a foreigner until she went to college. And homosexuality is still a taboo topic over there. Sure, it exists. But no one admits it. You don't talk about it unless you're like using a VPN online or you know the right places to go."

Karla explains that Lin Li's trip to Buena Vista was because she found out about Randall Williams and did not approve of Kristee dating a Black man.

"I wouldn't call her racist. It's the way she was raised. And even though she's spent thirty years in the States, she has never dropped those cultural norms she's saddled with."

"But if Kristee is gone, why is it so important to keep this from your mother?"

Karla takes a breath. "Because it's not related to her disappearance. And if this goes public, my mother will be embarrassed. She'll believe Kristee's death was related to the bad decisions Kristee made in her love life, and what do you expect she will do after that?"

"I don't know."

"She's going to spend the rest of her life making sure her only surviving daughter doesn't make the same mistakes as her oldest daughter. She's going to ensure my life is a living hell. I've already got an obligation to care for her, especially now that Kristee's gone." She spreads her hands. "But I need to live my own life, too. Which I can't if my mother is looking over my shoulder, telling me who I can love and who I can't."

I nod. "What do you want me to do?"

"I'm worried that if I release the phone to Perez, Kristee's relationship will be public. Plastered in the media for my mother to read." Karla says. "Can you talk to him? He's your friend, and I feel like if you explain the situation, it might go over better than a daughter asking the same thing to keep her mother from knowing."

I think about that. She's right about approaching Perez without her mother's knowledge. Perez would be leery of involving himself in a disagreement or secret among the two remaining members of Kristee's family.

But I'm still uncomfortable with Perez withholding the altercation between Kristee and Nikki. And he didn't share it with Williams either. Kristee and Williams were having problems, and now I might have discovered why.

I have no reason to doubt what Karla has shared. The phone texts don't lie either. But the revelation generates more questions than it answers. Why hasn't Nikki told me about her and Kristee? Is she trying to steer us in a different direction so that nobody will find out about their relationship? Why would she do that if everyone in town (including me, within the last 24 hours) already knew Nikki was gay?

"Did you check anything besides texts?"

Karla shakes her head. "I checked her email and her social media stuff. That's about it. Didn't see anything weird."

"What about her internet search history or location pings?"

"No. I mean I know how to check the internet, but I didn't mess with that. I didn't check anything about location. Can't Perez and his guys do that? I'm not so worried about that kind of information staying quiet. Just this one topic in the text messages."

I promise Karla to talk to Perez and see what I can do to safeguard Kristee's privacy. Karla insists she won't give up the phone unless she gets some guarantees.

As I climb into my truck, I catch sight of Lin Li removing a cardboard box from the back seat of her car. I'm somewhat surprised— my first assumption after her abrupt departure was that the errand was a made-up excuse not to talk to me. Not that I took it personally. Her absence allowed Karla to show me the phone texts. But the box suggests Lin Li actually completed the task.

I rest my hand on the steering wheel before leaving, pausing to rerun my conversation with Karla. Despite my misgivings about Perez's motives, I know I'll take Karla's request to him. His team has the tools and if the phone can shine light on Kristee's disappearance, then law enforcement should have it.

But the texts with Nikki nag at me. If she was involved in Kristee's disappearance, then why pester me and Perez to pursue the investigation? She wouldn't. But if she truly wanted to help us understand what Kristee was going through—the issues she was dealing with—then why hide the relationship? She's been ducking and weaving the whole time. *Why?*

•   •   •

I park behind Nikki's place, but stay in my truck. The black Honda, the car I saw in front of Planned Parenthood yesterday, is nowhere in sight. Nikki doesn't appear to be home, and I realize I don't know where she works. But I still have her number.

I scroll through my call history and tap on our recent call.

"This is Nikki."

"Nikki, it's Tyler Zahn." From the brusque way she answered the phone, I suspect she recognized my number.

"Do you have anything new?"

"Maybe. We've found her phone."

I hear Nikki breathe faster.

"Nikki?"

"Yeah, I'm here." She pauses. "Who's 'we?' The cops have the phone, or you have the phone?"

I wonder why the distinction is important. "Karla has the phone. She's going to turn it over to the Sheriff's Department next so they can run some forensics." I decide to push her a bit. "Good news, right? Maybe we'll find something about the business."

Nikki releases a small breath. "Right, good news. Thanks for letting me know." She raises her voice at the end of her sentence, as if she's getting ready to hang up.

"Nikki, I looked at the phone, too."

More silence.

"Do you mind if I swing by and talk to you about your texts with Kristee?"

A choked sob escapes from my phone.

"Nikki?"

"You bastard. I can't believe you read those. I can't believe you guys are letting the cops see those texts. That was between Kristee and me. That was personal."

"Nikki, I—"

"Shut up. You don't understand." Her voice fades, and she chokes a sob. Then she's back. "We loved each other. We were literally falling in love. Kristee was just coming to terms with who she really was, and I was helping with that. And then—" Nikki's voice breaks.

"Do you want to meet and talk?" Maybe giving her time to pull herself together might help.

"No, I don't." She pauses. "Did you know Kristee was going to tell Randy Williams their relationship was over? I don't know whether she was just going to break up with him or tell him about us, or what, but she told me she was ending it. And then—"

I'm expecting another off-phone sob, but Nikki keeps talking.

"Something happened. I think she talked to him, and he forced her to change her mind. I don't know what happened, but that's my guess. Kristee came back the next day and told me it was over between us. She said she didn't want to have anything to do with me." Nikki sniffs, but she's done sobbing. "She said it wasn't me—that it all had to do with her and coming to grips with herself, her feelings, and her sexuality. But damn, Tyler—she was cold. No negotiation. No tender goodbye. One day we were in love, the next she excised me from her life."

"I can't imagine how angry you must have been," I say, cautiously. Nikki's revelation is the closest thing I've heard so far to a motive for harming Kristee. Especially considering Kristee took out a restraining order on her.

Nikki must have seen right through me.

"Fuck you. Of course I was angry—but not like you're thinking. She broke my heart. I've never met a woman like her, and I believe in my soul she wanted to love me."

"I didn't mean to—"

"Yes, you did. What do you think we were arguing about on the trail the day she disappeared? I hadn't even been able to talk to her before that because of that goddamned restraining order." She pauses. "I'm sure you've heard about that. Anyway, it was me begging her to come back, and her telling me I needed to back off. I would never harm her. She was the one for me, and if she were still here, I would still be trying to win her back from that asshole Williams who doesn't even deserve her."

"I—"

Nikki cuts me off. "Do whatever. I don't care. I've told you everything about us."

I hear silence on the line and realize Nikki has hung up.

· · ·

"Here's the deal, Rick. Karla wants you guys to have the phone—so the forensic guys can look at it. She's got a few caveats, though."

Perez stares at me across the table at the Elkhead. He has yet to smile. This might be the first time I've seen him here without his signature slice of quiche. His hands curl around a cup of black coffee, just as mine do, and he appears to concentrate on my every word.

"What caveats?"

"There's personal information on the phone. Stuff she doesn't want to share with her mother."

"You saw it?"

"I did. But I don't want to share it with you until we come to an agreement about this information."

"Yeah, right." Perez peers over the rim of his mug as if checking to make sure it's coffee before returning his eyes to mine. "Is it personal about Nikki Kingston?"

I'm not trained in the art of subterfuge, but I do a pretty good job of not reacting to Perez's question. Instead, I volley one in return.

"Do we have a deal?"

"Screw you, Zahn." Perez glances around the room and I follow his gaze. The closest customers are two tables away. He leans forward. "You're a shitty liar. I wish I could have had a mirror in front of you so you could watch your own eyes dilate when I asked you that question. Why do you think I didn't tell you about the argument between Kristee and Nikki? Or anyone else? Why didn't I haul Nikki in for violating the restraining order on that mission? Do you really think I'm trying to hide something from you?"

I want to nod my head, because that's exactly what I am thinking. That Perez is hiding something. Something about him and Williams and their jealous squabble over a girl who may not have loved either of them.

Instead, I just stare at Perez. He stares back, and five seconds pass before he lets out a breath and shakes his head.

"Don't get me wrong—I'm not trying to make you feel like an idiot. I've known about Kristee and Nikki for a couple of weeks now. Their...how do you want to put it? Relationship."

My mouth drops a bit, and Perez must notice because suddenly he's practically apologizing.

"Listen," he says. "I know you guys were close. Good friends. She told me she sees you—saw you—as a father figure, or uncle, or whatever. You know what I mean." Perez gulps at his coffee. "I'm not sure she would have shared it with me except for the restraining order. I pressed her about what was happening, and she finally told me."

"Told you what?"

"That she thinks she likes women. She told me about her and Nikki, and how it wasn't the first time that had happened to her. Before she lived here in BV, she had another experience."

I remember Karla's story of the young woman in college, and I nod.

"She told me she needed time to process everything. She needed time to talk to Williams. Time to sort out her feelings." Perez takes another sip of his coffee and replaces the mug on the table. "And Nikki wouldn't give it to her. She was pressuring Kristee every day about coming out, admitting who she truly was, cutting ties with her traditional past—I think that meant breaking up with Randall—and embracing the new Kristee." Perez pauses. "It was too much. She had that, and business drama, and something going on with her neighbor. Lots of shit." He meets my eyes again. "She probably would have told you instead of me, but you were gone. Off at the Academy. And here I was, the guy working the restraining order and also her friend."

I glance away from Perez to the window facing the Collegiate Peaks. The sun tries to hide early in the Upper Arkansas River Valley, and already the snowfields on the avalanche chutes of Mt Princeton have gone from a sunlit white to a shadowy gray as the rays shine onto the floor of the Elkhead. I sigh and Perez notices.

"What?"

I turn back to Perez and meet his eyes. "I owe you an apology."

"What for?"

"You were just trying to protect Kristee's memory, right? You knew all this about Kristee, but determined it wasn't relevant to the case, and you squelched it. Am I right?"

Perez closes his eyes momentarily, then looks at me. "She asked me to keep our conversation between us. I worded the restraining order such that it was less about a 'bad break-up' and more about a 'misunderstanding.' And I figured it wasn't my business to tell you about her relationship with that woman." He pauses, then chuckles. "And there's no way I'm telling Randall about it. He'd never believe it, and if it came from me, he'd probably lay me out."

I nod in agreement. Except something nags at me. "But what if your concern about keeping a friend's secret is keeping you from fully investigating the case? What then?"

I watch Perez's jaw clench before he speaks. "You've been wandering around for a couple of days doing your own investigating. Do you see any way Nikki could have or would have harmed Kristee?"

"No," I say truthfully. Because I haven't.

"Let's say Randall found out about it and—even though neither of us can picture it—flew into a mad rage and went after Kristee. Could he have done it?"

"No. He was in Denver."

"So, there you have it. I've got twice the resources you do and can't find a connection. If I could, then all of Kristee's secrets would go out the window to bring the culprit to justice." He spreads his palms on the table. "And the same thing holds true for our deal."

"What do you mean?"

"I mean, I'll keep all the personal stuff quiet as long as it remains irrelevant to the disappearance. I won't tell her mother because Kristee wouldn't have wanted that. But the moment anything on that phone becomes relevant? Then all those promises go out the window. Do you understand?"

I do. And I predict Karla will agree, as well.

"Sounds like you've got a phone coming your way," I say, and I smile at my friend for the first time since I left for the Academy.

KRISTEE

BEFORE

Something's wrong. Slipping the key into my condo door, I listen for the tap, tap, tap of Amore's claws on the tile entryway and a whine of anticipation as he waits for the door to open. I hear nothing.

I swing the door open, and Amore is nowhere in sight.

"Amore?" My voice is tentative. It's a small condo. If he's here, he can hear me. I do a quick scan of my bedroom and the bathroom. The condo is empty.

Jacy. She must be walking him. I scold myself for worrying and bolt for the stairs. Jacy and Amore have spent a lot of time together over the last week, and I'm not surprised the teenager is growing attached to my dog.

I knock on her condo door and it whips open.

"What the hell you want?" Jacy's father squeezes a Coors Light in one hand and the door handle in the other. I almost smile because the only thing missing is a stained wife-beater t-shirt. Instead, he wears a long-sleeved flannel shirt with a plaid print and a pair of Carhartt cargo pants. His jaw is set, and I realize he must figure I'm here to discuss more parenting techniques.

"Is Jacy here?" I take a step backward. "My dog, Amore, isn't in the house, and I thought maybe she was walking him."

Erik shakes his head. "Nope. She's still at school for some kind of play practice thing." He leers at me. Not for the first time—but this is different. Instead of sizing up my figure and doing an internal assessment of whether he has a chance, this is more like a high school wrestler sizing up his opponent before the big match. Like he's trying to figure out if he could hurt me, and the only thing stopping him is the fear of getting caught. I see his eyes flit over my shoulder and I step back.

"OK. I'll keep looking. Can you let me know if you see him?"

He gives me a thin smile. "Oh, you bet. Top of my list." He steps forward through the doorway and onto the landing. I take another step backwards. "You know, Kristee…" He pauses, then asks, "It is Kristee, isn't it?"

I nod.

"You know, there's a leash law in this town, right? It's illegal for your dog to be out without a leash."

I nod. *No shit, Sherlock.* I mean, it's not as if Amore has gotten away. My condo was locked. If Jacy doesn't have Amore, then someone took him.

"I'm sure you'll find your mutt before someone reports you."

I glare at Jacy's father. Really? He's trying to play off his obvious abusive relationship with Jacy against an animal control law? Asshole.

I turn on my heel and head toward my car. Maybe Jacy accidentally let Amore out when she fed him. It's the only remaining explanation.

As I approach the parking lot, a silver Toyota pulls into the slot next to mine. A tall man with slicked black hair steps from the vehicle and looks my direction. I continue walking toward my 4-Runner and glance at the parking spot on the other side to see if we'll have a Toyota trifecta. Nope. Subaru Outback.

The man catches my eye. "Are you Kristee Li?"

I nod and instinctively check behind me to see if any of my neighbors are available to watch my interaction with a strange man in the parking lot. Jacy's dad has already closed his door and I see no one else.

Before I can answer, the man lobs another question. "Are you missing a dog?"

"Yes! Have you seen him? He's—" I'm walking toward the man, practically jogging now that he's mentioned Amore, but I stop talking when I round the back end of my car. There, pressed against the man's passenger-side window, is Amore.

"Oh, my God." I open the passenger door and grab Amore by the collar. "Where did you find him?"

"Trotting alongside Highway 24. Looks like maybe he had his eyes set on Salida." He pauses. "You're a lucky woman. Lucky he had a collar."

I bend and scratch Amore's head, and that's when it hits me. Amore's collar has his name and my phone number. And I didn't receive a phone call.

"How did you know where I lived?"

"Like I said, his collar—"

"His collar doesn't have my address. Just my phone number. So how did you find me?"

The man rests his hands on the car's roof. His smile has faded, and his eyes lock on mine. I glance at Amore. "Stay."

"See what you're doing now? I brought your dog back, and you're just standing there interrogating me. Doesn't seem very smart. Maybe you should stop asking questions if you got what you want."

I step back, glancing from the man to his car. Silver. Toyota. Just like the one from which Travis unloaded his little boxes.

This man is not kindly returning my dog, I realize. He's sending me a message.

I grab Amore's collar and walk him toward my condo without looking back. Behind me, the man snorts before calling out to me.

"You keep an eye on that dog, Kristee Li. He's a beaut. You'd hate for him to run into someone who's not as understanding as I am."

•   •   •

My cell phone rings as I drag Amore through my door. I could have just told my dog *we're going home*, and he would have followed me into the condo, but Travis's man has me rattled. Obviously, Travis told the guys about me. They must be worried I'll be a problem. But what kind of people abduct a dog? And is that son of a bitch Travis in on this?

I glance at the phone. *Karla.* Competing emotions slam me as I hover my thumb over the button to accept the call—relief at the chance to talk to my sister, and guilt because I'm sure the conversation will inevitably turn toward the missing tuition payments.

"What's up, girl?" Even though I am still reeling from the Amore episode, I go for nonchalant.

"What's wrong?" Karla says.

I sit back on the couch, propping my feet on the coffee table. Amore nails me with an expectant stare, and I tap the couch to my left. Less than a second later, I've got a dog's head in my lap. *What's wrong? Nothing's wrong now.*

"I'm good. I was coming up the stairs with Amore when you called and double-timed it to the door before I answered." There's no way I'm sharing with Karla what just happened. My rule is to never make my problems her problems.

"What have you been up to? School going OK?" I scratch Amore's ears.

"Everything's fine. A's in everything. Well, almost everything. My differential equations class is throwing me for a loop."

"You won't get help from me on that!"

"I know. I'll figure it out…" Karla's voice trails off.

"What is it, Kar?"

"How are you dealing with the fact that Mama is coming? Are you ready?"

I laugh out loud. "I was dealing with Mama when you were learning how to walk. You think I can't handle her?"

"I know. But I keep hoping it's going to be a reconciliation, not a battle. Why do you think she's reaching out?"

I'm silent for a moment, debating whether to share my thoughts on that with Karla or not. "I'll try and see if we can work it out. I promise."

"But?"

"But I don't think that's why she's coming."

"What's the real reason, then? You think she wants to talk to you about finishing college or something?"

"Simpler than that—and his name only has five letters."

"Amore? Your dog?" Karla pauses again and I can picture the realization dawning on her face. "Oh, shit, it's Randy, isn't it?"

"That's my guess. I can't decide which one bothered her the most, me having a girlfriend in college or the fact that I'm dating a man of color."

"Why is she like that? Why can't she just accept the people you choose to love?"

I mull over Karla's rhetorical question as if I can change the immutable. Mama Li is the stereotype of the stereotype for classic Chinese mothers—especially ones who have immigrated to the West. When she and the father I barely knew prepared for their journey to the United States, they might have traveled lightly, with just the shirts on their back, but they didn't skimp on packing up all the traditional, conservative values with which they were raised. Papa died, but Mama never weakened in her resolve to manage every aspect of our lives. She raised us on piano and violin and stood over our shoulders for hours until our homework was perfect.

"It's the way she was brought up. I honestly believe she thinks she is a good mother when she pulls stunts like this."

"Do you want me to come out with her? Maybe I can run interference."

I think about that. I'm picturing Mama and me in a staring contest trying to come up with something to say. Karla would make it easier. But...

"No. You've got school." I pause before continuing. "And now's not a good time to buy a ticket."

Karla says nothing. Neither do I. Just when I decide the silence is becoming too awkward, she speaks. "How's the new business going?"

And there it is. The topic I foresaw. College money.

"We're having some bumps getting started, but I think it's going to turn out OK." I'm silent for a moment and so is Karla. "Are you really interested, or is there another reason you're asking?"

Karla lets out a sigh. I've given her the opening to cut to the chase. "Well, I'm getting some emails about a late tuition payment. On the installment plan you set up?" Her voice trails off again.

"I'm aware of that. I'm running behind on this next payment. Don't worry, though. They'll send something through snail mail when they're really serious about their timeline."

"I've gotten two of those, as well."

Shit. I had transitioned from semester payments to a ten-month installment plan in order to make the payments more manageable. I hadn't accounted for the fact that the university's billing process for the installment program would be more responsive, as well. "OK. I need you to scan those letters and email them to me, got it?"

"Should I look at loans again?"

I'm down to nothing for savings. Zero.

And then I remember. I've got the money Travis gave me—and more on the way. The money Travis refused to take back.

Am I going to let my sister get kicked out of college? Or go into debt?

Hell, no. I put all thoughts of tiger mom out of my head. Tiger sister is in control now.

"Karla, we're going to pay. Send me the letters. I'll take care of it today."

I hang up my phone and stare out across the valley at my happy place—those towering peaks overlooking my home. Upright, regal, and dominant. Unlike me.

· · ·

Even though Amore is restless from the day's adventure, and I'm stressed about Karla's tuition notices, I still sleep like the dead. Reluctantly, I wake from a dream and smile at the weight of Nikki's arm

141

draped across me, just like the night she stayed over. I open my eyes and stare at the fur-covered paw next to my face.

"Amore!" I flip over and meet my dog's wide-open eyes. Not Nikki's.

I laugh and give Amore a shove. He pops to his feet on the bed and yaps. Ready to play.

"Kristee…" I say to myself, staring at the ceiling. All these thoughts weighing on me, and my mind is stuck on a crazy night with a crazy woman where nothing happened. *And why does part of me wish it had?*

I thumb Nikki's name on my screen and press CALL.

"Morning, Sunshine," she says. "Took you long enough."

"Long enough for what?"

"To call. What's our plan?"

Nikki is so far ahead of me, I'm at a loss. "I was just calling to say 'hi.' Thought you might want to grab a beer tonight? At the Lock-Up?"

"Depends. How about a beer and a movie? We could hit the drive-in."

I immediately agree. I've been to the local drive-in once with Randy, Perez, and Zahn to watch a climbing movie. It's fun. Friends crammed in a car with a cooler of beer. Plus, there's no place else in Buena Vista to watch a movie.

"I'll meet you at the Lock-Up at six. We'll have a couple and I'll drive to the show," Nikki says. "You want to hike ahead of time? This afternoon?"

"Raincheck on the hike. I'm meeting Randy in Fairplay." Today is date day. Time enough to meet halfway for lunch. Fairplay is only 45 minutes for me, and just shy of two hours for Randy, but we alternate on who has to drive the farthest.

"Aren't you the social butterfly?" Nikki teases. "See you at six. Save some energy for me."

I hang up the phone, and my belly tingles. Nikki is referring to our evening beer and movie event, but the way she said it makes me imagine other reasons I would want to conserve my energy. The same reasons that woke me this morning and inspired this phone call.

Argh. I glance at my watch, remembering I have to swing by The Aerie this morning before I get on the road to meet Williams. I need to pick up the other payment from Travis and get it into the bank.

Three hours later, I'm sitting across from Williams's comforting smile, listening to him tell a story about how he and his coworker had been on a missing child case and found themselves treed eight feet up with a foamy, barking dog holding them at bay. The story makes me forget my nervous errand run around Buena Vista, where I caught sight of at least two silver Toyotas—just like the one who brought back Amore. The first had a blonde-haired woman driver and an occupied car seat in the back. I lost sight of the other leaving town.

"I saw the mutt coming, a pit bull, you know, and I pulled my weapon."

"You were going to shoot the dog?" I stare at Williams in disbelief.

"It was like an instinctive reaction. He was coming for me, and I needed to protect myself." Williams has his palms upturned, implying his lack of alternatives. "But then the screen door bangs, and I hear the guy in the house yell the dog's name. 'Caesar.' So, the dog freezes and looks back at the house. I back up, and Jess, my partner, he does the same. I holster my weapon, and the guy yells the dog's name again. 'Caesar…get 'em.'"

"He sicced the dog on you?" My mouth drops open.

"Right, so I turn and it's obvious I can't make the Tahoe. And the tree's right there. So I run for the tree. The dog's right behind me.

I cover my mouth with my hand. It's not funny, but the way Williams is telling the story has me giggling.

"But Jess, he must have had the same thought, because I'm swinging up to the first branch and Jess, he's already got one leg over it. We're getting all tangled up together, and this pit bull is already at the base of the tree, barking and snarling." Williams pauses, his eyes wide. "And it's not that big of a tree. I mean, it's only like twelve feet tall, and it's bending with our weight, and the dog's got Jess's pants leg in his mouth."

"So what did you do?"

"I pulled my weapon back out, and I'm trying to line it up so I can take out the dog without shooting Jess's foot off when, finally, the guy back at the house, he sees what I'm getting ready to do and he calls out, 'Caesar, house.'" Williams grins wide. "The dog drops Jess's leg, wheels around, and trots up next to the man and sits down. End of story."

"Did you find the kid?"

Williams shakes his head. "That's the thing. It was the wrong address. All that for nothing. Well, Jess got the opportunity to order new khaki pants. Dog ripped a hole in them. I almost had to wash mine—thought I was going to crap my drawers."

I lean back, still laughing. Williams can tell a story, and I love it when he gets on a roll. I gaze across the table at him laughing with me, and it reminds me of how comfortable we are with each other. He's my best friend.

Williams's eyes meet mine and then shift to check out my empty plate. Another great meal at the South Park Brewery. I sense he's worried about the time and how long it will take him to get back to Denver, but as his eyes shift up from the plate and settle on my chest, I realize his thoughts are elsewhere.

"What's going on there, big boy?" It's a rhetorical question—I already know what's on his mind.

"Was just thinking we might have time for a nooner." He grins. "You in a hurry?"

I smile back, but inside I'm shaking my head at our different reactions to each other. I am so comfortable right now listening to Williams tell his stories and enjoying a sense of camaraderie. Of friendship. But Williams is looking at me, and I know he feels a different sense of closeness. Different from what I want. But similar to my feelings when I talked to Nikki this morning.

Williams wraps his arms around me in the parking lot. He's accepted the fact that a nooner isn't happening and seems to be trying to settle for a prolonged goodbye, which he knows I hate.

"Awesome lunch, babe," I say, pecking him on the cheek and turning my head as he tries to zero in on a long kiss. "Sorry, I just can't right now. Too much stuff running around in my head."

"I know. You got a lot on your plate." He steps back and looks me over from head to toe.

I can see he wants to mention the impending visit from Mama Li, but recognizes it as dangerous territory. Smart man. I smile uncomfortably as he looks at me, and my eyes catch movement behind him. There's a man leaned against a silver car, four cars down from Williams's Traverse. I step sideways to get a better angle on the car. It's a Toyota, just like the one in the alley behind The Aerie. Just like the car I saw leaving town.

The man twirls a dog leash in his hand, looking toward the string of shops abutting the brewery. The car looks familiar, but the man is a stranger. The leash, though…

Williams follows my eyes. "What's up, Kristee?"

I'm already walking, my confidence bolstered by Williams's presence.

"Can I help you?" I call out, striding the ten steps between Williams's Traverse and the man.

He turns his head toward me and stops twirling the leash. "Excuse me?"

"I asked if I can help you? Obviously, you're standing out here watching me. Do you need to say something?" My eyes drop to the leash in his hands. "Someone lost their dog?"

"Kristee—" Williams touches my shoulder and I shrug away.

"No. Let him explain."

The man looks from me to Williams and takes a step backward. "I'm just waiting for my wife and our dog." He nods toward the row of shops next to the brewery. "Tater is getting groomed. We're taking him for a walk when he's done." He holds up the leash and gives a slight shrug.

I glare at the man, then turn to Williams. He's squinting his eyes at me, and I realize how this looks to him, without any context. I haven't told Williams about the man in the alley behind The Aerie. Or about Amore being taken. And I'm not ready to share this yet, because the moment I take that step is the moment I have to return the money and explain why I'm such a dipshit loser and can't pay my sister's tuition.

I turn toward the man, who now wears a smile. A woman and a neatly trimmed Labradoodle are walking his direction. My mouth drops.

"Sorry," I mutter, and turn back to Williams.

"Have a nice day," the man says, but I don't think he means it.

Five minutes later, I'm on the road back to Buena Vista, checking my mirror for signs of a silver Toyota. Nothing.

Williams asked one question before he left. "What was that about?"

"I told you, I'm stressed," I say. "I don't want to talk about it now."

So we didn't. He left. And then I left.

The highway home is mostly straight. Fairplay sits up in South Park, a giant alpine meadow between mountain ranges. Rugged open country where the wind blows year around, and the elk cross the road like neighborhood kids on Halloween.

I still can't decide if the parking lot guy was watching me or not. It looked like the car. I kick myself for not getting a plate number. This is the third time I've run into a silver Toyota, and the only way I have to confirm if it's the same one is whether the driver looks the same? How hard can it be to snap a cell phone photo?

Come on, Kristee. Strangers posed as a couple with a dog, and set up a grooming appointment next to the place you met your boyfriend for lunch just so they could watch you exit?

I'm going nuts.

I palm my phone and check my home screen to see if I have service. Two bars. I hit favorites and select Perez. Waiting for his answer, I turn my eyes back to the road to check for elk. Zahn calls this route the Highway of Death. Perez was driving Zahn's daughter, Daria, back to the Springs last year when they hit an elk at sixty miles-per-hour. Totaled Perez's Jeep and put him on crutches for a week.

"What's up, Kristee?" Perez's voice booms over my car speakers. "You inviting me for a late lunch?"

I roll my eyes, thankful Perez can't see me. "No. Just had lunch with Williams in Fairplay. On my way back to BV."

"Oh, man. I'm the rebound guy again? You need some relationship counseling?" Perez teases me.

I laugh. "Oh my God, Rick. You nailed it. You're just the person I would reach out to for advice on a healthy, dynamic, loving relationship." I pause, and wonder if I'm pushing his humor limits by hinting at his divorces. Ah, screw it. "How's yours, anyway?"

"My what?" Perez mutters.

"Your relationship?" I listen to the silence on the other end of the phone and realize I've probably more than made my point.

"Thanks, Kristee. You know how to take a conversation from light banter to existential angst in zero point two seconds." He pauses. "So, what's up?"

I should have rehearsed this call before I hit speed dial. Now that Perez cuts straight to the chase, I'm questioning my resolve to tell him what's happening. *Something fishy is going on at my new business, and I accepted $10K to shut up about it. Am I in trouble?* I don't need Perez to tell me what a dipshit I am.

"Is it Travis? Your new business partner?"

My heart plummets. He already knows? But that's not possible. I take a tentative probe to see what Perez has heard.

"Yeah, I understand these kinds of issues aren't in your wheelhouse, but I wanted to run something by you."

"I knew it. I knew that dickwad when he was in high school, and he was trouble then. What's he done now?"

I breathe easier at Perez's question. If he's asking me what Travis has done, then he's unaware of the funny business. And there's no way he knows about the money.

"It's a contract law thing. Travis and I bought the building to use as office space rental. Short-term or hourly rentals, you know, like they're doing in the cities?"

"Right. Moving BV into the modern age like Vail or Aspen. I got it."

I roll my eyes even though Perez can't see me. "Right. So, after we close on the building, hire the contractors, and start remodeling, Travis carves out a piece of the real estate for himself. For a side hustle. Won't let me use it for our joint venture." I pause. "Does that sound right?"

"That sounds like Travis. That little shit never kept his word to anyone in his life. Slimy. I remember this one time when they were having prom at the high school. He asked this gal to go with him. Can't remember her name, but you know her dad, Curtis Evans, from Ace Hardware?"

"I know Curtis." I wonder where Perez is going with this.

"So, Curtis's daughter is all set, and Travis never picks her up. The girl's heartbroken and Curtis is beside himself. He calls Travis's folks and they tell him Travis is at the dance. So Curtis drives to the gym and checks things out. Turns out Travis asked another girl at the last minute and never told Curtis's daughter about it. Left the poor girl hanging."

"Harsh," I say. "What did Curtis do?"

Perez laughs. "He held it together better than half the fathers in town would do. He went home, comforted his daughter, then confronted Travis the next day. Handled the whole situation like an adult should. Of course, it didn't make any difference. Travis was a little shit then, and I doubt he's changed." Perez's breathing gets louder. "Yeah, the stuff you're talking about? That internal funny business? That's civil court action, contract law, and all that. Not my area of expertise. It sounds like you need a lawyer. Got an extra $10k to pay for one?"

I cough and shoot my hand up to my mouth. If he only knew about my extra $10k. He'd be telling stories about that little shit, Kristee Li, who tried to open a hi-falutin' business in BV and accepted hush money from her crooked business partner.

"No. You know I can't afford a lawyer. I put everything into this new venture, and I'm kind of operating on a shoestring."

"Well, maybe you guys will work it out. Let me know if I can help." And just like that, Perez is ready for the next topic. "How's old Randall doing, anyway?"

I sigh into the phone, frustrated that I couldn't bring myself to tell Perez more about my problems at The Aerie. Perez misinterprets my reaction to his question.

"That bad, huh? I might not know corporate law, but I am somewhat of a self-taught expert on relationship troubles. You want to share?

I laugh out loud at that one. Perez has been married twice and shares his alimony woes with anyone who will listen. I'm always amazed that he's not actively dating any of the women in town. He might have been zero help with my Travis situation and taken me on a non sequitur with the high school story, but Perez is actually a pretty funny guy and a good friend to have in your corner. I like him.

But not the same way he's always liked me.

I spend the next five minutes catching Perez up on Williams's activities and confessing to the stress I'm feeling over my mother's impending visit. Nikki calls while Perez and I are still chatting, and that starts my heart pounding again. I'm looking forward to seeing her in a couple of hours. I send her a *Can I call you later?* text as I wrap up my conversation with Perez. My head shakes as I press send.

I've gone from almost confessing my potentially legal issues to discussing my boyfriend and mother with a man who's crushing on me. Meanwhile, I'm all jittery about a potential date with a girl I'm suddenly crushing on myself.

And Perez thought Travis had high school issues? I'm a hot mess.

ZAHN

NOW

My brain works in mysterious ways. I figure it was the beer session and my associated ruminating that led to this whole Kristee/Nikki relationship thing breaking open. If I hadn't started wallowing in self-pity, I never would have tossed the rest of my beer away and headed downtown to talk to Travis, Nikki, and Karla. I might never have discovered the real reason Nikki and Kristee were fighting on that mountain.

So when I stop by City Market for another six-pack, I remind myself I'm just resupplying for further investigation. I grab a roasted chicken from the deli's warmer and a bag of frozen French fries. I've got some thinking to do, and a salad just won't cut it.

The elevation climbs six hundred feet from the Arkansas River to my house, which is nestled so close to the base of Mt Columbia that you can't see the summit. Although my mind churns on the drive home, trying to figure out how what I've learned pertains to Kristee's disappearance, I still can't resist admiring the way the sun casts a corona above North Cottonwood Creek and the Continental Divide as it settles in the west. I might envy the downtown residents of Buena Vista for their ability to walk to everything they need, but I always remind myself that they live between the mountains, while my place is among the mountains. I wouldn't trade it.

I throw the fries in the oven, adding an extra five minutes on the timer since I've skipped the preheating instructions, then pop open a beer and sit in front of my chicken and a roll of paper towels.

I stare at my can of inspiration before swiveling my eyes to the chicken. Perez is right. Kristee's love life is a surprise, but what does that have to do with her disappearance? After all, it was Nikki who brought the whole *I don't think she is lost* theory to our attention. I tear a wing from the chicken and gnaw on it, trying to reconcile the knowledge I've gained with the elusive facts regarding Kristee's disappearance.

And, of course, the moment my hands are slathered in chicken grease, my phone rings. By the time I've ripped two sheets from my paper towel roll and wiped my hands clean, the phone has rung three more times. I don't recognize the number.

"This is Zahn."

"Yeah, this is Travis. From The Aerie?"

Kristee's business partner. What does he want?

"What's up?"

"Yeah, so I just talked to Karla, Kristee's sister? She swung by to get the stuff that her mom couldn't fit in the car."

"Uh-huh."

"I asked her about Kristee, and she said they found her phone."

"Right." An internal alarm rings in my head. Why is this important to Travis?

"So, what will they do with it?"

My initial thought is to tell him the truth—that the cops are taking it for forensics to check for clues about Kristee's disappearance. But I'm afraid if I open with this revelation, Travis might stop talking.

"Well, Karla's checking it for Kristee's asset info—you know, life insurance, bank accounts, that kind of thing."

"So like emails and texts and stuff?"

"Yep."

Travis is silent.

"What aren't you telling me, Travis? Why do you care?"

"Uh, it's kind of personal. Her family might be embarrassed by some texts on there. Do you think you could get the phone? I could delete them, maybe?"

"Maybe. But I'd need to know what you're deleting before I ask Karla for the phone." I'm having a hard time imagining a situation where I'd help Travis with this...but maybe I can get him talking.

"No way." Travis's response is instant.

So much for that strategy. "I guess you can just wait and talk to the Sheriff's Department?

"Oh, fuck no." Travis says. "It's one thing if her family finds out, but it just doesn't make sense to get the cops involved, since she's already...you know, gone."

I take a pull from my beer and lean back in my chair. A lone deer meanders across my back yard, picking at green shoots poking between the pine needle carpet surrounding my horseshoe pits. I can almost hear the gears in Travis's head turning.

"Look, man, she was your friend, right?" he says.

"Right."

"So maybe you know this already. She was into drugs or something. That's what the texts are about. She got herself in trouble and tried to shift the attention over to me. There's a string of texts about that, and if you read it wrong, it looks like I'm involved."

I roll my eyes as the deer disappears from view. There's no way Kristee is involved in drugs. I know she's pretty open to others using them, and I've seen her turn the other cheek during a past case we worked together. But using them herself? No way. The only foreign substance I've seen her allow into her body is alcohol, and she doesn't drink a lot of that either.

Why would Travis fabricate drug use to get hold of the phone? The texts must do more than shift the blame. He doesn't want the cops to see the phone because he's trying to save his own ass.

This sounds like something for Perez and his team. But if I choose this route, Travis won't talk to me. He'll likely lawyer up, as well. I take another tug on my beer.

There is another alternative. If I agree with Travis's plan, I might elicit more information from him. Because this revelation—that something is wrong inside Travis and Kristee's business—makes sense. She had been stressing about the business since before it opened, but mentioned nothing more specific than Travis commandeering office space and changing the operating plan.

"Maybe we should meet," I say.

. . .

I smile as I hang up, wondering what Travis has on Kristee's phone that might help me break the case wide open. But by the time I finish the other chicken wing, I realize I'm not any closer to figuring this out. There's no case. All I've got is a bunch of people trying to cover their asses. Travis doesn't want anybody looking at whatever he's got going. Karla doesn't want her mother to find out Kristee might still like women. And Nikki—well, Nikki just seems nuts.

Before the Iraq War, our defense secretary had told the press *you go to war with the Army you have.* That's how I feel about my investigation into Kristee's disappearance—I've got to go forward with the information I have...not the information I wish I had. I finish my beer and reach for another.

Before I meet Travis, I need another look at Kristee's phone. Karla just showed me the Nikki texts and nothing else. I'm hoping she hasn't already given it to Perez.

. . .

"Just a second," Karla says. Her voice muffles. "I'm going outside, Mama. It's a personal call. A friend from school.

She returns to the phone. "Are you still there?"

"Yep."

"Yeah, I still got it. I'm supposed to meet Perez tomorrow and turn it in." She pauses. "I'm glad you called because I have something else I want you to look at."

"The Travis texts?"

"What? No, I just skimmed over those. Are they important?"

"I don't know. I want to look at them. What do you have?"

"Some weird stuff. In her browser's search history."

"You mean like from the Internet?"

I hear Karla snort or something.

"Are you laughing at me?" It sounds like she is.

"Sorry. It's just that…well, yes. The internet. It's what you use a browser for."

I knew that. But it's nice to hear Karla laugh, even at my expense.

We meet at the Stray Cat, a coffee shop I rarely frequent. Not many folks I know use it either—that's why I recommended it to Karla. The business sits three blocks south of Main Street directly on Highway 24, the route snaking north along the Arkansas up to Leadville. Perfect for a tourist, but too mainstream for a local.

I arrive first and end up waiting ten more minutes for Karla. Tourist trap or not, the aroma of fresh grounds smells like home. The server pours me black coffee, and I thumb through a real estate pamphlet, shaking my head at the prices before looking around to see who else is here. I don't recognize anyone. A bearded young man in one corner and a middle-aged woman in another have their heads buried in their laptops, and I figure they are doing the poor man's version of Kristee's business model. They can get a small desk and access to the internet by buying a cup of coffee. Probably cheaper than The Aerie.

Karla's late, and I figure she's working up an excuse to get out of the house. She finally pushes through the door, scanning the room for me, her eyebrows raising when she spots me in the back.

"You want anything?"

Karla shakes her head and then thanks me as I pull her chair out for her.

"So, what do you have?" she starts and then stops because she's interrupted me asking the same question.

I laugh, then lean forward. "I got a call from Travis. He's worried about some texts between Kristee and him. He wants to delete them."

Kristee's mouth drops open. "I'm letting the cops read my sister's texts about a woman she's having an affair with, and Travis is worried about shared office space secrets?" She lets out a breath. "I mean, come on. What could be that important?"

I don't really want to go into the whole drug thing until I see the texts, so I stay silent as she pulls Kristee's phone from her pocket.

"OK, let's see what we got." Karla thumbs through the phone and then pauses. "I've got their conversations here."

"And?"

"Just a minute." Karla's brow furrows and I see her scrolling on the phone. "Yeah, I probably should have read these closer." She hands the phone to me. "What do you make of these? I mean, there's a lot of back and forth, but I'm guessing the ones Travis wants deleted start with these."

I take the phone and start reading.

"The green bubbles are Kristee. The white bubbles are Travis," Karla says.

I told you I wanted to give it back. You wouldn't let me. So now you either let me or I'm keeping what I found.

What did you find?

I think you know. Or at least you know where I found it. D-2. I sunk your battleship.

Quit fucking around Kristee. You're the one in trouble.

This look familiar?

Kristee has sent a photo of the inside of a dark building. I can make out corrugated walls and a stack of boxes, but nothing else.

You have no idea what you are doing, Kristee. You need help.

I know exactly what I'm doing. And if you don't start talking with me, I know exactly where I'm going.

I examine the picture again before returning the phone. "What's that about?" I'm confused with the dialogue because I saw nothing in the conversation that referenced drugs. Tension courses in the subtext between the lines, but I see nothing incriminating. Unless the picture itself is what is important.

"I don't have any idea. But why let Travis delete these before the cops see them?"

"I don't think we should," I say. "I'd like to talk to him, though. Find out why these texts have him so wound up."

I stare over Karla's shoulder at the sepia pictures adorning the walls, memories of a Buena Vista a hundred years ago. The framed vistas of lettuce fields, railroad stations, and cattle ranchers likely remind patrons of simpler times when life appeared less complicated.

Shaking my head, I shift my eyes back to Karla. Life wasn't simpler back then. Putting food on the table, staying warm in the winter, and protecting your family probably consumed all your time. In comparison, the issues of today are definitely first-world problems.

Karla thumbs through the phone again, then pauses. She scoots her chair over next to me and shows me the screen.

"This is an internet search a week prior to her disappearing. Were you talking to her then?"

I try to focus on the sites Karla is scrolling past. "No. I talked to her the morning before she took the SAR mission, but I hadn't seen her in a couple of weeks before that. We had dinner and beers at the Surf."

Karla's thumbs pause. "OK. You can see here, she's got these searches on Duke's bursar's website. I can see where she's researching the payment regulations."

"That makes sense, right? She's probably trying to find out ways she can delay or lower the payment, right?"

Karla nods. "I think so. But check out these next entries. Look at some of these sites." She hands me the phone.

I squint at the URLs as if I'm trying to read Arabic. "These don't make sense to me. Can I click on them, or does that mess the history up?"

"Knock yourself out. They'll still stay in the history on the date she accessed them. Whatever you open just adds to today's history."

I tap the top URL and glance at Karla while waiting for the site to open. She's watching me closely, as if trying to gauge my reaction.

When the page expands on the screen, I see it's a cryptocurrency site—an educational, how-to essay on Bitcoin. I go to the next site and get something similar. Glancing up at Karla, I shrug. "It looks like she's trying to get smart on cryptocurrency? Was she into that? Bitcoin or some other cryptocurrency?"

Karla says, "No. Not that I've found. But look at the trend—she's obviously looking for ways to get money. She's got the cryptocurrency sites, there's the loan site, and there's even something she's typed in about how to leverage your business for cash if you're not the sole owner. Like the situation she's in with Travis."

"I guess this doesn't surprise me, Karla. She was having problems with the business and was concerned about your tuition. She was probably stressed about how to make it all work."

Karla's voice catches as she reaches for the phone. "Let me show you something."

I hand her the phone and watch her thumbs fly across the cell phone keyboard.

She stops scrolling and stares down at the screen before handing the phone back to me. "Look at these."

I take the phone and press enter on the site she has highlighted: *https://organtown.com.* My eyes narrow as I try to make sense out of what Kristee had been searching. The page opens, and red squares load one at a time in a column on the right side of the screen. I squint my eyes and hold the phone closer to my face. The squares are photographs, and each photo has a caption next to it. The first reads:

Human Lungs For Sale: $50,000

Then

Human Liver For Sale: $60,000

The third picture is of a heart. The last one shows a kidney.

I place the phone face down on the table, my mouth moving soundlessly, while glancing around the coffee shop to see if anyone is watching us. Everyone is drinking their coffee or looking at their phone or computer, absorbed in their own lives and dramas.

My voice returns. "What the hell is this? Why would she buy an organ? I thought this was about college tuition. You're telling me she needed an organ? What the hell?"

Karla shoves the phone toward me. "Keep looking."

I push the phone toward her. "Just tell me, Karla."

Karla picks up the phone and puts it in her pocket before resting her hands on the table and locking her fingers. I hear her voice as she looks straight ahead. "She wasn't interested in buying. Look at all the previous websites about earning money."

"You mean she was—"

"In each of these organ websites, she went to the home page first, then clicked on 'Sell Your Organ.'" Karla pauses and then turns to meet my eyes. "She didn't need an organ. She was trying to sell one for money."

•   •   •

The Aerie is only a five-minute drive away—a quarter-mile north on the highway and two blocks east on Main Street. I pull from my parking slot toward the exit, then see Karla jogging across the lot, waving her hand. I brake and check my rearview mirror to see a black SUV vehicle waiting on me to clear the entrance to the highway.

"What's up?" As if everything she's shown me so far isn't enough.

She thrusts Kristee's phone at me through the passenger window. "Take this," she says. "You might need it to make Travis talk. Just bring it back by tomorrow so I can get it to Perez and his guys."

I nod and take the phone. Glancing in my mirror, I spy the car still sitting there, and I'm surprised at their patience. I see Colorado plates and realize it's likely a local. Out-of-staters would blast their horn.

As I approach The Aerie, interior lights highlight the figure of a woman behind the reception desk. Travis is probably here, but I'm too wired to talk now. I need to get myself under control before I chat with Kristee's business partner.

I pull into the parking lot across from the police station next to the tennis courts—my normal parking location for yoga at the community center when I'm back in town. The car behind me continues straight. It looks like the same car from the Stray Cat—Colorado plates.

As I lock up my truck, I watch the car angle left down to the River Park, and release my breath as it parks next to the restrooms. In our tiny town, you could see the same car five times in a day. I'm just paranoid.

I still plan on dropping in on Travis, but I need time to process what I've learned. Kristee thought she had something on Travis. Travis says he's got something on Kristee. And Kristee is researching how to sell her own body organs? It makes no sense at all.

The land north of the tennis courts is a Frisbee golf course, and the paths that weave between the holes are popular with the locals for walking dogs. A perfect place to clear my head. At the end of the course I can loop to the east and finish the walk along the Arkansas River, before returning to my car or continuing on foot to The Aerie.

The Midland Hill perches to my right overlooking the Arkansas River, the reddish rock a sharp contrast to the silver and gray of the Collegiate Peaks on the opposite side of the valley. A border collie with a young couple passes me, walking the opposite direction toward my car. Five minutes later, a woman with a lab mix follows in the same direction. I realize I should have offered to walk Amore.

Ahead of me, a bench faces the mountains and I stop and sit. Kristee and her internet searches for organ websites are still stuck in my head. I watch another person working their way in my direction, the first walker I've seen without a dog. I pull Kristee's phone from my pocket and tap in the code Karla shared with me. Mimicking the steps Karla took to get to the internet search history, I scroll through the websites. If Karla uncovered organ sales just by scanning domain names, who knows what I might uncover? I know Perez's team can do this better than me—but I want to see it first. I've got eighteen hours with this phone before Karla turns it in, and I'm going to look at everything I can.

The walker I'd seen in the distance nears me, and I nod at the man as he passes. He's got the classic Colorado look for someone twenty years younger than me. A tightly quilted down jacket, hiking pants, and trail runners. Out for a stroll.

The man nods back and tilts his head at me as he passes. "Great day, isn't it?"

"It is." I return to Kristee's phone, then glance back at the man when he stops and turns around.

"Hey, I know this is kind of a weird question, but would you mind if I borrowed your phone?"

He's right. It's a weird question. And I'm uncomfortable with the speed at which he approaches me. I rise from the bench, and the man's eyes shift from mine to something behind me.

Before I can turn, a blow to my head staggers me. I reel forward and then I feel nothing.

KRISTEE

BEFORE

I lean on the balcony railing of my condo, Amore unleashed at my side, and gaze north to the Buffalo Peaks. A thousand feet lower than the Collegiates that dominate my dining-room view, the Buffalos are actually harder to climb. No established trail leads hikers to the top, and it's a seven-mile drive on rugged roads to get to the base before a would-be climber could start bushwhacking.

My phone rings, and I check the screen, expecting to see Karla's name. I've paid the first of the two overdue tuition installments, and I'm considering what I'll tell Karla regarding paying the other. I'm not sure that a simple *I've got it* will fly with my sister. She knows something is awry in my financial world.

But it's not Karla's name on the phone. It's Nikki, and the caller ID hits me like an ice cream headache. How can something so good cause pain?

Nikki slept over after our get-together three nights ago. And she's shared my bed every night since. I'm unsure whether it's infatuation or whether I'm head over heels in love, but every time I even think about this woman, I can't keep the grin off my face. I'm guessing Nikki feels the same way because she calls every three or four hours.

"What's up, girl?" I say.

"Just calling to see how my gal is feeling this morning."

"You know how I'm feeling—you just left like 45 minutes ago."

Nikki giggles before she speaks again. "I know. But I was thinking about you." She pauses. "And thinking about tonight."

And here comes the headache. I have to do something about this relationship. Either I embrace this woman I'm falling for and tell Williams what's up, or I sit down with Nikki and we talk through what we are doing. Decide if this is real.

But our budding romance is just the tip of my iceberg of worries. I've still got Karla's tuition payments hanging over me like the IRS on April 14. I've spent everything Travis gave me, stayed away from his office, and still sense that his goons are following me around. I had hoped The Aerie would bring me joy. Instead, it's dragging me down like a backpack with a broken waist belt. Especially now that I've used Travis's money.

And the cherry topping the sundae? I've got a mother visiting soon who I haven't seen in five years. Mama Li thinks she's on a mission to break up an interracial romance and instead is more likely to find me back in the kind of same-sex relationship that estranged us in the first place.

My perfect life—the self-possessed, self-made woman making it in the Colorado Rockies—is fucked.

I fix wistful eyes on the Buffalos, shaking my head at Nikki's question about this evening. I want to see her—another night at the Lock-Up followed by another night under my covers—but I have different plans for tonight. Since I can't seem to control my love life and there's no stopping my mother, I've decided on something I *can* do. Figure out what Travis is up to.

I don't appreciate the leverage he is waving in my face, and I'm sure it can't be legal. If I discover his angle, I'll have something on him. Whether I use that information to redeem myself with the law or to get more money from Travis for Karla's tuition…well, I haven't decided yet.

The first time I searched Travis's office, I had found the storage shed leases and keys. I recognized the business names on at least two of the documents. They operate here in Buena Vista, and I'm checking them out tonight. But I need an excuse for Nikki.

"Yeah, Nikki…I can't do tonight."

"Why?"

"It's been three nights in a row. I need a break." I give a short laugh. "You probably need one too. Don't you feel like I'm suffocating you? All this time together?"

Actually, it *has* been a lot of time together, and I wonder how Nikki feels about that. She's been on my mind nonstop and it's weird. I let out a breath. I do need a break—to get my shit together, but I don't *want* a break.

Nikki's voice is quiet. "Not really." She pauses, before continuing, "To be honest, Kristee, these past three days have been the best since I moved here. I can't stop thinking about you."

There it is. She feels the same way. Neither one of us is thinking straight…which sets off warning bells for me. Is this love? Or infatuation?

"I'm meeting Randy again. He's picking me up and we're hitting Leadville for dinner." Amore scrambles to his feet when he hears Randy's name. I'm lying to Nikki, but I can't think of a better excuse.

Nikki is silent. This is the elephant in the room. Nikki hasn't asked what our blossoming relationship means for my boyfriend, Randy. I'm grateful for her silence on the matter because I'm not sure what it means either.

Now I'm using Randy as a fake excuse to investigate my business partner, and the elephant is taking up the whole couch.

"You've got to give me some time to process what we're doing, Nikki."

"Oh my, doesn't that sound clinical? Processing. Are we having a process, you and me?"

"You know what I mean. Give me a chance."

Nikki's voice is firm. "I am. Have fun at your little dinner tonight. Consider this your chance. Your opportunity to tell Randy how you really feel. You know…about our process."

Nikki ends the call, and I glance at Amore, who has lowered himself to the balcony floor after figuring out I'm not talking to Randy, and put his head between his paws.

Exactly how I feel. "My life is so screwed, Amore."

. . .

I stand in front of a Hi-Alt storage shed ready to put my plan into action. I'd expected my covert mission to be a bit more challenging. Not that I'm going all 007, but I did wear dark clothing, entered The Aerie from the alley side with a flashlight, and took back streets to the storage facility. I stopped short of camouflaging my face or choosing a random route to the office, though. No one is paying attention to me at 2:00 am.

A camera perched at the end of the storage row angles my way. I know from scouting this place they have security cameras, but I've decided to ignore them. First, there's no way the owner of this rinky-dink eight-container facility has the bucks to pay someone to watch this footage 24/7. Second, it's probably set up to play back if someone reports something stolen.

I'm not here to steal. I need to see what Travis is doing. I ignore the camera and shove the key into the padlock. After sliding the door a foot to the right, I'm inside.

I close the door and power on my SAR headlamp. The container is only partially filled, with cardboard boxes lining the right wall and two rows of briefcase-sized Pelican cases on the left. It only takes me three minutes to rule out the cardboard boxes as anything suspicious. They're filled with computers. All the same brand. No monitors, no keyboards. Just computers. I don't understand much of Travis's crypto shit, but computers make sense.

The Pelican cases are a different matter. They're locked. Not with keys, but with padlocks linking the hard plastic sides together, two on each case. Using both hands, I lift one to waist level. It can't weigh over ten pounds. When I shake it, something inside shifts.

Duh. Who is going to lock up empty cases?

I shift my eyes to the row below me and count the remaining cases. There are nine more.

What are the odds of Travis and his boys noticing a missing case? I involuntarily snort at my question and quickly dim my light even though I'm alone. *Well, Kristee, I guess that would depend on what's inside the cases.* Which is the whole reason I'm here.

Adjusting my load, I move to the door, dousing my light before balancing the case in one hand and sliding open the door with the other.

Walking away from the storage shed, my first thought is returning the key to Travis's office. But it occurs to me I might need to return the case. Damn. I've got a long night ahead.

Amore's all wound up when I return. He's not used to my absence in the wee hours of the morning and crowds my legs. I position the Pelican case on the dining room table and turn for the door. Amore whines, and I soothe him. "I'm just going to the shed for some tools. I'll be back in like two minutes. Relax."

Amore stops whining and stares at me, motionless. I'm positive he'll be in the same spot when I return.

At the bottom of the landing, I hear yelling coming from Jacy's apartment. Instinctively, I check my watch, even though I know it's past three in the morning.

"You are grounded from now until you graduate from high school," Erik's voice bellows.

"How do you even know if I'll finish high school?"

I pause on the landing, wondering how Jacy's father will respond to that. All I hear is silence.

"Go ahead. Do it. I know how good it makes you feel when you slap me around." I wince at Jacy's mocking voice. It's like she's begging for punishment.

"What do you expect me to do, Jacy? I can't control you. I'm the dad. I'm responsible. Do I just let you run wild around town? Have people talking about ol' Erik Johnson, who can't control his loose daughter?"

I hear the door open, and I step behind the stairwell as Jacy barrels out of her condo with her father in trail.

"I'm staying at Janelle's," she shouts.

"Don't bother coming back." The door slams as her father returns. When I peek around the corner, Jacy is jogging across the parking lot.

At least she doesn't look hurt. And she's away from Erik and doesn't need my help.

I unlock my storage shed and grab my hacksaw. Closing up, I remember the snippers I found while plowing the previous winter. Industrial-sized, with foot-and-a-half long handles, they're perfect for fence repair. And maybe padlocks. I reenter the shed and rummage through my lost and found box. I call it that even though it's only filled with things I've found. The snippers are right on top.

My neighbors are silent as I climb the stairs to my home. Sure enough, Amore stands in the living room staring at the door when I enter.

"Did you miss me?"

At the table, I don't even waste time with the hacksaw. When I squeeze the snippers, I can see the sharp metal making a dent on the first lock, but nothing else. My arm strength isn't going to be enough to cut the hasps. I step back and reexamine the case.

A smile comes to me slowly, and I set the case on the floor, positioning the snippers on the lock again. This time, one handle presses against the floor. I step on the top handle, balancing myself with one of the dining room chairs, and lower my body weight.

Snip.

I position the snippers the same way on the other lock.

Snip. I'm in.

I lift the case to the table and unlatch the front. Part of me hopes these cases are where Travis stores his more expensive computer gear. Fancy hard drives or something. I don't know.

But the other part of me knows without a doubt that Travis is dirty. So I'm unsurprised at what I see when I open the lid.

Five large zip-lock bags filled with smaller plastic bags. I lift one of the larger bags closer and peer through the transparent plastic. Inside are small snack bags filled with white powder. I doubt it's laundry detergent. Good—now Travis isn't the only one with leverage.

I drive to Travis's office, locking the Pelican case in my car while I enter the back of The Aerie to return the key. Then I weave through the back roads, all four of them, to Highway 24, where I head south out of Buena Vista. At the halogen glow of the prison lights, I turn the opposite direction and head west toward our Search & Rescue bay.

If these guys are willing to steal my dog, there's nowhere safe in my condo to hide these drugs. And I'm not returning them to the storage facility. No way. Travis won't let me out of this situation I'm in, and now I finally have some leverage. If he backs off me and moves his operation out of The Aerie, I'll stay quiet. If he doesn't, I have the goods against him. Sure, I'll take some heat for accepting his money, but it's better than continuing down this path with Travis. Especially now that I've confirmed it's definitely illegal.

My breath deepens and my shoulders relax slightly. At least now I'm positive about Travis's angle. And it's not just crypto.

The SAR parking lot is empty except for a lone medical van we keep powered up outside the front door. No one has used it since I joined. Our go-to vehicles are inside, a lifted Toyota Tacoma for traveling light into rugged terrain, and our tech rig, an over-powered dually that can carry everything we need for a major rescue.

I punch in the door code and let out a tiny scream before recognizing the figure at the entrance. It's Bumbling Bob, our medical dummy, propped in a chair next to the doorway. This is the third time Bob has scared me, and I know I'm not the only one who thinks the joke is getting old. Z-man laughed his ass off the first time I told him about Bob.

Closing the door, I leave the lights off and switch on my headlamp. We park the vehicles in a massive garage off the classroom where I am standing. That's where I plan to stash the case. The challenge is finding the right spot—keeping it away from the stuff we use every day, but also hidden enough that a curious SAR member won't stumble upon it. I didn't have any padlocks to replace the ones I snipped off, but I've used my bike lock to secure the case. Good enough.

Staring at the racks on the wall, I spy a potential hiding spot. A five-gallon bucket labeled *Rodent Control* sits on the lower shelf behind a pile of ropes toward the back of the bay. But we don't do rodent control in the bay anymore—we recently signed a contract with the local exterminator. This bucket is left over from our kill-the-rats-ourselves days. I move the ropes, slide out the bucket, and curse. The case is too big to fit in the bucket. Not a good option.

I crouch and peer into the space I created when I emptied the shelf. There's plenty of room for the case. I see-saw the plastic container toward the back, then pause as my headlamp beam catches the tumbler on the bike lock. I don't want anyone getting too curious. I stand, scanning the bay with my headlamp, before pausing at the tech rig and smiling, remembering the zip-ties we used on a stretcher repair last mission. Back at the case, I run a tie through each buckle and pull it tight. A bike lock and two zip-ties won't deter someone intent on opening the case, but they might deter someone who simply stumbles upon it.

This is only temporary. Once Travis moves this gig out of The Aerie, we can discuss me returning his stuff to him.

After locking the SAR bay, I head back to my condo. It's past five now, and I'm far enough from Midland Hill in the east, overlooking my building, to see the pink glow of the sun crawling toward Buena Vista from South Park. I should be exhausted—but I'm not. Instead, I'm keyed up from breaking into Travis's office, finding the drugs, and deciding to hold them.

As soon as I open the door, Amore pops to his feet. That dog will sleep like the dead this afternoon. I strip off my clothes and climb in bed. Too wired to sleep, I stare at my cell phone screen.

"I. Need. Money."

I'm thinking this thought out loud, and Amore offers a whine at my voice. I glance at my dog, then back at the phone. What the hell. I type "*I need money*" into my browser.

Bitcoin ads fill my screen. I realize cryptocurrency is all the rage, even after its post-pandemic plummet, but I haven't done the research to find out more. Hell, the only thing I really understand is what Travis explained regarding his tumbling work. I type *Crypto For Dummies* and browse a couple of sites. *Crypto 101. So you want to invest in digital currency?*

I stare at site after site telling me how to invest money I don't have and turn it into more money. The explanations lose me when they shift to blockchains and every time I try to concentrate hard enough to understand the concepts, I'm reminded that I have nothing left to invest. How do you make money quick if you don't have money?

So, I type my question into my browser and stare at the results.

Selling Your Blood

Selling Your Semen

Selling Your Body

I laugh. I don't have enough blood to make the money I need for Karla's school. I certainly don't have any semen. I read the words *Selling Your Body* and laugh again. Probably not going to make my next fortune sleeping around, either. But I am curious to see what the business model looks like.

My eyes widen as the website opens. This is not a Do-It-Yourself prostitution site. It's a portal to sell your own body parts. A picture of a heart sits above a picture of a kidney. I check the prices next to each picture. $110K for the heart. Kidneys are $50K. I hover the cursor over a liver and wonder what makes them so expensive.

I'm dismayed at the depth of my depravity, and alt-tab over to my life insurance account. The one I emptied for my down payment on my share of The Aerie. Maybe there's a discount for prior policyholders?

I leap from my bed, startling Amore, and stride to my dining room table. The dawn wind is cresting off Mt Princeton, creating wisps of snow that curl like smoke as if the mountains are semi-dormant volcanoes, off-gassing for my pleasure. My heart pounds. I'd do anything to escape to my mountains.

I don't know what to do. My plan with Travis's drugs is to create breathing space. Make those men go away. Should I sell the drugs and use the money? There's no way. Even if my conscience would allow it, I know I would get caught. They'd garnish the money from Karla's school while Travis and I are sitting in the slammer.

I press a key on my laptop, and the life insurance website glares at me. Useless. I no longer own a policy, and even if I did, it only pays if I'm dead. And according to the fine print, suicide would void the policy. So how exactly would I engineer that? It would have to be an ironclad accidental death because if I bought a new policy and died a month later, they'd certainly be investigating it.

I switch back to my cell phone and the organ selling site. What looked crazy five minutes ago suddenly looks like an option.

An hour later, I've got some significant research under my belt. It's illegal to sell your organs in the United States. But it's not illegal in many other countries. *Organtown's* prices are pretty standard and that amount would get me out of my hole.

And most important? People donate kidneys all the time and continue to live healthy lives. I skim over my notes to see if I've missed anything, then sigh and push the papers away. What I'm missing is a sanity check. Is online organ selling even legit? I don't have anyone I can ask.

I start a to-do list on the side of my notepad.

- *Contact the organ website*
- *Check my passport*
- *Contact Duke for another installment extension.*

I take a deep breath and gaze over my computer at Mt Princeton. The wind has slackened, and the crisp outline of the aretes pointing at the summit jump out like etchings against the sky. I sense possibility for the first time in weeks. Maybe I can make this happen.

ZAHN

NOW

"You were just sitting there? Not doing shit?" Perez squints at me.

I nod slowly, from a bed at the Rocky Mountain Regional Clinic, our town's meager facsimile of a medical facility. The paramedics hauled me here after another dog walker found me face down near the park bench where the guy—I'm assuming it was a guy, just from the weight of the swing—clubbed me. By the time the ambulance arrived, I was already walking toward my truck while the motherly dog walker berated me for not waiting for the paramedics. I knew the EMTs from Search & Rescue, and they concurred I would not die anytime soon, but they also reminded me that protocol was protocol and hustled me to the clinic as a precaution.

The doctor says I probably have a concussion, and he's making me wait an hour or two before I head home. He won't let me walk back to where I left my truck, and that's why Perez sits in the chair across from me. Well, that and the fact that when I called him, he reminded me I was an assault victim and someone from law enforcement needed to take a report.

"No idea what the guy who hit you looks like?" Perez says.

I pause at that, recalling the man who wanted to borrow my phone. "Never saw the guy who hit me, but I saw their partner."

"Two people? And they didn't take your wallet, you said. Are you missing anything?"

Here it comes. Perez is going to love this.

"Yeah. They took Kristee's phone."

Perez stares at me, and I shift my eyes from the floor and stare back. Finally, he speaks. "Are you going to make me ask the question?"

"Because Karla wanted me to check for any other personal information before giving it to you. She asked, and I agreed." I don't share the text exchange between Kristee and Travis and the drug reference. I don't describe the websites Kristee visited involving organ sales. If they catch the guys who clocked me, then they'll find the phone and discover all this themselves. If they don't reclaim the phone, maybe I'll share what I found with Perez. After I investigate more.

"So, they didn't take your wallet. They didn't take your phone. But they took Kristee's phone." Perez's voice is so slow, even my concussed brain can keep pace. "This changes everything."

I recognize from Perez's tone that he won't be letting me check things out alone.

"Yep," I say.

·　·　·

The doc instructs me to wake myself every couple of hours and call the next morning, before sending me home with prescription Tylenol. I lay off the beer—more doctor's orders—and try to sleep. Perez interrupts my efforts with two random "Are you conscious?" calls at two and four in the morning.

I greet daybreak like I did during the bad years—sleep deprived and head pounding. The only things missing are the empty bottles next to my bed. I make my mandatory call to the doc, who says I'm good to go. Don't climb any mountains or get into any bar fights.

I hang up, and Perez's name flashes on my phone—his third call of the day. The first call while the sun is up.

"You can stop calling. The doc just cleared me."

"That's why I'm calling. I've got a job for you." Perez pauses. "If you're up for it."

"Kristee-related?"

"Yep."

"I'm in. What do you have?" I'm suddenly alert—and intrigued. It's felt as if Perez has been holding his cards to his chest for this whole ordeal, and now he suddenly needs my help?

Perez tells me of a couple living in Winfield, the old mining town that serves as the trailhead for Huron Peak for two-wheel drive cars and trucks that can't make the last two miles of rock-strewn, off-road track.

"Frank's lived up there for over 30 years. He's got a camera mounted on his garage pointed at the road and claims he's got every vehicle that used that road on the day Kristee disappeared."

I'm nodding my head because I know where Perez is going with this. The same road leading to Huron Peak's base forks into the main trail leading to the Apostles' northern approach. It's the same trail I used when I met Chad on the way to Kristee's memorial service.

But I stop nodding as I work through the logic. Kristee left her team on the north side of the Apostles. But they found her phone on the south side, by the rockslide. What exactly could they expect to find on this tape?

Perez is slow to answer when I pose the question. "Here's the deal. This guy called in the information about his tape a week ago. We had it on our follow-up list, but then we closed the case. Now that we've found her phone, we're rechecking some of our loose ends. It was never a front-burner lead."

"Why me? Why not one of your law enforcement types, Deputy Sheriff?" I emphasize Perez's title, reminding him I don't have one yet.

"Right. That's a fair question. Here's why. I talked to the Buena Vista Police, and they're letting me take the lead on finding those guys who took you out."

"Uh-huh." I'm still not tracking.

"If I find out why they stole Kristee's phone, we might reopen Kristee's case. Then I could free up more resources for leads like the one I'm sending you on."

"But in the meantime…" I let my voice trail off because I've figured out what Perez is doing.

"Right, in the meantime, I've got you champing at the bit to get involved and I want you out of my way while I'm looking for your assailants. How's that for a naked truth? Besides, I trust you. So how about you get off your lazy, un-concussed ass, and go watch some video?"

I laugh. This is the Perez I'm used to.

"Got it, sir. On my way."

"I'll call Frank and let him know you're coming. Wear your SAR jacket and bring your ID in case he asks."

"My ID doesn't—"

Perez interrupts. "Nobody knows what you guys can or can't do. Those IDs look official. Just take it."

It's a good forty-minute drive up to Winfield, twenty minutes up Highway 24 toward Leadville, and then another twenty on the gravel road bordering Clear Creek Reservoir and the creek itself. I'm familiar with this road because it's the primary access route to five fourteeners. I pass Missouri Gulch and the trail that splits to Missouri Mountain, Mt Belford, and Mt Oxford—three peaks I've summited both for pleasure and in search of stranded climbers. Less than a mile farther, I pass the remains of a cabin and the abandoned mining town of Vicksburg. At the road's end, I pull into Winfield, where the north and south forks of Clear Creek merge. The north fork leads hikers to the south side of La Plata, a challenging 14er as familiar to SAR teams as tying a double figure-eight knot. Every year we rescue more climbers off La Plata than any other mountain in our county. The south fork points to Huron Peak and the Apostles, where we lost Kristee.

As I scan the four remaining log homes, I spot a man standing on the porch of the closest cabin to the road. I slow my truck to a walking pace as the man steps off the porch and approaches me from the driveway.

"You Tyler Zahn?"

"That's me. I'm guessing you're Frank?"

He nods, and I shake his hand.

Frank points to a patch of grass next to his garage and waits for me to get out of my truck. I note the camera above where he stands, mounted on the corner of the garage and aimed toward the main road.

"That's the one?"

"That's it," Frank says. "I've got the footage inside. I checked it for that day and saw nothing unusual, but when I heard about your lost gal, I figured someone besides me ought to have a look-see at it." He pauses. "I guess that's you." He shakes his head. "Took you all long enough."

I don't have an answer to that, so I say nothing. It's Perez's problem, but it won't help if I say that.

We climb the steps and enter the cabin. Frank opens the door, and I hear a female voice from inside.

"Don't let the cat out."

Frank jerks, and I watch him turn his foot sideways to block a charcoal gray cat from escaping the house. He bends over, grabbing the cat by the nape of its neck and pulling it into his arms with one hand, while holding the door open for me with the other.

"Got to watch this guy," Frank says, with a twinkle in his eye. "If the cat disappears, I'm in big trouble."

We enter the cabin without losing any pets, and I meet Bridget, Frank's wife. She's a large woman and welcomes me with an equally large smile.

"Frank's been trying to get someone to review his footage for a week," she says, as Frank pulls up his video on the computer. "He spent good money on this surveillance system, and we've never had the slightest problem with intruders. It was a couple hundred dollars to purchase and install. I suspect he wants you guys to find something just to justify the cost."

I nod and smile, but on the inside, I'm not as optimistic as Frank and Bridget about whether we'll find anything. Unless Frank has a clip of Kristee walking down the road, I don't see us solving any cases today.

Bridget disappears to fetch coffee and Frank turns to me.

"This is the footage from the date you all reported the young lady missing. That Kristee gal. She was on your team, right?"

"Right."

"If we run it in real time, we'll be here all day. You have a time window you want to use?"

"Does this thing have night capability?"

"You mean like infrared? No." Frank shakes his head. "But my garage light is bright enough to see the cars."

I estimate if we watch at high speed from an hour after Kristee left Karla and Chad, that should cover whatever it is we're hoping to find. I guide Frank to that time frame, and he plays the footage.

As I expected, it's hours of nothing interspersed with an infrequent car flitting through the screen. Frank ends up running the footage at the highest speed possible, and we just pause it and zoom in when we detect movement on the road. The process is quicker than I expected because of the low traffic volume.

Seven cars and one bicycle into the footage, Bridget arrives with coffee and we take a break. We sip from mugs, and Frank asks, "What exactly are we looking for?"

I decide to be frank with Frank, but I don't share that joke with him—I'm sure it wouldn't be the first time he's heard it.

"I'm not sure. To be honest, we're just checking out everything because we have nothing. We just found her phone on the other side, down by North Texas Creek, so it seems unlikely she would have come back through here, doesn't it?"

"North Texas Creek is where the rockslide went, right?" Frank says.

I nod.

"Heard about that. You might never find her if she was down that side."

I know he's right. These mountains have claimed more lives from avalanches and rockslides than we will ever know. Gravity pulls down the rocks and snow. People disappear. The mountains rarely give them up.

Eight cars later, I ask Frank to pause.

He's got a dark-colored car driving by on the road, and the model looks familiar. Which isn't that surprising—it's a small all-wheel drive SUV and those things are everywhere. But still.

"Can you play the black car again? Frame by frame?" Something rubs my leg and I jerk, scalding my lips with the coffee. I see the cat rubbing against my boot.

"Bridget! Cat!" Frank shakes his head as Bridget appears in the doorway, scanning the room for the cat. "Sorry." He turns back to the screen. "It might not be black. Can't tell on black and white footage." Frank fiddles with his mouse and runs the car backwards, and then forward as slowly as he can make it go. "You recognize that one?"

"Maybe. Can you tell what kind of car it is?"

Frank zooms in on the grill and freezes the frame. "Looks like a Honda to me." He points to the *H* emblem on the front.

He uses the up arrow on his keyboard and shifts the picture up to the driver's seat. The driver wears sunglasses, and I can't tell whether it's a male or female. But behind the driver, I spy an oval shape on the back window.

"Can you zoom in on that?" I point to the shape.

"That's as close as I can get. Let me center the screen."

He moves the picture sideways, and I zero in on the inverse image of a sticker on the car's rear window. I can't read it, but I recognize the shape. It's our Search & Rescue logo.

"That's our sticker."

"Right?" Frank's nodding his head, but isn't as excited as I am. "We saw your group's Toyota Tacoma three cars ago. You guys were on a mission. Isn't it normal for your team to have some personal vehicles out?"

I can't argue with Frank about that, but it's the combination of the car's model, dark color, and the sticker that holds my attention. Because I've seen those three things together previously...on the back side of Nikki's house. Where she parks her Honda. And then I remember the last conversation I had with Kristee. She said she was taking a team out in a chopper. And she had. Kristee, Nikki, and Chad flew out for this mission in a helicopter.

How many other members of our team own a dark-colored Honda CRV with a SAR sticker on the rear window? If the answer is zero, then what is Nikki's car doing up here?

I wonder if it's even worth the effort to play the rest of Frank's footage for the day and ask him how much time he thinks it will take to review the remaining video.

"Hell, I can just run it through on hi-speed, and at least you'll know how many cars we're talking about," he says, clicking the mouse on the double arrow.

"Stop!" Frank has barely pressed the button, and the next vehicle grabs my attention. "That next car. How long after the Honda did this one come through?"

Frank scans the time stamps. "About one minute. You think they're together?"

I stare at the truck and try to figure out what prompted me to halt the video scan. I've seen something like it before. Long-bed truck, twin-cab. Another dark color I can't distinguish. I don't see stickers in the back window. I can't see the plates. But it looks familiar.

I take a deep breath, then release it. Now that I think I've seen Nikki's car driving out of here—which is highly improbable—I'm seeing suspicious vehicles everywhere.

"I've seen enough, Frank," I say. "Let's wrap it up."

KRISTEE

BEFORE

Two weeks pass, and my mojo is returning. A semblance of control. My problems remain unsolved, but things are in motion. Nikki is next to me on the couch, and Amore lies on my other side.

The kidney thing is no internet hoax. I reached out to the company in Thailand by phone. I talked to a former patient for an hour after they put me in touch with her. It's like they advertise: they pay you to travel to Asia, they pay for the operation, and they pay $50K for the kidney. A week of recovery and you're back in the states.

I'm cognizant that this potential plan of mine borders on the extreme. OK...if anyone found out, they would think I'm bat-shit crazy. But they also wouldn't understand the hole into which I've buried myself. If I do nothing, my sister drops out of college and joins the ranks of the failed Li family. Dead father, a disgraced former university professor mother driving for Uber, and me—gutter cleaner and snowplower. Oh, and don't forget...I also collude with a local drug dealer.

So, yeah, it's a little crazy. But you only need one kidney to live. According to my research, you can lead a normal life after the procedure. Climb mountains, raft rivers. Like the old Kristee.

I sent my passport in for renewal. I haven't signed the dotted line on my kidney, but I want to be ready to travel when I do.

My laptop perches on my thighs, and my feet rest on the coffee table, entangled with Nikki's. This is a first. I don't even own a television, yet here I am, snuggled up with Nikki watching a movie on my computer. I look at her.

"What?" Nikki shoves me.

"Oh, my God, I was just thinking how pitiful this would be if we were watching a rom-com right now. At least there's some action in this movie."

We're watching a show about a plane crash in the Rockies and two survivors' attempts to return to civilization. I'm pretty sure I've read the book, and it's not as if you can't figure out how it will end.

"You're not having fun?" Nikki gives me a fake expression of hurt, but I know her well enough to recognize her faux feelings always pack an inkling of truth.

"Loving it, girl. I haven't relaxed like this in a while." I give her a tap on the shoulder. "But I need you to rewind a bit. You made me miss some."

Nikki smiles and reaches over to rewind the show as my phone buzzes. She pauses and looks at me with a question in her eye.

I glance from the phone to Nikki and nod. She's thinking it's Williams, and she's right.

"I'm going to take it. We're paused, anyway."

"Whatever."

"Nikki, I'm sitting here with you, not him. It's not like he's my mortal enemy now. Show some confidence in us."

She stops messing with the laptop and heads into the kitchen, leaving me on the couch. I tap the phone, staring out the window.

"Hey," I say.

"Hey, yourself."

I watch the wind whipping the three cottonwoods outside my window. Fifty-mile-an-hour gusts are forecast today, and that's the reason Nikki and I are spending a Saturday inside instead of hiking in the mountains. I say nothing for a moment and Williams speaks again.

"What are you up to?"

I sigh. I broke it off with Williams two weeks ago, and he's not taking it well. My reasoning? We were trying too hard to make a long-distance relationship work. If we were going to move forward, something had to change.

Of course, I was lying through my teeth. If it wasn't for Nikki, I'd stay with Williams. I looked forward to my time with him, and the long-distance relationship guaranteed my cherished independence. It was a perfect set-up. If only my love for him included the sense of passion I feel with Nikki.

But I couldn't continue this charade with Williams anymore once Nikki and I started sharing the same bed. It wasn't fair to him. And it certainly wasn't fair to Nikki. The irony was that I was being honest with Nikki, but not with Williams. She wanted me to break up with him to spend time with her. I told her I would, and I did. But I couldn't bring myself to be that honest with Williams. I just wasn't ready for him to know my feelings for Nikki.

"Randy," I say. "We're still friends, but I can't do the casual conversations—just checking in on each other. Not yet. It's too soon."

"That's not why I called."

I say nothing.

"You said something has to change. To move forward in our relationship?"

"Right?" I'm unsure where Williams is going with this.

"I'm thinking if I move out there—not move in with you—but move to BV where we can spend more time together, that might be the change you're talking about."

This is a bad idea. And I'm the one to blame for Williams coming up with it. "You can't make that drive every day into Denver. We're talking about almost six hours on the road there and back."

"Not if I find a new job."

Guilt washes over me. Randy loves his job more than anything. *Except for me, it seems.*

I see Nikki's eyes flick up to mine. She can't hear Williams's proposal, or she'd probably flip. She just wants to watch the movie.

"That's the worst idea I've ever heard," I say. "Please tell me you're not serious."

"I am. I can find something to do. The prison's advertising jobs. I could work at the police department or with Perez and the sheriff."

I've got to stop this plan. The last thing I need is Williams discovering I left him for a female alternative and gaping firsthand at the carnage of my life.

"No, Randy. Just. No." My breath comes heavier now, and I'm sure he hears it on the phone. I glance up, and Nikki's eyebrows raise in a question. "I don't think I could live with the guilt of you dropping your career just to move out here by me."

Nikki doesn't drop the dishes she's carrying, but she sets them on the counter with enough force to make me jump.

Williams obviously heard. "You have company?"

My thoughts race as I try to produce another lie. "Just Amore bumping the chair in the dining room."

Williams is silent and I wait for him to speak again. He doesn't.

"Are you still there?"

"Oh, I'm still here, Kristee. And I'm thinking you're not being honest with me. Not about our relationship. Not about who's there right now." He pauses. "Maybe you don't want me there because I'll be too close to your newest interest. Is that it?"

He's not wrong about that, but what he says next floors me.

"You don't want me applying for the Sheriff's Department because you don't want your ex-boyfriend working with your new boyfriend?"

What the hell? "What are you talking about? You can't possibly mean Perez?"

The phone clicks.

"Randy? Williams?" He's hung up.

ZAHN

NOW

I meet Perez in the parking lot next to the Elkhead. He's too busy for a coffee. The deputy shakes his head as I share the results of my visit to Frank's video recorder at Winfield.

"We've been through this, Zahn. It's not Nikki. Everyone saw her get on the helicopter for the mission. People saw her and Kristee on the mountain. Everyone saw her fly out in a helicopter."

Perez misses my point. "I didn't say it was Nikki. I said it might be her car. Or someone else's on the SAR team. I want to check it out."

My friend sighs. "Knock yourself out. But you're not doing it in an official capacity."

I dangle my Search & Rescue badge in front of Perez and smile. "You mean like I was before?" I change subjects. "You find the phone?"

"No. Still working it."

I leave Perez to *work* it and brainstorm how I'll canvas the entire Search & Rescue team for someone who owns a dark Honda CRV. Our organization doesn't keep a personal vehicle log. I nod as Perez departs, then pull out my phone to try the SAR shared drive. I clear an error message as I log into my SAR account. *"Your cloud storage is full. Would you like to add more storage?"* No, I would not. *Who pays for that stuff?*

I thumb through the member files looking for personal vehicle information. A month after I joined SAR, our team assisted in a criminal investigation. We had to log our vehicles in and out with the Sheriff's Department. Maybe we have a spreadsheet for that.

My finger pauses above the screen. Why am I looking for someone besides Nikki with a dark-colored Honda? It would be quicker to ask Nikki if her car was out there. If it was, my search is over. If it wasn't, then someone else on the team probably owns a similar car. Which wouldn't be unusual or suspicious—I could rule out Frank's footage as a dead end.

Time to talk to Nikki again.

. . .

"When I asked you to keep looking at this thing, I didn't realize how deep you'd sink your teeth into it," Nikki says.

We've met at Riverside Park, and I'm looking over her shoulder at her black Honda. The shadow of a SAR decal shows in her back window—in the same position I saw on the car in Frank's video. Nikki follows my eyes and squints as she looks back at me.

"What?"

"I guess you know why I'm checking out your car." I read this line in a book. You show up on a doorstep and ask, "I guess you know why I'm here?" and the person is supposed to spill their guts, even though you have no idea what they've done wrong.

Unfortunately, my experiment fails.

"I guess I don't. What the hell is going on, Zahn?"

I pull another technique from my meager bag of tricks and just tell her.

"We found footage of your car driving away from the Apostles the night Kristee disappeared."

Nikki stares at me, her eyes widening at first, like when you round a corner at night and a couple of deer are staring at your headlights, then narrowing as she takes the offensive. It's a tell, and I suspect it's her car. But I need to make sure.

"Found footage?" she says. "In Winfield? They barely have electricity."

"I didn't mention Winfield, Nikki."

"Cut the shit, Zahn. Yes, my car was there. I loaned it out."

"Explain."

Nikki looks at the ground and shakes her head without speaking. Finally, she meets my eyes and I can tell she has an explanation. I'm just not sure if it will be true.

She takes a deep breath and leans back against her car. "We all got the alert for the mission at the same time, right? So, we responded to the bay. I drove my car." She pats the Honda. "When I arrived, Kristee and Chad were the only ones there. The helicopter was already on its way to take the first team to the Apostles."

I nod.

"So Kristee was not happy that we were in the same room, let alone on the same team, but I was ecstatic. I hadn't talked to her because she wouldn't answer the phone, and I figured if we were on the same mission, then maybe I'd finally have some one-on-one time with her. I told her I'd behave myself—finally, she just said 'fuck it' and told Deb she'd take me on her team. So that's how I ended up on the helicopter."

"What about the car?"

"Right, I'm getting to that. So, we're loading up the helicopter and Chris Atkins—you've met Chris?"

I nod. Another young guy I recognize by face, but haven't really met.

"Chris shows up in his Nissan sedan, and I realize he's going to be waiting around until they have enough guys to form a team, so I ask him a favor. I ask him to take my Honda up instead of riding with the other guys in the tech rig."

"Why? Why would you need your car, and why would he agree to it?"

Nikki nods, as if expecting my questions.

"Right. This is going to sound weird. But as soon as Kristee agreed to take me on her team, I started working out how I could find alone time with her."

My thoughts freeze as I hear this. Alone for what? Was Nikki actually crazy enough to hurt Kristee?

Nikki gauges my expression, and she must see something, because she immediately scrambles to explain.

"Not like that. Not like you're thinking." She's gone from nodding to shaking her head over and over. "I told you I loved her. After the mission, I wanted to drive back to BV with her. So we could talk. Maybe straighten things out. When she told me I could be on her team, I felt like it was a thaw in our relationship. An opportunity I could use to understand where her head was."

Maybe. It sounds like a stretch to me, and I'm sure Nikki can hear the skepticism in my voice when I ask, "Why would Chris agree to your request? What was in it for him?"

Nikki laughs. "Oh, he didn't hesitate at all. I explained I wanted to drive back and would trade rides. He was all over the chance to ride the helo out."

I nod. That's the first thing Nikki has said that makes sense. SAR members love to hike, but will do anything to avoid the long drives to and from the trailheads where we start and finish.

"Did Kristee know? Did you tell her about your plan for the two of you to drive home together?"

"Hell, yes, she knew. You talked to Chad about the argument he saw me and Kristee having, right?"

I nod.

"That was what it was about. I asked her to ride home with me, and she went off about how our relationship was over, and how she had all this stuff going on in her life, and she couldn't handle a psycho ex-girlfriend having a mental breakdown on top of it all." Nikki's mouth hangs open, and she stares at the ground by her feet. "Can you believe she said that? Psycho? Mental?"

Actually, I can. But now isn't the right time to say so aloud.

"So how did you get the car home? Did Chris drive it or you?"

"I drove it."

"But they saw you board the helicopter."

Nikki nods. "Which direction did it depart?"

"I didn't arrive until the next day, so I wasn't there. But it would have left to the north. The helo can't make it over Lake Ann Pass on departure." Realization dawns on me. "The helo let you off at the Winfield parking area? Why?"

"It was no big deal for them. Thirty seconds to let me off at my car and load up Chris."

"Why didn't you have Chris drive it back? Since you didn't have Kristee with you, anyway?"

"No way. A deal was a deal, and I wouldn't ask him to drive it after I had promised him the helicopter ride." She looks up at me and her voice softens. "There was another reason, too."

She pauses and I wonder if I'm supposed to guess or something. "What?"

"Kristee has…or had…my extra key to the car. I don't know. Once I'd told her about my driving plan, and she took off and we couldn't find her…I guess in the back of my mind I thought I might come down the mountain and my car would be gone. That's what I was hoping for. That she took my car—and then I'd know what happened to her."

I say nothing and she finishes her thought. "But it wasn't gone."

●　　●　　●

I consider Nikki's story as I drive home from Buena Vista. It's possible she's telling the truth. It's just as possible she's hiding something. But if she's not lying, I can't figure how, or if, the story relates to Kristee's disappearance.

Checking the road for traffic, I tap my mounted cell phone for messages. Nothing. I tap another icon for email and check the road again. I'm aware of the phone-distracted driver crisis in our state—hell, in our nation—but I guess I fall into the mainstream, believing the warnings are for other idiots, not me.

I've got two emails. The first is from Perez. *Call me if you figure out the Honda thing.* The second is from my phone provider offering me a package to update my storage for my phone backup. I exit email and turn my attention to the road. I'll call Perez when I get home.

A revelation pops into my head so suddenly that my foot instinctively taps on the brakes. I glance in my rearview mirror and see the car behind me slowing as well in response to my sudden change of speed. He probably guesses I spotted a deer or something. I punch on my hazard lights and pull to a stop on the shoulder.

Storage. Phone backup. I've been ignoring the cloud messages and advertisements on my phone because I'm uninterested. I don't keep anything important enough on my phone to require a back-up.

But what about Kristee?

We might have lost access to her phone, but I wonder if Karla has checked Kristee's laptop for phone backup. I snatch my phone from its holder and dial Karla's number.

"It didn't occur to me," she says. "Can you stay on the line? I'll look right now."

I wait on the side of the road and wonder whether her mother is in the house, watching Karla tackle Kristee's laptop yet again. Lin Li seems to be tired of these false leads and my refusal to let her daughter's case go cold—she's lost interest in any alternative explanations for Kristee's disappearance, and I keep wondering why.

Karla returns, and her voice is excited. "It's here. All of it."

KRISTEE

BEFORE

I need to talk. Not with Williams, because those feelings are still confusing, and he mistakenly believes Perez and I are running around together. If he only knew the truth…

Not to Perez. He's a good listener, but the things I need to unload carry legal repercussions. Plus, if Williams found out I am actually meeting with Perez, he'd go ballistic.

I smile when I spot a text from Zahn. Yes.

Coming home for the weekend, you up for a hike?

I consider Zahn's text. Hiking is tricky. Nikki would understand me eating with Zahn—he's too old to be a romantic rival—but if I go hiking with him, she'll want to join. She wants to go everywhere with me these days. Everywhere.

Got some work stuff to do Saturday and Sunday. I'd let you take me out to dinner, though.

I laugh aloud as I send the message. If hiking's tricky for me, dinner is probably trickier for Zahn. He's a straight arrow and likely considering whether it's proper for him to take me to dinner. Both for my reputation and because he still thinks Williams and I are dating.

He takes a good three minutes to answer my text.

OK. How about the Surf Hotel at 5:30 on Saturday?

I laugh aloud. No danger of things getting carried away at a 5:30 dinner. He'll be home in time for an 8:00 bedtime.

Meet you there. Thanks.

Nikki and I hike on Saturday. I spend half the time worrying we'll run into Zahn and that I'll have to explain my lie. I spend the other half rehearsing the conversation I want to have with him at dinner.

I want to discuss The Aerie. And Travis. I need a solution for this dilemma which includes no one going to prison. If I get arrested, my Thailand plan is out the window. If Travis gets arrested, I've lost my two-thirds business partner and my future income. But I can't bring my money problems into the dinner conversation with Zahn, because I know how he is. He'd give me the shirt off his back, or probably mortgage his house, if I told him I needed money. He's that kind of friend.

And I'm the type who would rather die of shame than ask for help, let alone accept it. I can't do it.

"You're quiet today," Nikki says, as we pause halfway up the Midland Hill for a water break. "You sure you're up for a night out after your special friend's dinner?"

I snap my head toward Nikki and check her expression before letting out a sigh. She's teasing me again, but doesn't seem to be angry. My offer to meet up with her after my dinner with Zahn seems to have mollified her disappointment at not being invited.

"I'm good. Just thinking about work. Tonight will be fun." I grin. "If you can keep up."

Nikki smiles back. "That's what I'm talking about."

I love her smile. I love her energy. Everything about Nikki reminds me that the intimate relationships I'd been in since college were just OK. And now that I've tasted a genuine connection with someone I care for, I realize that just OK is not good enough. There's a lot I didn't know about love.

What seems strange to me is receiving that love full force right back at me. Nikki treats our relationship the same way she attacks life. Head-on and at full speed. Since we started dating, she's taken over my calendar and monopolized my time. I'm not used to having to explain where I'm going and what I'm doing. Especially if it's something I need to do alone.

I can't stop thinking about her either—but we're still learning our boundaries.

•   •   •

Zahn is waiting at the table and stands to hug me. I can't remember the last time I've eaten at the Surf, one of BV's more upscale establishments. The wrought-iron, stone, and stucco construction is faux European, but the cuisine and prices are the equivalent of dinner in New York City. The hotel is primarily a place for tourists and businesspeople to meet—not a typical hangout for the locals unless it's Mother's Day or a daughter is getting married.

I nod at Zahn's choice of seating as we return to the table. He positioned us overlooking the river, with the sun still reflecting off the same Midland trails Nikki and I hiked earlier, the river rapids tinseling a silvery gray in the shade. Zahn reaches for my chair, then glances at me and grins, moving over to his own seat. He knows I'm not big on men opening doors, pulling out chairs, or protecting me from traffic, and he probably just remembered he didn't want the dinner perceived as a date.

We order drinks, and the menus remain face down for fifteen minutes as he brings me up to date on how the Academy is going. Zahn rarely enjoys talking about himself and immediately tries to steer the conversation toward my business and life. I push back—eager to keep him talking so I can procrastinate.

"Is it what you expected? Can you see yourself doing what Perez does every day?"

Zahn sips his IPA and smiles. "Not every day. I'm training as a Reserve Sheriff, remember? If I wanted to do it full time, I'd have applied for a job there." He pauses for a moment, gazing toward the water, before turning his head back to me. "But, yeah. I like it. It kind of feels good to be doing the actual day-to-day work instead of running the whole show. Like in the Air Force—I enjoyed being in charge of the squadron, but my favorite days were out flying the line. With this job, it'll just be me and my rig and my weapon. I think I'll like that."

I nod, remembering Zahn's difficulties that led to his Air Force retirement. A clash of personal and professional tragedies unmoored him and robbed him of his confidence in his own leadership. After leaving his family and wallowing his life away as a contractor in Florida, Zahn finally picked himself up and moved to Colorado for a restart.

"You'll be great," I say. "Finish the damn program already and get to work back here."

Zahn nods and grins. "That's the plan." He reaches for his beer and leans back in his chair. "Are we done talking about me yet?"

I plaster a matching grin on my face, but my gut twinges. Here we go.

"Your business or your love life? I need an update on both," he says.

My business partner deals drugs, and I've ditched my boyfriend for the girl next door.

Shit. These revelations might send Zahn scurrying for the door without me even bringing up the real crazy one. *Did you realize you can get $50K for a kidney these days? No, I'm serious.*

I choke on my beer, imagining his face if I vocalized my thoughts. Zahn has gripped the arms of his chair like he's ready to come administer the Heimlich, and his concern sends me into a coughing fit.

I pull myself together, grateful I've inadvertently given myself a couple of extra seconds to assemble my thoughts.

"Yeah." I cough once, and then I'm good. "Yeah, I'm OK." I give one more cough. "What do you know about tumbling?"

"Tumbling? Like gymnastics?"

I snort, and will myself not to cough again. "No. Tumbling cryptocurrency so you can't track where it came from."

Zahn shakes his head. "You lost me at crypto. I read an article about that Dogecoin currency once—you know, the one they started as a joke but hit $8B later on? I don't get it. Why do you ask?"

I'm not ready to bring up Travis's drug connections yet. My tumbling question is a probe to see if he might understand the economics behind what I suspect Travis is doing.

"Just seeing if that might be one of your secret specialties. My business partner is into it, so I've been trying to bone up on it."

"Sorry. Wrong guy."

I nod and give Zahn a smile. "If you can't give me business advice, I guess that leaves my love life. Have you talked to Williams lately?"

"Why? You guys having problems?"

I've known Zahn for three years now. Yes, he's old school. Yes, he sometimes fits the stereotype of the conservative military veteran. But I know one thing he's not. He's not judgmental. I don't know if it's because his folks raised him that way, but he's just naturally understanding. Maybe he realizes that he's not qualified to cast the first stone.

I could tell him about Nikki and my feelings for her. I need to tell someone. Zahn wouldn't judge me.

But I don't.

I've crafted a public identity here in Buena Vista. The cute little tough girl who rafts rivers, climbs mountains, and saves hikers. What's assumed is that the cute little tough girl is straight. The community saw me date locals when I first moved to town, and they've watched Williams and me together. I'm not ready for everyone to meet—and judge—the new me.

Nikki disagrees. But it's easier for her. She moved to this town as a strong, proud, gay woman. She's comfortable in her own skin. Hell, I'm not even certain I'm gay. I've fallen for Nikki, and she's not the first woman I've loved. But I loved Randy, too. I still love him—I think. But definitely not in the way I love Nikki.

My uncertainty worries me. I worry that my attraction to Nikki might be a combination of romantic infatuation and a longing for the powerful love I felt with Terry in college. Nikki and I have only known each other for a few weeks. But, oh, what crazy weeks.

"We're taking a pause," I say. I toss in a partial truth. "This long-distance thing has been tough, and we're reevaluating it."

"It must be really tough. He's always been head over heels for you. I'm guessing this was mostly your idea?"

Zahn's question provides me a way out of tonight's conversation. I can't tell him about Nikki. That one is too personal for me. I can't reveal the drug thing at the office. I can already hear the advice from the reserve sheriff in training. *Kristee, you need to call the cops. It doesn't matter how deep you're in, he's going to get caught and when he does, you'll go down with him.*

And I can't accept that answer. I've spent two rounds of Travis's money on Karla's spring school bill and am preparing to pay most of the remaining balance with the surgery in Thailand. Once I get Karla squared away for the rest of her semesters, I'll come clean.

"Yep. My idea." I nod. "And you know why?"

Zahn shakes his head.

"Because when I mentioned these long-distance challenges, Randy started making noises about quitting the Marshals and moving to BV. Finding a local job."

"Really? He'd give up the Marshals?"

"Right? That's what I thought. I mean, it's his whole life. So that's when I decided we'd take a break." I sip my beer before continuing. "Me deciding on a pause keeps him in the Marshals and my conscience clean." Bile tickles my throat. My own lies are making me sick.

Zahn nods. "I can see that. I'm sorry to hear it, but I can see your reasoning." Then he smiles and his head shakes.

"What?"

"Better not tell Perez." Zahn grins. "I think he still carries a torch."

Damn, Zahn sounds like Williams. Everyone has to mention Perez when they talk about my love life.

"Ha ha." I give a thin smile, and add one more lie, like an extra olive in a martini. "I think I'm done dating for a while."

Although disappointed at my confessional failures, I still garner comfort from my friend's smiling face. We finish dinner and the conversation slows. The sun has finished racing up the Midlands and a silvery moon is turning the river luminescent.

As we say our goodbyes, Zahn's eyes seem to be questioning me, as if he's wondering why I opted for dinner as a get-together. I'm sure he assumes I wanted to talk and is wondering why I didn't. I doubt he believes my rocky relationship with Williams is the primary reason, but I don't give him an answer—just a quick hug as we go our separate ways.

ZAHN

NOW

I prop my elbow on my dining room table, notebook splayed open, gazing across my Colorado front lawn through the living room window. Out west, we don't have enough water to support manicured grass. A stand of Ponderosa pine fronts my house, towering over a carpet of brown made up of cheatgrass and pine needles, but I don't mind the lack of green on the ground. The trees maintain the color just fine with their remaining needles. And I certainly don't miss mowing.

I try to remember the last lawn I mowed. Maybe ten years ago when I was still together with Sheila and the kids? Before we lost our son, Jacob. After that, I lived alone, and it was one-bedroom apartments with a lawn-mowing service.

Reluctantly, my eyes return to my notebook pages. My notes stretch far beyond my initial scribbles on the day I joined the search for Kristee, especially after my meet with Karla and our careful investigation of Kristee's cloud account.

Unlike the discovery of Kristee's phone, we didn't hide these discoveries from Lin Li. The cloud storage program is arranged differently, and there's no danger she will stumble onto Kristee and Nikki's text exchanges.

"Money. See if you can find more information about her accounts. And the life insurance. See if she really borrowed against her life insurance," Lin Li had directed.

Karla and I weren't sure what we were looking for, either. When she'd called to let me know she had accessed Kristee's cloud storage, she just assumed Kristee's phone was the only thing copied on there. She hadn't dug into the data.

During our deep dive into Kristee's cloud account, when Karla left for a bathroom break, I reviewed Kristee's browser history. I typed in *Stedbriar* and found her initial research on the life insurance company. Then I scanned Kristee's follow-on searches. I heard the toilet flush as I read the words *suicide provision* and *how to hide suicide life insurance* before quickly closing out the search history. Karla didn't need this. We spent the afternoon pouring through the data, while Lin Li popped in and out of the room, checking on our progress.

Now I sip my coffee and review what I've copied into my notebook from my session with Karla.

Lincoln Mutual life insurance-she borrowed against it for the business. Nothing there.

* Check out Stedbriar life insurance. Looks like she bought another policy.

International calls to Thailand. Number is associated with organcity website.

Passport renewal—did she actually get her new passport back before she disappeared? Was she planning a trip to Thailand?

I flip the page to my personal notes—the ones I haven't shared with Karla.

Was Kristee doing all this for her sister? To solve the tuition problem?

My head whips up from my notebook as my peripheral vision catches movement in my living room window. I spy the tail end of a figure stepping onto my porch. Expecting the doorbell, I'm surprised when the door opens, and a voice calls out, "Hello? Dad?"

I'm out of my chair and walking toward the foyer when my daughter, Daria, pokes her head around the coatrack and calls out, "Anybody home?"

My reply catches in my throat because surprise visits haven't been a part of our relationship. Last spring was the first time we had been together in seven years. After my divorce, things went sour and, over time, twice-a-year visits dwindled to none.

But we reunited over a prolonged college break last year. Except for Perez totaling his Jeep with Daria inside, a crazy neighbor kidnapping her, and a broken collarbone from a horse accident…it was a perfect vacation. Not. But we definitely bonded. Or re-bonded, one might say.

"Is everything OK?" I wrap my arms around Daria, pulling her close and burying my nose in her hair. "It's been a long time."

"Like six weeks," Daria scoffs. "Did you forget about the Harvard Lakes hike with Kristee?"

I step back, keeping my hands on her arms. "It's great to see you. I'm just surprised, is all." I tilt my head. "Too busy to give me a heads up? Or a text?" No one Daria's age likes to talk on their phones.

Daria tilts her head with what looks like doubt in her eyes. "Actually, I was worried that if I told you why I was coming, you might ask me not to come. This way, I'm here. No questions."

We move toward the kitchen, and I punch the power button on the water kettle. "Still drinking that green tea stuff? I have some from your last visit."

Daria stands at the dining room table, staring at my notes. She looks up, blank-faced, and nods, before returning to my work.

"That's a project I'm working on."

Daria looks up again. "I know. That's why I'm here."

"I don't know that I need any help. Aren't you supposed to be in class?"

"Perez says you might need help. And I don't think he was talking about needing an assistant on your project." My daughter's eyebrows furrow. "He's the one who told me you're investigating Kristee's disappearance." She pauses. "He's worried about you."

I abandon my efforts at tea and stride toward the table, pulling the notebook from Daria. Now I know why she's here. Perez.

The deputy suspects me of emotional overreach, and he's been assigning me work he thinks is unrelated to the case. Probably trying to vector me away from something. That's the part I haven't figured out.

But hinting to others that I'm going off the deep end? Telling my daughter that I need help? The man claims to be my friend. That's too far.

I stare at Daria as these thoughts race through my head, searching for the words to defend myself. But I say nothing. Daria's a smart girl. She will understand why I refuse to walk away if I talk her through the evidence.

So that's what I do. I drop a tea bag into Daria's cup and fill it with hot water before handing it to her. We sit at the table, and I show her everything I've uncovered on Kristee since she disappeared. I reveal the relationship between Nikki and Kristee. Daria seems surprised at that. I tell her about Randall and his belief that Perez still harbors feelings for Kristee. When I describe the money challenges Kristee was having with Karla's tuition and the information regarding organ selling, passports, and life insurance we found on Kristee's phone—and the suicide research—Daria's first reaction is disbelief.

"Karla was with you when you found this stuff?" Her voice sounds skeptical.

"Everything except the suicide research," I say. "I didn't tell her about that." I squint my eyes at Daria. "Does it matter if she was there? Do you doubt what I found?"

"It just sounds a little strange, Dad. And…" her voice trails off.

"And, what?"

"I just don't see the connection." She pulls my notebook toward her and looks at the scrawled pages. "Even if everything you tell me is true—"

I gesture toward my notes and Daria sees how upset I am.

"I'm not saying you didn't find what you found," she says. "It's your interpretation of it and how it relates to her disappearance that I'm talking about."

"What are you talking about?"

"Nothing you're telling me provides a motive for anyone else to make Kristee disappear." Daria pauses. "And I refuse to believe she took her own life. Or ran away."

The evidence I've gathered might not be clear, but it's certainly beyond suspicious. I remember what I've forgotten to share with Daria.

"I haven't told you about the Travis situation." I watch Daria's face carefully, unsure if I can handle an eye roll at this point.

In Daria's defense, I detect sympathy in her eyes, as if she's willing to listen to anything I have to say if it might bring me comfort.

"Who's Travis?"

"Daria's business partner. I think she might have stumbled onto some kind of drug connection involving him." I thumb through my notebook. When I find my transcription of Kristee and Travis's text exchange, I show it to her.

She scans the words, then looks up at me. She still has sympathy in her eyes.

"It doesn't say drugs, Dad. This could be anything. Do you think this links to Kristee's disappearance? Like her business partner waited for a random Search & Rescue mission and then took her out? Really?"

The pungent aroma of Daria's tea wafts between us, but she doesn't drink. I stare at her and say nothing.

Daria returns the favor before finally speaking.

"Perez is worried that you're digging for something that's not there. That you're making people nervous."

"What do you think? Based on what I've shown you so far?"

Daria shakes her head. "I'm not doubting what you've found, Dad. But can't you see why people might take you the wrong way if you've been running around town trying to link up a lesbian relationship, a drug business, and organ sales in Thailand? None of this makes sense, and it sounds kind of wacko."

I squint at Daria and realize she's right. It's not the evidence that's the problem—it's the optics. No wonder I'm getting nowhere with this thing.

"Everyone liked her, Dad. Name me one person who would ever threaten her."

I say nothing. Daria has nailed Kristee's personality. Everyone loved her. But still...with drugs and dealing, it isn't like a sparkling personality earns you a free pass. But as I nod, I see Daria's expression shift.

"Dar? What are you thinking?"

"Nothing. It's just when I said that no one would ever threaten her, it reminded me that someone actually did." She furrows her brows.

I flip my notebook to the front, where I have my list of names. "Who?"

Daria shakes her head. "No one on your list. And I'm not trying to add a name to your files either. You've got enough there. It's just…well, Kristee told me about getting threatened a couple of weeks ago, and I'd kind of forgotten about it."

I look at Daria and wait.

"It was Jacy's father."

"Jacy, the 'watch the dog' Jacy? The one who lives downstairs?"

Daria nods. "Have you ever met her dad? Erik?"

I remember when Karla and I ran into him in the parking lot. Me shielding her after Erik stepped from his enormous truck and bellowed after Jacy. Then turning to us…*What the fuck are you looking at?*

I nod. Big guy. Loud voice. Big truck…

Big truck? Like twin-cab, long-bed big. And maroon. A dark color just like the vehicle following Nikki's car out of Winfield on Frank's footage.

I open my mouth, then clamp it shut. *Listen, Zahn. Listen.*

I nod at Daria's question.

"Right, kind of hard to forget, isn't he?" Daria gives a nervous laugh. "So, Kristee told me about a run-in she had. Where he was in a fight with Jacy, and Kristee intervened."

"Like physically intervened?"

"She didn't say. She said she saw Erik grabbing at Jacy and pulling her back into their apartment as Jacy was trying to leave. She got away, and when Erik ordered her back in the condo, Kristee intervened, and invited Jacy to her place for a minute."

I nod. "I can imagine how that went over."

"Exactly. Kristee told me Jacy didn't want her involved, so she told Kristee everything was OK. But when Erik told Kristee to mind her own business, Kristee brought up the cops and accused Erik of assault."

"Whoa."

"Yeah, then she said it started getting really close to…how did she put it? Real close to going western. He stepped into her face. Told her to go ahead and go to the cops. But if she did, Kristee could be certain that Erik would turn his attention from Jacy to Kristee."

I'm unsettled by what Daria has shared with me. "You didn't think this was important enough to tell me?"

Daria's gaze has shifted from me to my notebook. She sighs. "To be honest, I'm not really comfortable telling you now. I'm guessing that you're going to add Erik's name to your little list there and start investigating him, too."

Of course I am, but I know better than to admit that to Daria.

"Look," Daria says. "Kristee told me about it because I'd met both Jacy and Erik before. She felt like she had a responsibility to Jacy, so she was going to keep an eye on them. But she kind of blew off the whole threat thing. She compared it to the story of the snake that bit the fox carrying him across the river. Erik couldn't help threatening her. It's in his nature."

I try to speak, but Daria's on a roll. "Even if I would have thought about that confrontation before today, I don't think I would have related it to Kristee's disappearance." My daughter stares at me, her eyes turning hard. "Kristee disappeared on a Search & Rescue mission—a random event at a random place while her neighbor was probably at work. How could they possibly be related?"

Except I spotted his truck on scene at the search site, I want to say, but for once, I let my brain get ahead of my mouth. I don't know for certain that it was Erik's truck on the video. Not yet. And if I accuse Erik of being involved in Kristee's disappearance, Daria will tell Perez to send in the men with the white jackets.

"You're right," I lie. "Hard to see a workable link there. But I've seen Erik yelling at his daughter myself. I might mention it to Linzmeier down at the BV police. Not related to Kristee. But for Jacy's protection."

Daria nods, but wears a skeptical look on her face. I'm unsure if it's because I mentioned Linzmeier—the BV police officer who made lewd comments to her during a traffic stop last spring—or because she doesn't trust me to drop the Erik angle.

"What?"

"Wait a bit, Dad. Until some of this Kristee stuff blows over."

"You just got done telling me there was no way they are related." I ask the question I shouldn't. "What gives?"

Daria says nothing.

"What?" I repeat.

"It's you, Dad. When Perez called me up, he said the county's buzzing about you and your theories. You don't think the cops in BV haven't heard Tyler Zahn's conspiracy stories?

I'm furious. It's one thing to have Perez publicly discounting my efforts. It's another to have him on the phone with my daughter, explaining why everyone thinks I'm losing it.

So, I do what I do best when I'm close to losing my temper. I let out my breath and plaster a smile on my face.

Daria watches me, and I can tell she's not fooled.

"Can I spend the night?" Her voice sounds tentative.

"I'm not letting you drive all the way back to Boulder in the dark. Let's go downtown and grab a bite. Your room's ready."

Daria nods.

I widen my smile.

Neither one of us is fooled.

KRISTEE

BEFORE

My office—if you can call it an office, because it's basically a cubicle set up in the tiny space behind our receptionist, Bree—does nothing to add respectability to my predicament. Especially when I picture Travis leaning back, admiring the mountain view in his private room down the corridor. At least Bree's voice, drifting over my cubicle wall as she greets new customers and explains what The Aerie offers, lends an air of credibility to our business.

I feel off, and can't decide if it's from my failure to open up to Zahn at dinner or the pasta primavera. Or, maybe, it's just being back here in The Aerie.

A window. Is that too much to ask? The gray fabric framing the half-walls of my sitting space is a poor substitute for the crystal-blue Colorado sky draping the mountains outside our office doors.

When Bree pokes her head in, informing me I've been requested to give a new customer orientation, I leap from my chair. I'll grasp any excuse to leave my cubbyhole. Any excuse, that is, but another meet-up with Nikki. She's ignored my hints at easing back on our together time. In fact, she's been doubling down, and The Aerie is one of the few places where I can take a break from her almost cloying attention.

I turn the corner and find two men flanking Bree. My stomach cramps. The taller one is familiar, a shadow of a beard covering his face. The other is a stranger—overweight, sporting a black polo shirt and cargo pants. I glance back at his partner, and it comes to me. He's the one in the RAV-4 who stole my dog. I'm ready to give him an earful, then pause. RAV-4 man obviously senses my oncoming outburst and has shifted his eyes to the shorter man. Although I'm no thug-code expert, it's clear the men don't want to talk in front of Bree. And if the men are here to discuss Travis's sidebar business, then I don't want her to hear either.

"You want to see the Alpine office?" I offer.

RAV-4 man gives a tight smile. "That would be great. We've got about a week's worth of work and want to see if your space meets our needs." The heavyset man looks at me through lidded eyes and says nothing.

I nod at Bree and lead the two men upstairs. RAV-4 man walks directly behind me and the heavy scent of cheap aftershave speeds up my pace. I enter first and when I turn around, the shorter man has closed the door. He's more than heavyset, but he hasn't given his name, and *RAV-4 man's partner* is too long. I think about Travis's trailer down by the river and silently christen him *Double-wide*.

"Take a seat," RAV-4 man says.

"I'm fine."

"No, you're not. And I wasn't asking. Sit down."

Seating protocol strikes me as the wrong issue upon which to make my stand, so I sit at the four-person table next to the desk. RAV-4 man sits across from me, and his meaty partner sits between us—like we're a sandwich. I almost giggle and realize it's because I'm scared. Neither of these men have threatened me...yet, but they carry themselves with an unnerving confidence and arrogance.

"I guess you remember me?" RAV-4 man says.

I nod.

"Have you taken my advice?"

I give him a blank look.

"About the questions. Not asking too many questions."

"I guess so. I've just been ignoring whatever you do with Travis."

RAV-4 man stares at me for a second, then glances at his partner before continuing. "Are you sure about that?"

I try not to flinch at his question because I sense where he's going with it. They've been to the storage container. They know something is missing. Maybe.

"I'm sure."

RAV-4 man lets out a breath. "I hope so. Hope you're not snooping around into other people's business. That would create a problem for us, you know?"

I nod.

"We're the ones who take care of problems. In our business, we're the only ones who take care of the problems." He pauses. "Are you a problem?"

"No."

"Travis made a mistake. He thought you might be a problem, and he tried to do our job."

I try to make sense of this. Travis is after me?

"Paying you off." Double-wide sneers. "Shit."

"That's right," RAV-4 man says. "He gave you money to shut you up. We're not happy about that."

"Why? I haven't said anything."

Double-wide rises and walks toward the door, checking the window before turning to RAV-4 man and nodding once.

"Of course you haven't," RAV-4 man says. "And you won't. Not a word." He pauses. "But that's not how we guarantee silence. With money." He reaches across the table and lays his hand across mine. I flinch and try to retract my hand, but he holds it tight, his damp palm stuck to my skin. I sense movement over his shoulder and spy Double-wide holding a pistol in one hand below his belt.

"What are you doing?" I tug my wrist again, but RAV-4 man has me tight.

"You will return the money Travis gave you. It wasn't his, and that's not how we operate."

"I don't have it. I already used it. And I'm not talking." I give up on my hand and let it fall limp while fixing RAV-4 man with my best withering stare.

"Oh, we're not worried about you talking. If you prove that stupid, we will deal with it using our standard operating procedures." He glances at Double-wide, who tilts the pistol my direction and mouths *pow pow* with his lips. "No, we're not worried. But we will take our money back." He pauses. "We'll give you a week." He pulls my hand across the table and leans forward. "Do you understand?"

I say nothing. The gun in Double-wide's hands, RAV-4 man's iron grip on my wrist, and his ultimatum have rendered me speechless. It's one thing to be the no-nonsense, show-no-fear leader during a mountain rescue. It's another when evil sits across from you, holding your hand.

RAV-4 man drops my hand and rises from his chair. "We'll be in touch. And we'll be close by until you get that money." He pauses. "Oh, and keep an eye on that pretty dog, right?" He smiles and opens the door for Double-wide. They exit the room and I slump in my chair.

What have I done?

• • •

I can't stay at The Aerie. Bree escorts our two visitors from the building, then quizzes me about their reserved dates for office space. I still can't speak as I rush through the main door, leaving Bree convinced she works for the rudest boss ever.

Buena Vista's afternoon winds are on hiatus today, and a block from The Aerie sweat is already beading on my forehead. I don't mind. I need to purge my frightening interaction with Travis's goons, and I wonder if I have time to take Amore on a run. My pace quickens—of course I have time. I'm the boss, right? Not really, it seems.

I barrel up the sidewalk to my condo and find Jacy hunched forward in the chair outside her door. I wonder why she's not at school, but it occurs to me I've got enough of my own issues without bringing up my neighbor's problems. Jacy rarely walks Amore until the afternoon, so it's not like I'm in charge of how she spends her day.

"I'm still walking Amore at 3:30," Jacy says, looking up from her book.

I stop short. My neighbor sports an abrasion under her left eye, the top of it trending blue.

"What happened to you?"

"Car door. It happened at school."

I keep staring at Jacy. There's just no way. Bellowing dad. Recalcitrant middle-schooler. Car door, my ass.

"Yeah, right. We need to do something about your situation, Jacy."

Jacy touches her bruise, and I recognize fear in her eyes.

"It's not my dad. Things are better with that. It really was a car door. There's a guy on the track team, and he takes some of us home after practice."

"Even if I thought that was true, Jacy, I'd still be a little leery about a high-schooler driving around middle-schoolers in his car. Does that seem right to you?"

Jacy shrugs. "He's cool. He's not weird or anything."

I fix a doubtful gaze on her as I step past. "I'm always around. You can come to me. Any time."

Jacy shifts her eyes back to the pages of her book. "Everything's fine."

I continue up the stairs.

Amore circles around in the living room as I come through the door. Happy—or maybe even surprised? I don't normally come home before lunch, so he's unsure what's next.

"You wanna go for…?" Amore wheels about my living room letting out excited yowls. I should have changed into my running clothes first because now he'll be spinning around for the next five minutes.

Fifteen minutes later, we're running south on a trail along the Arkansas River. I'm striding out and already sweating again, still looking for that breeze. Amore is in his element—he can run this pace for an hour.

Travis's men scare me. I just assumed Travis's hush money was coordinated—something he worked out with his partners once I stumbled onto what he was doing. I catch a bug in my mouth and cough before spitting it out. It didn't occur to me that Travis might be protecting me by paying me off, so that I wouldn't have to deal with guys like the ones I met today.

I picture Double-wide and the pistol he'd vectored my direction. I have no doubts he'll use it if I don't pay back the money. Strangely enough, I'm not worried for my safety, but about what happens to Karla and school if I'm suddenly out of the picture. The installments I paid will take her through next semester, but after that? There's nothing. My life insurance is void, and my kidney plan somewhat relies on me being alive to take payment for it.

Alive. I skid to a stop, and Amore continues to the end of his leash before his neck jerks around from my sudden halt.

"Sorry, boy." I drop my hands to my knees.

Alive. The thought triggers my life insurance research from yesterday. I'd dismissed another policy because of the strict suicide policy. But what if my death wasn't suicide?

Amore whines, ready to run again. My fear of Travis's men trickles away like a ten-minute rain shower in our dry mountain valley. Suppose I didn't pay those men? What if I threatened to tell the cops? I picture Double-wide cocking his pistol at me, and I smile. The bad men can't risk me selling them out. They'd get rid of me.

And, boom! My new policy solves Karla's school issues.

Obviously, details remain. I need to activate the policy. And make a payment or two.

I sigh. First a kidney. Now my life? Is this how far I've sunk?

But it's not as crazy as it sounds. These are the cards I've been dealt: The kidney is Plan A—my course of action if Travis's men allow me to live. The life insurance is Plan B. For something out of my control.

That's why they call it insurance—just in case.

Amore strains at his leash, pulling me forward in a walk.

I jog again and a brief pang stabs my gut. *Plan A: selling a kidney? Plan B: my murder?* I shake my head and laugh.

The pang subsides, and confidence swells inside of me. Because I am strong. I'm taking care of my sister. And I will not fail.

ZAHN

NOW

I send Daria back to campus the next day, elated at the impromptu visit—I'd missed my girl—but I'm miffed at Perez for pulling the *maybe he'll listen to his daughter* card. Daria isn't five minutes out the door before I've got Perez on the other end of my phone.

The wind sweeping off the Collegiates creates a sound like a jet flying overhead as I stand in my driveway and listen to Perez try to explain himself.

"You're going overboard, Zahn. Yes, you were assaulted. Yes, the phone theft is weird. But all these other rabbit holes? With Nikki and Kristee's private affairs, and now Karla says you guys are looking at her internet history? Come on, man."

I barely make out Perez's words, but understand enough. He's defending himself for calling Daria by mocking my research. Angry as I am, I figure it's the wrong time to bring up Erik following Nikki's CRV out of Winfield. And I'm surprised Karla has been talking to Perez.

"Did you go talk to Karla, or did she come to you?"

"Oh, so now you think Kristee's sister had something to do with it? I guess Daria's talk didn't help?"

The roar of the wind distorts Perez's words, and we're getting nowhere.

"I've found something new. Meet me downtown." I've changed my mind. I don't care if Perez thinks I'm nuts. He's the one who sent me off to look at Frank's footage. It might be time to bring up Kristee's neighbor.

"Can't. I'm booked all afternoon. Tomorrow too. Let's rally up in a couple of days. Give you time to think things through."

The wind has died enough for me to get Perez's message. He doesn't want to hear any more crazy theories from me.

"Yeah. I'll call you." I hang up. "Shit." I tilt my head, gazing at the swaying treetops above me. "That didn't go well."

Part of me sees where Perez is coming from. No one doubts that I've discovered things about Kristee that aren't common knowledge. I uncovered trouble with her business. Her relationship with Nikki. No one else knew those things.

Except Perez.

I lower my head and stare at the gravel in the driveway. He knew about them. He's known about everything.

I still haven't shared the text exchanges between Travis and Kristee. The ones Travis says refer to drugs. Did Karla share those texts?

Here's what I can't figure out: if Perez is privy to the text exchanges, is he steering me away because he knows they don't relate to the case? Is Perez, as a friend, keeping me from making a fool out of myself?

Or is he vectoring me off track because he knows something he doesn't want me to find out? I'm not crazy enough (yet) to think Perez was involved in Kristee's disappearance. Hell, he was the one who called me when we lost her. But I believe he would blur the truth once again to protect her memory. He's a loyal friend.

And he still loves Kristee. I know that. Even Randall, the man who stole Kristee's heart, suspects how much Perez still cares. How far would Perez go to keep others from finding out how much he loved her?

Meanwhile, I have unfinished business with Travis at The Aerie. We had planned on discussing the drug texts—before I got clobbered on the head and lost Kristee's phone.

The receptionist at The Aerie introduces herself as Bree and puts me in the chairs by the front windows while she pages Travis. I smile at the façade of a sophisticated business communications system—Travis's office is only twenty feet from the Bree's desk.

"He'll be with you in a few minutes."

I nod and gaze out the window. Kristee and Travis couldn't have chosen a better location. The Aerie sits between the outdoor gear shop and the ice cream parlor. Across the street, a renovated theater hosts high school plays, and rumor has it, they're trying to attract even higher caliber stage performances. Buena Vista offers limited choices for new businesses. The Aerie got lucky.

Whether their concept works remains to be seen. Buena Vista is flush with teleworkers, but our town is smaller than Breckenridge or Vail. With Kristee gone, it will be interesting to see whether The Aerie survives.

"Tyler, my man. What's up?" Travis strides toward me from his office, a fake smile plastered on his face. I wonder when I became *his man*. Was it when I drilled into him about whether he had a lawyer to figure out Kristee's half of the business, or was it when he called up and accused Kristee of stealing something from him? Either way, I can tell he wants me out of his office.

Why? I missed our previous meeting where we had planned to discuss deleting the texts from Kristee's phone, because someone smacked me on the back of the head and stole it. Shouldn't Travis be slightly curious why I never showed?

"Just touching base with you. You said you wanted to talk?" I glance at Bree, who's watching us closely. "About some communications with Kristee?"

Travis also looks Bree's way and seems to change his mind about rushing me out of The Aerie. "Yeah, I heard about what happened to you. Unbelievable." He nods back toward the hallway. "Come on back. You want coffee?"

I decline the offer and follow Travis to his office. What I really want is answers. I'm not surprised Travis heard of my assault. It's a small town. I'm just surprised he hasn't tried to reconnect with me to discuss the phone texts.

"Grab a seat." Travis motions to a chair facing his desk and sits across from me. "So, what do you want to discuss?"

I gaze around the sparse office. The air smells of fresh paint and the walls are blank—no pictures, certificates, art. "You're the one who called. About Kristee's phone?"

Travis nods. "The papers said someone assaulted you and stole your phone. I assumed there was nothing to discuss if the phone was gone." He pauses. "Is there?"

Something locks into place in my head. I read the newspaper article. Travis is right. The article said *my* phone was stolen. It didn't say someone stole my friend's phone from me.

Now I have a choice. I can share this knowledge with this idiot who just gave away his involvement in the theft, or I can leave without Travis suspecting I'm on to him—an option that allows me to continue looking at Travis and his business from the outside.

But if I leave too soon, he'll be suspicious.

I lean back in my chair. "If you thought Kristee was framing you and drugs were involved, why didn't you go to the police?"

Travis rolls his eyes like he's just walked into my room at the senior citizen's center and discovered it's his turn to change my bedpan.

"Come on, man…you read the texts, right? I told her she needed to get some help. To deal with her stress. I'm not going to turn my business partner into the cops. Friends help friends get help. They don't just roll over on them." He gives me a dismissive look. "What kind of friend are you, anyway?"

I can't answer that. I'm either the sort of friend who upsets family and friends because he won't let his dead friend rest in peace…or I'm the type of friend who won't rest until the real reason behind his friend's death—or disappearance—is discovered. Maybe I'm both.

"What about the business end? What have you worked out with Kristee's mother?"

Travis spreads his palms on his desk and gives me a thin smile. "She's selling." He tilts his head. "Did you know Kristee redeemed her life insurance policy to stake her partnership with me? I didn't realize that. Her mom came in and explained it all. I felt terrible for her. And for Kristee's sister." He nods. "I'm buying them out so I can put some money in their pockets—like that policy would have."

I keep my expression neutral, but Travis's explanation has raised another question for me. This time I can't keep it to myself.

"If you have enough money to buy Kristee's share, why did you partner with her in the first place?"

Travis's expression freezes as if the requirement for brain power has paralyzed his face. "Well, we are a business, you know. Businesses make money?"

"Not according to Kristee. She says you guys were still in the red. You made enough to buy her out. Just in the last month, or what?"

Travis's mouth is moving before I finish my sentence, as if he's come up with a better answer. "Got another investor. They're helping me out with this."

I nod again, wondering what kind of investor sees The Aerie's first quarter performance and then asks Travis, "How can I get a piece of that?"

"Anything else?" Travis no longer tries to disguise the fact that he's done talking with me.

"I guess not." I rise from my chair.

Travis walks me to the front door and out onto the sidewalk. "If you need anything, you let me know, OK? I'll keep quiet about Kristee's texts and her little problem. I hope you'll do the same."

I nod at Travis. *You're the one who orchestrated the phone theft. Had me thunked on the head. You're the one hiding something with this business.* I'm going to keep quiet, all right. For now. But as soon as I have enough to put this scumbag away—something solid—I'm going to use it. Whether he had something to do with Kristee's death or not, I'm not happy with his threats to tarnish her memory.

KRISTEE

BEFORE

Nikki's laugh spills over my cubicle divider as she greets Bree, and I bury my head in my hands. The time we've spent together has been special, but it's also been too many hours for me. I'm a woman who values her alone time, and when I started dating Nikki, I forgot how important my solitude was. It's coming back to me now.

Plus, the more I consider my new relationship, the more I dread my mother's upcoming visit. Just over two weeks, and she'll be walking through my door. I wonder if we'll just pick up where we left off from my college days. Non-stop questions about my career, my relationships, and my plans. Or will she be contrite?

I give a half-laugh, half-snort—Mama Li contrite?—as Bree pokes her head around the corner. She raises her eyebrows at me and smiles. "Nikki's here. She wants to know if you have a minute."

I look past Bree and spot Nikki peering back to my cubicle from behind the counter.

"Break time," she calls. "Let's go get a coffee."

I nod at Bree and push back from my desk. "Guess it's break time." She steps back, allowing me to pass by and squeeze around the counter. Nikki moves in for a hug, and I dodge sideways, sticking my fist out for a bump instead. She wrinkles her nose and bumps my fist. I glance at Bree, who has returned to her desk. I'm not ready for public hugs yet.

Obviously, this bothers Nikki. We cross the street to the Elkhead, and she sulks, saying nothing. I stop at the door and pull Nikki to the side.

"I'm not really interested in coffee if you're not going to talk."

Nikki stares at me, and I recognize the hurt in her eyes. "I don't understand why it's got to be such a secret. I mean, you broke up with Randy—so what's the deal?"

"Not here. Do you want a coffee or not?"

Nikki nods, and we enter the Elkhead, grabbing a table in the back. I suggest we sit outside, but Nikki thinks it's too cold. The wind is blowing, and it's still in the low 50s. A typical Buena Vista summer morning, but I'm guessing she's still steamed at my hug dodge.

Nikki leaves her knapsack at the table, and we follow the aroma of freshly ground coffee to the counter.

"How come you're not at work?" I say as we return to our table. "Morning off?"

"I quit."

I set my coffee on the table and pull my chair forward. "What?"

"I didn't like how busy they were keeping me. Working through lunch. Cutting back on breaks. I felt like they weren't giving me enough time to meet you during the day."

I have my coffee to my mouth when she utters the last sentence, and I nearly choke as I draw in my breath.

"Wait a minute. You mean you quit because of me? We see each other every night." Which is true. Lately we've been alternating hosting each other. But the last two nights we've been at Nikki's place. Thank goodness she likes dogs.

"Not just you. I need more flexibility. I'm thinking about working from home. I'll have my own schedule. And if I need an office, I can use The Aerie. Wonder who I might run into there?"

I'm thrown for a loop. Nikki's work is Nikki's business, but I'm unhappy she's figuring me into the equation. My gut cramps, a pressing sensation, as if the Elkhead's walls are closing in on me.

"What kind of work?"

Nikki thrusts her phone my direction. "Check this out. This is a mortgage company operating in western Colorado. You get paid by the number of applications you process, not the number of hours you work. I heard about it from Kelly at SAR. She's got a friend who's raking it in doing this over in Frisco and Silverthorne."

I scan the website. The job sounds boring—nothing compared to her research work at the museum—but I say nothing.

"Check out the pay scales. I think it's on the benefits page of the site."

I swipe up on the phone and sense Nikki shaking her head in my peripheral vision.

"No, you have to hit 'benefits' to see it. Let me show you."

But I don't. Because when I swipe up, I get a row of open apps. The one right next to the browser app is the photo app. And the current photo looks familiar.

I tap the photo app as Nikki reaches across the table. "Let me—" she says before I interrupt her.

"What is this?" But I already know. Nikki's screen shows a picture of the two of us lying on her bed, our legs intertwined and our lips touching.

"What the hell?" I turn the phone screen to Nikki and rise to my feet. "What the hell is this?" My voice is loud and out of the corner of my vision, I see people turning toward our table.

Nikki rises to her feet as well and grabs the phone from me. The couple at the next table turns and eyes us. "Stop it," she says in a loud whisper. "You're making a scene."

"Give me that phone back."

Nikki scans the room again before returning her eyes to me. She looks as if she's made a decision. "Let's walk and talk. You're a little too emotional for public settings right now."

I step toward Nikki with my hand out, reaching for the phone. "Who took the picture, Nikki? I thought we were alone."

"Not here." Nikki turns, coffee in one hand and cell phone in the other, and exits the Elkhead.

My heart pounds as we round the corner and walk away from Main Street. Nikki strides ahead, and for a moment, I wonder if she's trying to escape our conversation. I run forward and grab her by the arm.

"How could you?" I'm not a crier, but my throat aches and the words sound choked.

Nikki stops and turns to face me. She takes a deep breath and I watch her try to stay calm.

"How could I what?"

"Take pictures of us. Without asking me. And how? Was someone in the room?"

Nikki gives me a look like she's insulted. "I'm making memories of us, Kristee. That's all. I took a frame from my video, so I'd have a picture." She stabs at her phone with a finger and shows the screen to me. "It's a beautiful picture. Look at it again." She shoves the phone closer.

I push back at the phone and instinctively scan for people watching or listening to us. "Put it away," I say. I stand staring at Nikki with my mouth open. It hits me. "You made a movie of us? Where did you stop the movie?"

"That's what I'm talking about, Kristee. That whole 'look around to see who suspects I'm a lesbian' thing you do? I did not ask if I could use my camera. Because I knew what you would say. You're so ashamed of your sexuality you won't even hold my hand in public. You wouldn't have let me shoot it."

I step forward toward Nikki and tilt my head up at her. "Damn straight, I wouldn't have." I point at the camera in her hand. "Those electrons are forever. A movie or a pic? It's like a tattoo. There's no getting rid of it."

"Why would I get rid of it? It's a testament to our love." Nikki's eyelashes literally bat at me.

"Because I'm telling you to. Right now. Delete it."

"You're upset. Don't you think we should sleep on it? We can watch the movie tomorrow and decide if you want to get rid of it." She grabs my arm. "Come on, Kristee—it's us. It's beautiful."

I pull my arm away and step forward again. "Right now, I don't feel like there's an 'us.' And sleep on it? Are you kidding? You went too far, Nikki." I spread my hands. "I can't believe you did that. I want you to get rid of it."

Nikki's eyes have gone cold, and I step backwards. She steps forward into the space I just vacated. "What are you saying?"

"I'm saying it's over. This is bigger than saying the wrong thing or having a little tiff. You violated me, Nik. On purpose. You violated my trust." My head sways side to side. "I need you away from me. At least for a while." I point my finger at her. "And you need to delete it all...right now."

Nikki presses her lips together. "Don't do this."

"Delete the movie."

Nikki is still shaking her head. "If I delete it, can we still try to work it out?"

Now my head is shaking. "You'll delete it right now. It's not a bargaining chip. And we're done."

Nikki still wears the emotionless smile as she replies. "Well, I guess it is a bargaining chip, then. Because if you're leaving me, there's no chance I'm getting rid of our last memories together. See you." She turns and walks away.

I race after her and tug on her arm. Nikki whirls and steps right into my face. "What are you going to do, Kristee? You can't even be seen loving me in public. Are you going to fight me in downtown BV now?" She jerks her arm out of my hand and keeps walking.

"You're psycho," I call out, and as I utter the words, I realize it's true. My obsession with Nikki was just that. An obsession, filling my thoughts and dreams, which hadn't yet faced the tests of a long-term friendship. But Nikki's actions are different. She's been hoarding our time for weeks: first every day, then every hour, and now every minute. Not normal behavior.

As I utter the words, Nikki freezes for a second without turning. Then she faces me, her thin smile widening, and whispers loud enough for me to hear. "What did you say?"

"I said you're crazy. You took this relationship too far. There's something wrong with you."

The smile disappears, and Nikki purses her lips. "Don't go there, Kristee. You don't want to go there."

I say nothing.

Nikki waves goodbye, but I notice she's waving with her cell phone in her hand.

Don't go there. Not while I have this.

I hear her unspoken words. She expects our relationship to continue…or else.

ZAHN

NOW

"Can you come over?" Karla's voice sounds tense over the phone. "Mama's going a little nuts."

I'm trudging back from my neighborhood's centralized mailboxes, a half-mile journey I often use to clear my head. Stuffed in my pocket is a flyer advertising new windows and two offers to refinance my mortgage—my typical postal service bonanza. Yesterday's fifty-degree temperatures have swiveled to seventy-five today. Rocky Mountain weather swings are matching my mood days. Wild fluctuations.

"What's going on?

"She says she's getting texts from Kristee."

I stop in my tracks, twisting my body to muffle the noise of the wind. "Did I hear you right?"

"I think so. Texts from Kristee. I checked her phone, and they appear to be coming from Kristee's number."

"Right. The phone they stole from me. Someone's messing with your mother."

"I know. I know. It can't be her. But Mama believes it is— remember, we didn't tell her about the phone…"

I hear the panic in Karla's voice, swelling like bags of potato chips in the local grocery store after the altitude change from Denver. Ready to burst.

"I'll be there in twenty."

When Karla lets me into the apartment, Lin Li is pacing in the tiny living room. She whips her head my direction as I walk past Karla and then thrusts her cell phone at me.

"I thought my daughter was dead. But here she is. Somewhere. Reaching out to me."

Karla's voice had sounded panicked. Lin Li's voice sounds manic. Her eyes shine and her chest heaves. I reach out and take the phone, scanning the text messages on the screen.

She's right—the texts appear legitimate. The bubble at the top of the screen reads "KL." Kristee and her mother might have been estranged, but at least Lin Li had her listed in her contacts.

I gesture toward the couch. "Let's sit down. Let me read these."

Lin Li raises her arms toward the ceiling like a staunch believer at church. "Why sit? The evidence is there. We need to tell the police."

I look down.

"She's texting about the business," Lin Li says. "About my share. She wants me to have the money because she's not coming back."

My head jerks. This confirms my suspicion that Travis is in on the phone theft.

I look at Karla, and she nods. There's no need to keep the information about Kristee's phone secret from Lin Li any longer. That phone is gone.

When we break the news to Lin Li, it's as if we're beginning again at the first stage of grief. She denies the discovery of Kristee's phone, and when we finally convince her it's true, she wastes no time moving on to anger.

"How could you possibly keep this from me?" Lin Li's eyes narrow at Karla, and I recognize the no-nonsense woman I first met. "You were going for the passwords, weren't you? Trying to get at Kristee's money so you could take it for yourself?"

I watch Karla's mouth drop open and wonder if she sees mine doing the same. I had expected Lin Li to blast us for hiding the phone discovery because she would have seen it as evidence Kristee might still be alive. Instead, the first thing that crosses her mind is that her other daughter is accessing Kristee's accounts.

The speed of Lin Li's transition from believing Kristee is alive and texting—to accusing Karla of gold-digging—is staggering. But I remember the shine in Lin Li's eyes when I arrived. The one I believed meant she was ecstatic Kristee might be alive.

I realize now she was spun up about the contents of the text message, not about who sent it. She wants the money from Kristee's portion of The Aerie, and suddenly it looked like her oldest daughter was giving her permission to take it.

Karla looks torn, and I realize her dilemma. Lin Li suspects Karla was using the phone to access Kristee's accounts, which means Karla doesn't have to explain that we were trying to hide Kristee's relationship with Nikki. Karla opens her mouth to speak and nothing comes out. I see tears rolling down her face.

"You should cry," Lin Li says, scowling at her daughter. "You should be on your knees begging forgiveness."

Karla's mouth drops again, and she turns on her heel and walks out of the apartment, squeezing out the door so Amore can't follow her.

"I don't think—" I begin.

"I don't blame you, Mr. Zahn. Both my daughters have deceived me, and this phone issue comes as no surprise." She sits on the couch, staring at the coffee table. "Now we must discover who sent the text messages and find out why they asked me this question. Perhaps I can get a higher price than what Mr. Travis is offering."

I stare at Kristee's mother in disbelief. A day ago, I was wondering if the downstairs neighbor was the wild card involved in Kristee's disappearance. Three minutes ago, I'm back to looking at Travis's business and wondering why he set up the theft of Kristee's phone. Now I'm staring at a mother unlike any I've ever met. One so focused on financial gain that losing her daughter means nothing except an opportunity for herself. And I'm no closer to discovering who actually made Kristee Li disappear.

KRISTEE

BEFORE

I sleep like an inmate's last night on death row. Every time I'm close to dropping off, I picture Nikki's cell phone shot of me with my tongue down her throat. It's amazing how what seemed a romantic tryst at the time feels so sordid after Nikki's surreptitious film episode. I dozed off once, just after midnight, but woke with a start less than thirty minutes later, roused by another dream involving kissing. I'm still lying in Nikki's bed, my arms wrapped around her, our faces close. But as I tug on her lower lip with my own, bristles poke at my nose, as if she's wearing a sandpaper mask. I recoil, and the unshaven face of RAV-4 man smiles back at me.

"I want my two dollars!" RAV-4 man laughs at his retro movie quote. I sense movement behind me, and when I roll over, there stands his partner, Double-wide, cocking his finger at me like the pistol he'd brandished at The Aerie.

I jerk awake, gasping for air, my heart pounding. Sleep remains impossible, and I lie in bed for the next four hours, rubbing Amore's belly, and staring at the ceiling until the sunrise's glow angles off the Collegiate Peaks on the far side of the valley. The anxiety pangs in my stomach have morphed into a permanent state of nausea.

I can't face this day alone. Not after what happened at The Aerie. Not after the blow-up with Nikki. I don't know how to fix my life. But if I bottle it inside, I'm going to explode.

I tap Perez's number into my phone.

"Hey, Rick. It's Kristee." I'm guessing any sheriff's deputy worth his salt is awake by this hour.

"Hey…everything alright?" The concern in Perez's reply confirms the unusual hour of the call.

"Yeah. Are you up for some coffee? I woke up this morning and realized I hadn't talked to my favorite deputy in a while." I'm careful with my voice. I need to talk to a friend, but I use the word *favorite* lightly, trying to avoid innuendo. Perez still carries a torch for me. My decision to date Randy never sat well with him. I'm lucky he still considers me a friend.

"I can do that. Can we hold off until about 9:30? I've got a staff meeting this morning."

I laugh. "Two months ago, and I would have been making fun of your little bureaucratic meeting schedule. Now that I have my business, I kind of empathize." I pause. "9:30's good."

"Elkhorn?"

That's our usual spot, but I don't want to meet him directly across the street from Travis and The Aerie. "How about June's? My treat."

"You had me at 'free.' See you there."

I can't go to the office. No way. I consider a run, but I'm exhausted from my sleepless night. I look over at Amore. "What do you think?"

My best friend must interpret my question as *"Walk?"* because he jumps off the couch and circles around the coat rack, where his leash dangles like a noose.

As I descend the steps outside my door, Erik steps from his condo, probably heading to work. I definitely need to time my departures better. He locks his door and as he turns my direction, he surveys me from head to toe. It's uncomfortable. And I'm not in the mood.

"You like what you see?" I pop off, and turn up the sidewalk toward the parking lot.

"I like the leash. Hate for you to lose that dog like you did last time."

I freeze in my tracks and whirl to face him. "Did you help that man take my dog last time? Was it you who showed him how to get Amore?"

Erik walks my direction, aiming at either me or his truck—I can't tell which. I hold my position and widen my stance.

He brushes past and I turn in his direction. "Answer me."

Erik doesn't turn, but I hear his voice. "Don't have time for your shit. Don't have time for your drama." He turns his head over his shoulder and leers at me. "Glad to see you're on your toes, though. As you should be." He continues to his truck, leaving me debating whether I just have a child-abusing, crazy neighbor, or whether Erik's colluding with Travis's bad guys.

I log a mile at a slow jog before easing to a walk. Amore tugs at the leash. Whatever problems I had sleeping last night didn't affect my hyperactive dog. I consider my planned breakfast with Perez. I can't just lay it all on him. *You know the Girl Scout who guides rafts, cleans gutters, and takes you hiking up 14ers? She also thinks she might have fallen in sideways with a crazy lesbian and a group of drug dealers.* That conversation wouldn't go well. And subtlety is not my forte.

I walk into June's at 9:25 and spot Perez sitting at a table for two. He rises when I approach, always the gentleman, wearing a wide smile. Pulling out my chair, he gives a sarcastic "Madam…" before returning to his seat. Perez knows I hate the chivalry shit.

"So…" Perez opens, but I'm not ready to dive into the reason I've asked him here.

"So. Why are you early? Thought you had a meeting?"

"I told the boss I had to check a lead on some drug stuff. Unfortunately, I missed out on the rehearsal plan for the children's parade next weekend." Perez makes a face and I grin.

"Oh, darn." I say, as our server, Mary Beth, approaches to take our order. Perez asks if June's has quiche, and Mary Beth snorts so hard she has to turn away from us. I'm pretty sure Perez knew the answer before he asked. He ends up ordering a cheese omelet. I always forget he's a vegetarian.

The thick aroma of bacon isn't helping my nausea, and I stick with coffee.

"Right. And enough of the small talk. What's going on?" Perez cuts to the chase.

"Wait. I'm not done asking questions. Are you really working a drug case?"

Perez looks out the window facing the street. "We're always working one drug case or another. Your rafting folks only see the cannabis side—all the stuff that's legal now—but the other stuff is out there."

"Where are they getting it?"

Perez turns his head back to me. "That's the issue. It used to be we were making all our busts for possession and use, right? People would go into the city—Denver or C Springs—and buy. Bring it home and use it, and we'd bust them for raising hell."

I nod. *I've been inside a storage shed in town that might show a different story.*

"But now we're seeing dealers. Busted a couple, and one of them talked. We thought the dealers networked from the Front Range. But this guy—the last guy we nabbed—he hinted they might distribute from right here in our valley."

"In Buena Vista?"

Perez nods. "We've just got this one lead, but we're poking around for more." He squints his eyes at me. "Why the interest? You hear anything?"

"No!" I say, just a fraction too fast. "The guys I know just sit around comparing the quality of the local edibles. Nothing like you're talking about."

Perez smiles. He's getting ready to needle me.

"What guys are you hanging out with? I can't picture Marshal Williams as an edible connoisseur."

Mary Beth delivers our coffee and gives Perez a five-minute warning on his omelet. I counter Perez's dig with the truth.

"Randy and I are on hold."

Perez's eyes widen, and he sets his coffee in front of him. His nose wrinkles as if he's considering the appropriate reaction. I decide not to wait.

"Spill it." I stare at him with a half-smile.

"I was just trying to decide whether to open with a statement: 'I'm sorry you're having relationship troubles,' or a question: 'You called me to breakfast to tell me you finally decided I'm the right man for you?'"

Fortunately, I'm between sips on my coffee, or I'm pretty sure I would have sprayed Perez as I laughed. I watch as he gauges my reaction and breaks into his own wide smile. It's not the first time Perez has used humor in dark moments to cheer me up.

I reach across the table and give his arm a pat, then pull my hand back. "You're the right friend for me, Rick. I hope."

"Ah, the platonic friend. A shoulder for you to lean on. My favorite role." Perez still smiles, and his sarcasm presses like a foam roller on sore quads—it hurts a bit, but it's good for me. To remind me I still have friends, even if they're unaware of the chaotic turn my life has taken.

"Just giving you a hard time." Perez says, his smile fading. "So, what's with you two? Long-distance thing finally taking its toll?" He pauses. "There's no way he's found anyone else…is there?"

"No. I broke it off. And yes, the distance thing mattered." Now I pause, as Mary Beth approaches the table and serves our food.

"Need anything else?" she says.

We shake our heads, and she disappears into the kitchen.

"It's me," I say. "I found someone else."

Perez's eyes widen again—not as wide as when I made my break-up proclamation, but he appears surprised.

"Who's the lucky guy?" His voice is flat. I sense he asks out of a morbid curiosity, already disappointed that it's not him.

Here we go. I take a breath and release it before speaking. "Nikki Kingston."

Perez has taken a bite of his omelet before my response, and now he freezes mid-chew. "Nikki Kingston from Search & Rescue? The girl

Nikki?" His mouth is full and his words come out garbled. When I nod, he opens his mouth to speak again, eyes locked with mine, then closes his mouth. He lowers his eyes to his plate and resumes chewing.

Search & Rescue doesn't have any boy Nikkis. None in the entire town, in fact. I've confused Perez. It's not that I've found someone else. It's that the *someone else* is a woman.

Finally, Perez returns his eyes to mine. I sense questions. I detect anger. I spy confusion. I can read whatever I want in his eyes, but I can't tell what my friend is thinking.

"Can I ask you something about this?" he says. I nod, and he goes on. "So, if you like women, what were you doing with Williams?"

I glance toward Mary Beth and raise my coffee cup. Perez has asked the one question I don't completely understand myself, and I need something to distract me while I consider my answer. Coffee.

Mary Beth fills me up, and Perez covers his cup with his hand. After she moves to the next table, I lean forward and answer Perez's question.

"It's not as simple as you make it sound, Perez. It's not just binary— liking men or liking women. Or, at least it's not that way for me." I eye him, hoping for a head nod, but he's just staring at me, waiting for more explanation. "I like Randy...physically, emotionally...and in a bunch of other ways." I let out a breath. "But I fell for Nikki for the same reasons. We've both kind of crushed on each other over the last couple of weeks." Perez nods, and I mutter mostly to myself, "Too much crushing, in fact." I'm thinking of the photo Nikki showed me at The Roastery.

"What do you mean 'too much?' Are you guys already over or something?"

I nod. "It went too far, too fast." I lean back and try to explain the last several weeks. How Nikki and I started hanging out. How it gradually started turning into something more. And then the tipping point where we began to spend every moment together.

"Nikki expected me to go public with our relationship. To tell friends. To touch each other in public. I guess for me it would be 'coming out' since everyone already knows Nikki is gay." I pause. "And

I just wasn't ready for that." I'm also not ready to mention the picture to Perez. Or the movie.

Perez reaches across and gives me the arm pat this time before retracting his hand back to his lap. I figure he's about as much into public displays of intimacy as I am.

He hitches his thumbs in his belt, keeping his voice low. "Look, Kristee, I'll admit it. I'm surprised. I didn't see this coming, and I don't want you to take my surprise as some kind of judgment." He pauses. "It's not. I don't pretend to understand what motivates desire in any of us, and I'm certainly not one to pass judgment on it unless someone is breaking the law." He shakes his head. "And you obviously aren't. I think all of us—you know, your friends—would understand. I think you should consider telling more people than just me. Especially if it's who you are."

I always sensed Perez would be okay with this. Disappointed for himself, maybe, but okay with me. And he's right about my other friends. I think they'd understand—except for Randy. But that's a whole different situation.

But this isn't a *coming out* conversation. I'm here to discuss Nikki and how to break it off with her. Now that we're done, I don't plan on revealing my sexuality issues. Especially one week before my mother's visit. Talk about a win-win. Mama will be happy I've broken up with Randy, the *African American*, and I can avoid informing Mama that I'm still attracted to women.

"I'm not going back to her," I say. "So, I don't want people to know. Especially with my mother coming. God, she'd throw a fit. We'd have another five years of no talking."

"So why are you telling me, Kristee? Why pick me to share this with?"

I nod. The crux of our discussion. "Because I'm not sure she's going to let me go without a fight. I told you how obsessed we both got. I'm through with her. But she's not through with me. That's all the detail you need." I pause. "My question for you is, how do I keep her away from me?"

"Well, after two divorces, I don't consider myself a relationship expert, but I would start off by telling her—"

"Rick."

"What?"

"I'm asking you as a cop. As a law enforcement officer. How can I legally keep her away from me?"

"Oh." Perez stares at me. "I see."

ZAHN

NOW

"Tell me more about Kristee's relationship with her mother," I ask Nikki while walking my loop around Elk Trace. I've got Lin Li on my brain and hope this phone call to Kristee's ex-girlfriend will answer some questions.

"You're supposed to be her friend. Why are you asking me?"

I say nothing.

"She didn't enjoy talking about her mother. Just like she didn't like talking about our relationship. No coincidence, either—those topics were linked."

I pick up an empty Gatorade bottle from the road's shoulder and jam it in my side pocket. I won't pick up my neighbors' dog poop, but we all try to keep the litter at bay. "Linked, how?"

"I mean her mother is a crazy-ass, hyper-conservative bitch. She was visiting because she was planning on breaking up Kristee and Randy—because he was Black. Kristee was having a cow about her finding out she was dating a woman instead. Said that she'd already experienced her mother's reaction to that situation."

I chew on that for a moment.

"Tyler, you still there?"

I stop on the shoulder of the road, turning so the wind isn't howling in the phone. "Yeah, the college girlfriend, right?"

"See? That's what I'm talking about—you're wasting my time. She already told you everything. You've just been playing me about not knowing Kristee was gay."

"Not true, Nikki. Kristee never told me." I don't see a reason to mention it was Karla. "I found out through my research into the case."

I crest the highest point on my walk, and my breathing eases as I round the corner toward home. This phone call is useless. Nikki doesn't like Lin Li. Big surprise. I don't like her either. I haven't found anyone who does.

So why am I trying to turn Lin Li's focus on Kristee's assets into something sinister? Since when is financial pragmatism a crime?

"So, there you have it. Was I too subtle about my feelings toward her mother?" Nikki says.

"No. I got it."

Neither of us speaks for a moment, and then Nikki says, "She's still in town, you know. I saw her yesterday talking to Kristee's neighbor outside the apartments."

I press my phone hard against my ear. I'm not the only pathetic soul who can't get over Kristee. Nikki's doing drive-bys?

"I know. I talked to Lin Li yesterday." I sigh. "I understand this is all hard, Nikki. Especially considering how close you were." Too close, I muse—or Kristee wouldn't have put the restraining order on Nikki. "She was probably asking Jacy to walk Amore when you saw her. They're still using her to help take care of him."

"That wasn't the neighbor I was talking about. Lin Li was talking to Jacy's dad. You know, Erik? The asshole?" Nikki lets out a dry laugh. "If I didn't like her before, I really don't like her now, with the way she was smiling and putting her hand on his arm. I wonder if she knows how Erik treated Kristee?"

"Wait a minute." I stop in my tracks. "You mean they were like having a civil conversation? I thought he never talked to the neighbors unless he was threatening them."

"Exactly. Not this time, though. He was smiling back at her like they were old friends."

"Huh."

"Right. Huh. Makes you wonder, doesn't it?"

If Nikki knew about all the things making me wonder, all the theories spinning around in my head, she'd probably feel relief. That she isn't the only crazy one in town when it comes to Kristee's disappearance.

I need to hash out this connection between Lin Li and Erik. I never thought Kristee's mother was involved with any of this until she started expressing her frustrations about not having access to Kristee's money. Erik was never on my radar scope until I identified his truck on Frank's film footage, following Nikki's car away from the Apostles.

But the two of them together?

"Thanks, Nikki." I hang up.

KRISTEE

BEFORE

I wake to Amore licking my face and sunshine streaming through my bedroom window. And a queasiness in my gut, like I've eaten a pizza slice after it's sat in my car for two days. I shove Amore to the side and swing my legs to the floor.

As I stumble across the throw rug to my bathroom, Amore nips at my heels, assuming my panicked shove was a play-date invitation. My stomach roils, and I throw up just as I kneel over the toilet. Not pretty.

I spend five minutes after my last heave waiting for round two. What is wrong with me? My stomach lurches again as I choke on a laugh. What isn't wrong with me? I just dropped a restraining order on my ex-lover, and I owe $10K to Travis's thugs today. Money I don't have. So a little nausea? I guess I'm not surprised.

Pounding at the front door ripples the toilet water, and I jerk my head from the bowl. Amore yaps once and stands sentry in the bathroom doorframe. I crawl to my feet and shift over to the sink to wipe my face and check the mirror. No need to rush—the men outside aren't going anywhere.

I run water over my hands and splash my face. Dropping the hand towel in the sink, I stare into my own vacant eyes reflected in the mirror.

"It's showtime," I say. Stress over Nikki and the restraining order isn't the only reason I didn't get a full night's sleep. I've come up with a plan to stall Travis's men. To buy more time. The problem is that it's a binary solution. Either the plan works, and I gain a reprieve from their relentless pressure…or they call bullshit and get rid of me. When they told me to pay up, or else, I didn't doubt their intentions if I failed. I still don't.

The hammering continues, and Amore barks twice before moving from the bathroom toward the front door. I follow, grabbing my phone and wrapping myself in a bathrobe on the way.

"Shhh. Relax." Right.

My door lacks a peephole—hell, half the BV residents don't even lock their doors—but I already know who's there. Releasing the deadbolt, I crack the door open and peer outside just as RAV-4 man wedges his foot in the opening and pushes the door the rest of the way open. Amore barks in a constant staccato, but stays in the dining room watching my reaction to the men.

RAV-4 man has the same three-day growth of beard he sported a week ago—I'm guessing he uses one of those *As Seen on TV* special razor attachments—and strides past me, dropping a paper bag on the counter between my dining room table and the kitchen. Double-wide closes the apartment door and stands in front of it with his arms crossed.

"Cinnamon roll," RAV-4 man says. "You hungry?"

"No."

He stares at me and then glances at Double-wide before shaking his head. He picks up the bag and tosses it to his partner, who snags it in mid-air.

"Guess I owe you a dollar," he says to Double-wide. He turns to me. "Much as I'd love to stay and chat, I think we should probably cut to the chase."

I swallow, but try to do it subtly in the hopes the men won't notice how nervous I am.

"I don't have the money."

RAV-4 man's smile fades, and he stares into my eyes. He almost looks sad as he turns back to his partner. "What the hell, are you like the shakedown whisperer? Now I owe you *two* dollars?"

Double-wide says nothing, but I can tell he's not surprised at my announcement.

"We're not giving you any more time, Kristee. I thought we made that clear?"

"I don't need extra time. I'm not going to pay."

At my announcement, the vibe in the room shifts. For a moment, no one moves. RAV-4 man's eyes don't leave mine, and for the first time since I've met the man, I see confusion on his face—as if I've told him I'd like to get to know him better.

I catch movement behind him as Double-wide pulls a gun. He wheels around and turns the deadbolt on my front door. It's time to explain myself.

I reach for my bathrobe pocket and RAV-4 man seizes my arm.

"What are you doing?" he says.

"I need to show you something on my phone." I pull it from my pocket and thumb to my photos.

"Fuck her phone," Double-wide says from the front door.

RAV-4 man doesn't turn, but extends his palm toward his partner. "No. I want to see this." He reaches for the phone.

I pull my phone closer to myself. "It will make more sense if I explain."

"How about I just pop you?" Double-wide says.

I thumb to a folder I've created and push the phone toward RAV-4 man. "Here's a picture of one of your drug stashes. In the storage shed."

"So what?"

I swipe to the left and show him the next photo. "Here's the car you drive. A white Toyota RAV-4."

RAV-4 man turns to Double-wide and shrugs.

I swipe again. "Here's you all getting into said car."

RAV-4 man grabs my phone and stares at the picture. Then he raises the phone in the air and sneers.

"You ain't getting this back."

"I think I am. Look at the next picture."

Double-wide looks over RAV-4 man's shoulder and shakes his head when RAV-4 man swipes the screen. "So she opened the case and saw the drugs. Big deal. We'll move them."

RAV-4 man shakes his head and holds the phone closer to his face. Then he walks over to the dining room table and holds the picture next to the veneer surface. He looks back at me.

"You took our stuff. You had it here."

I nod. "That's right."

Double-wide brings his gun up and points it at me. "Give it to us, now."

I try to keep my voice steady. "I can't do that."

He pulls the hammer back. "Then you'll die."

RAV-4 man steps sideways, ensuring a clear shot for Double-wide.

I take a deep breath. "Me dying would be a big problem for you." RAV-4 man opens his mouth, but I interrupt him. I've gone too far to turn back. "The drugs are with a friend. So are those pictures. As is my written narrative of everything I know—which appears to be a lot. If I disappear, my friend goes to the cops. If you try to take me hostage and negotiate with my friend, the cops will know."

Double-wide releases the hammer on his gun. RAV-4 man's gaze on me hardens. "You're bluffing."

Double-wide pulls the hammer back again. This is it.

"Try me," I say.

•   •   •

Twenty minutes after the empty-handed thugs leave my condo, my cell phone alerts with a SAR call. My hands are still shaking as I open the 911 app and scan the mission. *Missing hiker near Mt Harvard/Mt Columbia. Need hikers.*

If they had called me two hours before, woken me from my slumber, I wouldn't have considered responding. I've got enough drama in my life without a SAR mission. But my minor—although temporary—victory over RAV-4 man and his partner has me pumped with adrenaline. Without even thinking, I tap *Responding* on the app and head to my closet for my 24-hour pack.

Fifteen minutes later, I'm walking into the bay and checking in with Alex, the incident commander.

"Thanks for the quick response, Kristee. I'm sending you out with Monte and Nikki on Team 1. Monte's got the lead."

Shit. Twenty-four hours into my restraining order with Nikki and already fate slams us together. And I'm not even the lead. Not that I'm upset about that—Monte's a ten-year SAR veteran and knows his shit. But maybe I can use the team lead thing as an excuse.

"Where are we searching?" I scan the map on the screen.

"Main route of Columbia. Why? You don't like that plan? I figured that was most likely, since the Harvard route still has snow."

I touch my hand on Alex's sleeve and laugh. "Not critiquing your plan, Alex." I pause. "But I've got traction and even brought my snowshoes. Are you going to send a Team 2 on the Harvard trail?"

"That's the plan. I can hold you for that team if you want. I've got another hiker coming in five minutes I can send with Team 1. Sound good?"

I let out a relieved sigh. Conflict avoided. "Sounds great. You want me to scribe for you until we get enough folks for Team 2?"

"That'd be great. Team 1 is in the bay packing the truck. You go tell them the plan change, OK? They think they're waiting for you."

Shit. So much for avoiding conflict. I nod and walk into the bay. Striding toward the truck, I can't help but glance at the shelf containing the old gear and the Pelican case of drugs I stashed in the back. Nothing looks disturbed. I glance through the rear of the truck and see Monte and Nikki talking in the front seat. I've got time.

I saunter to the shelf and kneel on the concrete, stretching my arm over the boxes fronting the storage area. The pang in my gut dissipates, and I let out a breath.

"Looking for something?"

I recognize the voice. Nikki must have seen me enter the bay.

I stand and turn, keeping my back to my hidden contraband, my mind scrambling for an excuse why I'm rummaging through shelves.

"Just thinking we needed to get rid of some of this stuff." I gesture to a pile of coiled ropes. "Most of it's out of date and just taking up space."

"What the hell, Kristee? We're waiting for you in the truck. Let's go."

I stare at Nikki. "Not with you. You're supposed to know that. They were supposed to tell you." I move from the shelves to the center of the bay. "Alex is having me lead Team 2. You guys are supposed to wait five for another hiker."

Nikki smiles at me, but it doesn't resemble the smile I've gotten used to over the last several weeks. "Are you talking about that court order thingie?"

"Uh-huh."

"Come on, Kristee. You're not expecting us to comply with that, are you? I thought it was just something you set up, so when your mom comes and finds out about us, you can prove it's not your fault." Her smile fades. "You aren't really going to let that thing interfere with a mission, are you?"

Now I'm shaking my head. "I'm not going anywhere with you." I twist my head to the truck. Monte's silhouetted head still fills the canopy window. Lowering my voice, I add, "That thing with the camera? Without asking? And you not deleting it when I asked you to?" Now I step closer to Nikki. "That's not normal, Nikki. Not at all."

Nikki's eyes widen. "You want to talk to me about normal? *You*?" Her voice has also lowered, but she's punctuating her whispers with such force, I'm convinced Monte's 59-year-old ears can't help but hear.

"Normal was what we had when we were together," my ex-lover says. "Abnormal in intensity—I'll give you that—but normal that two women like us would feel passion for each other." She stares at me. "You felt it. I know you did, right?"

Nikki's not wrong about that. I felt it. An overwhelming desire to spend our moments together. But passion is defined by minutes, hours, and days. Love uses units like years and decades. I can't love a woman I don't trust. I've learned enough about myself over the last week to realize I was obsessed with Nikki—not in love with her.

I nod. "I felt it." I wait a beat. "I felt the passion. But it wasn't love, Nikki. And it never will be."

Nikki's face freezes, and I watch as she whirls back to the truck. She walks two steps, then whips around, jabbing her finger at me.

"I know everything about you. More than anyone else in Buena Vista. You want to halt all contact with me? Fine. But if you plan on preserving your precious little reputation in this town, you'll come back to me. I know everything that can bring you down."

Nikki strides to the open truck door. Before she climbs back in the truck, she calls out, "Think about that, girlfriend!"

Then she slams the door.

ZAHN

NOW

"Tyler, we need you. Can you come?" Karla's voice is a frantic whisper over my phone, and I squeeze the screen against my cheek to understand her as I pull onto the shoulder.

"What's going on?" I'm driving home from City Market. I ran out of beer the day before yesterday and had to resort to Jack Daniels last night to help my thought process on the case. Beer works better. Whiskey is dangerous.

"Erik's outside. He won't leave. He says Mama owes him money. I'm worried he might do something."

"Downstairs Erik?" I realize Karla and Lin Li can't know many other Eriks in town.

"Yes."

"Is he threatening you all?"

"He says if Mama doesn't pay up, he's coming in."

"You mean for Jacy's dog-walking?" I close my eyes. I didn't realize Kristee's family was so short on money. "Give me ten minutes, and I'll be there. I can pay him."

Shit. I check my rearview mirror and do a U-turn back toward town.

What Karla says next sends a jolt through me.

"It's not that; otherwise, we would have paid. It's something else."

"What?"

"He's just screaming now, but when he first arrived, he was very clear. He wanted to talk to Mama, and he yelled, 'I followed that bitch's car all fucking day. It's not my fault your daughter never came home. Where's my $500?'"

"Call the cops, Karla. This is serious."

Karla's breath sounds like a drum rhythm, but she says nothing.

"Karla?"

"I can't call the police. Don't you see? Mama must have done something wrong. I don't want the police. Can you come fix it?"

"I'm on my way."

I pound my hand on the steering wheel. I knew there was something off with Kristee's mom. And it was an open secret that Erik threatened Kristee multiple times. Why Lin Li would pay Erik to trail Nikki's car is beyond me. But it seems pretty clear that's what happened.

Did Erik go up the mountain after he followed the car to Winfield? Did he do something to Kristee? Most importantly, did Lin Li offer to pay Erik for more than following the car? What if Erik is couching his rant because Karla is listening and doesn't want her to find out her mother hired him to take out Kristee?

My mind races, and I laugh out loud. No wonder Perez thinks I'm nuts. This whole time I was torn between suspecting Kristee's partner, Travis, with his shady connection with drugs, and pondering whether Nikki was whacked out enough to act out revenge as the scorned lover. My suspicions toward Lin Li were niggles—nothing I had taken seriously. But now?

I can't leave the police out of this. It's gone too far. I turn at the single stop light on Main Street, four minutes out from the condo. I pull up Perez's number on speed dial, then pause. Perez might slow the process. First, he thinks I'm the one who's wacko. The local retired guy who won't let the tragedy go. Second, I'm in the Buena Vista PD's jurisdiction, so calling 911 is quicker.

I push the three digits into my phone and press the green button.

When I pull into the condo parking lot, Erik is pacing on the second-floor walkway in front of Kristee's apartment. I exit my truck and walk toward the stairway, glancing over my shoulder to check if the police are here. Not yet.

When I turn back, Erik is grabbing the railing with both hands, his angry eyes drilling into mine.

"Don't even think about coming up here, man. I recognize you. You're the one who meddles in everyone else's business." He steps toward the top of the stairs and grabs each rail like he's going to play Red Rover with me. I stop at the first step. I'm not going up. Erik would probably beat the crap out of me, and it wouldn't resolve the issue.

"The cops are on the way," I say, widening my stance. "I'll wait."

Erik's eyes widen a fraction. "You better." He turns back to Kristee's door, his voice muffled.

"Your daughter's asshole friend called the po-po. Looks like you'd better pay up, or we're going to have to explain our little contract to the cops."

My phone rings. Karla. I stab the green button and answer.

"Did you call the police, Tyler?"

I step back from the stairs for a better angle on Kristee's apartment. Karla stands at the window, her phone pressed against her ear.

"I did. I felt like I had to."

"Mama's paying him right now. I don't understand."

I shift my eyes from the window to the door, where Erik leans inside. He nods and backs from the door as it shuts. He stares at me again as he turns from the door.

"Move it," he says, then freezes and looks past me. I turn and spot a Buena Vista police department Ford Explorer with its rollers flashing, a uniformed officer stepping from the SUV. I recognize Linzmeier, a local cop, recently reinstated to the force after trouble at the local school last year.

"Hold it!" he barks. I turn to Erik, who remains motionless on the stairs, before glancing back at Linzmeier.

He nods at me. "Zahn."

I nod.

"You made the call, right?"

I nod again.

Linzmeier calls up to Erik. "What's your name?"

"Erik Johnson. Can I help you?"

Linzmeier glances at me before answering Erik. "We have reports you are threatening the women in the upstairs apartment and creating a disturbance." I nod at Linzmeier, but my head freezes when I hear a female voice behind me. I turn and see Lin Li, her head barely higher than the balcony rail.

"That's not accurate, sir," she says. "We had a disagreement about the amount of money I owed Mr. Johnson for detailing my car. We may have argued a bit loudly, but it turns out he was right. I paid the money and he is leaving." She looks at me and her eyes pierce mine. "I'm not sure what Mr. Zahn told you, but I can assure you he is overreacting."

I shift my eyes from Lin Li to Erik. He's looking past me to Linzmeier and nodding his head. I turn back to Lin Li, hoping to see Karla step forward and tell the truth about what happened. Tell Linzmeier why she called me for help.

I remember Karla's question when I arrived: *You called the police?* And I realize how this will go down. Linzmeier will go back and report a false alarm. The Sheriff's department will be notified. Perez will find out I'm chasing windmills again.

But I can't ignore what I've discovered. Kristee's mother paid the man who threatened her daughter to follow her daughter's girlfriend's car the day Kristee disappeared. What did Erik do for the five hours Nikki's car sat parked at the bottom of that mountain? And who can I convince to listen to me?

KRISTEE

BEFORE

Amore lies tucked between my legs on the couch as I stare at a blank television screen. Every day it's the same: I drift off to sleep with the best intentions for a walk or run with Amore, and every morning I wake up stressing over my business woes and the relationships I've ruined. The mistakes I've made. And I find no relief until I stagger to my bathroom, the urge to puke vectoring me to my knees in front of my new porcelain god. Then I crawl to this sofa with Amore and either stare out my window at the view that once filled me with joy, or stare at my television and remind myself I have no room in my life for entertainment.

A knock on my door interrupts my unhealthy meditation on the flat-screen and I groan to my feet and shuffle to the door. I peer out the living room window and spy Nikki raising her hand to knock again.

Shit.

She flinches as she catches me moving, and I duck toward the door. Too late.

"Don't even try, Kristee. I can hear you in there. I saw you in the window." She pauses a beat. "I just want us to talk. Can we do that?"

"You're not allowed to be here. You know that."

"You're going to call the cops on me? Really?"

I don't answer.

"Listen. I've thought about what's really making you upset. It's the video and the pic I showed you, right?"

I remain silent. She's partially right. I'm horrified at the video because she took it without asking. But she's missing the crux of the issue. Secretly videoing our intimacy is bad. But using it as a threat against me? That's mental. I can eventually forgive a person who has a mental problem—who needs help—but that doesn't mean I'll allow them back into my life, or pretend it never happened.

"I'm going to delete the video. Just talk to me. Please?"

If Nikki understood what really bothered me, she would have shown up and told me she had already deleted it. Not make it conditional on me talking to her again. I'll never know if she deletes all traces of the video or keeps copies. I have a hard time imagining Nikki relinquishing any leverage she might have over me.

"Please delete it. I'd like you to do that," I say.

"And we can start talking again?"

I want to tell her she needs help, but I remember her reaction at the SAR bay when I said her actions weren't normal. The way her eyes widened and her cheeks flared at being labeled abnormal. Like it wasn't the first time someone had called her crazy.

"No. You went too far, Nikki. Trying to use that video against me? I'm not ready to talk."

Silence permeates my condo. Thirty seconds pass. I'm ready to poke my head around the curtain again when her muffled voice seeps through the door.

"Not ready implies you might be someday. I'm going to get rid of the video. The picture. Everything." She pauses. "You think about us, Kristee. I'll be waiting."

Nikki flashes by the window, and she jogs the steps to the landing. I track her all the way out to her car, watching as she waves to Jacy coming up the walk. She clicks her key fob before turning back to my window. I duck behind the curtain again. She flashes a smile and my heart tears. How many ways can we smile at the ones we love? A false one to make the other believe you are happy. A playful one to encourage them. A sad smile to reveal our heart.

Nikki gives me none of those. Her smile is full of hope.

• • •

My daily nausea has been disappearing by noon, and today I choke down a slice of toast with avocado. The episode with Nikki has done nothing to calm my nerves or my stomach. I stare at my laptop and decide to research my undiagnosed ailment. Ask Dr. Google.

As my home screen illuminates, I spy a white number in a red circle on my email icon. I've got mail.

I scan my inbox. Two offers to remortgage my house, which I find humorous since I don't own one. One email from Williams. Odd...he usually texts. I move the cursor to the message and the email title below Williams's jumps out at me.

Contract Offer reads the top line, and it's from Winston at *organtown.com.* I double-click the email.

Dear Ms Li,

We have reviewed your file and are pleased to accept you as a candidate for our organ donation program—specifically, our kidney donation line. Please contact us directly so we can talk through the details and logistics, should you decide to accept our terms.

Sincerely,

Winston

The email is vague, but I understand why. When I finally contacted them in Thailand, they explained the online cash offers were legitimate, and I could expect to receive the money they advertised. But they also told me they never associate a money amount with my *donation* via email. Instead, if I am accepted, they notify me to call, and we negotiate over the phone. Then I sign the final contract via a secure electronic link.

But they accepted me! I'm ninety percent of the way to $50K. And that means I've found a solution to the rest of Karla's tuition problems. Something is finally going right.

My euphoria lasts almost five minutes as I toggle back to my original research on my nausea. I'm scrolling past the obvious non-starters: food poisoning, menstrual cramps, pregnancy, and focusing in on descriptions of various stomach viruses. Something nags me as I scan through the different causes of nausea, and I pause my cursor on the screen and lean back.

I count days from the last time Williams spent the night here. The last time we made love. It's less than two months ago. I hang my head, dismayed how my life has changed in just over fifty days. I've gone from a budding entrepreneur, guiding rafts and rescuing lost hikers, to a woman who's broken up with both a man and then a woman in the span of a month—and now a woman currently in a standoff with a drug ring.

I count the days to my last period and realize I don't remember having one since Williams visited. How did I miss that?

"Oh, God!" I lean forward again. "You've got to be kidding me."

Thirty minutes later, I'm back from the drugstore with a 3-count pregnancy test. Two more minutes, and the reactive strip tells me what I've known since I started counting the days on my fingers. I'm carrying Randall Williams's child. I pull out another strip and test again. Same result.

The fresh pain in my belly isn't nausea—it's the same cramping I felt after RAV-4 man and his partner threatened my life.

Stress.

It's not that I don't appreciate the miracle of life, or that I'm anti-kids, it's just…how could this happen now? I've never believed in the God of the Christian religion, and my mother never discussed her own parents' Buddhist upbringing. But I do believe in a universal balance—a karma—that encourages you to keep your head up when things don't go your way, because eventually they will. That's balance.

But this? This is unbalance. An elephant on the opposite end of my teeter-totter. This is life watching me drown in quicksand and instead of extending a branch, it's pushing my head below the surface and eliminating any hope of escape.

Maybe a false test? I shake my head and move to my bedroom. I knew the test results before I even bought the kit. I open my top dresser drawer and slide the remaining test under my clothes. My fingers brush against a piece of paper.

You deserve better—R

Randy's writing. But when did he leave the note?

I return to my computer and reread the email from *Organtown*. I pull up their website and scroll through every page, trying to determine if my pregnancy disqualifies me from the procedure. But they don't have the waivers and requirements online. I assume this information comes with the contract.

Will they remove a kidney from a pregnant woman? I really don't know. A US company performing this procedure would never consider it. But selling your organs is illegal in the US. Am I to assume *organtown.com* holds themselves to the same medical standards I expect in my country?

And that's when the answer occurs to me. I don't have to be pregnant. A Family Planning clinic sits north of town which deals with these situations. Or at least I assume so—I've never been there.

My mood shifts to the positive as I reach for the phone to schedule an appointment. I realize I need to relax. For once, one of my problems is under my control. I can fix this.

ZAHN

NOW

Karla phones the next evening, and I try to keep a civil tone while I stare at my half-full pint of Thick Haze gracing my dining room table. She's young, I tell myself. It's her family. But I'm still pissed she didn't tell the truth to Linzmeier. Especially after her call for help.

"Tyler, I'm sorry."

"There's something going on there. Why would your mother hire Erik like that?"

Karla pauses a beat. Her voice is quiet. "She wouldn't harm Kristee. She wouldn't harm either of us. Not her daughters." She's silent for a moment before continuing. "Maybe she found out about Nikki? And Kristee? Or suspected? And she was looking for proof."

I gulp my beer. Twice. And say nothing. A search and rescue mission—which you can't plan for—is not where you're going to prove your daughter is in a relationship you disapprove of. It has to be something else.

"But that's not why I called," Karla says. "I mean, yes, I called to say sorry, but I called for another reason."

I stay silent.

"The post office called about Kristee's mail."

"What about it?" I say. "How do they have your number?"

"They got it from Travis at The Aerie. They've been calling Kristee to tell her that her box is full, but of course the calls aren't getting through. They cross-referenced her name online and tied it with Travis, and called him to pass the message." Her voice rises an octave. "They didn't even realize she was missing."

I can't help laughing. The post office is a running joke for our downtown residents, so I'm actually surprised they took the time to track down Karla. I'm even more surprised Karla and Lin Li didn't notice the lack of mail sooner. "You mean you and your mother haven't seen her mail for over two weeks? Didn't you check it?"

"It didn't occur to us. I mean, what kind of town makes you go to a post office to get your mail? We figured if she had mail, it would show up somewhere around here."

I guess I can see it. Lin Li lives in Denver. Home delivery. And mail probably isn't at the top of your priorities when a family member goes missing.

"So…?" I'm impatient.

"So, most of it was junk mail. Mortgage companies, the local paper, that kind of stuff. Except for one from the State Department."

"Her passport?"

"Her passport."

My stomach drops at Karla's words, because in the back of my mind, I've fantasized that Kristee already had her passport. That she couldn't handle the stress and took off. That she's alive.

It's hard to imagine my friend running away from anything, but I had still carried a sliver of hope.

I let out a long breath. "How's that make you feel?"

"I guess I never really believed she would run. Not Kristee," Karla says, as if she reads my thoughts. She pauses, and the silence stretches between us. Finally, she speaks again. "You're mad about the thing with Mama and Erik. And you're probably not too happy with me."

"It's OK. Family can be tough."

"I found something else."

"In the mail?" I raise my pint, draining the last inch. The beer has lost its chill, but not its taste, and I savor the hoppy remnants, hoping they dull whatever bad news I'm about to hear. I swallow as Karla answers.

"No. In Kristee's stuff from The Aerie. The box Mama brought home. That's where I found the mailbox key. While I was looking, I found some notes Kristee took. I don't understand them—there's like math or a code or something—but I thought you'd want to see them. And there's something else."

"What?"

"A thumb drive. I plugged it into Kristee's computer and it looks like it's work stuff—from The Aerie. Except..."

I wait and she finishes her sentence. "Except for a password-protected folder I can't access."

I cradle the phone between my shoulder and ear as I pop another IPA. Part of me is tired of poking at Travis and The Aerie. I've got a solid lead on what happened to Kristee, and it leans far more toward Kristee's mother and Erik than it does with Kristee's business partner.

"Can you text the numbers to me? Or bring them?"

· · ·

An hour later, and Karla sits across my table, staring at the back of Kristee's computer while I peck away. I offer a beer. She declines and I catch a puzzled expression on her face when I sip mine, as if she lacks my faith in the power of alcohol as an antidote for desperation.

The numbers mean nothing to me. I run them through Google and come up empty—except for a *similar search* option pointing me toward crypto sites. The number of digits in each grouping appears to be the standard for crypto keys. But the more I search, the less I understand. I don't know how to decipher Kristee's codes. Some websites describe mining and make no sense. Others reference my *crypto wallet*, and all I can deduce is it's a secure place to keep your currency on the computer.

"Does Kristee have a crypto wallet on this computer?"

Karla seems as clueless as I am and shakes her head. "I don't think so. I didn't see anything that said 'crypto.'"

"What about the thumb drive? Did you look at that?

"I did. Everything except the password-protected folder."

"What's it called?" I click over to the F:/ drive representing the thumb drive Karla had found and click on it.

"*MISC*. Miscellaneous."

I double-click on the folder, and a password request pops up. "Did you try anything besides the one for her computer? Randall's name or Nikki?" I try both names with no luck. "Why would she password-protect miscellaneous stuff? Maybe this is her crypto wallet."

"Why would she have a crypto wallet? Just because Travis was into it doesn't mean Kristee was doing stuff with digital currency. We haven't seen signs of it anywhere else."

I grab another beer from the fridge and fill my glass, checking for Karla's reaction when I return. She's not looking at me. Instead, her eyes are focused on the paper next to the computer. The one with the undecipherable codes. I follow her eyes to the numbers.

"Did you...?" I start, and she shakes her head. Have we been staring at the password the whole time?

"No, it didn't even occur to me."

I let out a breath and pull the laptop closer. "Me either. Let's give it a shot."

We spend the next five minutes trying each of the three lines of numbers. Forward. Backward. Then the three lines together. Finally, Karla hits on the correct sequence—a group of five numbers from the first line, the second group of five numbers (and letters) from the second line, and the third group from the third line. And just like that, we're in.

Except that Kristee's encryption has left us more confused than before. The folder contains one file, a Word document entitled *BAY*. I double-click the file and open it. It's a single line of text, highlighted blue, a URL for something on YouTube.

"Any ideas?" I hover the touchpad cursor over the link.

"I have no clue. Click on it."

Ten seconds later, the smooth voice of Otis Redding's *Sittin' on the Dock of the Bay* fills my dining room.

Sittin' in the morning sun...

We listen to the first stanza and start the second one before I hit pause. I look at Karla. She stares back at me, shaking her head. "I have no idea. Keep playing."

'Cause I've had nothing to live for...

"Pause it there," Karla says. I stop the music and stare at the screen, afraid to look into Karla's eyes. I know why she had me stop.

Less than fifty percent of suicide victims leave a note. Kristee didn't leave one. None of us thinks Kristee would ever kill herself. But everything from the last three weeks has pointed toward foul play or suicide. And the final stanza sure sounds like a farewell. *'Cause I've had nothing to live for...*

"You don't think...?" Karla pauses.

I close the screen of the laptop and glance at Karla. "I don't. We can't be sure what this means. Maybe she was hiding something from Travis, and this was a red herring. Maybe we're missing the point. But if Kristee ever did something like you're thinking, do you think she would communicate her last words through Otis Redding? Did she even listen to this music?"

"Not this kind. This is like something she'd probably expect you to listen to...not her."

. . .

I wake with a start three hours later. Karla is long gone, but has left Kristee's computer behind so I can keep looking for clues. I sit up and turn on the light. Something has woken me. I usually sleep like the dead—even with my sudden increase in beer consumption over the last two weeks.

I poke my feet into my slippers and take a circuit around the inside of my house, checking out the windows for signs of any critters that might have roused me. I see nothing. I'm wasting time. *Wastin' time,* as the song from Kristee's *BAY* document had said. I pause on the way back to my bedroom. The song is not called *BAY*. It's called *Sittin' on the Dock of the Bay.*

Why did Kristee name the document *BAY*? Why not the full title? Or *Dock of the Bay*? Or *Otis*? Hell, if the post really was a suicide note—well, why not call it *Nothing to Live For*?

That's when it clicks. This isn't a message for Karla or her mother. This is for a friend. Someone who knows Kristee well enough to remember she's not a beach girl, an ocean girl, or a *sit on the dock of the bay* girl. She's an outdoorswoman who is defined by the time she puts into saving those who come unprepared for the Colorado mountains. Search & Rescue. And our Search & Rescue operates out of a large building that we affectionately call *The BAY*.

I pull on my clothes and grab my keys, tucking Kristee's computer under my arm as I head for my truck.

KRISTEE

BEFORE

Mama Li is here. She checked into the motel two days ago, and stress hangs in the air like wildfire smoke. It's been so long since we've spoken that we still haven't got past the "How are you? How's your job?" chit-chat. The long silences linger in the air as I sit at the dining room table with my laptop while my mother reads a book. We take turns releasing sporadic sighs while the other checks to see if it signals the starts of a conversation.

I make up my mind. I'm out of here as soon as my passport arrives.

It's as if I'm suspended in vitro, just waiting out my term. Travis's goons ignore me—for now. Nikki stays away—thank God. And then there's my baby. Well, Randy's baby, too, but I avoid those thoughts.

As I expected, the Family Planning clinic gave me options, but sent me out the door with standard advice: it's my decision. I made an appointment in Colorado Springs for the actual procedure.

But I canceled it two days later.

Here's why: I can barely look in the mirror anymore. I've gone from a woman known throughout this community as confident, self-assured, and someone people can count on when things get tough…to a pathetic, self-absorbed sniveler who isn't willing to accept the consequences for illegally accepting a payoff and who is afraid to discuss her confused sexuality with anyone. I'm a loser who's lost her morality.

After I cancel the appointment, I ask myself: *Is this the kind of person you want to be?* My stomach twinges, and I swear a voice in my head answers with a different question: *Is this the kind of mother you want to be?* And that's when I know. Something—someone—is growing inside of me. And it needs me.

I've decided to leave. And I'm taking my baby with me.

Over the last week, I've put together a backup plan in case the organ company won't accept a pregnant donor. A plan that requires Zahn's assistance. All that's left is to convince him to help if I need it. I'll tell him I'm working to raise money for Karla. For her college. So he doesn't question my motives. I'll leave out the drug situation—but I've left enough of a trail on the rest for him to figure things out if Thailand doesn't work for me.

Should I tell him about Nikki, Randy, and the baby?

No. I'm sure he'll figure most of it out the longer I'm gone.

"I'm walking Amore," I call to my mother, and herd my dog out the door, my phone already in my hand. What I have to share with Zahn can't be said with my mother sitting nearby.

"How long will you be gone?" I see skepticism in her eyes. This is Amore's second walk of the day.

"Twenty minutes. He needs to stretch his legs."

I scan for Jacy at the bottom of the steps, but instead find Erik occupying her normal spot in the chair by his door. He holds a Coors Light, and it's all I can do to keep from looking at my watch to calculate how many hours before noon he's started drinking.

"Day off?" I pause at the landing.

Erik stares at me as if I'm passing judgment. "Yup. You earn days off when you're working 12-on/12-off. You're probably unfamiliar with the concept."

So much for a fresh start. "Enjoy it. It's going to be a great day." I skirt past Erik and take the walkway toward the parking lot.

"Yeah, great day for poon tang." Erik's voice twangs loud behind me. "But you've got the monopoly on that, don't you? Not leaving much for the rest of us?"

I freeze, then turn and face him. "What did you say?" I don't know why I bother with the question—I clearly heard every word. My first thought is to inform him Nikki and I aren't dating anymore. Fortunately, my shocked outrage leaves me momentarily speechless. Erik doesn't deserve the details of my love life, nor does he have the right to pass judgment on my choices—even as reckless as those choices may have been over the last several months.

"I think you heard me. You've done a decent job of hiding it—but I've been asking around. You're a rug muncher."

My mouth drops. It's not that I'm naïve and imagine the entire world has moved beyond the misogynistic language of the past, but to hear this man—one who knows nothing about how to love a woman, whether it's a wife, a girlfriend, or a daughter—spew his words like a hangover purge makes the bile rise in my throat.

Erik stands and looks up at the concrete roof above him that forms the balcony in front of my second-story condo. "That your mama coming to visit? Does she know?"

It occurs to me he's enjoying this. He's goading me, hoping for a reaction he can use against me. And he's reminding me he'll make my life miserable if I share my child abuse suspicions with the cops.

I whirl on the sidewalk, tugging at Amore, and head off on my walk. Behind me, Erik's voice cackles. "Boy, howdy, I sure got the goods on you, don't I, honey? Uh-huh."

Unable to help myself, I spin on my heel to flip off my neighbor. A flash of movement on the balcony above Erik interrupts my immature response, and I see my mother gripping the rail and looking from Erik to me.

How much did she hear?

•   •   •

"Kristee, what's up?" Zahn's voice is clear and strong.

I'm still shaken from my encounter with Erik, but try to steady my tone. "Just needed to check in with the infamous Z-man. It's been a while."

"Perfect timing. Class doesn't start for an hour. Everything alright back there?" Zahn's voice sounds concerned, and I realize the only time I've called him this early is for a Search & Rescue alert. He's definitely guessed this isn't a normal "How ya doing?" chat.

I throw small talk at Zahn as I try to work my way around to telling him what's going on. Just when I'm finally ready—*there's something I haven't told you about*—my phone lets out a beeping sound and an echo on Zahn's end, as well. It's a Search & Rescue alert.

I read the screen and my heart swells. *Hikers needed. Three people missing from a planned hike yesterday in the vicinity of the Three Apostles...*

All thoughts of my fucked-up life disappear as I reread the message. I know exactly how to handle this. And I'm going to do it.

I tell Zahn I'm taking the mission. "I'll call you when the mission's over. I still need to talk. You might be the only one who can understand. Will you have time later? With all your Academy stuff going on?"

Zahn says he'll make the time and cautions me about the mission. *Are you kidding?*

I laugh over the phone. This I can handle.

ZAHN

NOW

It's well past midnight as I punch in the door code at the SAR bay and let myself into the building. I close the door behind me, turn on the lights, and about crap my pants like I've done the last two times I've come here alone. Bumbling Bob sits positioned in a chair facing the whiteboard at the front of the room, his arm propped on a knee in a sloppy rendition of Rodin's *Thinker*. I smile as I try to control my racing heart. Kristee would have appreciated the fact that Bob got me.

I pat Bob on the shoulder and slide past him to the door leading into the vehicle bay. That's where I'd hide something. Fewer people use the vehicle bay, and we've got stuff stored in there that hasn't been touched in ten years.

The cleaning supply closet is the first place I look. Definitely one of the least visited sites in the bay. I open several bottles of unidentified liquid and sniff them before realizing I don't know what I'm looking for—or what it smells like.

The vehicles make little sense, either, unless she's stuffed something up under the undercarriage and secured it. I grab one of our headlamps from the radio storage room and roll under the Toyota Tacoma first and then under our Chevy diesel tech rig. Nothing.

I stand between the trucks, shaking my head. Not only am I clueless about what I'm searching for, I still have no clue if the *BAY* from Kristee's computer is the SAR bay. The numbers she wrote relate to cryptocurrency, and they were the key to the password. Whatever might be hidden here relates to Kristee's business partner Travis and The Aerie. *Which is none of my business.*

I stop the negativity and take a breath. It was Travis's guys who thumped me on the head and took Kristee's phone. Sure, everything currently leans toward Lin Li and Erik, but something very wrong is happening at Kristee's business.

The perimeter walls are lined with shelves. A perfect place to hide something. I start at the southwest corner of the bay and begin working clockwise around the horseshoe bend of storage racks.

An hour fifteen later, I find something behind several coils of rope and a five-gallon bucket we've used for rat poison. I've bypassed several containers with padlocks because I have no key. But here sits a Pelican case locked with a bike lock instead of a padlock. We don't have bikes in SAR. We've got a grant application we sent up to state asking for money for electric mountain bikes, but as far as I know, they have not approved it.

I examine the case. Besides the bike lock, the hasps are secured with two zip-ties. I run my hands over the smooth black plastic. Dust bunnies blanket the ropes, and the bucket is caked with dirt—but this case looks new.

I grab a set of scissors from the front office and our fence snippers from the tool rack. The snippers are slow to gnaw through the bike lock cable, but the scissors instantly slice the zip-ties. I open the Pelican case. Shining the headlamp inside, I spot five plastic bags filled with smaller plastic zip-lock bags. I hold a bag directly in the beam of my light and see a white substance luminescing through the layers of plastic.

Bingo.

Even with the plastic five-gallon bucket labeled *Rat Poison* behind me, I'm guessing this isn't the rat poison storage container. I'm not a drug expert, but Perez and I have dealt with illegal substances before. Which means I'm not ignorant either. This is what Kristee is hiding.

I remember Travis's explanation.

She was into drugs…she was in some kind of trouble, and she was trying to turn the attention to me.

Is Travis right? Had Kristee gotten herself in over her head with a drug deal? I still can't believe that's the answer. Why would she lead me or her family to something she'd be embarrassed about? Doesn't make sense.

I return the SAR equipment to the shelves before hoisting the container. At the vehicle bay door, I lift a finger from the case to flip off the lights. I shuffle through the academic room and past Bob, where I use the same finger to flip off another set of lights. Propping one end of the case against the door, I twist the handle with my free hand, then quickly move it back to the container as the door swings open. I step through the frame and a weight pushes against the case, knocking me backwards. I trip on the sill and, as I try to break my fall, I let go of the case. I land on my wrists, the case in my lap, looking up at a silhouette in the doorway.

"What are you doing?" I push off the floor.

"Shut him up," a voice says, as a second silhouette joins the first. The first shape steps to my side, and I see the other pulling the door closed.

An arm moves in my direction.

Not again.

Cold metal crunches into the side of my head.

KRISTEE

BEFORE

Deb is working incident command when I arrive at the bay. "I was hoping you'd make it in quick. Can you take a team—Team 1—out with the helicopter?"

Does a duck take to water? Deb knows me better than to even ask. "You bet. Who else you got? What time does the chopper get here?" I walk to the whiteboard and snap a picture with my cell phone before reading what Deb has written:

Who: Party x 3: Michael Finch, Melody Schaub, Victor Schaub

What: Overdue hikers

When: Didn't return last night as planned. Vehicle still at trailhead

Where: Main route from Huron trailhead to the Three Apostles

Why: (hiker plan) They were trying to climb all three Apostles from west to east.

"The helo arrives in ten minutes. I've got you lined up with Chad Storms and Nikki Kingston. Everyone else is heading up on the ground." Deb's cell phone rings and she answers.

I freeze when she mentions Nikki, prepared to tell her that won't work. But I realize if I call bullshit, she'll replace me. Chad and Nikki are ready to go.

"That work for you?" Deb covers the cell phone with one hand.

I nod. I'm more than qualified for this mission. I can handle working with Nikki while I'm out there. The question is whether she'll be able to work with me.

Fifteen minutes later, and the three of us lift off from the meadow abutting the bay, the morning sun highlighting the Collegiates on the west side of the valley like a beacon guiding our helicopter up Cottonwood Pass.

"What's the plan, Kristee?" Chad's voice plays in my headset, and I glance at him, then at Nikki, whose lips are pursed. I had asked her at the bay if we could make this work, and she'd immediately taken offense.

"Of course. You're the one who doesn't want contact," Nikki had said, her eyes flaming.

"No chit-chat—it will all be business."

Nikki had rolled her eyes in response.

I turn back to Chad, lay out the map between us, and speak into my lip mike. "The hikers' plan was the standard route to the Apostles coming in from the north, and then hiking West Apostle, Ice Mountain, and North."

Chad nods. Nikki is expressionless.

"So, I figure if something happened, like an injury on West Apostle, we would have found out sooner than today. Someone else would have found them."

"Not if they got lost," Nikki says. "If they bushwhacked down the other side of Ice Mountain into the Texas Creek area, they could wander all day without running into anyone."

I nod, even though Nikki's logic isn't right. The Colorado Trail runs east-west in that part of the Texas Creek basin, and there are lots of other hikers. But there's no sense pissing her off.

"They were trying to summit all three." I nod again. "I agree it's easy to get lost if you get off the ridge between the peaks, but why would they?" I point at the map. "They're going to stay on that ridge to get to Ice Mountain."

Chad nods, but Nikki just stares at me. I sense she wants to say something, but thinks better of it.

"So, we'll offload at Lake Ann—that's the only place the chopper can land—and hike to the saddle between North Apostle and Ice Mountain. That's my first guess on where they might have gone astray."

Chad spreads my map across his legs and points at the gap so Nikki can see. "They could go here, here, or hike east on the ridge and come off here."

Nikki nods at Chad's map. Chad's nailed the plausible options, but I hope he's wrong. If you descend the wrong way from the east end—especially if you veer north—you might bushwhack for days without running into a road or a human.

The helicopter settles on Lake Ann's north shore, and we shuffle beneath the blades to a rally point. We instinctively duck our heads as the chopper soars north for the departure, using the downslope of South Clear Creek to gain momentum before disappearing around a corner. The mechanical sound and odor of the helicopter dissipates, replaced with the scent of fresh pines.

I'm home.

"Chad, can you pull up the InReach and tell them we've started hiking? And check that you're in tracking mode?" Tracking mode allows Deb to watch our progress on the big screen back in the bay.

"Got it," Chad says. "Already tracking."

I turn to Nikki. "You ready to hike?" She glares for a moment, then breaks out a small smile.

"Ready." Her grin widens. "This is what we do best, right?"

Damn her and that infectious smile. I can't help myself, and smile back. "Sure as hell is. Let's go find some hikers."

And we're off.

ZAHN

NOW

I'm trapped in a dream. I know I'm asleep, aware my experience isn't real, but can't wake myself up. Somehow I'm perched in a tree somewhere near the Apostles, I watch Kristee's mother, Lin Li, and neighbor Erik argue with my assailants—the men who knocked me out at the SAR bay. Probably the same men who stole Kristee's phone.

"It's a hundred yards that way," one man says, pointing through my tree and up the slope behind me. His partner stands next to him, drug-filled Pelican case in hand.

"No." Lin Li sounds adamant. "We planted her here. Start digging, Erik."

"Screw that, lady. I'm not doing nothing until I get my money."

"You made that perfectly clear when you almost gave us away to Mr. Zahn," Lin Li says.

"Zahn?" Pelican case man says.

"Zahn." Lin Li and Erik say together.

I lean forward, squinting at the people arguing, and fall from the tree.

All goes black.

When I open my eyes, I'm looking through the branches at a blinding sky. I close my eyes again.

"Zahn…Zahn? Are you awake?

This time, Perez's uniform fills my vision. He pulls back as my eyes open, and a bank of fluorescent lights causes me to squint again.

"What the…?" I croak. My voice peters out as I raise my head and take in my surroundings. I lay in a hospital bed. In a hospital room. A needle spears my left forearm with surgical tubing running to a machine at my shoulder.

"Relax, buddy. You took quite a spill. You've been unconscious for hours." Perez leans toward me again, his hand pressing on my arm as I try to sit.

I take in a breath to speak, then process Perez's words.

You took quite a spill…

Not, *Someone clubbed you over the head.* Or, *You've been assaulted.*

I twist my head toward Perez. "Did you get the guys?"

Perez squints at me, and I detect something in his eyes. Confusion? Or is it pity?

"What guys? We found you in the SAR bay early this morning when Will came in to grab a radio. You had an accident."

"No accident," I say. "They got me in the classroom. Took the drugs. You need to check for Kristee's laptop in my car. You need to…" I don't remember what I say next because everything goes dark again.

• • •

"Hey guys, she's over here!" I'm back in my dream—the same tree— and I twist at the woman's voice below me. Through the pinecone-laden branches, I spot Nikki on a small rise, pointing to a mound of fresh earth.

"Told you," says a deeper voice. It's the drug guy who pointed up the hill earlier. "You guys never listen to me."

"I don't know if I believe her," Erik says. He nudges Lin Li. "Do you? Do you believe your daughter's girlfriend?"

"Don't say that."

"Girlfriend, girlfriend, girlfriend…" Erik taunts.

I wake again, Erik's words echoing in my head, but the hospital room is empty. My head is clear now, and I'm ready to talk to Perez again.

Then I remember. The disbelief in his eyes, as if I were delusional. I struggle to a sitting position.

The screen is lit next to my bed, and I try to decipher what the steady beep and bouncing lights tell me. It can't be too bad, or I wouldn't be alone. Next to the remote on the side platform of the bed is a button marked "Call." I press it.

A minute later, a nurse walks in, smiling, with a clipboard in hand. "You're awake, Mr. Zahn. Good for you! How do you feel?"

"Like someone clubbed me over the head. But better than before. Can I get some water?" I pause. "Is Rick Perez still here? We were just talking."

"I'll get you a glass. You want some ice chips with that?"

I nod.

"You were talking with Perez yesterday," she says. "He hasn't returned today, but asked us to call if you woke up. Are you feeling up to talking to him again? That was quite a fall you took."

Here we go again. A fall. Not an assault. Not an attack.

I sigh. "Yeah, I'd like to talk to him again. What's your name?"

"Oops, sorry for not introducing myself. I'm Rhonda."

*Help me, Rhonda, help, help, me Rhonda…*the tune rattles in my head as the nurse leaves the room.

·   ·   ·

Perez stares at me, shaking his head. "Listen. I hear what you're saying, and you're obviously in better shape than yesterday, but your story isn't making sense." He pulls a chair next to the bed and sits. "You say men attacked you in the classroom, took a case of drugs, and probably stole Kristee's computer from your car. Do I have that right?"

I nod. "I'm not just saying it. That's what happened." I prop myself on my elbows and adjust my bed into a sitting position.

Perez says nothing and I keep talking. "Look, I found something on Kristee's computer that pointed me to the SAR bay, and when I searched, I found a case of drugs. They must have followed me there and attacked me on the way out."

Perez stares at the floor next to my bed, his brows drawn together. Not taking notes. Not even nodding.

I reach for his arm. "What?"

"Can I tell you what we found?" Perez's voice is soft. My jaw clenches at his patronizing tone. Perez doesn't wait for my response before continuing.

"Will found you in the bay. Between the Tacoma and the trailer. You were unconscious, with blood on your head, the floor, and the trailer hitch." He pauses. "Your blood. On the trailer hitch."

I open my mouth, but Perez interrupts. "There's no sign of forcible entry to the bay. No other injuries to you besides your head." He pauses. "Not that your bump from the hitch isn't serious enough." He stops for a moment, like he's getting ready to drop the clincher.

"What about the—" I start. Nurse Rhonda walks into the room with a tray of food. Perez steps back to make space.

"Lunch time," she says. "Sorry for interrupting."

I wave my hand. "Can I hold off on that? Maybe stick it over there until we're done?" I point at the counter next to the sink.

"No problem, Mr. Zahn. Buzz me if you need anything else." She leaves the tray and scoots from the room as if she senses she's picked an awkward time.

"So, what about the—"

"The computer?" Perez finishes my sentence.

Shit. He has an answer to that, too?

"We talked to Karla to tell her about you," he says. "She told us about the computer. You two checking it out."

I nod and say nothing.

"But she said she took it home that night. She showed it to us." Perez finishes.

This time I don't nod. My mouth goes slack, and I widen my eyes at Perez. There is no question in my mind—absolutely none—that I had Kristee's computer with me when I drove to the SAR bay. And it's not as if Karla forgot it at my house. I specifically asked her if I could hang on to it. The men who took me out must have returned the laptop and made her lie about it.

Perez leans back, shaking his head, as he watches me process this revelation. The pity from yesterday is back. "Listen. This has been hard on you. It's been hard on all of us."

"Cut the bullshit, Perez." I prop on my elbows again. "Someone took Kristee out, and you know it. There's too much stuff surrounding this case to ignore it. And I'm close. The drugs, her mom after the money. And Nikki. Crazy-ass Nikki. I'm not saying it's all connected. But I am saying there's no way she disappeared on her own. Someone took her down."

I stop, not because I've run out of things to say, but because I've said it too fast and need to catch my breath. I pant in front of Perez and I sense no empathy—no sign that he agrees with any of my suspicions. He simply looks sorry for me. That's when I realize he's not done talking. That he knows something I don't.

"Let's hear it," I say. "You've obviously got something else to share."

Perez reaches into his pocket, retrieving his cell phone. "We got a lead yesterday morning. While they were moving you here to the hospital."

I reach for the phone and Perez pulls it back. "Let me just tell you what we got first, and then I'll show you," he says.

I retract my hand and nod.

"You remember when I first called you about Kristee? To tell you she was missing? You were at the Academy." I nod again. "We interviewed those hikers on Ice Mountain that watched the rockslide. Got no information on Kristee…they never saw her. Our teams met them as they descended from the North Apostle-Ice Mountain gap." He pauses, then keeps talking. "They mentioned meeting another group of hikers on Ice Mountain. We could never track them down. When we put out the 'anybody with information concerning…' calls after Kristee disappeared, we got nothing. No other hikers called up."

"Until?"

"Until yesterday. Turns out the other hikers were from upstate New York. They hiked out the opposite way over West Apostle and then went home. Heard nothing about Kristee being missing. In fact, they heard nothing until yesterday when they read about the search on the internet and ran the math."

"Did they see something?" *Of course, they saw something, otherwise why would Perez be telling me this story?*

"Not at the time. But after they read about it, they reran the footage of the video they shot on Ice Mountain. This time they noticed something." Perez presses a button on the phone and hands it to me. "Press 'play.'"

KRISTEE

BEFORE

We're standing on the ridge bridging the gap between North Apostle and Ice Mountain—Chad, Nikki, and I—when we get the call.

Team 1, Trailhead.

I pull my handheld mike toward my mouth. *Trailhead, Team 1, Go ahead.*

Team 1, we just got a call on MRA-1 from Team 2. Did you copy?

I drop my mike and turn to Chad and Nikki. "I didn't pick up anything on mine. Any of you guys packing one? Did you hear anything?"

They both shake their head.

Trailhead, Team 1, that's a negative. What's up?

Yeah, they've made contact with the lost party. They backtracked off West Apostle last night, and one of them sprained an ankle on the descent. They spent the night three miles south of the Huron trailhead.

I glance at Chad and Nikki and roll my eyes.

"Shit," Chad says, "the chopper probably dropped us off a mile from their campsite." Nikki is silent, but leans forward, resting her hands on her knees.

I raise the mike to my lips. *Trailhead, Team 1 copies. You got anything for us? Are we mission complete?*

That's affirmative, Team 1. If you want to give me an ETA to Lake Ann, I'll check if I can get the chopper back for you.

Roger that. We'll be about an hour and a half. I flick my eyes to Chad, and he nods. I lower the mike and reach for the volume button on the radio when Trailhead makes another call.

Trailhead copies. Also…we got a message for you, Kristee.

I raise the mike. *Go ahead.*

Erik's here and said to tell you he's talked to your mother, and she's fine. He says he's got your back?

Erik? I respond, dropping protocol. Trailhead can't mean Jacy's dad?

He says he's your neighbor. He's up here, standing next to Nikki's car.

I whip my eyes to Nikki, who gazes at the valley toward the trailhead. "Why is your car at the trailhead?"

Nikki glances at me, then looks away. "I-I sent it up with Chris Atkins. I told him if he drove it up for me, he could have my return spot on the helicopter."

"So why is Erik at your car? How do you even know him?"

I hear rocks falling and watch as Chad wanders toward the south side of the ridge, scanning the scree field below. He turns back to me and calls, "Mini rockslide. Nothing big." I nod and turn back to Nikki.

"I don't know him. Just what we've talked about…when we used to talk. How mean he is—and the stuff with Jacy." I don't sense subterfuge in her eyes—she seems just as confused by Erik's presence as I am.

Keeping my eyes on Nikki, I radio Trailhead. *Roger, Trailhead. Copy the message.*

"Tell me again why you'd rather drive than ride the helo?" My voice is louder than before, and Chad pivots from his vantage point.

"I thought maybe you'd ride back with me. Since we're out here, you know, together, we could do some talking."

My breath releases with a whoosh, and I adjust my pack before turning to Chad. "Let's go. Chopper's on its way."

Chad buckles his waist belt and flourishes a hand. "After you all."

I take the lead, and Nikki tucks in behind me. We pick our way through the slick scree, using our hands on rock outcroppings wherever possible to keep from sliding. Neither of us speaks. After five minutes,

I glance back to check on Chad and notice he's allowed distance to build between us.

As we hit the tree line, Nikki sniffs behind me, and I turn as she wipes her nose. She stops when I stop and raises her head to look at me. Tears run off her cheeks.

"What the hell, Nikki?"

"I'm sorry. I'm so sorry."

"How about you spend less time apologizing, and more time getting your shit together? We're still on a mission. There's no crying in SAR," I say, turning back to the trail.

Her next words freeze me in my tracks.

"I'm sorry about your mother. That stuff on the radio."

I turn slowly, speaking in a quiet voice. "What do you know about my mother?"

Nikki backs up a step. "It's…well, I'm just guessing what Erik must have told her. About me and you. What else could it be?"

I step forward. Erik's voice echoes in my head. *Rug muncher.* How did Erik make the leap from Nikki and I spending time together to suspecting a relationship?

"When did you tell him?" When in doubt, bluff, I figure. "About us."

"After we fought. I came by and you wouldn't open the door. Erik and I talked, and when he asked what was going on, I told him."

I lock my eyes on Nikki. "You. Told. Him?" I look past Nikki at Chad, sitting on a dead tree thirty yards back. He obviously wants no part of this conversation.

Nikki covers her face with her hands. "He didn't believe me, and so I showed him the video."

This time I step forward and thrust my hands toward Nikki's shoulder straps, pushing her backwards. She moves a foot back, but her heel strikes a rock and suddenly she's sitting on her butt against the slope, my face crowding against hers.

"Keep talking," I say.

Nikki's lips quiver, and it takes a minute before she can speak between sobs. "That was it. He wanted to buy it from me. The video. But I wouldn't do it." She looks up at me, doe-eyed. "I wouldn't do that to us."

. . .

Fifteen minutes later, I reach the top of the ridge gap where Chad had spotted the small rockslide, breathing hard from my non-stop solo uphill surge. My quadriceps burn, and I'm gulping air, like I'm trying to overload my physical senses so my mental ones won't kick in. But I have nowhere else to go when I bridge the gap. Left is the North Apostle summit. Right leads to the top of Ice Mountain. I need more than climbing another 13-er summit to make things right.

My stomach cramps from the climb, and as I press my hand against my belly, I remember it's not just my body I'm straining. Another one grows inside of me. Every physical pain, every moment of stress—I'm not feeling these things alone anymore.

I survey the trail behind me. No sign of Nikki or Chad at the tree line. I turn back and stare south over the edge of the gap and the talus-strewn slope below.

I'm furious at Nikki for her betrayal—again. She violated my trust when she shot the video. Now she's doubled down by telling Erik about it. By showing him. The thought of that pile of pulsing testosterone grunting over our intimate moment sickens me. There's no doubt in my mind he's told my mother everything.

I stare south at the mountain peaks trailing to the horizon like an endless stream of whitewater rapids, imagining my life if I could simply hike away. If I could leave my tainted business and my wrecked relationships behind. It's not as if I would leave alone. I caress my stomach again. We're a team, now.

No passport yet, my practical side warns, steering me back to sanity. I can't leave yet. Not if I want to leave the country.

I turn again, toward Chad and Nikki, toward the helicopter landing site, toward the end of this mission and real life. I descend the trail toward my teammates. Maybe I can try to make it another week without Travis's drug escapade reeling me into trouble with the law, without my neighbor assaulting me, or without Nikki reminding me how psycho she is.

I laugh out loud. Hell, I'm not even sure I can make it through today.

Skidding to a stop, I burst into tears, surprising even myself. Crying is just not me. But as I raise my arms to the sky, my body racking in sobs, I realize I can't face it all. Some of it, maybe. But all of it? There's no way.

I wheel back up the trail, breathing through my nose and concentrating on filling my lungs for the brief climb while controlling my tears. At the gap, I peer over the south side at the rocky slope, dropping at a precipitous angle. The first couple hundred yards are a gravelly scree before the slope transitions to larger and larger boulders from past rockslides. I press my hand on my belly. I can do this—I can slide with the loose gravel to the rock field, then pick my way to the trees below. I stare off in the distance and spot the thin gray ribbon of highway where Cottonwood Pass crests the Continental Divide. My new goal.

I'm unsure where we're going. But I know where we're not going. We're not going home.

I lower myself off the ridge and allow my feet to slide with the gravel. I lean back as my momentum builds so I'm descending on my ankles and then the sides of my feet, trying to slow myself. Like a blue slope skier suddenly hurling too fast on a black diamond run, I quickly discern I can descend the slope in short hops by pressing against the mountain.

Skidding to a stop, I reverse and lean my feet into the mountain in the opposite direction. Behind me, a Z-pattern forms in the raw earth, where I've scraped away undisturbed scree.

Stop. Switch direction.

Stop again. Switch again.

I glance forward, and the boulders below loom large in my vision, the individual trunks of the trees sharpening as I get closer. A rush of rocks passes me, and then another. I check my six at a small rockslide accelerating faster than I am. A three-inch layer of scree envelops my boots and knocks me off my feet and against the mountain. It seems unfathomable this tiny flow of rocks can be dangerous, and I claw against the slope, trying to bring myself to a stop.

I slide another twenty feet before my feet jam against the start of the boulder field. A sharp pain shoots through my ankle as I jolt to a stop— a contact injury that's going to leave a bruise, but not a bone or ligament issue. I'm still good.

Pushing myself upright, I twist my head to confirm the rocks have stopped, then turn downhill again and pick a line through the larger rocks leading me to the trees. It's closer than it looked from above. Maybe a two-minute scramble between the boulders, three if I'm extra careful. Once I'm in the trees, it's a simple matter of working my way downhill to Texas Creek, following the water to the trail, and then an uphill climb to Cottonwood Pass.

As I catch my breath, I consider my options when I finally reach the road. Turn left and catch a ride back to Buena Vista to face the music. Or right, to a new life, a new future, with nothing to my name but the everything that grows inside me.

A sharp crack jerks me to the present. It's hard to describe how I recognize this noise as more than a branch breaking off a tree, more than a firecracker or a gunshot. It has a resonance that causes me to freeze for a fraction of a second before turning in the sound's direction. I've heard it before. In an IMAX theater. It's the same explosive snap a glacier makes when it cleaves into the ocean below. Like the earth is breaking.

I turn my head. The source of the sound is already in a slow-motion descent. The cliff side between the gap I descended and Ice Mountain has sheared off and is descending the mountain like a sheaf of spring snow cascading off the metal roof of a house.

And gravity is funneling it through the same chute it's used for millions of years.

Right where I am standing.

I whip my head around and laser focus on my chosen rock-clogged route to the trees.

And I run.

I run for myself. I run for my baby. I run for our lives.

ZAHN

EPILOGUE

I sit at my table, staring through the living room window, watching the Ponderosa pine shadows elongate westward as the sun rises. I'm taking my time debating whether to rise from this chair and pretend the day means something, or spend a third hour sipping at tepid coffee and trying to untangle my thoughts.

I'll get up, eventually. Karla and Lin Li asked me if I'd take Amore and I agreed—he's draped across my feet under the table right now. He's going to need a walk, and I need the excuse to move.

I expected the dreams to stop when I returned from the hospital. Instead, I jolt awake, always after midnight, my heart racing, and my plaid pajamas drenched in sweat. The first night it happened, I stumbled to my dining room table and popped a beer before I remembered I was on painkillers. Even I know the dangers of becoming too numb.

The dreams alternate. One night, I spy Kristee in a Thai market. I'm never clear why I'm in Thailand, but I remember why Kristee wanted to go. For the rest of the dream, I'm chasing her through Bangkok, trying to stop her from harvesting her organs. I never do.

Other nights, Kristee returns to the Apostles and she does get caught. I observe from a distance, never sure if I'm perched on a neighboring mountain or watching events unfold on Perez's cell phone.

Regardless, I spot Kristee just as the side of the mountain cleaves away and surges toward her. I scream for Kristee to run, but the echo of the sharp crack and the roaring crescendo as it aims for my friend drown out my warnings. No matter how loud I yell, the lead boulder unerringly finds Kristee's back just as she nears the trees. And then I wake.

I don't dream of Travis's men—the ones who put me in the hospital. Security footage from the SAR bay finally proved me right and Perez and his team put the men—and Travis—behind bars...and later apologized to me for not believing me. Drugs, assault, threats to Karla if she told the truth about the computer—plenty to keep them in the slammer. But no evidence they harmed Kristee.

I'm never certain how to interpret the dreams. Because the video Perez shared with me doesn't tell me how Kristee disappeared. It just explains how she didn't disappear. Perez's narration as he sat next to my hospital bed replays in my head.

So, the party filming stood on Ice Mountain, looking south from the summit. They were videoing each other reaching the top. The phone camera guy heard the rockslide—you see the view pivot. There's the front edge of the slide, right? (Pause) Now, focus here, on the screen's far left. Do you see the figure here? (Pause) Wearing a pack. SAR ball cap, white in the front with red bill? This is her. This is Kristee.

Now, watch as she moves...she's in front of the slide, heading for the edge of the boulder field. She's aiming for the trees. The rocks catch up with her here...as she drops out of sight. That's where we've got the teams searching now. (Pause) We're going to find her, Tyler. We're putting this to rest. For you. For Randall. For her mother and sister. (Pause...choking sound) Hell, for me.

Perez sounded so confident that it was over. But he was wrong. After a week of searching with dogs and pry bars and lengthy discussions on whether heavy equipment can reach the bottom of the slide to move rocks—it can't—they still didn't uncover my friend's body.

That's why I say the video only proved what didn't happen.

Kristee wasn't killed for the drug operations Travis ran in the Aerie.

Kristee wasn't killed by an irate neighbor, worried she'd report him for child abuse.

Kristee's mother didn't get rid of her daughter for money.

Kristee's crazy girlfriend didn't snap and make Kristee disappear.

Everything I believed to be true turned out to be wrong. Kristee left her Search & Rescue team after a fight with Nikki, and a rockslide got her. As simple as that. My friend, the intrepid SAR team leader I respected so much, had a bad day, made a poor decision, and paid the price for it.

Once I accept this premise, I'm also forced to accept that Perez is right. That I've let my personal attachment to Kristee cloud my judgment for the entire case. From the start, Perez's theory was that she had an accident. She was lost or hurt—and now dead. But from the time I involved myself in the case, I've blindly pursued every nefarious lead I found. Anything to prove it wasn't Kristee's fault. I had suspected someone out there needed my friend to disappear...and made it happen.

A woman's figure slides past my window, and I hear a knock. Amore yaps and heads for the door. I look at my sleepwear and shrug, deciding I'm decent enough for company. Rounding the corner of the mudroom, I peer through the front door glass and recognize Nikki squinting back through the glass at me. I stop for a moment before reaching for the handle and Nikki sees it. I can almost read her thoughts. She wants to talk. She knows I don't. And she's debating what to do if I refuse to open the door.

I solve her problem by turning the handle. And instead of asking her what she wants, I swing the door wide, wave her through, and ask, "Coffee?"

• • •

"I'm sorry, Tyler," Nikki says. "For everything."

"How's it your fault?" I pour Nikki a cup of coffee, and return the carafe to the drip machine. "It's not like either of us ever suspected it was an accident."

"But I made it all about me. I was convinced her leaving had to do with our relationship."

As I return to my chair at the table, I don't point out the fact that Kristee leaving the team in the field had everything to do with her relationship with Nikki. If they hadn't fought, Kristee wouldn't have taken off alone.

Nikki seems to take my silence as an invitation to keep talking. "And this video will shut up those sons of bitches saying she took her own life."

"How so?" The video is semi-viral on social media. The hikers had posted it right after they sent it back to Perez, and even though the Sheriff's department made them pull it down, it was too late. Amateur videographers have analyzed it from every conceivable angle, and now everyone has an opinion on where to look for Kristee's body.

"Did you see how fast she moved?" Nikki says. "Never underestimate the power of a mother bear when her young are in trouble."

A mother bear? "I'm not sure I follow."

Nikki leans back in her chair. "Come on, Tyler. You went through her phone. Her computer. I'm sure you knew…?"

I shake my head.

"She was going to have a baby. Kristee was pregnant."

My head stops shaking and I stare at Nikki. At first, I'm speechless, a hundred thoughts tumbling through my head. Regaining my composure, I try to frame my questions.

"Why didn't you tell me this when we first met? When I started asking questions?" I lean forward, my elbows on the table. "Why now?"

Nikki also leans forward. Only two feet separate us across the table. "I didn't know when we first started talking. I just found out through the clinic."

I remember my trip into town when I saw Nikki's car at the Family Planning Clinic. Wondering why Nikki was there. I think about asking her how she discovered the pregnancy. Surely the information is confidential. But the persistent smile on her face is throwing me off, and I change tack.

"You're practically beaming here, Nikki. Why does Kristee being pregnant make you happy?"

"Don't you see?" Nikki laughs. "It explains everything. It explains what happened between us. She said she left me because I was moving too fast. That I was too obsessive for her." Her eyes shine. "I never believed that was the reason. People always say things like that when they're covering for actual reasons."

I have no doubt that Nikki is in full denial. Combine Kristee's restraining order with what Nikki just ranted—*people always say those things*—and I'm guessing Kristee's pregnancy was probably only part of the reason she left Nikki.

Nikki's not finished. "I wondered if she was having second thoughts about breaking up with Randy, but now I know the truth. She was breaking up with me because of the baby. She couldn't handle our new relationship and impending motherhood." Her smile fades. "I could have helped her."

•   •   •

After Nikki leaves, I sit at my table and replay the video. Then again. And again.

Nikki was right—Kristee had a palpable desperation in her dash for the trees. Someone worried for their own life might have glanced over her shoulder to gauge how much time they had left. Someone trying to save another's life wouldn't have wasted the fraction of a second it would take to turn one's head.

Kristee never turned.

I freeze the frame as the lead boulder fills the screen where I'd last seen Kristee's figure. There was no way to see her last moments. No way to tell if she was lying under that boulder right now or whether she'd miraculously found cover in the trees. What if she had?

That's when I realize Perez and Nikki and Daria have been right, in a way, about me. I've driven myself to the edge over the last weeks trying to figure out what Kristee was running from. Trying to narrow down who would do her harm and figuring out how to bring them to justice.

And I was wrong.

Just as my friends and family had warned me, I had convinced myself that discovering *who* made Kristee disappear would ease the pain of another death in my life.

Instead, I should have focused less on what she ran from and more on what she ran toward. I replay the video over and over, and watch Kristee's will to live play out on my dining room table. Before Nikki told me about the baby, I had thought Kristee believed she had nothing to live for.

I was wrong.

Kristee left nothing behind for her family, her friends, or her mountain community—but she carried everything worth living for inside her.

ABOUT THE AUTHOR

Over a 30-year Air Force career, author Cam Torrens delivered combat supplies and personnel across Europe, the Middle East, and Africa. He piloted the first mobility aircraft into Iraq during the Iraq War, served as the United States Air Attaché at the U.S. Embassy in Beijing, China and spent four years as the Professor of Aerospace Studies at Virginia Tech.

Father of six, Cam and his spouse live in Buena Vista, Colorado where he serves as the Vice President of the Chaffee County Writer's Exchange and volunteers with the Chaffee County Search & Rescue team.

False Summit is his second Tyler Zahn novel. The first, *Stable*, was released in July of 2023.

Don't miss the first Tyler Zahn Novel...

CAM TORRENS

STABLE

SOMEONE IS TAKING THEM...

A TYLER ZAHN NOVEL

NOTE FROM CAM TORRENS

Word-of-mouth is crucial for any author to succeed. If you enjoyed *False Summit*, please leave a review online—anywhere you are able. Even if it's just a sentence or two. It would make all the difference and would be very much appreciated.

Thanks!
Cam Torrens

We hope you enjoyed reading this title from:

BLACK✿ROSE
writing™

www.blackrosewriting.com

Subscribe to our mailing list – *The Rosevine* – and receive **FREE** books, daily deals, and stay current with news about upcoming releases and our hottest authors.
Scan the QR code below to sign up.

Already a subscriber? Please accept a sincere thank you for being a fan of Black Rose Writing authors.

View other Black Rose Writing titles at
www.blackrosewriting.com/books and use promo code
PRINT to receive a **20% discount** when purchasing.

Made in the USA
Las Vegas, NV
02 June 2024